HELL TO PAY

A Detective Loxley Nottinghamshire Crime Thriller

By
A L Fraine

Copyright & Info

This book is Copyright to Andrew Dobell, Creative Edge Studios Ltd, 2025
No part of this book may be reproduced without prior permission of the copyright holder.

All locations, events, and characters within this book are either fictitious, or have been fictionalised for the purposes of this book.

Publisher - Creative Edge Publishing

Creative Edge Studios Ltd
PO Box 503
KT22 2PL
info@alfraineauthor.co.uk

ASIN: B0BRYWKLHD
ISBN-13 : 979-8373491600

Book List

www.alfraineauthor.co.uk/books

Acknowledgements

Thank you to Crystal Wren for your amazing editing and support.
Thanks to Kath Middleton for her incredible work.
A big thank you to the Admins and members of the UK Crime Book Club for their support, both to me and the wider author community. They're awesome.

A big thank you to Meg Jolly and Tom Reid for allowing me to use their names in this novel. I really appreciate it.
Thank you also to the Authors I've been lucky enough to call friends. You know who you are, and you're all wonderful people.

Thank you to my family, especially my parents, children, and lovely wife Louise, for their unending love and support.

Table of Contents

Book List 3
Acknowledgements 3
Table of Contents 4
1 7
2 14
3 31
4 42
5 53
6 64
7 84
8 96
9 112
10 123
11 131
12 144
13 152
14 159
15 165
16 178
17 182
18 188
19 198
20 204
21 212
22 222
23 227
24 232
25 240
26 248
27 254
28 269
29 279
30 294
31 301
32 311

33	320
34	333
35	337
36	342
37	349
38	373
39	378
40	382
41	391
42	395
43	403
44	415
45	427
46	437
47	441
48	448
49	454
50	462
51	471
52	484
53	489
54	492
55	500
56	505
Author Note	511
Book List	511

1

"Oi!" she bellowed from the roadside as the man threw the car into gear. Its front wheels spun, kicking up dirt that hit her legs. "Don't you bloody…" But it was too late. The car sped up the short side road, the rear door closing as it went, before it turned left, onto Mansfield Road and back toward Clipstone.

"Shit." Penny watched it go for a moment as it merged into the flow of traffic in the darkness, its rear lights mixing with others until she couldn't tell which was the car she'd been in, and which wasn't. She couldn't believe the shithead had left her here, out on a sideroad towards the edge of the village, in the darkness of the night. She knew where she was and she knew it was only a short walk back to where she'd left her friend, but the nerve of that guy!

They really were shitheads, sometimes.

Having picked up all the crap that he'd thrown onto the side of the road to get her out of the car, she stuffed it in her bag with a grunt. Then, with a frown, she pulled her money out and counted it.

With a sigh that seemed to affect her whole body, she realised she was short. He'd taken some of her money.

"Fuck!"

She shouted into the night, voicing her frustrations and the headache that the missing money would bring down on her. It was the last thing she needed, and just one more annoyance to add to the mountain that was already weighing her down. She needed to get back and find Izabela. Abel had asked her to keep an eye on Izabela, and she couldn't well do that here, half a village away, could she?

Feeling a sudden rush of anger, she kicked a small twig and shouted.

"Fuck!"

Frustrated, tired and alone, with a ten-minute walk ahead of her, Penny sighed and tried to let her worries and stresses drain from her body, but it wasn't easy. She had to somehow think of a way to hide the missing money from Abel, which would be a headache in itself. Although, she guessed she could see how Izabela was doing. Maybe she'd be able to liberate some cash from Izabela by offering to hold her bag or something.

There'd be a way for her to make it right, there had to be.

She'd sort it.

To her right, something moved in the corner of her vision; she caught sight of a figure walking along the main road, looking her way. Half a second later, they were gone, stepping out of sight before she could get a good look at them.

For a moment, she felt very alone and vulnerable, at least partially because she'd just been taken advantage of by that idiot. He was long gone by now, though, and there'd be no tracking him down.

Men were just fucking shitheads.

With another laboured sigh, she turned to her left and gazed out over the huge stretch of open grassland between the sideroad she was standing on and the industrial and residential estates beyond. Standing tall, about a hundred metres away, was the last surviving derelict building of the Clipstone Colliery, marked by its distinctive Headstocks—a pair of huge metal towers made from massive steel girders, topped with humungous wheels that... Well, she didn't really know what the wheels did, but she guessed they either lowered a lift down into the mine or carried the coal back out. Maybe both? She didn't know, but what she did know was that the structure made a great navigation point that you could see from all over the village.

But, standing in the darkness, surrounded by empty grassland, the towers and the smashed up, abandoned buildings they rose out of, took on a more menacing feel, as if they were towering dead monoliths, silently watching her from their lofty position. Her gaze slipped further left, out beyond the village to the rolling hills beyond and the slowly gathering mist in the valley. A shiver rippled up her spine as she looked upon the nearby gates that led into the fenced-off former Colliery. They seemed almost skeletal and black in the darkness.

The dead, useless husk of a building reminded her of the finality of things. They were nothing but a reminder of a time long past.

According to what she'd heard, however, they were going to be redeveloped, and the construction machinery parked up just inside the gates seemed to confirm that.

A rustle in the nearby bushes caught her attention, snapping her out of the daydream she'd slipped into. She turned, putting her back to the remains of the Colliery, and peered into the bushes that separated her from the houses beyond. This side road wasn't long, but it was quiet, unlit, and she decided she didn't really like it here.

Stuffing her hands into her pockets, she set off up the road towards the main thoroughfare and the streetlights that lined it. She cursed the mud that had caught around the heels of her shoes when she'd been thrown out of the car. They looked a right state now.

She paused for a moment and went to try and knock off some of the mud onto the kerb, only to stop and peer into the undergrowth beside the road.

She had a funny feeling she was being watched.

Squinting in the dark, she tried to get her eyes to adjust while hoping she was wrong. Had some pervert seen the car and stopped to have a good old look, hoping to get an eyeful? She had visions of some scruffy guy leering at her with his hand down his pants. The image sent a shiver up her spine in disgust.

"Is someone in there? Getting your rocks off, are yeh? Yeh dirty bastard." Feeling revulsion at the thought of the voyeur, she raised her hand, flipping him off before turning away and striking out again.

A rush of footsteps on muddy grass thundered towards her like an ominous drumroll.

Catching one foot behind the other, Penny stumbled as she turned. The shadow rushed in, swinging something.

Pain exploded across her skull, and her legs lost all their strength. Gripping her head, she crumpled to the floor, feeling something warm and wet oozing through her hair.

The world swam. Nothing made sense. She lay on the cold floor, feeling the damp concrete seeping into her clothing while a similar but warm wetness covered her head and fingers.

She felt the ground shifting beneath her, or was she being dragged? It hurt, but not as much as the incredible, indescribable pain at the top of her head. Something wasn't right up there. She could feel the top of her head, and it felt different. There was a soft bit, a bit that should have been hard, but wasn't. She probed with her fingers, wincing in pain, her stomach twisted in knots. It felt... broken. She felt sick, and retched, bringing up disgusting bile that burnt her throat. This stranger had smashed her skull in.

She needed help. Someone had to help her and stop whatever was happening.

"Plee... ples... Help meh..." She couldn't form her words properly, and her vision was blurred. Everything was pain and terror. "Help, I nee... help."

Bushes closed in around her, obscuring the stars and the clouds scudding across them.

What was this person doing? Why were they doing this? What did they want? She had a thousand questions but no answers, and every time she latched onto a thought, it seemed to slip away.

Something metallic caught the light and flashed. It looked long and pointed. It looked dangerous.

Penny tried to fight, but all her strength had gone as the figure knelt above her and lowered the blade to her neck. The cool metal pressed against her skin, against her throat.

"No, no, no, please, no." Was she saying this out loud or not? She couldn't tell.

The figure gripped the blade, put all their weight behind it, and cut.

2

Rob stopped his car short of the security barrier and wound down the window of his Ford Capri. The man on security duty stepped out of the small boxy building and wandered over. He looked the car over, nodding with a pouting bottom lip as he approached.

"Nice car," he commented.

"Thanks," Rob replied, his voice guarded, wondering where the guard was going with this, if anywhere. In an attempt to keep him from passing any further comment, Rob held up his ID. "Here you go."

The guard peered at the warrant card and then nodded. "Very well, Inspector. I take it you've been here before?"

"A few times."

"Then you know the drill. Sign in at reception. They'll tell you where to go."

"Thanks," Rob replied as the guard nodded to someone behind the tinted glass. A second later, the barrier rose up, wobbling in its housing. It looked like it had seen better days, but then, that was most police buildings, wasn't it?

Rob drove in, and as he navigated his way into the car park, he spotted Scarlett leaning against her purple Polo with her arms crossed. She saw him and waved. Rob turned into a parking space close by. A glance in his mirror revealed Scarlett walking over.

Gathering his things, Rob climbed out of his Capri, he smiled at Scarlett as he inserted his key and locked the door.

"That must get annoying," Scarlett commented, nodding to his hand.

Rob shrugged. "You get used to it."

"Mmm, give me central locking any day of the week."

She had a point, but it was part of the charm. Something which Belle had in spades compared to the bland, all singing, all dancing, modern cars of today. "You've scrubbed up," Rob commented, noting her freshly pressed skirt suit, heels, neatly arranged hair and the make-up she wore.

She raised an eyebrow. "It's our first day here. I want to make a good impression." She nodded to him. "Unlike some."

It was Rob's turn to raise an eyebrow at Scarlett's good-natured dig. "I'm setting expectations low, so they underestimate me," he answered in a conspiratorial tone.

She gave him a hasty up-and-down inspection, tilted her head and said, "I see. Consider my expectations set."

Rob had been here many times before and didn't see a need to try and make any kind of impression. Quite the opposite, he wanted to blend in. It turned out that Bill Rainault had been right. Busting his own DCI had painted something of a target on his back in the weeks since making the arrest.

"I'll enjoy watching you chase down some local scrotes in those." Rob pointed to her impractical heeled shoes, something he'd not really seen her wear before.

She seemed to stiffen as she took in his comment. "Why would I run anywhere in these, when I can get you to do the running for me?"

Rob shrugged. "Fair enough." Her heckles were clearly raised, so he decided not to pursue this line of banter.

"Also, piss off. I'll wear what I want, and I doubt we'll be banging any heads together today."

"Okay, okay."

"Don't disrespect the shoes."

"I'm sorry. I won't."

"Good." Her tone was clipped. There was a moment of uncomfortable silence between them as they walked towards the nearby building, following the signs for the reception. "Besides, I have some flats with me," she quipped.

"You've come prepared."

"I take this job seriously, you know."

"Oh, I know. Unlike some," he commented. "Curby's due before the courts in a few weeks by the way, just after Orleton."

"I heard," Scarlett replied. "Hopefully, they'll both be sent down for a long time."

"One can hope. Christ, it's early. I hope Nailer doesn't make a habit of these early starts."

"We're meeting Nailer now, right?"

"We're meeting the whole team, I think. Nailer made his choices as to who he wants on it," Rob explained, having heard from Nailer recently while they were finishing up the Sherwood Murder case.

The case had been one of the most intense Rob had ever taken on, not least because he'd been seconded to the East Midlands Special Operations Unit, which deals with the most serious and violent crimes in the area. His former boss, Superintendent Landon, who was now running the Nottinghamshire arm of the Unit, had brought Rob in after he'd responded to a call where a body was discovered in Sherwood Forest. That case led to the eventual discovery that his boss, DCI Peter Orleton, had been the murderer. He'd been corrupted by a local gang, and after the arrest of Peter, they eventually tracked down and arrested Curby, the gang leader, following a tip-off.

"I take it I'm on the team, then," Scarlett stated.

Rob smiled. "You've made something of an impression, I think."

"Maybe I'll make another impression today."

"I'm saying nothing. You look very nice."

"Once bitten, twice shy?"

Rob grunted in reply.

Scarlett smiled. "Well, thank you. It's good to see that you can be a civilised human being when you want to be."

"It takes a lot of effort." Rob sighed dramatically and then pulled open the main door into reception for her. He followed Scarlett in, taking in the space with its main reception desk and the Nottinghamshire Police logo inlaid into the floor.

Rob held out his ID to the uniformed receptionist, and Scarlett did the same. "I'm DI Rob Loxley. We're here to meet DCI John Nailer."

"DCI Nailer?" the woman asked.

"That's right."

"And you are?" She looked up at Scarlett.

"DC Scarlett Stutely," she answered, while the receptionist looked over her screen.

"Okay, can you both sign in please?" She tapped on the signing-in book as she checked the screen of her PC. "I see. Okay, so you're being transferred here. Alright. Well, DCI Nailer is due to meet you at the EMSOU office this morning. So if you go through that door to the end, turn left, head upstairs and come back this way, you'll find the office. It's sign posted. You can't miss it."

"Thank you," Rob replied, and with a glance at Scarlett, they made their way across reception to the door, and opened it with their IDs.

As Rob went to step through, a uniformed officer appeared in the doorway from a side corridor. "Oh, sorry," he said.

"That's okay," Rob replied but noted the frown that had suddenly appeared on the officer's face. The frown turned to a look of disgust.

"Grass," the officer muttered under his breath and made sure to bang his shoulder into Rob's as he stopped waiting and barged through the door, past Rob and into Scarlett. She yelped and grabbed the frame to steady herself as the man strode through.

"Bloody hell," she gasped.

"I think he recognised me," Rob said, watching the man walk off. This was far from the first time he'd encountered other officers who disagreed with what he'd done, and he guessed it wouldn't be the last, either.

"No shit, Sherlock."

"You okay?"

"I might be reconsidering my choice of footwear, but other than that, I'm fine."

Rob smirked. "Come on."

They set off along the corridor, passing other officers going about their morning's work. These strangers nodded or smiled at them, but Rob felt sure he caught a couple who recognised him as their smiles turned to frowns, which were followed by whispers that he struggled to make out.

But this was hardly a new thing for him, and although he noticed it more since putting Peter away, it was a familiar feeling that he was very much used to.

"Rob?"

The female voice came from a side room he'd just passed. Feeling on guard, he considered ignoring it, before finally slowing and looking back.

Scarlett caught his eye and gave him a questioning look.

Rob shrugged. A moment later, a woman dressed similarly to Scarlett appeared. She was a little shorter, though, with softer features and mousy hair rather than Scarlett's blonde.

"Rob! I thought it was you."

"Matilda." Rob recognised her and relaxed. "Fancy meeting you here."

"I could say the same," she replied with a raised eyebrow.

"I've been transferred. I'll be working here from now on with EMSOU."

"Oh, congratulations. I thought for a moment that… well, maybe you'd been shunted off to some desk job, somewhere."

"Nope. Not yet, anyway. There's still time, I guess. But no. What about you? You're here early... or should I say, late?"

"Early," she confirmed, flashing her smile at him.

"I didn't know you came out here?"

"I get around." She smiled. "I'm out here a fair amount. I've been to most of the stations around the city by now."

Rob nodded approvingly. "Excellent..."

Beside him, Scarlett coughed.

"Oh, sorry. This is Scarlett?" Rob asked. "This is Matilda, Duty Solicitor to the stars."

Matilda scoffed. "Hardly. Nice to meet you, Scarlett." She shook the DC's hand.

"Likewise. Should I continue on and leave you two to it?"

"No, no." Rob glanced at Scarlett, who was giving him a curious look. He wasn't sure what she was trying to tell him but guessed she wanted to get a move on. Rob turned back to address Matilda. "Sorry, we're due to meet our new DCI upstairs."

"Well, I'd better not keep you," she said with a smile. "I'll see you around?"

"Sure," Rob replied. "See ya."

He walked up the corridor with Scarlett in silence until they turned the corner and made their way toward the stairs. He could sense the pregnant air around them as if Scarlett wanted to say something but was holding it in. He was about to ask about it when she suddenly spoke up.

"Well, she was certainly flirting with you."

"What?" The comment surprised him. "No. She was just being friendly. We've sat across from each other in interviews, and she's joined us on some pub nights before. That's all."

"No, no, no, no. Trust me." Scarlett looked him in the eye. "She wants a little more from you than that."

Rob held Scarlett's gaze for a few moments as he considered her words. He wasn't sure what to think about that at all. "You think?"

"Oh, I'm certain," Scarlett deadpanned, adding an unnecessary eye roll.

Rob pulled a face as he thought about it. She could be mistaken, of course, but Scarlett did seem to be a good judge of character. He sighed, fully aware of his singleton status, which was at least partially by choice.

He'd had relationships before and wasn't necessarily against the idea, but he had reservations. They were a tie for a start. He also knew far too many officers who ended up single due to the demands of the job, and then there were the ever-present shadows cast over him by his family.

It might have been years since he'd had any serious communication with them, apart from occasionally and accidentally running across them, but they still played on his mind more than he cared to admit. They knew what he did for a job, and he knew their interest in the police was... Well, it was complicated, and Rob's position as a detective presented them with a potential opportunity. An opportunity that he suspected his family had tried to exploit on more than one occasion, including through one girlfriend that he believed had been more than what she appeared.

Did he want to take the risk of exposing himself to that again, or worse still, exposing an innocent woman to the potential dangers that would come with getting too close to him?

For years his answer to that had been a resounding no, and as of right now, he had no desire to change that.

"Okay, well, I appreciate your insight."

Scarlett eyed him as they climbed the stairs, clearly curious. "You're not interested?"

Rob shrugged. "I dunno. I'm... I have a lot going on right now."

"Don't we all."

"Mmm." It was a poor excuse, but he did not want to get into this now. Luckily, she seemed to pick up on his hesitancy.

"Alright, well, it's none of my business, I suppose."

"Yup."

They reached the upper floor and set off along a corridor. Following the signs that pointed towards the EMSOU offices, Rob spotted DCI Nailer and DS Nick Miller chatting in the hall.

"Aaah, Rob, Scarlett, you made it," Nailer called out as they approached. He smiled at them, beaming. "Sorry for the early start, but we have a busy day ahead."

"That's okay," Rob lied. He heard Scarlett quietly scoff beside him. "Wouldn't miss this for the world. We're ready and raring to go."

"Are you indeed?" Nick asked. "So, you're ready for a day of hard graft as the newest members of the East Midlands Special Operations Unit? You're ready to get your hands dirty?"

Rob frowned at Nick's curious tone and decided to throw it back to him. "Are you?"

"Of course."

"Good. I am too."

"Excellent." Nick sported a shit-eating grin. He knew something Rob didn't.

"What are we missing here?" Scarlett asked, giving voice to Rob's suspicions. Nick seemed entirely too pleased with himself for Rob's liking. "What's going on?"

"Well," Nailer began and reached out for the handle on the door beside him. "Welcome to our new office." He opened the door and walked in.

Nick waved them in, suggesting they should follow Nailer.

With a suspicious frown, Rob did as Nick suggested and stepped through the door with gritted teeth, expecting a surprise of some kind.

The lights flickered on, illuminating the shadows the outside light didn't reach through the closed blinds. The room was modest in size, but beyond a general impression of its dimensions, it was tough to make out the layout, because the room had been filled with boxes. Filing boxes had been piled up throughout the room, with a few winding pathways between them that seemed to have been made entirely at random. Dust floated in the shafts of light, and there was a musty smell that seemed to hang in the air.

Rob stared at the clutter in silence for several seconds. "What the hell's all this?"

"Don't tell me that's our caseload," Scarlett asked.

"Um, no. Well, not all of it anyway," Nailer replied. "From what I understand, after the temporary disbanding of the Nottinghamshire Unit, their unused office became a dumping ground for files and evidence."

"So, guess what," Nick asked, "we get to do on our first day here."

Rob rolled his eyes. "Oh, crap."

"I knew I'd worn the wrong bloody shoes for this," Scarlett groused.

"They're very nice shoes," said a voice from behind them. Rob turned to see three more people walk in, led by a woman in a trouser suit with short hair. Behind her, two men followed and fanned out.

Rob recognised the female officer, DC Ellen Dale, and DC Tucker Stafford, a short, stocky man who was carrying a little extra weight. The third man Rob hadn't seen before, but he had a trim physique, a shock of light brown hair and wore by far the trendiest suit of them all, complete with waistcoat.

"You know Ellen and Tucker," Nailer began.

"I do." They'd been working with Nailer for a while, so he was familiar with them.

"Morning Rob," Ellen said with a smile, offering her hand. Rob took it. "Congratulations on your promotion to DI."

"Thanks."

"Likewise," Tucker added, also shaking his hand. "Congrats."

The third man also offered his hand. "DC Guy Gibson. Nice to meet you. I've heard a lot about you."

"Not too much, I hope."

"Only what John and these two have told me..." He indicated Nailer and the others. "Plus the general talk about the station, of course."

"I see," Rob remarked guardedly, and glanced at John Nailer.

"Don't worry. I won't hold it against you. Your boss was clearly a bent copper and needed dealing with."

Rob nodded, feeling himself relax again. "Thanks."

"So this is the full team," Nailer announced, gesturing to them all. "We'll be working under Superintendent Landon with this office as our main base of operations, although our work will take us all over Nottinghamshire and possibly beyond into the other counties of the East Midlands. So we might need to set up temporary hubs to deal with each case, but we'll cross that bridge when we get to it. In the meantime, as you can see, we have some work to be getting on with."

"We're shifting all this crap?" Tucker asked.

"I'm afraid so," Nailer confirmed. "We need to make space to work, which is why I got you all in so early, before we get called out. Some of it will stay up here, but we've arranged another room to move it to for now."

"Remind me, what happened to the previous unit?" Scarlett asked. "I've heard talk but..."

Nailer grimaced as he shuffled on the spot and stuffed his hands into his pockets. "That's a long story..."

"So tell the short version." Superintendent Evelynn Landon walked into the room. "They deserve to know."

"Fair enough, ma'am," Nailer replied before turning to address the group. "I just wondered if perhaps you should be the one to talk about it."

"No, no. Please, you go ahead." Landon waved dismissively at his comment.

"Okay. Well, the previous branch of the Notts EMSOU had embarked on an operation that targeted an Organised Crime Group and one of their drug supply lines. The gang had a few simultaneous shipments coming in, and it was decided to hit them all at once. This was after months of surveillance. Phone tracking and tapping, undercover work, the works. If they pulled it off, it could have crippled the gang's drug operation for weeks, or even months. But what they didn't know was that the gang knew they were coming. They were walking straight into a trap." Nailer sighed. "Four officers were killed during the course of the operation, and many more were injured."

Evelynn Landon stepped forward. "It became clear that we had a mole in the force, perhaps more than one, who were feeding information and intel back to the gang. The gang knew we were coming. They'd prepared, and we paid a heavy price. An internal review concluded that the Nottinghamshire EMSOU needed to go through some changes. It could not continue as it was. So the remaining officers were reassigned, and the office mothballed while the brass consulted about what to do. They eventually assigned me to resurrect the unit, and I was tasked with building things back up from nothing."

"That's why you seconded me to the EMSOU?" Rob asked.

"That's right," Landon confirmed, looking over and smiling. She was a short and stern-looking woman. Her white and black uniform only served to enhance her official aura. "I'd already recruited Nailer, and when you took the Sherwood Murder case, he suggested we allow you to run it. We wanted to see how you got on."

"I take it we passed your assessment," Rob asked.

"You did indeed. You went above and beyond, actually. I was impressed, and I'm looking forward to having you on the team. You too Scarlett. Your first case with the Notts force really saw you thrown into the deep end."

"Thanks. I did my best to follow my instincts and see the case through to its logical conclusion. No one is above the law, not even a DCI."

"You hear that, Nailer?" Tucker asked with a wry smile. "She's got your fuckin' number."

Landon smiled. "All this does mean, however, that we need to clear the office of all this..." She waved her arms at the piles of boxes.

"Wonderful," Rob moaned.

3

Rising from his slumber, Emmett slowly became aware of the room around him and the early morning light streaming through the partially open curtains.

He squeezed his eyes shut to block out the intense glow and cursed the extra drinks he'd indulged in the night before. He wasn't a young lad any longer, and his body couldn't tolerate being abused like it once had. The pounding headache, churning stomach and aching limbs all made their protests known as he lay in bed. But, it was Tuesday, and he had work to do today. He couldn't afford a lie in.

Why on earth had he gone out drinking on a Monday night, he wondered, silently chastising himself for making such a stupid choice.

Thinking back, though, he knew the reasons why he'd done it and he would no doubt do it again until his situation changed... or until she changed.

As curiosity filled his mind, Emmett rolled over to peek at the other side of the bed.

It was empty. Valerie was up. He'd have a few minute's grace before he'd need to deal with her nags.

Good.

She'd probably be pissed off. She hated him going out all the time, doing his best to avoid her. But screw that. She was the one who'd changed. She thought she could control his life. Well, he'd show her!

He sighed, feeling sad despite his bravado.

She'd changed. She wasn't the woman he'd married all those years ago. At least, he thought that was the case. Maybe she'd always been like this. Once upon a time, he'd seen her as an entrepreneurial go-getter who wanted to get out there and make a difference. He'd found her endless energy and desire to better herself attractive. It had been part of what had drawn him to her. He liked that part of her.

But, she'd changed. He was sure of it. That desire for a better life seemed to morph into something more mercenary and toxic. She wanted to control him, to run his life and keep him on a tight leash. But Emmett didn't want to play her game. He hated this new, domineering side of Valerie.

He needed his freedom and resented her trying to control him and mould him into something different. He was who he was, and no one, not even Valerie, was going to change that. He was also aware of the irony of wanting Valerie to change when he didn't want to, but she wasn't the woman he'd fallen in love with. That was for certain.

All this was why he was going out drinking on a Monday night. He wanted to extend a long middle finger to her desire for control. He wanted to show her he'd do as he damn well wanted. Sure, it might not look good for the local District Councillor to be seen out drinking and getting plastered on a Monday night, but he didn't care. This was his life, and he'd live it however he damn well wanted to and screw everyone else.

If that embarrassed Valerie, then so be it. He was learning not to care what she thought of his antics. He needed control of his life.

The thought made him grin. Control? Hah! There was a distinct lack of that, last night. At least he wasn't well known enough to make the front page of any local or national tabloid.

He smirked. That was at least one saving grace of being an unknown local councillor. He didn't like the idea of being followed by the press and having his every move scrutinised, that was for sure.

He lay in bed as long as he dared until the ticking clock and the pressure in his bladder became too much, and he forced himself up. Emmett squeezed his eyes shut as he tried to banish the dizziness that washed over him. Hopefully, some paracetamol would sort him out and allow him to get through the day.

He heard movement downstairs and felt a sudden urge to hide in the bathroom until he felt better. He wasn't quite up to dealing with her crap just yet.

Grabbing his things, Emmett dashed into the bathroom and locked the door behind him, resolving to ignore his wife until he was damn well ready to deal with her.

After fifteen minutes of blissful silence, alone in the bathroom, letting the water from the shower hammer against his shoulders and wake him up, it was finally time for him to face the music and see what Valerie would say to him.

Dressed and ready, he made his way downstairs and into the kitchen, where Valerie sat waiting. A partially drunk mug of coffee—he could smell the beans—sat before her, its steam long since faded. Her eyes flicked up as he walked into the room, and fixed him with a penetrating gaze.

He felt his stomach drop as his confidence abandoned him. She looked pissed off.

No! He would not be made to feel like some kind of monster by her. She was the one who'd changed, not him. She was the toxic one. He just needed to remember that and keep his wits about him. That was all.

"Dare I ask where you were, last night?" she muttered, her voice low.

Emmett took a breath, sucking in the warm kitchen air as he tried to steel himself and remember all the perfect arguments that he'd run through in his head.

He knew how he wanted this conversation to play out. He knew what he'd imagined himself saying and how she should react to him, but as usual, it never quite worked out like that.

"I don't know. Dare you?" He grimaced. That sounded far more combative than he'd thought it might and a lot less clever. He walked to the cupboards and started to make breakfast. Cereal, milk and a nice glass of fresh apple juice.

"You were drunk again. I smelt it when you came back. It's disgusting."

"I had some drinks," he admitted and cursed himself for trying to explain to her why he'd been out. Did she deserve an explanation? No, she didn't. "So what?"

"So what? Christ, you're an idiot. You're a councillor, Emmett. You work for the government. You can't be seen getting blind drunk. It doesn't look good... for you or me."

He scoffed at her comment. He wasn't "blind drunk". There weren't gaps in his memory. "No one cares."

"I care."

"About yourself. About your image."

She shrugged. "Of course. What you do reflects on me, Emmett, and you know I'm dealing with massive contracts. I can't have your idiotic antics backfire on us. This has to stop. Both for my... for our sake, and the community's."

"The community? So you know what's best for everyone, do you?"

"I have a fairly good idea."

"Is that right? Well, I don't think everyone wants the Colliery renovated into a leisure facility. What about those people? Hmm? Did you consider them when you sold it?"

"You're getting side-tracked. What's that got to do with us?"

Emmett sighed. He wasn't sure why he'd gone off on a tangent about her involvement with the sale of the former Colliery, other than his encounter with Nigel Wild the previous morning, perhaps. The former miner had made his feelings about the renovation perfectly clear over the years as the Coal Board that Valerie worked for, pushed for the sale of the site. Nigel seemed to delight in calling him scab whenever they saw one another in the street, and yesterday was no different.

In hindsight, he shouldn't have engaged with him and confronted him. Nigel seemed upset over something and for whatever reason, the man decided to take that anger out on him.

The scuffle on the street that followed had been embarrassing, but after the local hairdresser Colleen and

Father Aaron had stepped in, it soon stopped and Emmett was able to walk away. He remembered walking past the social club that Nigel ran moments later and sneering at the dilapidated building. It desperately needed modernising, even a lick of paint would do wonders for it.

It was just another example of the investment that the town desperately needed, something which Valerie, despite her flaws, was working hard to procure.

"Nothing," Emmett hissed, as conflicting feelings rampaged through his mind.

"Then stop deflecting. What did you get up to last night? Beers and a takeaway, was it?"

Hazy, blurred memories from the night before, and the fun he'd had, flashed in his mind's eye. He smiled at them.

"I told you, I had some drinks with some mates, that's all. You can't complain, anyway. You were with your friends last night, moaning about me, no doubt."

"Not as late as you were out."

He remembered sneaking in and hearing her in the shower upstairs. So, he'd stayed downstairs and kept out of her way, only going up to bed when he felt sure she was asleep. Were those the actions of a coward?

Emmet finished pouring out his cereal and went looking for the milk and apple juice, only to find that the juice was all gone.

He sighed. "We're out of juice."

"Then you'd better buy some more," she explained as if talking to a child.

"Obviously."

Annoyed that he'd be going without his morning drink, he moved to the table and sat down to eat his breakfast. He could feel her eyes on him the whole time, watching him, judging him. He glanced up, and she looked away. He stared at her for a long moment, taking in her features. Her narrowed eyes, set jaw and pouting bottom lip. The thought that occurred to him made him feel bad, but he just couldn't help his feelings.

She'd let herself go. She didn't seem to care about her appearance anymore. She never dressed up, wore make-up or appeared to make any effort for him at all.

He found her ugly.

Ugly.

That was not a word he thought he'd ever associate with her, and the realisation made him feel terrible, but there was a part of him that felt liberated by it too. He didn't find her attractive anymore and didn't want to be intimate with her.

Was he a bad person for thinking like that? Was he the toxic one?

He shook his head. No, he wasn't. He wasn't the one who'd changed their whole persona into a domineering, controlling bitch, thus driving him away. This was her fault, not his.

Everything he'd done from the moment he'd noticed her changing was *her* fault. She was the one who'd caused all this. She was the one to blame. He was the victim, not her.

Across the room, at the breakfast bar, Valerie got up, dumped her mug in the sink, and walked out of the room without another word or even a glance his way.

Emmet went to take another mouthful of cereal but couldn't face it. Instead, he found himself staring at the spoonful for several seconds before dropping it into the bowl. He was neither in the mood nor was he feeling physically up to eating much this morning. Last night's kebab was weighing heavy in his stomach, so he picked up his bowl and walked around to the sink.

He swore upon seeing the mug she'd left for him to put in the dishwasher. No juice, and now this? With a grunt of frustration, he reached for the washing-up gloves, but they were gone, too.

The list of things she'd done to annoy him this morning was growing and showed no signs of slowing down. Cursing her, he rolled up his shirt sleeves, and went to scrape the cereal into the bin. But it was full. It hadn't been put out last night and as a result, was starting to overflow.

"God damn it," he hissed, keeping his voice low so as not to draw her attention. Was she on protest or something? After scraping off the cereal and setting the bowl to one side, Emmet grabbed the bag from the bin and tied it off, his movements jerky with emotion.

Pissed off, Emmett yanked open the side door and made his way, with the bag of rubbish, around to the front of the house where the wheelie bins were, close to the road, and lifted the lid of the general rubbish one.

He froze as he went to lift the bag, his gaze fixed on what he'd found inside the wheelie bin, not quite believing what he could see... what was staring right back out at him.

He blinked several times, wondering if the beers from the night before were making him hallucinate or if he might still be asleep, and this was some kind of terrible nightmare. But no, it wasn't, and that thing was still in there, partially wrapped in a black bin liner, but ripped open enough that he could clearly see it.

"Holy shit," he gasped as the reality hit. Feeling suddenly ill, he retched but fell short of actually being sick.

Turning away, he closed the lid behind him. Was it real? Was this a prank? Emmett looked around. He took in the street and his house, briefly convinced that there would be a hidden camera somewhere, and this would all be revealed as some kind of joke.

But no. The road was as it usually was at this time in the morning, quiet with a few people going to work. There was nothing out of the ordinary at all. Everything was achingly normal. Frustratingly so.

With the lid closed, it was almost as if it wasn't there. Maybe he could leave it, and the bin men would take it away without realising what was in there.

But no. he couldn't do that. He couldn't ignore this and go about his day, his conscience wouldn't let him. He needed to report it. He needed to raise the alarm... if it was real.

Feeling a sudden urge to see it again and confirm that he wasn't just dreaming, he lifted the lid.

Sure enough, there it was. A motionless, pale, severed head of a woman, splattered with dried blood, staring out of a ripped black plastic bag.

As he watched, wriggling maggots that must have already been in the bin, eating the discarded food, ate into her skin and eyes, feasting on the flesh.

It was real. This was really happening. There was no denying it. His life would never be the same again.

4

"What's the count?"

Sergeant Meg Jolly sighed as she looked at the stats. "Three anti-social behaviour reports, one burglary, two reports of criminal damage, one report of drug dealing—which is markedly less than usual—and three violent offences were all reported last night. Less than half of them were dealt with on the night shift."

She screwed up her face as she contemplated the numbers and wondered if there really was any hope for humanity when people were doing this every night, causing trouble and causing pain to their fellow man or woman. It was tiresome, and with the reduced budget and fewer officers, half of the remaining reports wouldn't be dealt with today, if ever. The situation was maddening at the best of times. Instead, they were forced to pick and choose what they dealt with, which was a mix of assessing each individual report and taking a whole range of factors into account, such as the severity of the crime, its location, who the perpetrators were, etc, etc.

It was harsh and distinctly unfair, but what else could they do? They physically just couldn't respond to everything. It was impossible.

"It never ends, does it," PC Tom Reid stated.

"Never," Meg replied, her tone flat. They'd not really started yet, and already she'd had enough.

"Well, let's see how many of them we can get to, shall we?"

Meg smiled at the man's optimism. This was their first time partnering, following a reshuffle, and she was curious to see how they'd get on. He seemed nice enough and sympathised with her point of view, so that was something.

"I'm guessing less than we'd like."

"Most likely. Let's hope for a quiet day though, shall we?"

Meg grimaced at his use of the Q-word. Wasn't he aware of the stigma surrounding that word? Still, she couldn't fault his optimism. "Sure, why not. One can hope." Meg consulted the sat nav. They were close to their first call.

"Remind me of this guy's name?" Tom said. "Who are we going to see?"

"Kevin Arnold," Meg replied. "Say's he's been assaulted by some local scrotes who were out causing trouble. He's reported incidents before, but it's never really come to anything before."

"The British justice system, working as it's designed," Tom groused.

They pulled into the street and worked their way along it until Meg spotted number twenty-four. "There, that's his place." She pointed to the basic, boxy house with its dirty pebble dashed exterior.

"Mmm," Tom grumbled. "Looks like the locals are out to greet us."

Meg glanced at the handful of kids out and about on bikes, wearing sports clothing, hoodies and puffer jackets. All of them looked like tiny hooligans. They'd be abused by these locals the moment they left the car. She was certain of that.

"Right, let's go and see what's what, shall we?" she suggested, forcing herself to take a more positive outlook on the situation. She climbed out and popped her hat back on.

"Oi, oi," one of the little toe rags called out. "Does anyone else smell bacon?"

Another kid made pig noises while his mates laughed.

"Original, as ever," she muttered as she rounded the car and passed close to Tom.

"The oldies are always the best." He waved for her to go first. "Age before beauty."

She smirked. "Nice."

"I've got all the best jokes stored up here." He tapped the side of his head.

"Well, as long as you have space 'up there' for some police work, we should get along fine." Meg walked up the path to the front door and knocked.

A moment later, she heard a muffled voice from inside. "Who is it?"

"Mr Arnold? It's the police. We're here to talk to you about what happened last night."

"It's about bloody time," he grumbled and set to unlocking the door, as the sound of metal bolts slamming back into their housings could be heard. Meg counted four separate bolts, plus the door's main internal lock before the handle twisted and the door opened.

Whoops and jibes were shouted at him by the kids as he appeared. The old man seemed to cower back inside, clearly terrified. "Come in, come in," he said, backing away.

"Thank you, Mr Arnold." Meg saw the man's split lip and facial bruising and felt terrible for him. No one should have to live in fear like this, not at his age. He was little more than a prisoner in his own home. "Shall we go and sit down?"

He nodded enthusiastically and led them through to his front room, where he gingerly took a seat. Meg and Tom took the sofa.

"You reported that you were assaulted late last night," Meg began, having pulled out her notebook. "We're sorry we're only just getting to you, but hopefully, we can get this sorted out."

"I hope so."

"You live alone, Mr Arnold?"

"Aye. It's just me." Mag caught his glance at the nearby cabinet where she could make out photos of him and a woman she assumed was his wife.

"Okay," she said warmly. "This isn't the first time you've reported a problem, is it?"

"No. They're terrorising the street. This used to be such a lovely place to live. We all used to get on, and visit each other. But it's not like that anymore. It's changed, and not for the better. My poor wife, I'm sure they drove her to her death with the fear and stress of living here."

Meg felt her chest tense with emotion but choked it back. She felt so sorry for him. Best to plough on. "So, what happened last night?"

Kevin sighed. "They were being particularly noisy last night, shouting and riding back and forth, knocking on doors, throwing stones." He shook his head as he stared into the middle distance, his tired eyes glistening. "It's too much. I can't live like this."

Meg went to reply, but found herself choked up. She coughed to try and clear the lump in her throat.

"Let's focus on last night," Tom suggested.

"Right you are," Kevin agreed. "I'd been listening to it for hours. In the end, it just got to me. It touched a nerve. I couldn't sit back and ignore it, so I went to the door, opened it, and gave them a piece of my mind."

"You shouted at them?"

"Yeah. Of course, I did. I couldn't take it anymore, so I told 'em to piss off."

"And then what happened?" Meg felt sure she could take a wild guess as to what the consequences of that were.

"One of them walked over and started mouthing off at me, calling me all kinds of names. Swearing at me. It was... terrifying."

"And then what happened?" Tom asked.

"Well, I wasn't going to stand there and take that, not in my own home," he answered. "Not on my property."

"So, you're saying things escalated?" Meg took notes as the man spoke, jotting down key moments and details.

He didn't like that I was standing up to him," he confirmed. "He didn't take it very well, and before I knew it, he lashed out. He punched me, splitting my lip. Then he laughed and went back to his mates."

"And who was this person," Tom asked. "Did you recognise them? Do they live locally?"

As Tom continued to ask about the details of the case, Meg heard her radio squawk into life. "All units, this is control. We have an urgent call out to Clipstone. Is anyone local?"

They were in Forest Hill, just a short trip over to the village, no more than five minutes away. Meg excused herself and left the room.

"Control, this is unit six over in Forest Hill. We're close to Clipstone," she announced over the radio. "We can be there in five, maybe ten minutes."

"Roger that, six. This is a suspected 10-54. Investigate and report in. Be prepared to secure the area and wait for backup. No one in or out. Copy?"

"Control, Six, copy that." An urgent 10-54? Meg ruminated, wondering what was going on over in Clipstone. Whatever it was, they needed someone pronto, and they were the closest. Unfortunately, it would mean leaving poor Mr Arnold for a later date.

And here was the issue they dealt with every day. It really was never-ending. No matter how small or large the list of incidents any given shift took on, new ones were continually being added. They were constantly playing catch-up. As desperate as she was to help Mr Arnold, the 10-54 took precedence. She hoped Tom was about finished, so they could get going. She'd be sure to check in with Mr Arnold, though, and follow it up as soon as humanly possible.

Walking back into the room, she stood by the door with her hand on her radio. When Tom looked up, she tapped it and briefly tilted her head towards the door.

"Alright, Mr Arnold," Tom said. "Thank you for those details. There's not a lot more we can do right now. We'll look into it and see what further action can be taken, okay?"

"Okay," Kevin replied, still shaky. He looked defeated as if accepting that nothing would be done.

"Have you had that looked at?" Meg asked, noting the wound closure strip on his lip.

"Yeah," he confirmed. "I'm okay. There are still good neighbours around here, despite the idiot kids. If they could just be brought under control, this area would be so much nicer."

She couldn't disagree with him about that. It was always the few that ruined it for the many.

Within moments, they'd excused themselves from the house, with Kevin locking the door behind them, and returned to their car. Meg felt pleasantly surprised that the kids hadn't keyed or egged it. Maybe there was hope for them yet, she thought.

"We need to get over to Clipstone," Meg announced once they were safely inside the car. "We've got an urgent call out."

"What's up?"

"10-54," she replied and fixed him with an expectant look, wondering if he could remember his codes.

"A body?" he replied.

"Aye. Let's get going."

He threw the car into gear. "Looks like my wish for a quiet shift has gone up in smoke."

"You should know better than to use the Q-word, Tom."

"I jinxed us, didn't I."

"Looks that way," Meg agreed as they set off, briefly followed by the local kids on their bikes, who threw insults their way. Meg focused on the drive over, making sure Tom didn't take a wrong turn while monitoring the radio and keeping control up to date with their progress until finally, they pulled onto Edmonton Road on the southern side of Clipstone. It was one of the nicer roads in the small, former mining town, on the opposite side from the iconic Headstocks further up Mansfield Road. Red brick houses and bungalows lined both sides of the road with their well-kept lawns and water features. It was all very middle class.

Pulling up, Meg spotted the house and two people standing outside, their arms crossed, looking distinctly uncomfortable.

"Here we go," Tom muttered before climbing out of the car. Meg followed, and together they walked around the car towards the house. She glanced back and forth, taking in the quiet road and morning traffic. A passing commuter craned his neck to get a better look at the conspicuous police car as he drove by.

Approaching the man and woman, Tom took the lead.

"Mornin'. What seems to be the issue? You've reported finding something. Is that right?"

The look in both their eyes betrayed their shock. They'd seen something nightmarish this morning, and yet the scene looked distinctly ordinary.

"Yeah," the man replied. "It's um... it's in there. In the wheelie bin. The green one." He pointed.

"The green one," Meg replied. She was closer than Tom and moved over to it. She reached into a pocket on her vest, cursing that she only had three pairs of latex gloves today, and snapped a pair of them on, hoping this wasn't a wasted use.

"That's the one," the man said. Beside him, the woman, who was probably his wife, put her hand over her mouth and looked away. The man cringed as she reached for the bin before he looked away too.

Was it that bad?

Concentrating on what she needed to do, she gingerly took hold of the edge of the lid, touching as little of it as possible and trying to stay away from the obvious handle to avoid smudging any fingerprints that might be on there.

Confident of her hold, she lifted the lid.

The sight that greeted her was a grisly one. She felt her stomach turn on seeing the severed head, its lifeless eyes open and staring out accusingly. Beside her, Tom leaned in to get a look.

"Jesus," he whispered.

"That's about the worst thing I've seen in a while," Meg muttered and carefully replaced the lid to better contain the evidence. "Call it in. We're going to need the whole circus here for this one."

5

Placing the umpteenth box down on the storage room floor, one of several they were moving most of the excess boxes to, Rob made sure to let his legs do most of the work and tried to avoid using his back. It was already aching like crazy, and he didn't fancy putting it out completely and having to claim some sick days on his first day in the EMSOU.

They'd been moving boxes for a few hours, and although it felt like the middle of the afternoon, it was still reasonably early in the morning.

On the plus side, their office was starting to clear. Tucker was firing up the computers, seeing what worked and what didn't, while the others continued to shift boxes, clear desks and generally try to make some room for them to work once their shift officially started.

Placing his hands at the small of his back, Rob leaned backwards as far as he could go, flexing his spine as he tried to work out the kinks. He'd sleep well tonight, he thought. That was for certain.

With a sigh, he left the room, closed the door behind him and turned to set off back to the office.

"Well, well, well, what have we here?" said a voice he recognised but didn't immediately place.

Rob looked up, and a beat later, his heart fell as he recognised Inspector Bill Rainault from the Professional Standards Unit (PSU), better known as Anti-Corruption. To Rob, he also had the dubious honour of being the lead member of the anti-Loxley club, he thought jokingly. Having left Nottingham Central Station, he'd optimistically thought that he'd left Bill, and his constant harassment, behind.

But, here he was, and he seemed to be enjoying himself.

"I was hoping we'd run into one another. It's good to see you again."

"I can't exactly say the same," Rob grumbled, sticking his bottom lip out.

"Oh, Rob. I've missed our little chats these last few weeks. So I'm thrilled you've finally made the move to Sherwood Lodge. It means I can keep my beady eye on you."

"It is beady."

Bill's eyes narrowed, and any mirth dropped from his voice. "I'm watching you, Rob."

"I'm so thrilled for you." Rob wasn't impressed. "Although I do question your workload if you have time to wander these corridors looking for me. Are your superiors keeping you busy?"

Bill sneered. "You're very much a side project, Rob. Don't you worry about that. But it's a project that I'm passionate about."

Getting into the swing of things, Rob couldn't help himself when he answered, "I've always wanted to be someone's passion. But I'm sorry, I just don't swing that way. Your love for me will remain unrequited, I'm afraid."

"You can joke all you like, Loxley. That's fine by me." He sounded haughty.

Rob decided to change tactics, and see what happened. "So, I take it you work here?"

"I go wherever my work takes me, Loxley. But yes, my head office is here, at the Lodge. Just upstairs, actually. Nice and close."

Rob glanced up and then back down at Bill. "Cosy."

"I know. We'll be seeing a lot of each other." He smiled. "How are you settling in? I'm guessing you've noticed how some officers react to people who arrest their own, right?"

Rob didn't like his tone. "Maybe."

"Get used to it because that stain lingers." He grinned again. "Well, as much as I'd love to, I can't hang around here all day talking to you. Some of us have actual police work to be getting on with. I'm sure I'll see you around again soon." With a final smug grin, Bill turned and wandered off with a swagger that said he didn't have a care in the world.

"I'll look forward to it," Rob grumbled, annoyed that he hadn't managed to escape Bill's obsession with his supposed links to organised crime. It didn't matter how many times he proved he was a victim of circumstance and that he had been estranged from his family for over two decades at his point, Bill didn't care. To Bill, he was a corrupt cop, feeding information and worse back to the criminal underworld, and he'd do everything in his power to expose Rob and his operation.

The issue being, there was no operation, so there was nothing for Bill to find. But Bill wouldn't accept that and just kept digging. It was infuriating.

He watched Bill walk away before he set off back to the EMSOU office with a sour taste in his mouth. That brief interaction had tainted Rob's otherwise pleasant morning. This was supposed to be a new start for him, but it looked like some of the old issues would continue to haunt him, no matter what he did.

He was probably being naive. It was unrealistic to expect the problems he'd had at Central Station to disappear just because he'd moved to a new unit. But, he had hoped to put some distance between him and the PSU's resident crusader, Bill 'The Sheriff' Rainault.

Annoyed and frustrated, he wandered back into the EMSOU office space with his hands in his pockets and a dark cloud hovering above him. Spotting Scarlett, he meandered over and caught her eye.

She did a double take and stopped packing the open box beside her. "Everything alright?" she asked with narrowed eyes.

"Bill works here," he muttered, keeping his voice low. "I've just seen him."

"Oh, crap," she answered and leaned up against the desk beside Rob. "I'm sorry. That sucks."

"Yeah, it does. I was hoping I'd left him behind."

"No such luck, then, I guess."

"Seems that way."

"What did he say?" Her tone was curious.

"The usual crap," Rob replied dismissively. "He's looking forward to seeing how I get on with the new unit, that kind of thing. You know what he's like."

"Yeah, I do." Her voice was serious. "I know exactly what he's like."

There was a pause between them as Rob remembered her describing the encounters she'd had with Bill during her first few days on the Sherwood case and how he'd accosted her a couple of times, trying to poison her against him. He thanked his lucky stars that she'd refused to believe Bill's crap.

He wished he could have seen the look on Bill's face when she'd stood her ground and basically told him to piss off, but in much nicer terms.

There was a pregnant pause between them. Rob felt like he needed to say something but couldn't settle on anything as his mind whirled with random, troubling thoughts.

"Well, there's only one thing for it," Scarlett said suddenly. "You've just got to press on as if he's not here. You can't let him win. You've come so far, Rob. So far. You finally got that promotion that's been eluding you for so long, and you've been transferred into a new unit after catching a high-ranking corrupt cop red-handed. That's nothing to sniff at, is it?"

"No, I guess not."

"You're damn right it's not. So let's show him what we're made of; what you're made of. You're better than he is."

Rob smiled at her undimmed enthusiasm. "Thank you, Scarlett. You're just what I needed, and you're right. Don't worry, I wasn't about to top myself or anything. It was just a little unexpected, that's all, and a little raw."

"Sure. No problem. I understand."

"You're right, though. I just need to keep going and let my actions speak for themselves."

"Screw him," she sneered.

"Yeah, screw him," he mimicked.

"Screw who?"

Rob turned to see Guy wandering over. "No one," Rob replied and clamped his mouth shut, preferring to keep his issues with the PSU to himself for the time being.

"Fair enough." Guy turned and looked across the office. Rob did the same. "It's looking better, isn't it?"

Finally, after several hours of work, they were able to look across the whole office unobstructed, and although there was still clutter and boxes, and the desks needed clearing and sorting, it was starting to look like a space they could work in.

"Yep," Rob agreed. "It's certainly getting there."

"Aye." Guy turned to them and smiled. "I'm looking forward to working with you both. I heard all about the Peter Orleton case. That was some crazy stuff. Did you ever suspect him?"

"Honestly, not really," Rob admitted. It was something he'd thought several times since Peter's arrest, and it made him question his observational skills. How could Peter get away with that level of deception for so long? If he'd noticed what Peter was doing earlier, then maybe they could have saved some lives. But he knew better than to go down that road, both because only madness lay there and also because Peter had been corrupt for years. He knew what he was doing. He was intelligent, subtle and crafty. Recriminations were pointless at this stage. "He kept it very well hidden and not just from me."

"He had everyone fooled," Guy said. "I mean, we've all probably interacted with him at some point, and none of us realised what he was doing. And if *you* didn't spot it, how could any of the rest of us?"

"He was very good at hiding what he was doing," Rob agreed. "Very good. Still, that doesn't seem to stop certain other officers holding a grudge against me."

"No, I don't suppose it does. Sorry, you're having to go through that."

Rob shrugged. "I'll survive."

"I'm sure you will," Guy added before turning to Scarlett. "Hell of an initiation into the Notts force for you."

"It's been full-on," Scarlett agreed. "But, Rob's helped guide me through it. I doubt I would have been transferred to EMSOU had I not been assigned to him."

"Sounds like you owe him." Guy gave Rob a conspiratorial smile. "I think there's a drink or two in that for you, matey."

Rob smirked and grinned at Scarlett. "I'll keep my fingers crossed."

"Not ganging up on me, are you?" Scarlett asked.

"No, no. Never," Rob replied.

"Don't worry." Guy winked at her. "I'll buy you a drink later, if you like."

"Will you now," Scarlett asked, raising an eyebrow at him.

Was he flirting with her, Rob wondered. He found it amusing, knowing he was barking up the wrong tree with Scarlett.

"Down, boy, down," Ellen said as she walked over. "Leave the girl alone."

Guy shrugged. "I'm just being friendly, that's all. Don't read anything into it."

"Yeah, right," Ellen scoffed before she turned and moved closer to Scarlett. "He's harmless, really. Don't worry about him."

"I won't," Scarlett answered. "But, I'd gladly accept a drink from a work colleague. Far be it from me to look a gift horse in the mouth."

Ellen raised her hand as she gave her an approving look. "High five, sister."

Scarlett slapped Ellen's hand.

In the distance, Rob heard a ringtone sound and turned to see Nailer taking a call in his office. The others seemed to notice too.

"Oh, is it that time already?" Ellen asked.

Rob checked his watch, and sure enough, their official shift start time had been and gone by now, meaning they were officially on duty. "Looks that way," Rob confirmed.

Moments later, Nailer finished the call and strode out of his office. He searched for and spotted Rob before he walked over.

"Looks like we're jumping right into it," Nailer said as he approached. "We've just been called out to a report in Clipstone. Someone has discovered a severed head in their wheelie bin this morning."

"Really?" Rob asked.

"Eww." Scarlett squirmed.

"Welcome to Nottingham," Ellen added.

"Yep," Nailer confirmed. "That's what they told me, and as we're back on call, they want us up there ASAP."

"I'll go," Rob offered.

"I was about to ask you," Nailer said. "Take Scarlett with you, too. Report back as soon as you can, and I'll start to get things arranged here. We'll need a local incident room set up, so I'll start looking into that." He turned to Guy. "Are we nearly done clearing the room?"

"I think so, sir," Guy answered. "Tucker's firing up the PCs, and most of the boxes have been shifted. But I think we'll be in a mess for a while."

Nailer agreed with a quick nod. "Yep. That's my assessment too. Okay. Rob, Scarlett, off you go. Let's make a good first impression as the new Notts EMSOU."

"On it, sir," Rob confirmed.

6

The pool car sped north up the A60, out of Nottingham towards Mansfield before veering right and taking the A617, and then various smaller side roads as they skirted the edge of the urban sprawl. They were making for Forest Town, and from there, they'd head east, into Clipstone.

"Yeah, you're probably right," Scarlett said from the passenger seat. "He probably was flirting with me."

"It was obvious," Rob said. "Ellen spotted it, too."

"I saw," Scarlett replied. "It was flattering, but he'll end up disappointed."

"Oh aye, but you could get a few drinks out of him before you crush his dreams beneath your heel."

"I never turn down a free drink," she confirmed. "A red. Merlot, in case you're wondering. Hint hint."

"Hint taken," Rob said, smiling. "Mine'll be a pint."

"A pint of what? Beer, lager, cider... vodka?"

"Beer or lager will do me. I'm not fussy."

"I'll make a note," she replied.

"I'm not a big drinker, mind," he admitted. "I'm not the biggest fan of getting blind drunk. I don't like losing control." There was more to it than that, though. He wasn't lying, he didn't like losing control, but he also didn't like being vulnerable. His history and his family left him with something of a target on his back, and the idea of running into his brothers, or worse, his father, and not being in full control of himself was enough to keep him sober most of the time.

He could never confirm his suspicions, and it had been years since anything had happened, but there were moments during his early days on the force when he'd sensed or suspected his family's meddling. His former girlfriend, Natasha Hunt, was certainly suspicious. His distrust of her was the main reason they were no longer together because, in every other way, she'd been perfect, and he'd fallen madly in love with her.

Sometimes, he thought back to Natasha and wondered if he'd been wrong. Had his paranoia got the better of him? Had their relationship been yet another victim of the fear surrounding his family and what they would do to get to him?

He had no way of knowing.

"You don't like losing control? Hmm. Is that an age thing? Because that doesn't bother me too much."

"It might be. What about you? Do you enjoy the occasional tipple?"

"I'm a social drinker," she answered. "I've not been properly drunk in years, not since uni, really." She stifled a laugh. "We didn't get much work done that first year. We spent most of our time going from student night to student night. Each evening it would be a different club or bar. It was fun early on, when we had the time, before the work kicked in."

"I didn't go to university," Rob replied. "Sounds like fun, though."

"It was, for the most part. Did you do any further education?"

"A bit," he admitted, thinking back and remembering his mother Annabel and how she'd protected him from his family's influence for as long as she could, getting him through school before she disappeared when he was seventeen. Back then, he'd hated it when she forced him to attend his classes. But looking back now, he appreciated what his mother did for him. She'd put her life on the line to protect him from his father and brother's influence, and he didn't want to betray her.

He'd nearly slipped through the cracks after she left, getting roped into working with his brothers for a few months until the incident and Nailer's intervention.

His life had changed that day.

"Just a bit?" She sounded curious.

"I went to college in Nottingham, and then did my police training, so..."

"I see," she replied, as they left Forrest Town and moved up Mansfield Road, into Clipstone, before finally turning right onto Edmonton Road. Ahead, a collection of police vehicles blocked the street. Blue and white police tape fluttered in the wind, marking the inner and outer cordons patrolled by uniformed officers wearing high-viz jackets. Driving slowly up to the outer cordon, Rob found a place to park.

"I can't say I'm looking forward to this one," Scarlett remarked. "A severed head in a bin? Just the thought of it makes my skin crawl."

Rob agreed. There was something wrong about seeing parts of a body separated from the whole, but he'd never seen a decapitation before, so this would be a new one on him. "Don't go losing your breakfast over this."

"I won't," she remarked as they climbed out of the car and made for the cordon and the nearest officer. As they approached, Rob pulled out his warrant card, and Scarlett did the same.

He showed it to the uniformed officer. "Morning," Rob said.

"Good morning, Detective Inspector." He glanced at Scarlett's ID. "Constable."

"Morning," she said.

"You'll want to talk to the Sergeant over there." He pointed.

"Thanks," Rob replied.

"Detective?"

The voice came from his right as Rob ducked under the tape, followed by Scarlett. He turned to see a shaven-headed man with dark brown skin, darker freckles, and warm friendly eyes, wearing the white collar of a priest with a black shirt. He smiled as he caught Rob's eye.

"Can I help you?" Rob asked.

"Are you the detective on this case?"

"One of them," Rob remarked. "How can I help?"

"Good morning. I'm Father Aaron, the local priest. I just wanted to make myself known to you because there's already been a lot of talk about this girl's head in the bin. People are understandably worried, and I'd love to put their minds at rest."

Rob raised his eyebrows at the priest's comments, shocked that word had got out so quickly. How did this priest know more than he did? Rob wasn't sure how to answer.

"We understand that," Scarlett cut in. "But right now, we need to focus on this scene and the case. We will come out with a statement soon, but until then, I'd recommend against spreading any rumours or gossip. It doesn't help anyone, least of all the victim."

Grateful for her help, Rob nodded along with Scarlett's words.

"Of course," Father Aaron replied. "I will be a paragon of discretion. You can count on me. Please let Mr and Mrs Wilkinson know they are in my thoughts and prayers."

Rob forced a smile. "Of course, thank you." Rob turned away, but Father Aaron had more to say.

"Oh, one other thing," he called out. Rob sighed. He turned back to find Father Aaron waving him closer. Rob approached the priest, wondering what bombshell the man of the cloth was going to drop this time. "When you have a moment, I'd like to talk to you about something. But, it can wait. You have more important things to deal with right now."

"Yes indeed," Rob replied. "We'll talk later."

Father Aaron smiled warmly before he turned and walked away, apparently satisfied with the conversation they'd just had.

John watched him go, wondering what the hell that man thought he was doing.

"How does that happen?" Scarlett asked as they turned to walk deeper into the police cordon. "How does he find out about that?"

Rob grimaced as he considered his answer. "I can think of dozens of ways, but it's probably come from either the couple who found the head or from one of our officers. Someone who's taken a bribe to spill the beans. My money's on the civilians, though."

"After what happened with Peter, you don't think it's a corrupt cop? I'm surprised."

"I'm full of surprises. I'm also well known for arresting a corrupt officer. Would you want to take the chance of ruining your career for a few quid, knowing I'm working the case?" They approached the Sergeant. She saw them coming and turned to greet them.

"Fair point," Scarlett replied. "I guess we'll see."

"Detectives," the approaching Sergeant called out. "Good morning. Looks like we have a doozy for you today."

"So we've heard. I'm DI Rob Loxley, and this is DC Scarlett Stutely. My DCI, John Nailer will be SIO." Rob frowned for a moment as he recognised the woman before him. It's Sergeant Jolly, isn't it?"

"Aye, sir. Megan Jolly." the dark-haired female officer replied. "I recognise you. Loxley, right? You took the Sherwood case."

"Yes, that's right. Good to see you again, Sergeant. Are we going to make a habit of meeting like this?"

"With the greatest of respect, sir, I hope not. But only because I'd rather people not get killed."

"How very selfish of you." Rob gave her a wry smile.

"I know. I should think of my needs and no one else's."

"That's the spirit."

"Correct me if I'm wrong," Scarlett cut in, "but, I think we have a job to do? I mean, far be it for me to tell you what to do and all, but..."

"But black humour in the face of tragic circumstances is a requirement of being a police officer."

"Oh, do shut up," Scarlett groaned. Megan looked surprised at Scarlett's presumptuousness, her eyebrows climbing up her head.

Rob shrugged and nodded to the second officer before addressing the Sergeant. "Are you going to introduce me?"

Megan waved towards Scarlett. "I was about to ask you the same thing."

"I'm DC Scarlett Stutely," Scarlett said, offering her hand.

"You're a feisty one," the Sergeant replied. "Megan Jolly, and this is PC Tom Reid."

"A pleasure," Scarlett replied.

"Nice to meet you, Tom." Rob turned back to Sergeant Jolly. "What's your involvement in this, then?"

"We responded to the call from the couple who live here. We were first on the scene, and I've taken command of the response. I will defer to you, of course, Inspector."

"Thanks. But please, carry on. You're clearly doing a bang-up job. Tell me about the situation right now?"

"The street's closed off," Megan replied, "and we have officers doing the door-to-doors. We've moved those living closest out entirely, and the couple who found the remains are being driven to Sherwood Lodge by request of DCI Nailer. They should be there shortly."

"The DCI's been in touch?"

"He has."

"I see, and what about the remains and dealing with the crime scene?" Rob asked. "Where are we?"

"The Police Surgeon has been and gone, photos have been taken, and Scene of Crime are doing their thing. They're your lot, actually. East Midlands Special Ops?"

"Aye," Rob confirmed, pleased that things were already well underway. "If you were first on the scene, I take it you met the couple?"

"We did. Emmett and Valerie Wilkinson."

"Then tell me what you thought of them. What was your impression? You saw how they acted upon seeing the authorities for the first time. What did you notice?"

"Both were visibly distressed," Megan answered. "Emmett was the one to discover the remains when he took the morning rubbish out and seemed very upset over the whole thing. I suspect he was in shock. Valerie seemed similar but was more grossed out over it than Emmett was."

"She gagged a couple of times early on," Tom added. "She didn't want to go near it."

"And how were they with each other?" Scarlett asked.

"They weren't hugging or anything," Tom replied. "Emmett didn't comfort Valerie at all. They were just standing there with their arms crossed."

"I wouldn't want to make assumptions," Megan added. "But, they didn't seem close and barely spoke to each other. But, I suppose this is quite a stressful situation?"

"Everyone reacts differently to these things," Tom agreed.

"Okay, thanks. That's helpful." Looking up, Rob saw one of the people in the white forensic suits standing waiting for them beside the tent. "We'll go and take a look."

"Right you are," the Sergeant replied. "Your CSM is Alicia Aston."

"Thank you, yes, I know Alicia."

Meg smiled. "I'll be around if you need me. I need to coordinate the house-to-house."

Excusing themselves, Rob walked over with Scarlett beside him.

"I'm not looking forward to this," Scarlett muttered. "I'll be having a large wine tonight, I think."

Rob agreed. Nearing the tent, the waiting Scene of Crime Officer greeted them. "Sir," the woman said with only her eyes visible behind her protective glasses, before she turned and addressed his partner. "Scarlett."

"Alicia," Rob replied.

"Hi," Scarlett said in greeting.

"Good to see you again," Rob added.

"You too," Alicia answered. "It's good to have you two on the unit. Congratulations on that and your promotion, sir."

"Thanks. I just hope I can live up to what Nailer and Landon expect of me."

"I'm sure you will. I have faith."

"Me too," Scarlett added, she reached out and briefly squeezed his upper arm.

Rob blushed. He was grateful for their support, but it wasn't something he was used to, and it caused his Imposter Syndrome to flare up as he let the ladies compliments settle.

"So, what have you got for us?" Scarlett asked, filling the silence.

Alicia lifted her arms from behind her back and held aloft two forensic coveralls. "I come bearing gifts."

The pair pulled on the baggy overalls, over the top of their suits, before adding the shoe covers and masks.

"This is a grim one," Alicia stated as they walked towards the tent. "Don't get too close and keep to the step pads. Here you go."

Rob turned right into the tent through its open side, his body tense as he gritted his teeth. Centred in the tent was a green wheelie bin with its lid open. Work lights to either side lit up the gruesome contents as flies buzzed around, adding to the eerie feel of the scene.

Inside the bin, a human head sat atop the pile of rubbish. The head was clearly female with long, dark hair. Her eyes were open, and she stared lifelessly out at him, with dried blood splattered across her face.

"Well, I'm glad I had my breakfast several hours ago," Rob remarked.

"That is not pleasant," Scarlett added. "My word, the poor girl. Who would do this?"

"Someone who really didn't like her, at a guess," Rob replied before he frowned and looked back at the house the bin belonged to. "Actually, another important question would be, why here? Why this bin?"

"Certainly," Scarlett agreed. "People don't usually do this kind of thing without a good reason. It's not usually random."

"Not always, no." Rob made a mental note to find out who Emmet and Valerie were before he turned back to the Crime Scene Manager. "So what do we know so far?"

"We don't have any ID yet," Alicia replied. "So, we have no idea who this is. But, her teeth are all intact, so we might be able to get an ID from those in a few days. But that then begs the question, where is the rest of her? Because if we can find the rest of her body, then we can use her prints, which would be quicker."

Rob nodded along slowly as Alicia spoke, agreeing with her. "Have we checked the other bins? Maybe the killer dumped the rest elsewhere up the street."

"I believe they're looking in the bins," Alicia replied.

"I'll check with them in a moment. Anything else? Was the obvious the cause of death, or was she decapitated afterwards?"

"I'll let you know about that. There's evidence of a wound on her head, but we need to get the head out of the bin and have a proper look."

"Of course. What about time of death?"

"Hard to say without a more detailed look. The pathologist could tell you more, but I'd say late last night, at a guess?"

"Okay. Keep me updated."

"Will do," she confirmed. Rob stepped away with Scarlett in tow and looked up at the house again. "What do you think?"

"I think we have a dangerous sicko on our hands," Scarlett replied. "Also, we need more information. We don't know nearly enough to make any kind of assumptions yet. Who is this girl? Why was she killed, and why was her head dumped here?"

"Agreed." Rob spotted Megan nearby, talking to some other officers. "So let's see what we can do about that, shall we?"

He strode over and waited for Sergeant Jolly to finish talking to the other officers before she finally turned to him. "What's up?"

"Who are Emmet and Valerie Wilkinson?" he asked, referring to the couple who had discovered the head.

"Aaah, yes. Well, that is interesting. Emmet is actually a local District Councillor for Edwinstowe and Clipstone, and Valerie works on the Coal Board, which is based in Mansfield."

"They both work for the government?" Rob clarified.

"They do," Meg confirmed. "Have done for years."

"So there are going to be people who disagree with their politics," Rob mused.

"Undoubtedly."

"That puts a new spin on it," Scarlett replied, making a note of what Megan had just revealed. "I think our list of suspects has just expanded."

"It certainly has," Rob agreed. Politics across the country and even the world seemed to have become ever more polarised of late, and it wouldn't be the first time he'd dealt with a political disagreement that got out of hand if this case turned out to be along similar lines. This potentially made things a little more complex and sensitive, which was not an idea he relished.

"Ma'am, sir?" It was PC Reid, walking over from the outer cordon.

"What's up?" Megan asked.

"We have a member of the local Neighbourhood Watch over here, demanding to speak to the person in charge." Tom looked over at Rob. "We've tried to send her on her way, but she's being persistent. Calm, but persistent. I think it might be worth you having a chat to her."

Rob sighed. "Do you, indeed?"

"Well..." Tom started.

"I'll go," Scarlett cut in, and then looked up at Rob. "We should engage with the community."

"No, no. You're right. We'll both go," Rob conceded before he turned back to Megan. "You've done a great job, and I'd like you two to be on hand for a while. We're going to need help with all this."

"Of course, sir," Megan replied.

"Great. I'll get one of my unit to come down and help with the house-to-house. We need to expand it right across the village and check everyone's bins, in case we find the rest of the victim."

"Of course."

"Great, okay, where is this person?"

"She's over here," Tom said, leading the way.

He soon spotted the woman. She glared at Tom as they approached, her eyes then flicking to himself and Scarlett as they drew near.

"That her?" Rob asked.

"That's the one," Tom muttered under his breath. "Good luck."

"Thanks," Rob replied.

"Are you in charge?" the woman snapped, her arms crossed. She appeared to be in her fifties and sported a severe expression, accentuated by the harsh bun tied at the back of her head.

"I'm the senior detective here, yes." Rob took a breath, making a conscious effort not to get riled up by a local busybody.

"I'm Janette. I'm on the Clipstone Neighbourhood Watch leadership team, and given what you've discovered in the Wilkinson's bin, it's clear to me that you need to talk to us and keep us up to date with what's going on. This is a serious matter."

"I agree, this is very serious, and we will be working hard to make sure we find the person or persons responsible." Her tone was a little too self-important for Rob's liking, but he let it slide for now.

"You need to work with us. We know this town better than you do. We'd be a valuable resource against someone killing young girls."

Rob frowned. So, she knew too. "You're well informed, I see."

"This is a small community, Detective. We all know each other."

"What else do you know?" he goaded her.

"I know this town is going to the dogs. I knew it was only a matter of time before something like this happened."

"Going to the dogs?"

"We have drug dealers out on the streets, kids hanging out on street corners mugging little old ladies. And then there are the prostitutes bringing all kinds of unsavoury people here. She's probably one of them, you know. Your victim. Killed by one of these perverts. This town isn't what it once was, not with all these criminals, paedophiles and immigrants. So yeah, it's going to the dogs."

Rob stiffened at her words, raising his eyebrows in shock. Conflating criminality or sexual deviance with people fleeing war and persecution undermined her credibility and took things a little too far.

"An immigrant or refugee isn't necessarily a criminal," Rob replied.

"Did I say they were?" She grunted. "You're twisting my words."

Rob shrugged. She was technically right, but by including them in that list, she was putting herself on thin ice.

She continued, "This town has gone downhill since we started letting these people in to leach off our system. Even the local pastor is one of them."

"One of them?" Rob wasn't certain what she was referring to, although he had his suspicions.

"Don't be naive," she snapped.

"Don't be racist," Scarlett barked back at her, clearly thinking the same thing that he was. He flinched at her words, but understood her frustration.

"How dare you!" the woman yelled.

Rob raised his hand, signalling Scarlett to stop and back off.

"I am not racist," Janette continued. "All I want is a world where we're all treated equally. Right now, people like you and me, good, hard-working British people, don't get the same opportunities these illegal immigrants do. We should get the same access to benefits, jobs and housing. We've been paying into this system for years, but instead, it benefits these people who come here illegally on a boat. It's a disgrace, is what it is, and towns like ours are paying the price. Crime is rife around here. Doris, up the road from me, she was robbed while she was in her own home the other week, and did you guys do anything about it? No, of course not. Why would you? You don't care about us, the one's who're funding your salary and pension."

"Miss…" Rob cut in.

"Mrs, actually," Janette replied. "Mrs Radcliffe."

"Mrs Radcliffe." Rob took a steadying breath. "I understand your frustration at the criminality in your town. I get it. But I think you should be careful about conflating it with unrelated issues. That said, this case is going to need the support of the local community, and we will make sure to keep the town's Neighbourhood Watch in the loop. That's the best I can do."

Janette pressed her lips into a thin, disapproving line, betraying her annoyance and frustration. However, after a moment's thought, she nodded. "Fine."

"We'll be in touch," Rob added.

"Thank you, officer."

Reluctantly, she turned and walked away. Rob watched her go.

"She could be trouble," Scarlett said.

"She's annoyed and frustrated and taking it out on anyone and everyone. That's all."

"She's also a bigot," Scarlett stated.

Rob sighed. "Perhaps. I don't much care about the politics of it. We're here to do a job and find the killer. I'd recommend putting aside any personal thoughts about Mrs Radcliffe for the time being. She could be a valuable resource or witness."

"I know, you're right," Scarlett grumbled. "She probably hates me already."

Rob glanced back at her. "I'm sure you'll cope."

"I might not sleep tonight."

Rob smiled. "I find that unlikely. Right, let's get back to the Lodge and leave the scene to these guys. We'll be back soon."

7

"Well, that sounds delightful," DCI Nailer commented as Rob and Scarlett sat in his office, going over the details of what they had discovered so far.

"It's certainly an odd feeling, looking at a disembodied head," Scarlett replied. "It feels wrong, somehow."

"I'm sure it does," Nailer agreed. "So, we have the head of a young woman dumped in the bin of a local District Councillor and his wife, who is also employed by the government. We don't know who this girl is, and we don't have the rest of her body, either. We've got a house-to-house search going on to look for the rest of the victim, and witnesses. Is that about right?"

"That's about the size of it, sir," Rob confirmed. There's plenty of community interest in this, too."

"I'm sure there is," Nailer replied. "So, we need to find out who this girl is, why she was killed, and why she was dumped in that bin and no one else's. Do you think it's related to the Wilkinsons and their jobs working for the government?"

"That is certainly one theory," Rob confirmed. "We all know how divisive politics can be, so it's not unlikely that someone took offence to something either Emmett or

Valerie was doing and decided to make their displeasure known."

"Emmett and Valerie are here, right?" Scarlett asked.

"Downstairs, yes. We have them in a break room with a family support officer. No one's spoken to them yet. You'll get first crack at them."

"Thanks," Rob replied.

"Anything else? Any CCTV or anything?"

"We're looking into that. I have no idea what local cameras are available, which ones work, and if we can get the footage. There might also be some personal security cameras, of course. The door-to-door will hopefully bring those to light. I've asked Guy and Nick to head over and coordinate that."

"Excellent," Nailer replied. "I've arranged for us to set up a local incident room at the Clipstone Village Hall. The priest was happy to help, but grumbled about the extra work he'd need to do to rearrange the other bookings."

"We met him at the crime scene," Rob commented. "He seemed nice enough, and quite well informed."

"The village grapevine working overtime?" Nailer asked.

"Yeah, maybe. I'm not too concerned."

"Okay, good to know. We'll start using the hall today and coordinate the investigation from there."

"Clipstone isn't too far away," Scarlett commented.

"No, it's not. But it's always better to be local for these kinds of things. That said, while I don't think we'll need room and board for the nights we're there, it might be worth having a bag of spare clothes with you, just in case we pull a late one."

"I'll need to pop home then, to grab a few things," Scarlett commented.

"Me too. I've not got anything here," Rob agreed.

"That's fine. Going forward, you need to keep a bag here," Nailer replied. "I'd suggest interviewing the Wilkinsons first since they've already been waiting for a while, but after that, go and get what you need and meet us at the Village Hall in Clipstone."

"Will do, guv," Rob replied.

"Thank you, sir," Scarlett added before they walked from Nailer's office back into the main room. Nick and Guy were already gone, but Tucker and Ellen were still working at their desks. The room hadn't changed much since they'd left for Clipstone, apart from a few more loads of boxes shifted into storage.

If they were constantly setting up local incident rooms, Rob wondered how much time they'd actually get to spend working here, in their own office. But, Nailer was right. Being local meant they were in the heart of the community, easily accessible for people who might want to come forward, and in close proximity to any new developments. He could see the benefits.

Rob turned to Scarlett. "Right then, let's head down and see the Wilkinsons."

They gathered their things and made their way downstairs.

"I hope we find the rest of that poor girl, whoever she is," Scarlett commented as they walked.

"Yeah, I know. Me too. Maybe Emmett or Valerie can help with that? It's a small town. They might know who she was."

"You never know your luck, providing neither of them is the killer, of course."

"I'll be keeping an open mind, as always."

They made their way to one of the break rooms that were kept sparsely furnished, with just sofas and a drinks machine. They served multiple purposes, from being actual break rooms for officers in the building to use to casual interview and meeting rooms. Here, they could speak to victims or the relatives of victims in a more comfortable environment without making them feel like they were being interrogated.

Finding the right room, Rob knocked on the closed door. A moment later, it was opened by a woman in plain clothes. Rob guessed she was the assigned EMSOU Family Liaison Officer. The woman smiled at them. "Hello? Yes?"

"I'm DI Loxley and this is DC Stutely..." Rob said, waiting to see if she recognised their names.

"Aaah, yes. The new detectives in the unit." She relaxed, letting the door open wider, revealing Emmett and Valerie sitting inside. "I'm DC Heather Knight."

"You're the FLO, I take it?" Rob asked.

"Correct. Come in, come in. I'll keep out of your hair. Would you like a drink?"

"No, no. Thank you."

"I'm good," Scarlett said.

"Very well." She waved toward the couple before closing the door behind them and taking a seat at the back of the room.

"Good morning," Rob said in greeting.

"Hello," Scarlett added.

"Hi," Emmett replied, but he didn't smile. He seemed almost hollow, and there was a haunted quality to his eyes.

Valerie, who was sitting a good metre away from Emmett, attempted a smile, but it didn't touch her eyes, despite her best efforts.

They were both clearly shocked and upset by the morning events, which was hardly surprising.

"Are you…" Emmett began.

"We're part of the investigation into the remains you found in your bin, yes," Rob confirmed. "I'm Detective Inspector Rob Loxley, and this is Detective Scarlett Stutely."

"Hi," Scarlett said. "How are you bearing up? Are you okay?"

"How would you feel if you'd found… that… in your bin?" Emmett asked.

"Upset and scared," Scarlett confirmed.

"Then you know how we feel," Emmett said. He took a long breath. "It's… I just don't know what this world is coming to. I really don't. I don't understand people anymore. Who would do this to…" He waved his hand in the air. "This girl, whoever she is. Or anyone, for that matter? Who goes around cutting heads off people? I just… I don't…"

"We understand," Rob sympathised. "This has been a massive shock to you both. We get that. But we need to talk to you, ask some questions and find out if there was a reason behind it. Is that okay?"

"Of course."

"Please, go ahead," Valerie added.

"Alright, let's go through the events leading up to the discovery. What did you both do yesterday and this morning?"

"I was working all day yesterday," Emmett replied, answering first. "After work, I went out with a few friends, we had some food and drinks, but that was about it."

"Do you know any timings?" Rob asked.

"Erm, let me think. I left work about six, went to the Social Club, had a few drinks. Then my mate, Charlie, left so I got a

Chinese before going to the Dog and Duck to meet up with another mate. I got home about quarter to eleven, I think."

"Were you with him?" Scarlett asked Valerie.

"No," Valerie confirmed. "I worked too, and went to see a friend at about seven thirty. I didn't stay as late, though. I was home before nine, so I watched some TV, then had a shower and went to bed. I was tired."

"Valerie was in the shower when I got back," Emmett added. "I stayed up a little later before I went to bed. She was already up when I woke up."

Valerie shrugged. "I woke up first, so I got up, got dressed, and went downstairs to get myself a coffee. Emmet appeared while I was drinking it."

"Is that right?" Scarlett asked while Rob looked on.

"Yeah, that's right," Emmett confirmed, shooting an annoyed look at Valerie. "After I had my breakfast, I sorted my stuff out and went to put some things in the bin. That's when I discovered it."

"I see," Rob said. "And you called us?"

"That's right."

"I'll need to speak to the friends you saw last night," Scarlett said to both of them before taking down their friends' details in her notebook. As she copied down the contact details, Rob decided he needed to know the answer to a question that had been bugging him since visiting the crime scene. He waited for Scarlett to finish.

"May I ask, have you told anyone about what you found this morning?" Rob asked.

Emmett frowned and then glanced at Valerie. Her eyes flicked sideways before she rolled them with a sigh. "Yeah. I messaged a couple of friends about it before the police arrived."

"I see," Rob replied. "Well, if you could refrain from telling anyone else anything about the case, for the time being, that would be most helpful. We need to control the release of information."

"I did tell her," Emmett muttered, twisting up his mouth in annoyance.

"That's okay. What's done is done, but we're all on the same page now, I hope."

Emmett nodded.

"Yes," Valerie said.

"Okay, great. So, as I understand it, you're a District Councillor, Mr Wilkinson. Correct?"

"That's right," he replied. "Do you think the, um... the head is related to that?"

"Do you?" Rob asked. "Do you know of anyone who might want to intimidate you or scare you? Do you have any enemies?"

"I have people who disagree with me," he answered. "But that's just politics. Our government policy is shaped by people holding different views and thrashing them out. That's what democracy is all about. But, if you're asking me if I know anyone who might be capable of this, then I would have to say no. I don't know anyone who would kill and chop someone up to send a message. That's insane."

"What about you, Mrs Wilkinson?" Scarlett asked. "You work for the government, too, right?"

"Yes. That's right. For the Coal Board," she confirmed. "But no, as Emmett said. I don't know anyone who could do that."

"What about enemies? Is there anyone local who might disagree with something you're doing?"

"I've been involved in the selling of the Headstocks in Clipstone to a private developer," Valerie replied. "I suppose that might upset some of the old miners."

"Headstocks?" Scarlett asked.

"The mining buildings in North Clipstone," Valerie clarified.

"I see."

"This is an old mining town," Emmett added. "There's plenty of former miners living here, and many of them still bear grudges going all the way back to the strikes in the eighties. I still get called scab occasionally because I worked through the strikes." He shrugged. "It's part of my history, and I'm proud of what I did back then. But would any of the people who disagree with me on all that, do this? I'd have to say no. I don't believe they would."

"You're sure about that?" Rob pressed.

Emmet took a breath and went to speak, but the words died in his mouth. He took a breath before answering. "I mean, how much do you truly know anyone? If pressed to the very edge, I suppose all of us are capable of some pretty horrible stuff."

Rob nodded in agreement. Having worked in the police for years and seen all kinds of people do some pretty horrible stuff. There really was no one type when it came to killers and those who committed violence. He'd seen the most unassuming people who wouldn't hurt a hair on anyone's head turn around and viciously attack someone because they'd been pushed to the absolute brink. People can only take so much before they turn. He'd seen it time and again, and he was sure he'd see it many more times before his career was over.

Was it possible that someone in this town, who perhaps disagreed with something Emmett or Valerie did, would kill someone and then dump the head in their bin just to send them a message? Certainly, it was. *Someone* had placed that head there, that was for sure.

But who, and why?

"Okay, fair point," Rob agreed. "Would you care to put a name to anyone who you've had issues with?"

"No, not right now," Emmett replied.

"Me neither," Valerie added when Rob glanced at her.

"Okay," Rob replied, a little annoyed that they wouldn't pin this on anyone. It was such a bizarre killing, it felt odd that these two didn't harbour any suspicions.

"We're going to need you both to make full written statements before you leave, detailing the events leading up to the discovery of the remains in your bin. You can do that with Detective Knight."

"Okay," they both replied.

"In the meantime," Rob added, "is there anyone you can stay with for a few days while we deal with the crime scene?"

"Or we can put you up in a hotel for a few nights," Scarlett added.

"I'm sure someone will have us," Emmett replied. "Mark and Claire maybe..."

"No." Valerie snapped. "We can't put someone out like that. We'll take a hotel room, please."

"Really?" Emmett asked, turning a reproachful eye on his wife. "I'm sure it'll be no problem."

"I'm not burdening anyone with this. We need our own space." Valerie pressed, before turning to Rob. "No. We'll stay at a hotel. I assume you'll fund it?"

"We'll cover the costs for a few nights at a hotel of our choice. Just until this blows over, and you can move back in."

Emmett grunted in frustration as he slumped back into the sofa, looking away from his wife. He didn't look happy.

8

"They're having problems," Scarlett stated. She sat in the passenger seat of Rob's Ford Capri, gazing out the window while Rob drove south through the city towards his apartment. The day was mild and grey, and the morning traffic had calmed down now that rush hour was over. No more parents desperately trying to get their kids into school on time.

It had been a full-on morning already with the clearing work at the office and now a sadistic murderer on the loose up in Clipstone. Rob wondered what the rest of the day would bring.

"You noticed the tension between them too, then," Rob replied as they drove south along the A60 through the heart of Nottingham and approached the River Trent, where Rob's apartment block was located.

"Difficult not to," Scarlett replied. "They were sitting about a metre apart and didn't seem to agree on anything. It seems fairly obvious to me."

"True. Although, that could be caused by the stressful situation they find themselves in."

"Yeah, it could," she agreed.

"Do you think one of them is to blame? Have we already spoken to the killer?"

"Mmm, I don't know. What's the motivation? Is one of them having an affair, maybe? But if so, wouldn't they know the victim?"

"Probably." Rob thought about it for a moment. "Okay, then how about that woman from the Neighbourhood Watch…"

"Janette."

"Yeah, her. She mentioned the town had a problem with prostitutes and that the victim was probably one of them."

"Yeah, she did." Scarlett's eyes narrowed in thought as Rob drew closer to his housing block. "And Emmett is a local councillor who could do something about them, maybe?"

"So, is someone pissed off with his lack of action on the issue?" Rob asked. "Is someone trying to intimidate Emmett or Valerie?"

"Interesting. Or maybe Emmett is using the working girls… He could be the killer," Scarlett suggested. "Maybe he has tastes that Valerie can't satisfy."

"That's messed up," Rob commented. "But, if we are dealing with prostitutes, then we're likely dealing with their pimps, and that leads to gangs. Are they sending a message to Emmett?"

"So this might be a gang killing," Scarlett said as Rob pulled into the parking space at his home. "I've already had enough of gangs to last me a lifetime, after Peter and the Top Valley boyz."

"I know what you mean, and all this conjecture doesn't take into account the possibility that this was all just random, and there's no reason why the head was found in Emmett's bin."

"True."

"We have too many variables right now. No motive, no ID and only the couple who found the remains and called it in as suspects. I think this is going to get a lot bigger before we find out who did it."

Scarlett nodded her agreement before they climbed out of his car.

"You know what," Scarlett said as she closed the passenger door. "She's growing on me." She placed her hand on the edge of the bonnet and ran her fingers along the paintwork.

"Of course she is." Rob smiled. "She's a beauty and a charmer." He locked the driver's door. "Have you locked it?"

"Oh," Scarlett exclaimed before opening the door, pressing the button and locking it shut. "That, I'm less of a fan of. I always forget I need to do it manually."

"But that's the beauty of her. She's old school and built to last."

"Oh, I know, don't worry," Scarlett agreed. She patted the bonnet one last time. "Right then, let's get your stuff, then head to mine."

"Right you are," Rob agreed before leading her through the locked outer door where he grabbed the morning's mail before walking up the stairs to his second-floor apartment. Rob glanced at his neighbour's door and briefly wondered if Erika was around? If he was going to be up in Mansfield and possibly staying up there for a few nights if things got busy, he'd need someone to feed Muffin, his cat.

He paused for a moment, unsure how to proceed.

"Everything okay?" Scarlett asked. Noticing his hesitation.

"Yeah, I just need to arrange for someone to feed my cat, so I was wondering about asking my neighbour." He jabbed his thumb towards the door.

"Do you know them?"

"Kinda," Rob replied. "Her name's Erika. She's nice. We've chatted a few times, and she's always friendly."

"Okay. And there's no one else you can ask?"

"Not really," Rob conceded. "Plus, she lives next door, so it would be easy for her."

"Then, the only question you need to ask yourself is, do you trust her?"

Rob screwed up his mouth in thought. She was right, it was the only question he needed to know the answer to, and he felt sure he did. "Yeah, I think so."

"Then ask. What's the worst that can happen?"

"She says no," Rob muttered. "No, no, that's not the worst thing. She could say yes, and then steal all my stuff and disappear."

"And you think that's likely, do you?"

"Well, no, but you asked what the worst thing she could do would be, so... No actually, she could rent it out to squatters, or have a party, or..."

"Rob!"

"You asked." He smiled. He was having fun with her, and from the roll of her eyes, she knew it.

"Just ask her, for Christ's sake."

With a final cheeky smile, Rob turned to the door and knocked on it. He waited for a few moments and knocked again until it became clear that no one was home. "She must be at work. I thought she might be."

"Do you have her number?"

"No," Rob revealed. "I'll write a note and pop it under her door with a spare key."

"That works." Scarlett shrugged. "Right, come on then. I want to meet your kitty."

"I'm sure he'll be pleased to meet you." Rob walked across the landing towards his door.

"You know," Scarlett began, "I never took you for a cat person."

"As I said, I'm full of surprises." He grinned at her before unlocking the door and stepping into his flat. Scarlett followed. As he walked in, Muffin jumped down from the back of a nearby chair, his tail raised as he meowed loudly in greeting. "Hello, you. I bet you're wondering why I'm back so early."

Rob scratched Muffin behind his ears, much to his cat's delight.

"Look, I've brought you a new friend," he said to the black cat.

"Hello," Scarlett said and crouched beside Rob and Muffin. "Aww, aren't you a handsome fellow." She petted him and continued cooing.

"Are you hungry?" Rob asked.

"Who? Me?"

"Yeah, you."

"I thought you were talking to the cat for a moment."

"No, he's got his food. I can whip up a quick cheese toasty for us both."

"Oooh, yes, please, I'm starving," she replied, still stroking Muffin, who was bumping into her legs and purring loudly. "Oh, Muffin, you're getting fur all over my tights."

Rob set to work, grabbing some bread and cheese and warming up the toasty maker.

"You've made a friend there, I think."

"He's lovely," she replied before looking up. "You old softy, you. I'm seeing a whole new side to you."

Rob pulled a face as he loaded up the machine. "Brown sauce?"

"Yes, please."

With a quick drizzle of Worcester Sauce, Rob closed the lid on the machine. "I'll go and grab my things."

"Yeah, yeah."

Leaving her to the affections of his cat, Rob dashed into his bedroom, grabbed a bag, and started to load it up with a few changes of clothes. He followed that by grabbing a wash bag and a selection of toiletries. By the time he was back in the open-plan living-room-come-kitchen area, Scarlett had already plated up the toasties and was tucking into hers.

"Come and have yours. You don't want to let it go cold."

Rob joined her at the table, noting that Muffin was still threading himself around her feet. "Thanks. So, he finally let you go, did he?"

"I pulled myself away."

"Do you have any pets?"

"Not right now," Scarlett answered. "But, I'd kind of like a dog."

"Oh? Anything in particular?"

"Um. A beagle, maybe? Something small-ish. But, not like a handbag dog."

"Okay."

"Do you like dogs?"

"Depends if it's trying to bite my hand off." Rob shrugged.

"A pet dog wouldn't do that. Especially if it was trained."

"I guess. I've never owned one." Childhood memories flashed through his mind as he considered Scarlett's question. He remembered the dogs that his father kept. His dad had loved dogs, but he had a specific use for them. He trained them to be obedient but vicious guard dogs that he'd occasionally use to intimidate others. He'd seen his father set them on people he didn't like several times. The animals had scared Rob when he was younger, and as he grew up, he never wanted one of his own, preferring the idea of a cat.

He didn't feel like sharing this part of his history with Scarlett, not yet, at least. He'd keep this to himself.

"And you've no desire to?" she pressed.

"No. We're happy." He glanced down at Muffin. "Aren't we, Muff?"

He saw one of Scarlett's eyebrows shoot up in a curious look. "That's an unfortunate nickname."

"Well, he is a pussy."

Scarlett smirked. "I... guess so."

Rob tucked into his lunch, savouring the mature cheesy taste mixed with the tang of brown sauce.

"You know, I realise I've never asked, where's home for you?"

"The Park Estate," she answered around a mouthful of toasty.

"Oh. Really?"

"Mmm-hmm."

"Nice." Rob decided not to hide his surprise. The Park was a private estate in the centre of Nottingham with huge houses and restricted access. It catered to the rich and well-to-do and until recently, didn't even appear on Google street view. It was where the wealthy and powerful of the city lived, complete with its tennis and squash clubs, famed Victorian houses and gas street light network. Maybe one or two of the force's senior officers might live on The Park, but it was out of reach for most officers and residents of Nottingham, due in part to the "Park Rates" that you paid in order to live there.

Scarlett shrugged. "Chris has a good job, so..."

"I bet." He got the impression there was more to it than that. She was holding something back, but it wasn't his place to pry. He focused on finishing off his toasty instead, catching Scarlett up as she polished off the last of hers.

"Right then," Rob said, getting up. Depositing the dirty plates in his dishwasher, he set it to a quick cycle before grabbing the spare key and a slip of paper. It only took him a moment to scribble down a quick note about feeding Muffin, complete with his phone number, before he grabbed his things and announced to Scarlett that he was ready.

She was crouched beside Muffin again, running her hand over his fur.

"And you call me a softy," he commented.

"Alright, alright," she said, standing up. She walked out, saying goodbye to Muffin as she went.

Rob bent down to briefly pet Muffin. "You might have someone new feeding you tonight, so you behave, okay? No puking on the sofa. Got it?"

Muffin meowed loudly as if in protest.

"That's enough of your sass, young man. I've been watching you, you know. I've seen you sucking up to Scarlett. Just remember who feeds you every day, alright?"

Muffin snuffled and purred.

"Better. Now, be good."

Rob left the flat and locked the door before he caught Scarlett giving him a curious look. "What?"

"You are such a cute teddy bear. I'm never going to be able to look at you the same way again."

"Oh, goody." He walked down to the entrance and slipped the note, along with his key, into Erika's letter box. Satisfied, he turned to Scarlett. "Right then, let's head over to yours, shall we?"

"Let's do it," she agreed as they made their way downstairs and back into Rob's black Capri. "Do you know Lenton Road?"

"By the castle?" Rob asked, feeling confident he was right.

"That's the one. Drive into The Park through there. You can't enter through Peveril Drive without your vehicle being registered on the ANPR system."

Rob had heard of the Automated Number Plate Recognition system that the estate used, which they used to control raising bollards on the southern entrance.

It wasn't a long drive along Sheriff's Way, Wilford Road and then Maid Marian Way before they turned in to The Park along Lenton Road. Immediately the roads were quieter, with fewer cars parked up, and the houses took on a grander, Victorian style. Rob had passed through the estate before, usually as part of work, and had often eyed some of the houses with envy. Although, there wasn't a lot of garden space in many of them.

Scarlett directed Rob to Clumber Crescent and into the gated driveway of an imposing house. A large Land Rover was parked ahead of them on the pea gravel.

"Oh, he's in." She sounded surprised. "Looks like you might get to meet Chris."

"The Fiancé?"

"Yep," she confirmed with a smile before they both climbed out of the car and set off across the driveway towards the red brick building. Rob eyed the pea gravel reproachfully. He hated the stuff. It made so much noise and was difficult to walk on. Ahead, Scarlett was having particular trouble in her heels.

They soon made it, though, and she led him inside.

"Babe," she called out from the hallway.

Rob heard movement, and a moment later, a man who was perhaps a little taller than Rob walked in. He sported a short messy blonde hairdo along with a physique that suggested he worked out and took care of himself.

"Hey," the man said to Scarlett. "You're back early."

"It's just a fleeting visit. I'm picking up a few things." She gave him a quick kiss.

"Oh, like what?" He looked a little confused. "We're not married yet, you can't leave me," he quipped.

"Well, for a start, I'm changing out of these heels." Rob smiled as she glanced back. "Don't you start," she snapped, giving him a look.

"I didn't say anything."

"You didn't need to." She looked up at her partner. "Oh, and this is Rob. Rob, Chris."

Rob took a step closer and offered his hand. "Nice to meet you."

"And you. I've heard a lot about you," Chris said before he turned to Scarlett. "Can I help you?"

"No. I'm just grabbing a bag of clothes. We've taken on a case up in Mansfield, so If I can't get home and I'm there overnight, I've got a change of pants." She grinned. "I won't be a moment."

And with that, she was off up the stairs.

Chris watched her go and then turned to Rob. "Women."

Rob laughed. "Yeah. Nice place you have here."

"Thanks. Yeah, it's not bad. It's a roof over our heads, anyway."

"Hope we didn't interrupt anything."

"Nah. Only work."

"What do you do?" Rob asked, curious.

"Oh, it's boring stuff compared to what you do. I work for a consultancy firm, we work with companies and help them mould their business plans for growth and... well, like I said, it's not exciting. Lots of meetings and sitting in front of a computer."

"We do a lot of that, too," Rob replied. "It's probably nowhere near as exciting as you think it is."

"You have moments of excitement, though. The most thrilling thing that happens in our office is if the water fountain breaks, or a PC blue screens."

Rob shrugged. "I guess. But it just becomes a job at the end of the day. So I hear you're getting married. Congratulations."

"Yeah, thanks. We got engaged a few months ago before we moved up here. We've got a lot to organise. Are you married?"

Rob chuckled to himself. "No. Never got there. Can't say I'm that interested in it, either."

Chris shrugged. "Fair enough. It wasn't something I put much thought into, I guess. I always thought I would get married at some point, but it wasn't something I was actively looking for. Not until Scarlett came along, anyway. But, it just felt right, with her, you know?"

"Not really."

"No, I guess not," Chris muttered. "Can I get you anything? A drink?"

"No, I'm fine, thanks, though."

"Okay."

Rob wasn't trying to make him feel uncomfortable, but from the awkward silence and the way Chris shifted from foot to foot, he seemed to have achieved it.

"So, Mansfield, then," Chris said eventually. "Big case is it?"

Rob shrugged. "I can't go into too much detail, but yeah. A murder. I'm sure it'll be on the news."

"Oh. And you're working up there?"

Rob narrowed his eyes. "As the East Midlands Special Operations Unit, we cover the whole of Nottingham, but also the rest of the East Midlands too. Derbyshire, Leicestershire, Lincolnshire, Northamptonshire and Nottinghamshire. Depending on the case, we might set up a local incident room and work locally. It just makes things easier, but it will mean that Scarlett will keep having nights away. Sorry."

Chris shrugged. "Fair enough. She did mention something about that to me before, but..."

"But you weren't listening." Scarlett clattered down the stairs as she spoke, now wearing trousers and different shoes. She rolled her eyes.

"Love you, babe," Chris crooned.

"Love you too," she replied. "Right then, I'm ready."

"Are you dashing off?" Chris asked. "I can make tea."

"I'm good," Rob replied. "Thanks, though."

"Sorry," she said, rushing up to him and planting a big kiss on his lips. "Hopefully, I'll see you tonight, alright?"

"Sure thing."

She smiled before the pair separated and they made their way out of the house.

"Don't work too hard," Chris called out after them as they left the house.

"I won't." Scarlett smirked as they stalked back onto the pea gravel. "Sometimes, it's as though he doesn't know me at all."

Rob smiled. "He's nice."

"Well, now I have your approval, we can get married," she snarked.

9

Izabela rocked back and forth. She sat perched on the edge of her dirty mattress, hugging her legs as she stared across at the empty mattress beside her.

Penny's Mattress.

Like hers, it was strewn with unwashed sheets and in desperate need of a clean, but that wasn't the worst thing about it.

No, the worst thing was that Penny wasn't on it.

She'd disappeared at some point during the middle of their evening on the street and hadn't returned. She'd gone off with one of her johns and didn't come back. Izabela had been working her own little patch under the watchful eyes of Abel, her pimp, and couldn't go hunting for Penny without pissing Abel off something rotten. She tried to keep him calm at all times in an attempt to avoid his flying fists. But Penny going missing would annoy him, and he'd probably take it out on her.

Penny had been Izabela's minder and the one who'd brought her into Abel's stable of working girls. She acted as both her protector and Abel's eyes and ears.

She was under no illusions that Penny would be spying on her and reporting back to Abel. But, she just accepted that and went about her routine, keeping her head down and the money rolling in.

Her cut wasn't much, but at least it gave her some cash to do with as she pleased.

The acrid stench of burning crack wafted across the room, filling her nostrils and awakening the familiar cravings she'd buried deep down inside. Pressing her eyes closed, she mentally wrestled with the monster inside that shouted and wailed for her to go over there and take a drag on Candy's pipe.

It wasn't easy, though. Izabela hugged her legs tighter, to the point of pain. She tensed up, rocking back and forth with her eyes squeezed shut. *No, no, no*, she silently repeated to herself in her head. She didn't need it. She didn't want it. It was what Abel wanted. Once she was hooked on it again, there would be no getting off it, not without help.

She heard one of the other girls muttering to Candy, asking where she got the rock and if she could have a puff.

"Please. Just one puff. Come on, Candy. You don't need it all. Please? What do you want me to do? I'll do anything. Please?"

And so it went, with Anna offering money, sex, favours and anything else she could think of for a hit on Candy's pipe. In the end, Candy was so high that Anna managed to grab the pipe without Candy realising. Shortly after, both girls had collapsed to their beds, utterly wasted on whatever tiny amount of Crack Candy had found through her Ghostbusting—a slang term for when a crackhead went hunting for discarded rocks of crack by getting on their hands and knees and searching.

Izabela didn't mock them for it. She'd been there, she'd done it. She'd been so hooked on that poison that she'd done literally anything to get her next hit. Those were memories she did her best to shut away and not think about. They were dark, sad memories, and she did not want to return to them.

And yet, she'd willingly put herself back into this position after getting out. After she'd left Radek and got clean, she'd gone right back into the game, but this time with Abel. Different pimp, different gang, but the same old crap.

What else was there for someone like her? She was an illegal immigrant with no passport—because Radek had taken it when he'd trafficked her—and no rights. She didn't know how to do anything other than sell herself for money. Money she desperately needed for her mother back in Poland.

That was what she told herself, anyway. That was the story she'd constructed as she went about this life, like a ghost. She'd not spoken to her mother in months, and apart from sending money through the post—something she'd done on a handful of occasions—she had no idea how to contact her mum. She couldn't remember her phone number, and anyway, she didn't own a phone. Abel wouldn't allow that.

This was not the life she wanted, nor was it the one she'd been promised by Radek and his gang. They'd promised to get her into the privileged west. They'd take care of her, and give her the new life she wanted. But they'd lied.

Thinking back over the horrible things she'd done, and been forced to do, she almost didn't recognise herself anymore, and wondered if her mother would, too. She was disgusted by what she'd become, embarrassed and ashamed. Her mother wouldn't understand, she couldn't know what she'd been through. It had all been by degrees, steadily, over time, until she looked in the mirror one day, and she realised she didn't recognise the person staring back at her.

She couldn't reveal to her mother what she'd become, what she'd done with her life. So letters, often anonymous ones, were what she'd resorted to. She didn't even want a phone. Not really.

Some of the girls had them, secret ones that they kept hidden, even from each other. Some of the girls would use that knowledge to curry favour with Abel, ratting each other out for a hit of crack or some other favour.

There was no trust between them, not in this kind of situation. It was everyone for themselves.

And yet, she'd come to almost rely on Penny. She'd been her guide and the person who brought her into Abel's gaggle of women. She knew she couldn't trust her, but still, she'd clung to Penny as if she was a life raft. But she was gone, and she could feel herself starting to drown.

But what had happened to her? Was it the John? Had he taken her away and killed her? She'd suffered violence at the hands of a client before. She'd been hit, gut-punched, slapped and thrown about by these men who paid her for sex. She'd even once been strangled, which had been a terrifying experience. So it wasn't hard to imagine a John getting his rocks off by killing the girl he was banging.

But that wasn't the thought that terrified her. Not even the idea of Abel coming back and being upset with her scared her as much as the idea of Radek being responsible for her death.

When she'd escaped, she'd left him without a trace. She'd disappeared, and she'd been one of his better earners. She'd seen Radek get angry before. She'd seen him turn girls and guys black and blue with the punishment he doled out for what she thought of as minor infractions.

Abel was violent, but Radek was a monster, and he'd be furious with Izabela for escaping his stable of girls.

Had he found out where she was? Did Radek know she'd joined Abel's girls? Was this his way of taking revenge against Abel, or sending a message to her? And if so, what would he do now? Who was next to feel his wrath?

The idea was terrifying, and she wasn't as protected as she'd once been. Abel didn't offer the same kind of protection that her saviour once had—the man who'd taken her in last time.

Maybe she should go back to him. He'd been good to her once, saved her from Radek, got her off the crack, helped her. He might help her again.

Maybe...

She wasn't sure, but circumstances might make the choice for her.

Downstairs, the front door slammed.

"Penny," Izabela gasped. She dashed from the room. She ran across the tiny landing and started down the stairs, hoping against hope that it would be Penny.

Abel was standing just inside the doorway.

Izabela froze halfway down the stairs silently praying that Abel would ignore her.

Three other girls quickly clustered around him, begging him for crack cocaine. One of them was pulling on his belt and zip. "Please, Abel. Please. Just one hit, that's all I need. I'll do anything, whatever you want. I just need a hit." The girl stuffed her hand down his trousers.

"Not now." He threw her off, slamming the girl into the wall. He'd hurt her, but he didn't give her a second look. Instead, he was staring up the stairs at Izabela. "Down here, now."

She hesitated.

"Get down here right now, bitch."

The fire in his eyes scared her, and she saw no other option but to do as he asked. She started down the steps under the uneasy gaze of the other prostitutes. They sensed it, too, his simmering anger and knew she was on very thin ice. She needed to be careful.

As she descended, he sneered at her in disgust, then walked through to one of the side rooms, clearly expecting her to follow. She glanced at the gang member sitting beside the front door, scrolling on his phone. He was there to keep the girls from running away, but he wasn't needed for most of them. Many came from outside the UK, and Abel had confiscated their passports, promising to release them once the girls had made him enough money. It was probably a lie. Most were also addicted to crack, and other drugs, and Abel was the only supplier they knew.

They were illegal immigrants who didn't know the country, didn't want to get caught by the police in case they were deported, and had a laundry list of reasons keeping them here with Abel.

For these desperate young women, he didn't need someone on the door. They weren't going anywhere. They were also self-policing, with them snitching on each other, ratting the others out for an extra high or other favours. She'd seen one girl try to get out, only for several of the others to pin her down and beat her senseless until Abel turned up. They knew from personal experience that if one of them got away, they would suffer the consequences.

No, the guy on the door was only for the few who might attempt to run, like her—new recruits who couldn't yet be trusted—and to answer the door when needed.

"In here," Abel barked.

Izabela followed, wrapping her arms around herself as she walked into the room. He didn't scare her as much as Radek did, but she had no illusions about how dangerous he was and what he would do to protect his own interests. She'd do well to be careful.

"Where is she?"

Penny. This was about Penny. "I don't know where Penny is. She went off with a John and... didn't come back."

"The bitch has taken my money," he growled. "Fuckin' cow. Who was this John?"

"I don't know. I didn't recognise him."

The slap came out of nowhere. His hand shot up and caught her across her cheek and jaw before she knew what was happening. A shockwave of pain exploded across her face. She yelped and gasped for breath, reaching up to touch her face.

"I want to know where she is." His tone was laced with warning.

"I do too. I don't know who she went with, but I might recognise him if I see him again."

"Make sure you do," he hissed. "I need you out on the street, making bank. You'll never get home or help your family without money, will you? What will your mother think of you, huh? If her girl can't help support her family, what use are you?"

"I'm... no use..." she squeaked, hating that she answered him.

"Exactly. And don't you get any ideas, either, because I will find the run-away bitch, and she will suffer, I can promise you that."

"I know."

He eyed her, his face a mask of thunder and rage. Suddenly he was on her, grabbing her by the throat and slamming her against the wall. "I mean it. Because if you try anything, I will take great pleasure in making you suffer. You won't know what hit you. I'll turn you into a plaything for my boys. You'll think you've been fucked by a freight train. You got that?"

Izabela swallowed her fear back down. She felt sick to her stomach as she gripped his hand, desperately wanting him to let her go. "Okay, okay. You're hurting me."

"Are you sure you don't know where Penny is?"

She tried to shake her head but could hardly move. "No. I don't know anything. It might be..."

His grip tightened. "Might be what?"

"Radek? It might be him. Does he know I'm here?"

Abel frowned as he stiffened before he looked away in thought.

"If he knows..." she continued, leaving the comment hanging. A moment later, his grip loosened, and she sucked in a deep breath. "Might he... do something?"

He let her go and took a step away, thinking things through. Izabela leaned against the wall, her hand on her bruised throat as she sucked in life-giving air. In that moment, she knew. She couldn't stay here. She needed to get away. Abel would hurt her, abuse her, and maybe even kill her if she stayed. If Radek started killing Abel's girls, she'd become a liability, and it might be Abel who killed her just to keep Radek's crew off his back. If she stayed here, she was a dead woman. That was for certain.

He turned back, still frowning. "No. I don't think so. I think you'll say whatever you need to protect yourself. That's what I think."

"No," she pleaded. "That's not..."

"Shut up. You're working Forest Town tonight. You'll be with Candy, got it?"

She nodded as he went to walk by her. As he passed, he lashed out and slammed his fist into her gut. Doubling over in pain, it took her several moments before she could take a breath.

"I'll have less shit from you from now on."

She nodded, unable to speak as the agony flooded through her body.

Then he was gone, leaving her with her thoughts and the beginnings of a plan to escape.

10

The Village Hall sat on the western edge of the Clipstone Welfare Sports Field, which was basically a large area of grass in the centre of the village, marked up with the lines of a football pitch. Several buildings lined the southern side of the block, which was surrounded by a road, and suburban housing around that.

Rob pulled up to the side of the road between the hall and the green, noting the small car park at the front was already full of police vehicles, vans and pool cars. Nearby, locals were standing watching as the team's equipment was unloaded, supervised by DC Guy Gibson. They'd probably never seen anything like this happen in the village before and might never again. Several members of the press could be seen, too, talking to the locals or watching proceedings.

As he stopped, Guy took a break from directing the people unloading a van and walked over.

"The circus has come to town," Rob muttered before Scarlett lowered the passenger side window.

"Hey," Guy said. "There's more parking round back. You might be better round there."

"Right you are," Rob replied.

Guy smiled. "You took your time getting here. We could have used your help."

"Sorry, we had to make a stop," Rob replied.

"Yeah, his cat needed feeding," Scarlett added. "Couldn't wait."

Guy raised an eyebrow. "Whatever, just get parked up and come help."

"Will do," Rob confirmed. He drove around to the rear of the building and turned onto a track that led to a makeshift car park. It was little more than beige gravel surrounded by trees and bushes. There were a few more cars parked up, and he recognised Nailer's as one of them.

"Turning up in force in a small town like this," Rob mused. "We're going to cause a stir."

"Of course we are," Scarlett replied. "It's only natural. The press can be useful, though."

"And annoying."

Scarlett shrugged. "That too. Like you, really." She grinned.

Rob couldn't help but smile. "That's what I am to you, is it? Useful and annoying."

"Pretty much. Like most men, you have your uses, but you often just get in the way."

Rob nodded. "I won't argue with you today. I wouldn't want to be annoying."

"See, you're getting it." She climbed out of the passenger seat.

With a laugh and a shake of his head, Rob got out, too, before they locked the car. "Right then, let's see how much mess we've made of the place."

"I'm guessing a lot," Scarlett speculated.

They walked around the building to the front entrance, passing civilian workers and uniformed officers alike, before they got inside.

The main hall was set up with desks and laptops, but there was plenty of open space too, and it didn't strike Rob as being the main incident room. He spotted an open door leading to another room, and there were people coming and going through there as well.

Nearby, Nailer was talking with Father Aaron and Nick. Ellen and Tucker were close by too, moving tables and helping to set up.

Rob wandered over to the DCI.

"No, no, it's fine," Father Aaron said. "We want you here. It's the perfect place for you. I'm happy to host you."

"But we've caused you some problems," Nailer stated.

Aaron conceded the point with a reluctant nod. "Well, yes, this has caused a few headaches. We're going to have to contact the people who had things booked up and find a new venue or refund them. It's annoying, but we'll cope. This is far more important. We're not work-shy, you know."

"Alright," Nailer replied. "Thank you for being so accommodating and on such short notice."

"Of course, it's no trouble," Aaron replied. "In fact, I've been wanting to talk to you about something I saw the other day. I think it might be relevant as it involved Emmett Wilkinson."

"Of course. My colleague, DI Loxley, will be able to accommodate you. I believe you've already met?"

Father Aaron turned to Rob and smiled in recognition. "Yes indeed, at the Wilkinsons'."

"That's right. Good to see you again, Father."

"And you."

Rob turned to Nailer. "Have we got anywhere set up for interviews?"

"The back room will be our main incident room, but there's nothing in there yet and it's probably best for now. It'll be more private." Nailer signalled to one of the uniformed officers. "Can you show Father Aaron through to the incident room and make sure it's clear of people, so we can talk to him in private?"

"Sir," the man replied and guided Father Aaron away.

Once the priest was out of earshot, DCI Nailer turned to Rob and Scarlett. "All sorted?"

"Aye," Rob confirmed.

"Yes, sir," Scarlett said before continuing in a brighter tone. "I met Rob's cat."

"Oh, nice," Nailer said before he addressed them both. "Right then, we're not far off being set up, now. This will be our base of operations. The back room will be our private incident room for smaller meetings and such, and we'll use this space to deal with the press and hold any meetings with the larger community, and so on. We'll also divide off a separate space for interviews. Okay?"

Rob nodded. "Sounds like we've ruffled some feathers already."

"We have, but we were always going to. It's unavoidable."

"Any developments?"

"Not yet, although, maybe Father Aaron can give us a lead?"

"One can hope," Scarlett replied.

"The prodigal son returns," Ellen said as she wandered over with Tucker. "What do you think of the place?"

"It'll do," Rob said. "You?"

"The town seems a little provincial," Ellen replied. "Not sure what they'd think of a gay like me."

"I'm sure they'll be very accepting," Rob replied.

"She's the only gay in the village," Tucker said in a mock Welsh accent, mimicking a comedy sketch. He smiled, returning to his usual midlands accent. "I like it. Father Aaron seems like a top bloke. He's done us a fuckin' favour letting us have this."

Rob had forgotten about Tucker's potty mouth. "He has," Rob agreed.

"Well then," Nailer said. "You'd better get in there and see what he's got to tell you."

"Guv," Rob confirmed and led Scarlett across the room, through a short corridor, and into another, smaller room with a central table and a whiteboard on the wall. Father Aaron waited for them on one of the hard plastic seats around the table.

They took their seats and readied their notebooks. "So, you wanted to talk to us?" Rob asked.

"I did. Sorry, maybe I should have mentioned this earlier, but you seemed a little busy when I saw you on Edmonton Road."

"We were busy, but if you have important information to tell us, we'll always make time."

"Of course. That's a lot like my job."

"Indeed," Rob confirmed. "So, what do you want to tell us?"

"Well, after all this with the bin and what Mr Wilkinson found in it, I thought you'd like to know about something I saw yesterday morning."

"Go on."

"Okay. I was at the parade of shops on Mansfield Road, and I saw a confrontation between Emmett Wilkinson and Nigel Wild. I didn't catch it all, but insults were flying, and it started to get a little violent before myself and a few others stepped in to stop it."

"They were fighting?" Rob asked, his interest piqued.

"Nearly. Nigel grabbed Emmett by the scruff of his neck before I stepped in."

"And what was this about?" Scarlett asked.

"Well, I've not been here long, but I've heard from others that these two have a history of this, which I believe dates back to the miner's strikes, as they were on opposite sides of the picket line. Emmett worked while Nigel went on strike."

"I see," Rob said. "And what was said during this confrontation?"

"I'm unsure how it started, but Nigel called Emmett a scab and a Judas. I think that was the word that caught my attention, predictably."

"Understandable. Go on."

"Well, Nigel was about to hit Emmett when he saw me and stopped. He did, however, threaten to hurt Emmett and then told him to watch his back."

"Nigel threatened him?"

"He did. He said, 'I'll smash your face in... again.' So maybe he's hurt Emmett before?"

"And if he has, we might have a record of it," Rob replied, sitting back to think about the implications. Clearly, there were issues between these two men which were big enough to cause them to fight in the street. Rob didn't like the idea of Nigel telling Emmett to watch his back. "So, who is this Nigel Wild?"

"He owns the Clip Club. It's a social club at the end of the parade of shops by the car dealership. He took it over after his mining career ended, I believe."

"And both he and Emmett were miners in the eighties?"

"I believe so. Again, I don't know the details, but that is what I've heard from asking around. I hope that was useful."

The man who found a severed head in his bin was threatened the day before by a local man, Rob thought. *Yep, that's classified as useful.*

11

Sitting at the desk in the back room, Rob tapped away on the laptop, logging into the PNC database and running a search on Nigel Wild. The internet was a little slow, and it took a few moments for the information to appear on the screen, but he was soon looking at the records they had of Nigel and his brushes with the law.

Rob scanned the list of cautions and such before the door to the room opened. Scarlett walked back in after escorting Father Aaron out, followed by Nailer, Nick, Ellen, Tucker and Guy.

"Productive, was it?" Nailer asked, referring to the meeting they'd just had with the village priest.

"Very," Rob replied. "Turns out that the day before he found the head in his bin Emmett Wilkinson was attacked and threatened by a local resident he's had a long-running confrontation with that goes all the way back to the miner's strikes in the 1980s. The man who threatened him is called Nigel Wild, and he was a miner at the same time as Emmett, back in the eighties. Nigel went on strike, but Emmett didn't, which was the start of the animosity. Nigel picked up a few cautions and such from the strikes, nothing major, but he did attack Emmett several years ago. Emmett wasn't seriously hurt, and no charges were brought against Nigel, but he reported it to the police, so we have a record of it."

"Did Emmett mention any of this when you spoke to him?" Nailer asked.

"No," Scarlett answered. "He said he's had some disagreements with people who don't subscribe to his politics, but he didn't name names and said he didn't know anyone who'd do this."

"And yet, the day before, Nigel threatened him," Nailer mused.

"Yep," Rob answered. "According to Father Aaron, Nigel grabbed Emmet by the scruff of his neck, threatened to beat him up, and told him to watch his back."

"That's a clear threat."

Rob shrugged. "Maybe he didn't think Nigel would go through with it? Maybe he's used to people shouting abuse at him in the street?"

"Or maybe he just wants to see the good in people," Scarlett added.

"Or he's protecting Nigel," Guy said.

"Whatever it is, this needs more investigation. This is a clear threat, and given its timing, it's highly suspicious." Nailer turned to Rob. "So, where does this Nigel live?"

"He's the owner of the Clip Club, a social club on Mansfield Road, and he lives above it."

"Where did this altercation take place?" Guy asked, narrowing his eyes in thought.

"Just up from his club, on the parade of shops," Rob said.

"There's a camera just opposite there, so we might actually have footage of it."

"Good thinking," Nailer said. "Right then, this is what we do. Rob, Scarlett, go and speak to Nigel, find out what his story is. Ellen and Tuck, I need you to make your way back to the Lodge and find Emmett. I want to know why he didn't mention this incident or his long-running feud with Mr Wild."

"Can do, guv," Ellen confirmed.

"Nick, get out there and continue with the house-to-house that's going on. I want you in operational control of it. You might want to speak with people on that parade of shops too, the owners and such, see if there's anyone else who can corroborate Father Aaron's story."

"Sir," Nick answered with a nod.

"Guy, I need you to get that footage from the camera. If there's video evidence of it, I want it."

"Sir?" Scarlett spoke up. "We also need to speak to Emmett and Valerie's friends, the ones they saw the night before they found the remains. I just want to confirm their stories."

"Yes indeed," Nailer replied. "Guy, can you do that? Give them a call and see if you can confirm Emmett and Valerie's movements?"

"I can," Guy replied. "I'll see if I can get their phone tracking data, too."

"Excellent. Scarlett, liaise with Guy on that."

"Sir," she replied and started scribbling in her notepad. "I'll just note down their friends' details."

"Thanks," Guy replied.

"I'll be here, getting this place set up, dealing with the District Council, keeping the Superintendent up to date, and coordinating between you all. Right, we all know what we're doing. Let's get to it."

"Sir," they all chorused and rose from their seats. Rob got up and nodded to Scarlett.

"Let's go and meet Nigel, shall we?" They quickly made their way out and around to the back of the Hall before jumping in Rob's car and setting off.

"What do you think about this new development?"

"I think it's like we discussed before," Scarlett answered. "We both knew there'd be more to this than met the eye, and we were right. There is. As for what I think of Mr Wild and what happened between him and Mr Wilkinson, I'll withhold my judgement for now. I'd like to meet the man first."

"Me too. But it doesn't sound good."

"No, it doesn't."

"I knew there'd be more going on here. Emmett was too blasé about things when we asked him if there was anyone he has issues with."

"Maybe. I just think he's used to it. I think you have to be, as a politician. There are always going to be people who hate you. I bet Nigel isn't the only person flinging abuse at him when he walks down the street."

"He's only a District Councillor," Rob replied. "He's hardly famous, and I doubt that many people care that much about what he does."

Scarlett shrugged. "Yeah, maybe."

"I think the miner's strike stuff will be worse. Those who went on strike hated the ones who worked."

"I'm right in thinking that a scab is someone who doesn't join the strike and keeps working, right?" Scarlett asked.

"Right. And the miner's strikes were quite intense."

"That's a long time to hold a grudge, though."

"True," Rob agreed as they drove through the village. "But this was their whole lives. Clipstone and places like it were built on the back of mining. To the people who worked and lived here, it was everything. When the mining stopped, it sapped the life out of places like this. They've never been the same since. I bet Nigel is still a member of the union."

"You think?"

"I'd put money on it."

"But, do you think someone like Nigel would kill over it?"

Rob took a breath as he considered his answer. "That, I don't know. But, if Nigel already had murderous tendencies, it's not a stretch to think he'd use them to freak Emmett out, is it?"

"I suppose not. You would have thought he'd just kill Emmett, though, or Valerie. Not someone else and dump the remains in their bin."

A new angle sprang into his mind as Scarlett voiced her scepticism. "Unless he was trying to frame Emmett for the murder," Rob suggested.

"Ooh, sneaky," she replied. "That would be nasty. Ruin him and frame him for murder."

"Let's withhold judgement for now, though. I think we're only just getting started picking away at the layers of this."

"Probably," Scarlett agreed.

Moments later, they pulled into the side road that ran along the front of the parade of shops and parked up close to the Clip Club at the end. Rob could see it was closed, but hopefully, Nigel would still be in. They climbed out of the car and made their way over. It was late morning, and the street had a smattering of locals going about their business, walking along the pavement and visiting the local shops. It seemed busier further up, where Rob could see a small supermarket.

They approached the Clip Club next to the car dealership at the very end of the parade. No one paid them much attention.

"Seems quiet," Rob commented as he ambled towards the front door. The lights were on inside.

"Do you think he's in?" Scarlett asked.

"Let's find out." He knocked and waited, listening to see if he could make out movement from within. After a moment, he heard footsteps, and a beat later, the door unlocked and opened. The face of a woman appeared. She was bleached blonde, in her thirties, wearing leggings and a baggy jumper.

"Yeah?" She looked them up and down. "We're closed."

"We're with the police." Rob held up his ID. "Is Nigel in? We need to talk to him."

The woman peered at Rob's Warrant Card as the situation sank in. "Oh, sorry. I thought you were punters looking to get an early pint in."

Rob shrugged and smiled. "Not this morning. May we come in?"

She looked uncertain for a moment. "Err, yeah. Okay." She backed away and opened the door. "Nige?" she called out. "Some people here to see you."

Inside, a man in his late fifties with thinning hair and a slim build approached. "What's up?"

"Sir," Rob began, showing his ID again. "We just need a few minutes of your time. We have some questions."

"Oh, alright. What's up?" Nigel guided them to a nearby table while the woman went about her work, shooting curious glances their way.

"You're Nigel Wild, right?" Rob asked.

"That's right. How can I help you?"

"It's come to our attention that you had a confrontation with Emmett Wilkinson yesterday, just up the road from here."

For a moment, Nigel held his breath before he visibly deflated and sighed. "Yeah, that's right." It was as if he'd briefly contemplated denying it before changing his mind. "Has he made a complaint?"

"No, Mr Wilkinson hasn't reported you. It was a witness who came forward, actually, who saw the whole thing. Now, I can't go into too much detail, but we're looking into a serious crime that took place last night and involved Mr Wilkinson. Because of that, we need to follow up any leads such as potentially violent confrontations…"

"I didn't hurt him," Nigel snapped.

"Okay. But this wasn't the first time you and Mr Wilkinson have clashed, is it? You have attacked him before."

They'd caught him on the back foot. Rob could see him reeling as he fought to get ahead of them. "We've... we've had our disagreements."

Could he be any cagier? "So, you don't get along?"

Nigel bit his lip. "Look, this is a long-standing issue that goes back to the strikes. We just disagree about a few things, that's all."

"It sounds like it's more than that, Mr Wild. It must be serious if you're willing to attack him in the street."

"I was just pissed off, that's all. I was having a bad morning, and he was there. He was just in the wrong place at the wrong time. Look, I'm not going to mince my words with him. He's a self-serving twat, but it's not as if I'd kill him or anything. I've roughed him up once before, but that's all."

Rob frowned and wondered if he was telling the truth.

"Where were you last night?" Scarlett asked.

"Here, like always. Serving."

"And can anyone corroborate that?"

"Caprice, can," he replied and turned towards the bar where the woman was working. "Caprice, where was I last night?"

"Working here," she replied.

"The whole night?" Scarlett added.

"Yeah," she confirmed as if it was a silly question.

She turned to Nigel. "So you didn't leave the building at all?"

"No," he answered.

"You disappeared just after nine for a bit," Caprice said.

"I went upstairs to do some paperwork," Nigel protested. "I didn't leave the building. You came and got me."

"What times were these, roughly?" Scarlett asked Caprice.

"Between ten-past-nine and maybe ten-to-ten?" Caprice replied.

Nigel looked a little shocked by Caprice's comments as he turned back to them. "I was here the whole time. But yeah, I do other things apart from serving the whole time. I have staff to do that."

"Of course," Scarlett said. "But, there's no one that can confirm you were in the building the whole time?"

"I don't know." He seemed offended.

Rob sat forward. "What was it you were pissed off about before you confronted Emmett yesterday morning?"

"I... I don't know. I came down to find the place wasn't as clean as I'd like, and... I think it was just a bad morning. That's all."

The way he spoke suggested he was holding back. Rob frowned at him. "A bad morning? So, there wasn't something specific that was causing the mood?"

"Not that I can pinpoint, no." *That was a lie*, Rob thought.

"You're sure?"

"Quite sure." Nigel seemed to have recovered from the initial shock of having to answer these questions and looked a little more self-assured in his answers.

Rob nodded along with him but found it difficult to believe what he was saying. There was more here, but Nigel seemed keen to keep it to himself, and right now, there was only tenuous circumstantial evidence linking Nigel to the murder. After all, they still didn't have the rest of the body.

There just wasn't enough to arrest Nigel for right now. His history with Emmett was a concern, but why would Nigel kill an unrelated girl when his issues were with Emmett? It didn't make sense. "Alright, Mr Wild. Thanks for your help."

They got up.

"Excuse me?" Scarlett called out to the woman. "Can I take your full name and address, please?"

"Caprice Randell," the woman answered before reciting her Clipstone address.

"Thanks," Scarlett replied with a smile.

Rob nodded to Scarlett, grateful for her studiousness. "Cheers," he muttered before turning to Nigel. "Thanks for answering my questions. We'd appreciate it if you didn't leave the area for the time being while our investigation is underway."

"What's all this about?" Nigel asked. "What investigation?"

"I saw it mentioned online," Caprice piped up. "Something about a body in someone's bin, was it?"

"Body in someone's bin?" Nigel sounded shocked. He frowned as he thought it through, and then a look of realisation flashed across his face. "Do you mean Emmett's bin? And you think I did it?"

"I'm afraid I can't comment," Rob answered.

"Holy crap," Nigel exclaimed. "I wouldn't do that. I wouldn't kill anyone. Tell them, Caprice."

She shrugged. "No, I don't think you would. Not really."

"See!"

"I didn't accuse you of anything, Mr Wild." Rob smiled in the most reassuring way he knew how. "Thank you. But don't worry, you're not under arrest at this time, Mr Wild. We're merely following up the leads we have, okay?"

After a few more calming words, they left the club and made their way back to the car. Rob got in and closed the door before pausing as he looked out at the façade of the social club. "He's not telling us everything."

"I'm inclined to agree," Scarlett replied.

12

"Busy mornin'," Ellen said as she drove them into the Sherwood Lodge grounds and made her way through to the car park.

"You can fuckin' say that again," Tucker said from the passenger seat. She'd been working with Tucker under Nailer for a while and knew Rob and Nick well enough, even though they had been part of Orleton's unit. Rob and Nailer had a long-standing friendship, and Nailer seemed to be something of a mentor to Rob. She wasn't entirely sure why that was but saw no need to question it.

When Nailer had asked her to join the EMSOU, she'd jumped at the chance, along with Tucker, eager to climb the ladder even further.

"What do you think of them all. The team, I mean."

"Yeah, they're alright," Tucker answered. "Can't say I know Guy much, but I've seen him around, and Nailer knows him. I've got no bloody idea about Scarlett, though."

"She seems nice. Feisty, maybe, and she's sticking close to Rob."

"I'd have thought that would piss Nick off," Tucker commented. "Rob too."

"Maybe he's taken a shine to her? I don't blame him. She's a beauty."

Tucker laughed. "I don't think Rob's interested in her like that, and why are you letching over her, you tart? I thought you had a girlfriend."

"I do," Ellen confirmed. "But I can appreciate another woman's beauty. Chrissy would too. She wouldn't begrudge me for indulging in a little window shopping."

Tucker laughed. "Lord have mercy. Window shopping?"

"We do it together when we're at a coffee shop."

"Wow, it's a whole new world," Tucker replied. "I had no fuckin' idea."

"Just because you're all uptight..."

"Me?"

"Yeah, you." She laughed. "How was it talking to Mr Aaron? Did it bring back memories?"

"Father Aaron," he corrected her.

"Sorry. Father Aaron."

Tucker shrugged. "Brought back a few memories, sure. That's a few years ago now, though." He looked a little wistful for a moment as he thought back. She knew little about Tucker's past. Only that he used to be a member of the clergy then his father died, and eventually, he joined the police with Nailer's support. So now he was giving back to the community in another way. "Come on," he said as Ellen parked up. "Let's go and see what Emmett has to say for himself, shall we?"

"You sound suspicious of him."

Tucker screwed up his face for a moment. "No. Not really. I can't say it sounds like the bastards being honest with us, though, does it?"

"Not really," Ellen admitted as they made their way towards the building. She'd called ahead before they'd left Clipstone to make sure Emmett and Valerie were still at the Lodge and to keep them there for the time being. Luckily, they hadn't gone and were just finishing off their statements.

Tucker's obvious deflection when she'd pried into his past a moment ago amused her. Tucker seemed to dislike talking about what happened between his time as a priest and when he'd joined the police. She guessed there were some difficult memories there for him. She guessed he'd perhaps been thrown out, although, for what, she didn't know. But it wasn't her place to pry. If he wanted to keep that to himself, that was up to him.

After all, not everyone was as open and upfront as she was.

They made their way inside and signed in before moving through a nearby security door and making their way towards the room they knew Emmett and Valerie to be in.

"How's it going up in Clipstone?" DI Bill Rainault asked as he walked towards them, coming the other way down the corridor. He stopped, apparently expecting a conversation.

Ellen felt her heckles rise immediately, fully aware of his obsession with Rob.

"Fine," she answered, seeing no reason to give him anything more.

"You're all up there, right?" he pressed on. "The whole of the EMSOU, in Clipstone?"

"Yes, with Rob," Ellen replied, pre-empting him.

Bill smiled. "Indeed. So, nothing to report?"

"Not to you," Ellen replied, waiting a beat before adding a final word filled with contempt. "Sir."

"Fair enough," Bill replied with a knowing smile. "See you around."

With that, he turned and strode off, continuing the way he'd come.

"Slimy fucker," Tucker commented.

"He is, and with Rob on our team, he'll be all over us from now on." She looked back at Tucker. "We need to be on guard."

"Mmm," Tucker answered, clearly thinking things through.

Ellen pressed on up the corridor and on reaching the room, knocked on the door. Moments later, it was answered by the assigned FLO, Heather Knight, who Ellen recognised.

"Aaah, hello," the Liaison Officer said. "Come in. We were wondering when you'd turn up." She led them inside. "They were just about to leave for the hotel."

"That's okay," Ellen reassured them. "This should only take a few moments."

Heather shrugged. "Be my guest."

Ellen focused her attention on the couple, who, she noticed, were keeping some distance between each other. Their body language didn't suggest a loving relationship as they sat there with their arms crossed, not looking at one another and with a permanent frown attached to their foreheads.

Ellen decided to start with a light compliment to engender some trust. "Thanks for waiting. We really appreciate it."

"That's okay." Emmet allowed a brief smile to pass over his features. He seemed the more annoyed of the pair.

"Okay, great," Ellen replied, trying to keep the tone light. "I wanted to ask you a few questions about Nigel Wild."

"Oh, him?" Emmett moaned. "What's he done now?"

Beside him, Valerie frowned. "Do you think..." Valerie asked, putting two and two together quicker than Emmett.

"We're not thinking anything right now," Ellen reassured her, keen for her not to get any funny ideas. "We're just asking questions, and we've become aware of a run-in you had with Nigel yesterday morning. Is that right?"

"Oh, that. Yeah, he threw some insults at me, and I..." Emmett sighed. "I didn't take it well, I guess."

"We've had a witness come forward who says Nigel was attacking you. He threatened you. Is that right?"

"I guess so," Emmett confirmed, "but look, you mustn't blow this out of proportion. Yes, we had a few cross words for each other yesterday, but that's all it was, and I'm not sure he'd actually hurt me, or anyone else for that matter. Besides, it's not the first time he's called me a scab for what I did back at the mine. It's not a big deal."

"He threatened you with violence," Ellen pushed.

Emmett shifted in his seat. "He did, but..."

"Why are you defending him?" Valerie asked, turning to Emmett. "He's been causing you problems for years, all because you did the honourable thing back during the strikes. He can't let it go, whereas we have moved on."

"It's a big thing for him..." Emmett explained. "He wouldn't have hurt me."

"He attacked you last year, Emmett. Actually hit you, and he won't leave it alone. I don't know why I didn't cotton on earlier, but he's the obvious culprit." Valerie turned to Ellen. "I assume you've arrested him?"

"We're talking to him," Ellen replied cautiously.

"Talking to him?" she snapped. "He's a menace to this town. People like him should be locked up, so they can't go around hurting people. Have you heard of that club that he runs? It's a dive, from all accounts. There are frequent fights and trouble there. Is it any wonder, given who the man seems to be?"

"I understand your frustrations, Mrs Wilkinson, but we have procedures to follow. Rest assured, however, we're looking into it."

"See," Emmett exclaimed, "they're looking into it. Now leave it alone. Nigel didn't do this, I'm sure of it."

"Hmm," Valerie grumbled before looking back at Ellen. "I will pray for you tonight, Detective. I'll pray that you find this killer quickly and without further people being hurt."

"Aaah... Thank you," Ellen said, uncertainly.

"That's very kind of you," Tucker answered with more conviction. "I'll pray for you, too. You've been through a lot today. I hope the Lord has mercy on you and takes you into his heart."

Ellen felt a little uncomfortable listening to Tucker, but he was preaching to the choir with Valerie, so she let it go.

"Thank you, officer," Valerie replied. "It's lovely to know we have a man of faith on the case. It's very reassuring."

"I will keep you updated on things," Tucker replied.

"We will liaise with you through the Family Liaison Officer," Ellen added, keen to keep Tucker from getting too involved. They needed to stick to procedure.

"Of course," Valerie replied.

"Thank you, officer," Emmett added.

13

Reaching the door at the end of the corridor, Bill glanced back and watched DC Ellen Dale and DC Tucker Stafford walk into the side room and close the door behind them. He didn't much care for their attitude and could tell from that interaction alone that Ellen, and probably Tucker as well, would be on Rob's side.

They were not people he could use to his advantage.

Silently cursing to himself, he turned right and made his way back upstairs, wondering what he could do to keep a better eye on what Rob was up to. Who could he use? Who'd work with him?

Scarlett and Nick were both out of the question. They had both made their opinions of him and his mission clear, and he still remembered Scarlett's rant to him on the stairs of Central Station. Her venom had taken him by surprise, and it was only later that he realised that he should have said something.

He was her superior officer, after all. She should not be allowed to speak to him like that.

But, he knew he was on thin ice with his personal investigation of Rob. Even his boss wasn't too keen on it, often citing the number of times Rob had passed vetting. If he went to his boss over how Scarlett had spoken to him, and his boss found out he'd been trying to get Scarlett to turn on Rob, he'd be screwed. Scarlett would get away with a slap on the wrist, whereas he would likely be reprimanded by his DCI, or worse, his Super.

No, he needed to do this himself, use the resources he had at his disposal, and when he had proof of Rob's malfeasance, then he could present it to his superiors.

He was a lone crusader, he thought, smiling to himself, and he needed someone up in Clipstone to help him.

On the EMSOU team that Nailer had appointed, there wasn't anyone he really knew of or had any link to. He knew some better than others, such as Nick and Nailer, but that wasn't saying much.

Walking into the PSU office, Bill wandered around to his desk. He'd become fiercely protective of his little corner of the room, liking that there was only a wall behind him, so no one could peek over his shoulder at what he was doing. It was a small measure of privacy that he valued. Especially when he was looking into what Rob was up to.

Relaxing into his chair, Bill pulled out his phone and started to scroll through his contacts. He needed someone who could keep a close eye on Rob, without drawing any suspicion. He needed to operate under the radar and blend into the background noise. He mentally ticked off the names as he scrolled through them until one jumped out at him. He stopped scrolling.

Vincent Kane.

Bill grimaced as he considered the options. Kane was a journalist who had no love for Rob, and Bill felt certain that he would jump at the chance of a juicy story. He could feed details of the case to him in return for Kane following Rob and reporting on what he saw.

The idea carried weight, sure, but it did mean working with a member of the press, and passing information over that he really shouldn't. It wasn't ideal, but he needed someone up there today, and this would achieve that goal.

With an annoyed sigh, Bill hit the call icon and put the phone to his ear.

Two rings later, the line connected.

"Mr William Rainault, as I live and breathe."

"Inspector Rainault," Bill corrected him. He didn't like Vincent's tone. Was this a mistake? Would he regret doing this by bringing Kane into his personal mission? He hoped not.

"My apologies, Inspector. What can I do for you today? It's been a while. When was the last time we spoke?"

"A couple of years ago, I think."

"Indeed. How's Jon?"

Bill could detect the spite in Kane's voice, and it made him smile. "He's no longer with us."

"What?"

"He's moved down to Surrey. He's with the police down there now."

"Oh. For a moment there, I thought you were implying that he'd left this mortal coil."

"I'm afraid not."

"Aaah, well, it was a nice feeling while it lasted. Go on then, what can a bottom-feeding journo like me do for an upstanding public servant like yourself?"

Kane's sarcasm was annoying. "I was hoping we could come to some kind of deal, Kane."

"A deal? What kind of deal? That sounds a little underhanded."

"It's nothing of the sort, Vincent. I take it you remember Rob Loxley?"

"Loxley? How could I forget?"

"Well, he's on a case up in Clipstone, and I'd like someone up there, watching him. I thought you might be interested."

"Did you now?" Kane answered. "Well, let me think. The last time I tangled with the Nottinghamshire Police, it didn't go so well, did it."

"No, but that was a while ago, and this time you'll be working with me," Bill reassured him. He understood Kane's hesitancy, but he'd be perfect for what Bill needed.

"What are you saying, that you'll protect me?"

"I'll be on your side, and I'll give you access to the story. It's a juicy one, plus, it's Loxley, and I know your feelings about Jon's friends."

"Are you sure about that?"

"Don't play coy, Kane," Bill snapped. "I know you don't like Loxley and have your suspicions about him, just as I do."

"Maybe I do, maybe I don't."

"I'm offering you an opportunity, Kane. Are you sure you want to look a gift horse in the mouth?"

"Tell me more about this case, and how privileged will this information be? I can't imagine you have unfettered access."

"I have my contacts."

"I can imagine." He sounded suspicious, but Bill wasn't about to hand his contacts over to him.

"How about a little taster?

"Why not. Go on, tempt me."

"A district Councillor woke up this morning and found a woman's severed head in his bin," Bill said, reading through the confidential report on his screen. "No ID on the woman, yet, but they're looking into it."

"A District Councillor?"

"Emmett Wilkinson," Bill added.

"Emmett. Aaah, yes. I'm aware of him, and his wife, Valerie. She works on the Coal Board."

"I'm aware," Bill replied. "I can send you more as it comes in, if you manage to get something for me, of course."

"Sounds like an interesting case, I guess."

"You guess?"

He heard Kane sigh on the other end of the line. Kane was interested. He felt sure of it.

"Okay, fine. I'll do it. Clipstone, you say?"

"Loxley is part of the East Midlands Special Operations Unit now. They've set up a local incident room in the Clipstone Village Hall, so you should be able to catch up with them there. I'll be in touch with more as it comes in, okay?"

"You better be. The last time I poked my nose into the business of Loxley and his boss, Jon rewarded me with a broken nose. If that happens again, I'm going private, and you're paying, got it? Plus, I'm blaming everything on you."

"You're not scared of Loxley, are you? A big tough guy, like you?"

"Oh, do fuck off," Kane snapped back and hung up.

Bill smirked quietly to himself and turned his screen off. He was taking a risk with this, feeding the press information. He could get fired if he was found out, but he needed this. He needed to finally pin something on Rob, once and for all.

A few moments later, a text appeared on his phone from Kane.

'On my way.'

"Of course you are," Bill muttered.

14

Paul pulled up to the kerb on the side road, yanked on the handbrake, and with the van in neutral, turned off the engine.

Only then did he relax back into his seat and take a moment to let his cares fall away.

He was starving and only had a few short minutes to eat his packed lunch before he needed to get out there and finish off the day's deliveries.

Two-hundred-and-forty-seven of them, today alone.

He'd managed one-hundred-and-fifteen so far, which put him about on schedule.

He felt pleased with that. He hated when he fell behind because of traffic, roadworks or an irate customer. However, it was made much easier now they were allowed to just leave things on people's doorsteps, sometimes with a confirmation photo. That sped things up immensely compared to when they had to knock and wait at each and every door. But, with every step forward, there was inevitably another step or two back.

The increase in speed meant they needed fewer drivers, and each driver could fit more deliveries into the day. This led to job losses and a greater workload for those who remained.

Far from being work-shy, however, Paul didn't mind working hard, but in his opinion, this did edge into the territory of exploitation.

Still, the customers didn't seem to mind it too much. Some hated that they left the parcel on the doorstep, and it did seem to come with an increase in Porch Pirates, stealing deliveries from doorsteps, which wasn't great.

Aaah, whatever. All he wanted was to do his job and get paid. That's it. As long as he got paid, he didn't care that much about the rest of it.

He also wanted his lunch and quickly grabbed his sandwich box. Pulling it open, the smell of cured ham wafted into his nose, making his mouth water in anticipation as the aroma of barbeque sauce followed it.

Lovely.

On top of his wrapped sandwich, he found a note from his girlfriend, scrawled in her usual loopy handwriting.

'Love you', it read.

Paul smiled, placed the note to one side, and pulled his sandwich out of its clear plastic bag. The first bite was always the best, especially after a long morning's work.

He let his mind wander as he took several more bites from his fix of carbs. He'd parked up in Clipstone, on the side road by the Headstocks. He'd used the road a few times in the past to take a break and have something to eat. It was usually quiet, and he could get half an hour uninterrupted to eat before he needed to push on and finish his route.

He spent the time gazing out of his passenger side window, admiring the former mining complex and its distinctive silhouette against the grey sky. Some thought it was a bit of an eyesore, but Paul quite liked it. It was a reminder of the industry that the town was built on, a link to the past, and he hoped they wouldn't knock it down if they ever got around to redeveloping it.

Taking another mouthful, he let his eyes wander over the scene and peered into the bushes on his right. After a moment, he realised he'd been looking at something sticking out from under one of the bushes without really knowing what it was. He couldn't make sense of it and frowned while shifting in his seat to get another angle on it.

Suddenly, like one of those optical illusions, it clicked into place, and he understood what he was looking at.

It was a shoe. A woman's heeled shoe. A fancy one, too. But wasn't *just* a shoe, because there was a foot in it too, the leg it was attached to disappeared off into the darkness beneath the overgrown bushes on the verge.

"What the..." Paul gasped, confused and curious. He took another bite of his sandwich, waiting to see if the foot moved.

It was probably a homeless person taking a nap, but would a rough sleeper really wear high heels?

It didn't make much sense.

As he finished his sandwich, he started to look around, over to the nearby main road and such, wondering if anyone else had spotted it. Was this some kind of prank, maybe? But as the minutes passed, and the foot remained still, a knot of panic started to grip his chest. This felt wrong. Very wrong.

Something wasn't right here.

Checking the time, he felt briefly conflicted about what he should do. Investigating and maybe reporting this was clearly the right thing, but he also had a job to do, and he wasn't sure how his manager would react to him acting the hero when it was probably some idiot with a hangover. But then, his manager was an idiot with delusions of grandeur, so no matter what he did, he'd be in the wrong.

No, he needed to investigate. It was the right thing, the only thing to do. What if this person needed help, and he was the only one who'd spotted them.

Cursing his conscience, he opened the door and climbed down from the van. A little closer to the foot, and without the dirty windscreen in the way, he could see it quite clearly now.

"Hello?" he called out. "You alright in there, miss?"

No answer came, and the foot didn't move. Paul frowned as a sinking feeling settled in his stomach. *I have a bad feeling about this*, he mused, borrowing a line from one of his favourite Sci-Fi franchises.

Moving closer, he walked until he was level with the foot. The skin was pale and dirty. The shoes were a gaudy red colour, bright and happy, standing in contrast to the scene that was giving Paul very bad vibes. He'd heard stories on the news of people discovering dead bodies, and the thought made his skin crawl. But he couldn't help thinking that this was exactly that. Was his day about to get turned upside down, all because he'd chosen to park up in one of his favourite places to take a break? He had a horrible feeling that it was. But, he needed to be sure. Lifting his leg, he gently tapped the foot with his toe.

"Hey?"

The foot barely moved at his touch. Silent. Still. Dead?

"Shit, shit, shit," he muttered and crouched down to look under the bush and get a better look. It was dark back there, but he could see more of the body. He could see her other leg with a matching shoe on her other foot, the rest of her body somewhere beyond

He reached out again and tapped the platform of the shoe. "Hey, miss? Wake up. Are you alright? Can I help?"

Still nothing.

Standing up, Paul scanned the scene and thought he saw a way through to get a better look. He hoped against hope that the woman was asleep or unconscious, but that weight in his gut said otherwise. Deep down, he knew what he'd discovered. Paul knew what he was about to see, but he couldn't accept it until he saw it for himself. He needed to see it.

Paul pushed through between two bushes and looked left where the woman's head should be.

It wasn't there.

Her shoulders and chest were there, covered in dark red splatters, but her head was missing. Her neck just ended in a ragged wound of torn skin, fleshy muscle and gleaming bone.

Paul turned away in disgust as his sandwich threatened to make a sudden and unscheduled reappearance.

"Oh god, oh god…" he muttered as he returned to the road and stumbled back to his van. He collapsed against the front grille and sucked air in desperate gasps. He'd never seen anything like it and hoped never to see it again. With trembling hands, Paul pulled out his phone and dialled 999.

Well, that was his day screwed.

15

Rob turned right onto the side road, just off the main Mansfield Road through Clipstone. Several police vehicles were already on site. He spotted a few marked cars, a SOCO van, and another van he didn't recognise. The officer on cordon lifted the tape and allowed him to drive through and park up just inside. They were right beside the main road where passing cars slowed, their drivers peering out, wondering what was going on.

To be thorough, they needed to put in a diversion and block off the road. They'd need to get that sorted.

"Do you think this is her?" Scarlett asked from the passenger seat.

"Sounds like it, doesn't it," Rob answered, remembering the report that had come in. Someone had called 999, saying they'd found a headless body in Clipstone. Who else could it be?

Rob's phone started buzzing as he climbed out of the car. Frowning at his pocket, he plucked the device out and read the caller ID. It wasn't a number he recognised. A mobile, judging from the 07 prefix, but that's all he knew.

"One moment," he said to Scarlett.

"Really?" Scarlett asked, incredulous.

"She's dead, she's not going anywhere."

Scarlett rolled her eyes. "Fine."

"Hello?" Rob said down the phone after hitting accept.

"Rob, it's Erika, your neighbour."

He recognised the voice. "Oh, hi."

"Hi. So, I err... got your note. I'd be happy to feed Muffin if you like. That's fine."

"That would be amazing, thank you. I can see there being nights where I'm back just far too late, or not at all, and I need someone who can pop their head in and make sure he's not clawing the place to bits and feed him. Is that okay?"

"Totally fine. Yeah. Happy to. Just let me know when you need me to pop over, and I'll make sure he's okay. This is my number, obviously."

"Okay, great. His food is in the cupboard under the sink, just so you know."

"Thanks."

"Alright, that's great. I'll be in touch. Thanks again."

"No worries. My pleasure," Erika replied. "See you later."

"Bye."

She hung up.

"Ready now?" Scarlett said with an impatient look on her face.

"Just about," he replied, saving Erika's number to his phone before stuffing it back in his pocket. "Sorry," he said, looking up at Scarlett.

She rolled her eyes and chuckled. "You and that cat."

"What? I'm doing the right thing."

"I know, I know. Come on, let's see what's waiting for us."

Rob glanced back at the cordon and noted the small crowd of people who'd already gathered to watch. They were too close, in his opinion. But they'd sort that soon enough. Turning on the spot, he looked through the temporary metal fencing surrounding the old Clipstone mining buildings with their iconic Headstocks. Is this where the victim had been killed, in view of these iconic structures?

"Right, let's go take a look, shall we?" Rob wandered over and found Sergeant Jolly who was organising the scene. He was pleased to see a familiar face who understood what they were dealing with. "Afternoon."

"Afternoon, Inspector. Constable," she added to Scarlett. "Looks like we've found the body to match the head."

"Busy day," Rob commented.

"Tom said it might be a quiet one first thing this morning," she replied. Sighing and shaking her head. "That'll teach us to use the Q-word."

"That's a sackable offence, isn't it?"

"Something like that. The body's over there, in the bushes"

Rob followed her outstretched hand to see the gaggle of white-clothed SOC officers going about their business beneath a tent.

"Okay."

"The man who found her is Paul Stokes. He's a delivery driver who was on his lunch break. He's back there."

Rob looked where she pointed and saw the man. "How is he?"

"A little shaken up, which is understandable, but he's been great so far."

"I'll have a quick chat with him."

"Of course."

"That cordon, it's a little close."

Megan sighed. "Yeah, I know. We did the best we could when he first got here, but we need to arrange a diversion so we can push it out. I've got my boys on it already. Tom's coordinating getting the diversion signs up. We should have it sorted in the next half an hour."

"Punishment for using the Q-word?"

"Something like that."

Rob nodded, impressed. "Good work."

"Thanks."

They wandered over to the man who had discovered the body. He was sitting sideways in the passenger seat of a marked police car, his feet on the road and a silver heat blanket around his shoulders. A uniformed officer was crouched beside him.

"Paul Stokes, is it?" Rob asked, flashing his warrant card.

Paul looked up. He looked pale and tired, his eyes haunted by what he'd seen. "Yeah."

"How you doing?"

"I've been better. It's not every day you find a headless corpse."

"No, I guess not. So you were just parked up here, were you?"

"Aye. Just having my lunch, like. I've parked here loads of times before. But, I was just eating my sandwich and spotted something weird under a bush. So I investigated and… well, found that." He waved in the general direction of the body. Paul shuddered as he pulled his hand back under the blanket.

"So, you don't know who it is? You've never seen them before?"

"No, never. I can't see her face, so… But, it can't be anyone I know. It just can't. It's some girl, though, I think. Young, at a guess. Looks like she's wearing clubbing clothes, you know? Like she was out on the town?"

"I see. And did you touch the body at all?"

"I tapped her shoe with my boot and fingers. I thought she was asleep or something, so I tried to wake them up. But her foot was stiff, and cold."

"Alright. We're going to need to bring you in, get your prints and take a statement, okay? But don't worry, you're not in any trouble. Do you need to call anyone?"

"I've spoken to my manager. He wants the van back. There's over a hundred parcels in there that need delivering."

"Okay, we'll see what we can do," Rob replied.

"Thanks."

"Sure."

Rob turned away and led Scarlett towards the tent.

"He's innocent," Scarlett remarked.

"Yeah, he's just having a bad day. Right, let's go and see if this body is who we think it is."

"He said 'going out' clothes," Scarlett mused. "Was she out on the town last night, maybe?"

"Maybe," Rob confirmed as they approached the tent.

One of the white-clad Scene of Crime officers spotted them and approached. Rob recognised the little of her face that he could see from earlier that day.

"Alicia."

"Loxley," she replied. "I think we've found the body that the head belongs to."

"You're sure?"

"About as sure as I can be until I get them side by side and compare the wounds. But I'd be surprised if this wasn't her."

"Okay, that's good. So we're dealing with one body, not two."

"Indeed," Alicia confirmed.

"What else?"

"Well, come with me." She led them closer, so they could see the body at a distance. It was still under one of the bushes, so Alicia asked one of the other SOCOs to pull the leaves and branches back, revealing the headless corpse. As Paul had said, she wore a tiny skirt, crop top, heels and a jacket, most of which were covered in blood. He spotted several bruises and marks on her thin, pale body.

"That's quite an outfit," Scarlett remarked.

"Yeah, it is."

"Any thoughts on time of death?" Rob asked.

"Based on her pallor, temperature and the stiffness of her limps, I would guess that she died late last night, between maybe six PM and midnight, and if you held a gun to my head, I'd say she was likely killed somewhere in the middle of that range."

"So, what, nine, ten PM?"

"Around there. It's always tough to say, of course. She's thin, not wearing much, and she's outside, all of which speed the cooling time. She's also stiff as a board, which helps. You can see the lividity too where the blood has pooled, so I'm confident in saying this is where she was killed and left."

"What about the bruising I'm seeing?"

"They're old," Alicia answered. "She's got a few of them, but they weren't caused by the murderer, I don't think. She's also sporting some track marks on her arms."

"Drugs," Rob muttered to himself as he peered at the old puncture marks on her inner forearms where she'd been injecting herself.

"Yep. I'd guess she was a heavy user as those look recent, but I'll know more when toxicology comes in."

"I see. So, sexy clothes, bruises and drug use…"

"I know where you're going with that, so let me add in this." She walked to a nearby table where several items were spread out with markers beside them. One of them was a small handbag. "This was on her, wrapped around her body, so I'm fairly sure it's hers. There's no ID in here, but there is a small stack of cash, a can of pepper spray, and a lot of condoms."

"She's a pro," Scarlett said, giving voice to Rob's thoughts.

"That would be my conclusion," Alicia agreed.

"Are we sure of that, though," Rob asked. "I'm inclined to agree, but we need to be certain of it."

Both women nodded. "Agreed," Scarlett said. "We shouldn't jump to conclusions, but the evidence seems fairly damning."

"I'd be surprised if she wasn't," Alicia said.

"Me too," Rob added. "No ID yet?"

"Not yet," Alicia confirmed. "But it won't be long now. If she's a working girl and she's been doing it for a while, I'd hazard a guess that she's been picked up before for something."

"Meaning we'll have a record of her," Scarlett added. "How soon will we know?"

"Her post-mortem is booked in for tomorrow," Alicia said. "I'd guess you'll have fingerprint ID by then."

"Excellent. Good work, keep me up to date."

"Will do," Alicia replied as Rob turned to walk out of the tent. Outside, he spotted Nick Miller waiting for them. Rob had asked him to follow on to help with the scene and expand the house-to-house based on this new discovery.

"Rob," Nick said in greeting. "Do I dare go and have a look?"

"Be my guest, but it's not pretty."

"Maybe later. What's it looking like?"

"We think she was a working girl," Rob said. "It's a conclusion based on circumstantial evidence, such as her clothing, the contents of her bag, and the tell-tale signs of drug use, but it seems likely."

"We've already had another local mention a problem with them in the town," Scarlett added.

"Janette," Rob said, remembering her name.

"She said she thought the victim would be one of them. Seems she was right."

"That may be so," Rob agreed. "I guess we'll find out."

"Alright. So let's do something about it," Nick suggested. "Let's be proactive."

"What did you have in mind?"

Nick shrugged. "Well, we're here, in town. I say we head out tonight and see if we can't speak to a few of them. See if anyone knows of someone who's missing."

"Sounds like a plan," Scarlett agreed. "I like it."

Rob nodded at Nick's forward thinking. "Alright, sounds good. In the meantime, I need you to focus on talking to the people in these houses." Rob pointed to the ones beyond the bushes where the body had been found and those on the other side of Mansfield Road. "Find out what they know. Did they see or hear anything last night, no matter how small. We need leads on this."

"We also need to expand that cordon," Nick said, frowning at the placement of the tape.

"Jolly's on it," Rob confirmed. "See what you can do to speed it up, though, okay?"

"Will do."

As Rob's eyes scanned the growing crowd beyond the cordon, his eyes settled on a face he knew. "Oh, shit."

"What?" Nick asked.

"What's up?" Scarlett added as she craned her neck to look too.

Rob sighed. "Don't worry about it. It's just a journalist I know."

"Oh, crap, yeah," Nick said. "That's Vincent Kane."

"Yep," Rob confirmed.

"Who's Vincent Kane?" Scarlett asked.

"He works for the Mansfield Gazette, and he hated Jon Pilgrim. He was always writing terrible things about him and hounding him on cases. He was a nightmare. Well, he was until Jon punched him."

"He punched him?" Scarlett asked.

"Kane broke a cordon and contaminated a crime scene, all to get a story," Rob explained. "When he mouthed off about it, Jon lashed out. He was given a slap on the wrist, and Kane got a broken nose. It didn't go any further than that due to embarrassment all round, but Kane kept his distance from then on."

"Kane also hates Rob and me by association," Nick added. "I'm surprised he's here, actually. He's kept his distance from police stuff for a while."

"So, you're saying, because I work with Rob, I need to be careful around him," Scarlett concluded.

"I wouldn't go anywhere near him," Rob said, fixing Kane with a cold stare as he spoke. "He's trouble."

Across the way, Kane noticed Rob's gaze and smiled.

"Isn't that a bit of a cliché?" Scarlett asked. "The troublesome reporter, I mean?"

"Probably, so what?"

"So, maybe we shouldn't paint all reporters with the same brush?"

"Believe me, I don't, but Kane is an idiot. Trust me on this one."

"Don't worry, I will," Scarlett confirmed with a cheeky smile. Was she purposely goading him into reacting? He shook his head at her, which only made her smile more. She knew what she was doing.

"So, what's next?" Nick asked.

"We need to process this scene and deal with the mountain of paperwork that it will undoubtedly generate," Rob answered, knowing the work that would need doing. "Our priority, though, is finding out who *she* is. We can't do much more until we know that."

"Agreed," Nick replied. "Maybe going out tonight and asking around will help with that."

"One can only hope. Right, let's crack on."

"Aye," Nick replied, leaving Rob and Scarlett to their work as he went to find the Sergeant.

"I hope we're not jumping to conclusions about the victim," Rob muttered to Scarlett as they made for his car.

"I don't think so. I think we're right about what this girl did for a living."

"Probably," Rob said, hoping they were wrong.

As they approached his car, Vincent Kane started to call out.

"Detective? Have you got any comments for the press? The British public has a right to know about any dangerous criminals in the local area. Detective?"

Rob ignored him. He had work to do.

16

Grabbing her coffee from the machine, Erika turned the device off and clutched the mug in both hands. She enjoyed the heat as it warmed her fingers. Leaning against the kitchen counter, she glanced over at the note she'd placed to one side, along with the key.

It was something of an unexpected development, for sure, but a welcome one too. She'd moved here, taken this flat, for a very specific reason, and this development played into that better than she could have hoped. But it didn't stop her from feeling nervous about it all.

She couldn't help but wonder if this might cause everything to backfire somehow and ruin it all. But she couldn't see how.

What she needed to do was to talk to the one person who she could share this news with and who understood its significance: her mum. But even that potentially had perils. Her mum might think things had gone too far and demand that she move out, or she cause other problems.

Her mother was quite adept at causing problems, that was for sure. And so she'd hesitated and hung on to the information for the afternoon, pondering the course of action she should take.

She'd called Rob because to do otherwise would be weird, and felt good about their little chat. He just seemed grateful that she was willing to help him out with his cat.

She'd naturally been nervous about the call and hoped she didn't come across as too enthusiastic or eager to please, but when she thought about it objectively, she knew she'd handled it right. She was sure of it.

Feeling desperate to share this with someone, she found she was powerless to resist any longer and gave in to the inevitable.

Pulling her phone from her back pocket, she quickly placed a call to her mother, before she had a change of heart, and waited as the line started to ring.

"Hello, darling," her mother sang down the line to her. "What's up?"

"Hi, Mum. How's things?"

"Alright. I'm just at home doing a little baking. Your dad's at work, looks like he's got a lot on right now."

Erika listened but didn't really take in what her mother was saying. It wasn't all that important compared to what she'd called about. Her mother's ramblings about the mundanities of life were boring, frankly, especially when she had such a huge development to tell her about.

Huge for Erika anyway and potentially huge for the family.

"Is everything okay, dear? You seem quiet."

"Yeah, I'm fine. Just a lot on my mind, that's all," Erika explained.

"Oh. Like what?"

This was it. This was the moment when she could either turn back and forget the whole thing, or come clean and tell her all about what happened this morning.

In the end, it was inevitable what she chose.

"I've been given the keys to Rob's flat. He wants me to look after his cat when he's away on cases."

There was silence at the end of the line. It stretched on for what felt like an eternity as her mother no doubt processed what she'd just been told.

"Oh. I see."

"What do you think?" Erika asked.

"I, err... Are you sure that's a good idea? I mean, this is risky, Erika. Don't you think? You could have said no."

"I couldn't. That would seem even more suspicious."

"Is that not better than the alternative?"

"And what's that?"

"You know what. You shouldn't get too close. It risks everything."

"It's just feeding a cat, Mum. I'm hardly telling him my life story... or yours."

"Don't joke about that, young lady. You know how dangerous this is. I've told you a thousand times about being careful while I've indulged your curiosity. But this... This seems a little foolhardy. I knew you shouldn't have moved in there. I knew it. It was bound to backfire."

"It's not backfired, mother. Everything's fine. He doesn't know anything. I'm just his neighbour, nothing more. This is why I moved here, after all, to be close to him and maybe get to know him."

"And if this need you have to know him ends up exposing us? Then what? What happens then?"

"That won't happen. Trust me."

"It better not."

"It won't."

17

Standing in the outbuilding, surrounded by the smell of old wood, oil and the countryside beyond, Carter watched dispassionately as two of his enforcers tortured another man hanging from a cross beam by his ankles. The man was naked and bleeding badly, his blood dripping to the earthen floor beneath him while he cried.

"Please, I don't know anymore. I don't know anything. Please stop. I'll do whatever you want. Just please, don't kill me. Let me go."

"And why would we do that, Vaughn? After what you did, why would we let you go?" Carter answered.

"Because I won't do it again. I won't tell anyone about this. You have my word."

Carter felt his phone buzz in his pocket and pulled it out. He recognised the name. "Boys. Shut him up."

"Sure thing, boss," Jonas answered and clamped one hand over Vaughn's mouth.

Satisfied, Carter answered the call and listened as the voice on the other end offered him some useful information. It only took a moment, and in less than a minute, the call was over, and Carter hung up. For a moment, he gazed into the dark corners of the outbuilding while pondering this new revelation. It wasn't groundbreaking by any stretch of the imagination, but it was a new development that Owen would certainly want to know about.

It did concern family, after all, and that was always important, even in this case. In fact, maybe, especially in this case. It might be that this could present a unique opportunity for the firm and take the family places that it needed to go.

But that was a long shot, and he had to admit that he didn't know enough about the details of it all to say one way or the other. That was for Owen, his brothers, and their dad to evaluate.

One thing he knew for sure, though, was that he needed to pass this on up the chain, and it couldn't wait.

Nearby, Vaughn started crying and carrying on again as Jonas released his mouth. "Carter, please. I've told you everything."

Carter sighed and realised that Vaughn was probably telling the truth this time. Maybe he'd been telling the truth the whole time. Either way, his usefulness was at an end, and they needed to clean up. He had more important things to deal with right now.

"Actually, I believe you have told me everything," Carter said as he wandered over to stand beside his two enforcers. "Which means your usefulness is at an end, my good friend."

"No, please. Don't do this," Vaughn said while Carter held out his hand. Jonas pulled out his Fifth Generation Glock 17 pistol and handed it over.

Carter ignored Vaughn's pleading as he ejected the magazine to confirm it was loaded and then pulled back the slide to check the breach. A 9x19mm Parabellum round was already chambered, waiting to be fired. Perfect.

"No, please, wait..." Vaughn cried as Carter aimed the firearm and pulled the trigger. The report echoed around the building as a short, thunderous bang that caused Jonas to flinch.

Vaughn jerked once as the bullet passed through his skull before falling limp. A new runnel of blood poured from his forehead onto the ground.

Carter gave Vaughn a last look before he shrugged and handed Jonas the gun.

"Clean this up," Carter ordered.

"On it, boss."

With a nod, Carter turned, walked towards the large wooden doors, and swung one open. They had seen better days. The rusty hinges creaked and squealed, not unlike Vaughn, as Carter lifted his phone again.

He placed the call and put the phone to his ear. It rang a few times before a female voice answered.

"Hello?"

"It's Carter. Is he there?"

"One moment, Mr Bird," the woman replied and put him on hold.

Carter sighed and leaned his shoulder against the door frame as he listened to the boys cutting Vaughn down from the cross beam behind him. They were out in the countryside, south of Mansfield and well away from anyone who could interrupt them. A few hundred yards away, the woods on his property loomed, hiding secrets that few knew about.

Vaughn would be another of those secrets in a few hours, once the boys had finished with him.

Seconds later, the line clicked.

"Carter, good to hear from you, my man. What's up?"

"I've just had some new information come my way from one of my contacts, which I think you should know about."

"Well, don't keep me waiting. What's all this about?"

"It concern's your brother, Rob."

Carter heard the brief hesitation on the other end of the line. "I see."

"Apparently, he's going up in the world. He's been promoted to Inspector, and he's now leading a team on the Nottinghamshire branch of the East Midlands Special Operations Unit."

"Is he now? How reliable is your source?"

"Very," Carter answered.

"And you're sure about that?"

"Of course. I wouldn't have called if there was any doubt."

"Alright, leave it with me. I'll be in touch. I think we might want to meet this contact of yours."

"Understood," Carter answered. He kept his reply calm and even, but inside, he was cursing. It might mean that his contact would start reporting to his boss rather than him, and he'd lose a valuable asset. He'd need to see what he could do about that.

"Good work," his boss added before the line clicked off.

"Shit," Carter cursed. It seemed this tiny piece of information was a double-edged sword. On the one hand, it made him look good, but on the other, it might also hurt the network he'd built up.

Grumbling, he turned and looked back into the barn. His men were standing on either side of a large metal barrel, of which Vaughn's feet were sticking out of the top. As Carter watched, Jonas unscrewed the top of a huge plastic container with gloved hands and started to carefully pour some liquid into the drum. Steam started to rise from the barrel as the corrosive chemical began to eat through Vaughn's flesh.

In a few hours, there'd be nothing left of him. He'd be little more than fertilizer.

18

"This is a long shot," Rob muttered as they walked out onto Mansfield Road opposite the parade of shops, and turned left.

"You don't think we'll get anything useful?" Scarlett asked.

"I don't know. I doubt we'll find our victim this way. And one thing I do know from my years on the force is, these girls will not like talking to cops."

"Then we need to try and look a little less suspicious," Nick suggested, giving Rob a knowing look.

"Let's be a little more optimistic about this," Scarlett added. "You never know what we might discover. Nailer seemed to go for it."

"I think you're over-egging the pudding, there," Rob said. "He said he saw no harm in us asking a few questions. That's a little different to being enthusiastically behind it. Besides, he was a little distracted preparing for his meeting with Landon."

"Should we be concerned?" Scarlett asked.

"I don't think so. He's just briefing her on our progress so far. I suppose us putting in the extra hours and working the streets for information makes him look good."

"It makes us look good, too," Nick added. "You're welcome, by the way."

"For what?" Rob asked.

"For making you look good. That was my idea."

"Ever the team player, Nick," Rob muttered.

"That's me."

Rob smiled and decided to change the subject. "I tell you what, I'm bloody hungry, I know that. I'm looking forward to this meal later."

"Where are we eating again?" Scarlett asked.

"The Dog and Duck," Rob said. "It's a pub just outside Clipstone."

"Nice?"

"I think so."

"You should view this walk as working up an appetite," Nick suggested.

"Oh, is that what I'm doing. I see," Rob replied sarcastically. "Well, that makes it all worth it, then."

"Will Nailer be joining us?" Scarlett asked.

"I think so," Rob replied.

"You never know," Nick added. "He might bill it to the police as an expense. Saves us from chipping in."

"Yeah, right, fat chance of that," Rob muttered. "Still, it'll be nice to hang out with you all." They needed to gel as a team, and group activities like this meal would help with that, making them more effective.

The sun had set, and the village had long since been bathed in shadows. Street lamps lit up the main road like a runway as cars drove by, either in towards Mansfield or out. It was relatively quiet on the street, but he could make out music playing in the distance. Looking back at the parade of shops, he could see people standing outside the Clip Club, the smoke from their fags lit up by the car dealership's lights. Between passing cars, he could hear the distinctive sound of people laughing and talking at the edge of his hearing.

He wondered if Nigel was there tonight with Caprice and his other bar staff, serving the locals?

Much further up, in the direction they were headed, the shadows of the Headstocks were just visible above the houses on the other side of the road.

"I think I can see some of these girls," Scarlett said and pointed.

They stopped and peered into the darkness. As a car passed, its headlights lit up a handful of girls, their bare legs almost glowing in the light, before the car passed and they were dropped into shadow again. There weren't many of them, maybe a handful across a couple of groups standing in the entrances of commercial properties on the opposite side of the road.

"There we go," Nick confirmed. "Right, I think we should spit up. We can talk to more of them that way, and we're less likely to scare them off."

"Agreed," Rob replied, wondering if they were out here in the cold night air for no reason. Was this likely to net them any kind of information at all? He had no idea.

"I'll go ahead," Nick said.

"I'll hang back," Rob added. "I'll take the ones furthest this way."

"Okay," Scarlett said. "I guess I'll be somewhere in the middle, then. A Scarlett sandwich."

Nick smirked and pressed on ahead while Rob stopped and leaned against a sight post, biding his time.

"Don't be so pessimistic," Scarlett said, fixing him with a glare. "We'll find out who she is, one way or another, and maybe this is how we do that?"

"Yeah, maybe," Rob admitted. "I have my doubts, but maybe."

"Maybe is better than won't, I suppose."

"Be careful. It's likely that their pimp will be around somewhere, and he won't like us interfering with his business. So watch your back."

"I'll be careful," she said. "Will you?"

"Always," Rob confirmed.

Scarlett grinned at him before she turned and walked on, keeping her distance from Nick as she went. Rob watched her go, letting her get a good way ahead before he set off.

He soon approached a pair standing outside a gated entrance. They were a few metres apart, shifting from one foot to the other while hugging themselves against the cool air. It wasn't a warm night, and they weren't wearing much. He felt bad for them, being forced to stand out here in the freezing cold, selling themselves to any old stranger who drove by. Rob shifted direction and made to cross the road during a gap in the traffic. The nearest young woman saw him coming when he was partway across and started preening herself. The young woman's stance shifted from self-preservation against the cool air to something much more confident.

She was selling herself.

"Hello, handsome. Looking for some action?" She spoke in a seductive purr and matched it with a smile, her eyes twinkling in the night.

"I certainly need your help," Rob replied and glanced around, looking for her pimp. There were several cars parked up along the street, and any one of the shadowy vehicles might hold people keeping an eye on these young ladies.

The one he approached might pass for someone in her twenties in this half-light, but he had a horrible feeling she was much younger than that. It was tough to know for sure with all the make-up she had on. Close up, she looked worn out, like frayed, well-used rope, about to snap. His trained eye spotted the track marks and self-harming scars on her arms she was trying to hide, and the poor complexion of a regular drug user. He felt sorry for her.

"I can help you with all kinds of things," she crooned. "What you after?"

All Rob wanted to do was to get her off the street, away from the predators, and find her the help she so desperately needed. But it wasn't that easy, and he had a job to do. "What's your name?"

"Whatever you want it to be."

Rob grimaced at the stilted, awkward conversation. There was no need to drag this out. He needed to know what she knew, and that was that.

"I'm looking for someone."

"I'd say you found someone, babe."

"Did one of your…" he struggled to find the right words, "fellow workers, disappear recently? One of the other girls I mean. I think one of them went missing. We're looking for her."

"We?" She frowned, looking suspicious. "Who are you?"

"A concerned citizen." It wasn't a lie.

"Are you pigs? I ain't talking to no pigs." Again, her demeanour shifted. She was no longer trying to entice him. Her arms were crossed over her chest, with a scowl fixed to her face. She backed away. "Piss off."

"I don't want to cause any trouble for you. I just need a quick answer, that's all. Did one of your group disappear recently?"

"If you don't want any trouble, then I suggest you piss off, mate. You're gonna get nothing but trouble round here. Go on, get lost."

The other young lady standing close by joined in. "Go on, fuck off. You're gonna lose us business."

"It's just a simple question."

"Which we ain't answering," the first replied. "We ain't doing nuthin' wrong. We're just waitin' for some friends. That's all."

Behind him, an engine roared. Rob turned to see a black car skid to a stop, its bumper less than a metre from his legs. The driver and passenger doors were flung open, and two men climbed out, one much bigger than the other.

"See, my friends," the girl said.

"Oi, fuck face. You need to piss off," the shorter, slimmer one spat. He seemed like the one in charge.

"Want me to teach him some manners, boss?" the larger one asked, confirming Rob's suspicions.

Rob backed up and pulled his warrant card, hoping to avoid the beating this man was obviously gunning for. "I'm police. I just have a few questions."

The large man hesitated and glanced over his shoulder. "Boss?"

Rob could see the smaller man processing this shift in power and hating it. He silently cursed. "Keep him back." The man turned to the girls. "Get in, now," he barked and ushered them towards the car.

"We need to find out about this missing girl," Rob called out, trying to make the girls see sense. "Someone's targeting prostitutes. You could be next."

"Ain't no whores here," the thug said.

Rob pressed on, "We're trying to help."

"We don't know what you're talking about," the smaller man snapped, his voice filled with spite. "We don't know about any missing girl or any prostitutes. I'm just picking up my mates, and you're harassing us."

"Then talk to us," Rob pleaded.

But it was no use. Within moments, the women were shut into the back of the car and out of reach. Rob glanced up at the bigger man who'd been blocking his way.

"Get lost," the thug rumbled.

"I'm only trying to help," Rob said and heard another engine roar behind him. He turned to see a second car picking up the three girls further up that Nick and Scarlett were talking to. Rob cursed as he returned his attention to the car before him.

The smaller man hurried around to the passenger side. "Get in. We're leaving."

Rob frowned as the men got into the car before the engine revved and it sped off back towards Mansfield. He pondered if he should have arrested the girls for suspected soliciting or the men for controlling prostitution for gain. He'd aired on the side of caution, for now, preferring to focus on the job at hand rather than expand what they were doing. Was it the right call? He wasn't sure about that, but there were so many unknowns that it was difficult to discern which was the right course of action.

Pulling his notebook out, Rob jotted down the number plate of the car so he could check it out later in case they needed to follow this up.

If his suspicions were right, and these girls were prostitutes, and the men were their pimps, they could be part of an organised criminal gang, and the cars might well be stolen, or the plates could be changed or fake. Whichever was the case, it would lead to a dead end.

Nick and Scarlett joined him as he returned his notebook to his pocket.

"Any luck?" Nick asked.

"No, nothing. She clocked me for what I was pretty quick and clammed up."

"Yeah," Nick muttered. "Mine too."

"I decided against arresting them," Rob added. "We want them to trust us, after all."

"Yeah. That could be counterproductive."

"How about you?" Rob asked Scarlett.

"Well, I might have something," she said, a hint of smugness in her voice.

"What did you find out?"

"Something about a local massage parlour. I heard one of the girls whispering to her friend, saying something like she wished she'd stayed at Phil's. Much less hassle at the parlour."

"Phil's?"

Scarlett shrugged. "That's what I heard."

"Alright, then, we need to see what we can find out."

"I told you it wouldn't be a write-off," Scarlett said.

19

For Nailer, the day had been a long series of meetings with local councillors, mixed with calls to the Superintendent and others, while getting reports from the team and general management. He was helped by the small team of civilian investigators they'd brought with them and the digital technology they used.

The day had flown by, and as his shift came to a close, he got a message that Landon wanted to see him personally to get an update.

With the group's meal at the Dog and Duck looming, he had little choice but to head south and hope he got back in time. Driving back to the Lodge, he thought back over the day and how the new team had worked together in these early hours.

Overall, the group had pulled together admirably during the day. It had been impressive to watch, and he felt reassured that he'd chosen well.

Rob had been a given, pretty much. When Landan had asked Nailer to join up, Loxley had been one of the first things they'd discussed. She had ideas and shared why she'd brought Rob on board early on.

But all that would come later once the team was settled.

Rob was a dedicated and skilled detective, and being an officer seemed to be his life. His background was both a hinderance and an asset, and it focused his mind in a way that was incredibly useful.

His long-term partner, Nick Miller, had also been an easy choice. These two detectives had impressed Nailer repeatedly over the years, and having Nick on his team for a few weeks following Orleton's reassignment only confirmed that he would be a great choice.

Scarlett was more of an unknown. Having only recently moved up here from Surrey, no one really knew her, which could have been an issue. But, her conduct on the Sherwood Murder case with Rob, her single-mindedness, and how she'd helped take down their own DCI without flinching stood her in good stead.

Also, Rob seemed quite taken with her, and if Nailer had to guess, he felt it was quite likely that Rob would stick to having Scarlett as his main partner rather than go back to Nick. It was a curious development, but Rob seemed to have a solid relationship with Scarlett, and they worked together well, all of which would be good for the unit.

Despite all these positives, however, she was still something of a relative unknown to Nailer, and he resolved to keep an eye on Scarlett until he knew her better.

Guy Gibson was a man Nailer had worked with a few times during recent years, and he'd been impressed with the young man and his work ethic. He was bright, intelligent and steady. He knew what he was doing, all of which would stand him in good stead with the team.

Ellen and Tucker had both been on Nailer's team for a while already, so when he was reassigned to the EMSOU, he knew immediately that he wanted to bring the pair with him. They were both gifted officers and would be assets to the team, in his opinion.

However, what he'd been less sure about was how well the group would gel. He'd picked out several strong personalities, and he could see some of these guys clashing if he didn't manage them.

It would be a challenge, but it was one he'd gladly taken on following Landon reassigning him to the unit.

Nailer parked up at the Lodge and made his way inside. It wasn't that far to Landon's office, but he needed this to be quick, so he could get back to the job at hand and the meal he'd committed himself to attending. He was soon through reception and making his way upstairs.

He'd been keeping an eye on the group during the day to see how they interacted and had been left feeling pleased with the dynamic. He could see that a couple of groups had already formed, no doubt from having worked with certain people before.

Rob, Scarlett and Nick seemed close, although Nick crossed the divide and hung out with Ellen and Tucker just as easily. Guy seemed to flit between the two groups—which made sense given he was the odd one out—but spent more time with Ellen and Tuck than the others.

But then, they were all DCs, and Rob was their Inspector, their boss. It made sense that the DCs would stick together. Nick, however, being the Sergeant, bridged that gap.

Only Scarlett seemed immune to that hierarchy, but that was probably because she'd worked with Rob on her previous case and was familiar with him.

He'd keep an eye on that dynamic to see how it developed, but right now, all was as he'd expected it to be.

Reaching the corridor that Landon's office was on, he marched over and knocked.

"Come," she called out.

Nailer opened the door. "I'm heading off, ma'am."

"Come in, John. Come in." Superintendent Landon clicked her mouse and then looked up. She smiled. "Sorry to pull you away, but I needed to find out how your day went after you pulled them in early to help clear the boxes? Did they gel as a team?"

"Yeah, I think so. As much as I could have hoped for, anyway, so I'm satisfied, and they're working well on this first case."

"Excellent. How's that progressing?"

"I'll find out more tonight when I get back and chat with them all over dinner," Nailer answered, keen to impress on her that he couldn't stay. "But, from the reports I've had in, I know they're making progress both on identifying the victim and rooting out suspects. They're working well together."

"Good. I must say, however, that as a team-building exercise, moving boxes is a little unorthodox. But, I can see the merits of it."

"Thank you."

"You're happy with your choice of officers, then? No second thoughts?"

"No, not at all," Nailer replied. "I'm very happy."

"That's good to hear. And how's Rob doing?"

"He's fine. Your plan to try him out on the Sherwood case worked perfectly, and there didn't seem to be too much resistance from the brass about promoting him to EMSOU."

"You didn't see most of it," Landon replied. "There were a few dissenting voices, but they saw the merits of my plan, even after the whole Orelton thing."

Nailer grinned. "Are they worried Rob might go after them next?"

Landon snorted. "Are you calling your superiors corrupt, DCI Nailer?"

"No, of course not. I'm sure they're all whiter than white." Nailer grimaced. "But when there's someone who has a knack for sniffing around other officers, it can make people nervous."

"Maybe they should be nervous." Landon's face was dead pan.

"Maybe," he conceded. "So, will you be diving back into Operation Major Oak soon?"

"There's no rush for that," Landon answered. "I will, but not just yet. Let's see how things go. Rob's family isn't going anywhere, and neither is Rob."

"I suppose not," he conceded.

"I just hope, when the time comes, he'll be as useful as I think he might be."

"Don't we all," Nailer agreed. "Don't we all."

20

Walking back towards Mansfield Road along Sixth Avenue, Izabela scanned the road, in front and behind. After finishing with her latest John, she'd found herself alone at the allotments in North Clipstone. After the previous two Johns, she'd been picked up and ferried back to her patch. They didn't trust her, and were keeping an eye on her. But this time, there was no one here.

No one was coming to get her.

Something was up. Something that had called her minders away, leaving her alone.

Keen to not let this unexpected opportunity pass her by, she set off back through the town, choosing an obscure route through back roads and cut-throughs, and kept her head down.

Remarkably, she reached the main road without trouble and found herself staring at the busy Clip Club beyond the car dealership opposite. People were standing around outside, drinking and smoking, enjoying the freedoms they took for granted. Freedoms that people like her had to fight for.

Standing beside the fence of the corner property, she considered her plan and wondered if she wasn't being utterly crazy coming back here. But where else could she go? She only knew a few people and only trusted maybe two of those. Perhaps just one, depending on how Nigel was with her.

The only person she knew for sure that she could trust was Caprice. She'd always been kind to her and helped her out whenever she could. She'd seen her since she'd left Nigel's care, and she'd been just as friendly as before.

But Caprice wouldn't be enough. She needed Nigel. He'd been key to helping her last time, and she hoped he would be able to help her this time too. He did, however, run hot and cold, and she feared catching him at the wrong time and being sent back onto the streets.

That's where Caprice came in. If anyone could talk Nigel around and get him to help, it would be Caprice. She'd seen how Nigel looked at Caprice. She'd noticed the signs.

She needed his help, and Caprice would be key in getting it.

Today's events had made her escape even more urgent than before. She couldn't wait any more and bide her time. Things were spiralling out of control.

The news had spread during the day amongst the girls, and it wasn't difficult for them to piece the jigsaw puzzle together. An unidentified girl had been killed in Clipstone. It was all over the news that one of the girls saw on her hidden phone. Another confirmed it after seeing the same story on Abel's phone. He seemed curiously interested in the story, and when Izabela found out, she knew instinctively that it was Penny. There was no other option, as far as she was concerned. Penny had been murdered, and Izabela knew who'd done it. It all worked and fit into place for her. She felt sure of it. It was so obvious.

But if that was the case, and her suspicions about the killer turned out to be true, then her life was in danger as well. She couldn't trust Abel to look after her, given how little difference it made to Penny's life. Besides, he didn't care for them. He made that perfectly clear through his actions, which left only one option, which meant escaping Abel and taking a huge risk.

So far, that risk seemed to be paying off, but the riskiest part was still to come, and she had no idea what she'd do if this fell through. To minimise the chances, she needed to get Caprice onto her side. That way, Nigel would find it so much harder to dismiss her.

Taking a breath, she waited for a gap in the sporadic traffic flow and jogged over the road before walking down Central Avenue opposite, away from Mansfield Road.

Passing the cars parked outside the dealership and the mechanics attached to it on Central Avenue, she came to the cut-through that led behind the dealership and the Clip Club, where Nigel and the employees parked. Without a backwards glance, she walked through as if she owned the place. She couldn't afford to look shifty and get questioned about what she was doing, nor could she afford to spend any more time than was necessary out on the street.

She walked through shadow, into the familiar back lot. Music and the sounds of people enjoying themselves could be heard from inside the building, but going in through the back door was out of the question. Instead, she scanned the rear lot, picking out Nigel's and Caprice's cars.

They were both here, it seemed. Turning again, Izabela appraised the space, wondering where to hide and wait for her chance. She'd been out here plenty of times during her stay in the Clip Club. It had been her refuge. The place she'd come to get out of the building and away from everyone else, remaining out of sight and safe from casual view.

She'd have gone insane without it.

But it didn't feel like a safe haven today. Instead, it felt like enemy territory, and she needed to hide. Walking over to the bins, she found a small pile of flattened cardboard boxes ready for pick up and recycling. It was the work of minutes to turn them into a small place for her to snuggle down and remain somewhat protected from the elements. It would do for the short term while she waited for Caprice to appear.

The cardboard provided little warmth or insulation, and it wasn't long before she found herself shivering and questioning her plan. The minutes dragged on endlessly as she waited, hoping that Caprice would appear alone. While she waited, Izabela busied herself with creating a small makeshift bed out of the boxes, using some like a mattress and the rest as a kind of covering in an attempt to keep the heat in and fend off the cold. As she huddled under the cardboard, she thought back to the other girls and wondered how much danger they might be in? If this was as she feared, and tensions were brewing between the rival gangs, how long would it be before outright violence erupted? He had to know. It was the only explanation for Penny's disappearance, and if he couldn't get to her, then he would surely lash out and attack anyone he could, such as Penny.

Minutes turned into hours as she shivered under the covers she'd created for herself. Peering out across the parking lot, she watched the rear door, hoping against hope that the one person she needed to see would appear. Caprice usually took out the rubbish. She'd seen her do it time and again. But would she do it again tonight?

When the door finally opened, it came as something of a shock, and for a moment, Izabela didn't quite believe her eyes as the familiar-looking blonde woman stepped out with several large black plastic bags clutched in her hands.

This was her chance.

Izabela slipped out from under the boxes and waited for Caprice to get much closer before she rounded the corner.

"Hey," Izabela said cautiously.

Caprice jumped and dropped the bags, letting out a stifled yelp as she turned. "Holy shit."

"Sorry. It's me. I didn't mean to scare you."

"Izabela?" Caprice sounded shocked.

"Hi."

"What the hell are you doing back there? You must be freezing."

"I err, I ran away."

Caprice frowned. "You what?"

"From Abel, I mean. I couldn't stay with him anymore. Look, I need help."

"Help?" Caprice glanced at the club with a troubled expression before she turned back, looking curious. "What kind of help?"

Sensing that she had a chance, she stepped closer. "I think my life is in danger."

The blonde frowned and narrowed her eyes in what looked like a mix of confusion and suspicion. "Why?"

She sighed. "You've seen the news about the murder?"

"Yeah, it's all anyone's talking about."

"I think that was my friend, and I think they're after me."

The look on Caprice's face turned incredulous. "Are you sure? How can you know that? That's a hell of a leap."

"No, it's not. I was one of Radek's girls, right? But I escaped. I got out, thanks to you and Nigel."

"And then you went right back into it," Caprice added, sounding tired.

"Yeah, I know."

"Why?"

"I... Because I needed money." She took a long breath, knowing she needed to be honest about this. "Because Penny convinced me, and... I guess I just didn't know any better." She sighed to herself, wishing she'd thought it through more, but hindsight was always clearer. It was always easy to look back and see the mistakes you made, but when you're in the moment, sometimes it's just not that obvious. Sometimes all you can see is trees, rather than the whole wood.

"I know," Izabela added. "It was wrong. I should have... I don't know, done something else."

"Anything else. You hurt Nigel and me by going back. We thought you knew better than that."

"I do... now," she admitted.

"And you want our help again?"

"Yeah..." she answered, but this was starting to feel like a lost cause.

"I don't know how he's going to react to this, Izabela." Caprice sighed and put her hands on her hips. "I don't think tonight is a good night to go and talk to him, either."

"No. Of course not. But I can't go back now because they're after me."

"That's a bit paranoid, don't you think?"

"Penny disappeared last night, and today, a girl was found murdered. It's her, I know it. It's Radek that did it. He found out... something. Maybe he knows I'm part of Abels' crew, or that Penny helped recruit me, or something. I don't know. But it's him. I'm sure of it. If I don't disappear, I'm next."

"You don't know that. You're speculating. It might not be Penny, and it might be totally unrelated to you. Maybe she escaped like you did. She might be halfway to London by now and a new life. You don't know."

"I don't care," Izabela snapped. She wasn't going to be talked out of this. "I'm not going back, and I'm asking for your help. Will you help me?"

Caprice sighed and seemed to think it through before she looked around, her eyes settling on her car. She pulled out her keys. "Yeah, sure. I'll help. Don't say I never do anything for you, though."

21

"It's quite comfortable back here," Scarlett said as Rob drove north out of Clipstone. They were in Belle, his 1985 Ford Capri Mark 3, 2.8 Injection, otherwise known as his pride and joy, with Nick in the front passenger seat and Scarlett in the back. "It's quite roomy for a three-door."

"You're just trying to butter Rob up," Nick said. "I've been back there. It's not that spacious."

"Well, clearly, my arse is smaller than yours," she quipped. "And I don't want anything from Rob. I was just passing comment."

"Thank you," Rob replied, choosing to take the compliment for what it was. "I appreciate it."

"Again, what are you after, Stutely?" Nick asked.

"Nothing," she answered, her tone flat.

Rob smiled as Nick looked over at him. He jabbed his thumb towards Scarlett. "This is what you've been working with while I was with Nailer?"

"I have a name, you know," she said.

"Yep. *She* is *who* I've been working with," Rob answered.

"I'm right here, you know," Scarlett added.

"Don't ignore her," Rob warned him. It was all just good-natured ribbing, but he was perhaps pushing things slightly. Rob glanced back at Scarlett. "I'm still trying to house-train him."

"I can see that. Does he always talk to women this way?"

"No, just you," Nick quipped, his tone light.

"Huh-ho!" Scarlett exclaimed.

"I'll have to get you two working together on something," Rob mused to himself. Enjoying the friendly banter, knowing it was all harmless.

When she answered, Scarlett's voice dripped with sarcasm. "Oooh, I can't wait."

Nick turned back to her. "Hey, it means we can talk about the boss without him listening in." He grinned and winked at her.

"Oh," this time, she sounded excited, "well, as I said, I can't wait,"

Leaving Clipstone behind, they drove northeast along Mansfield Road, past fields on both sides until they drove through the smaller village of Kings Clipstone and veered right. As they left the village behind and headed east, the Dog and Duck appeared on their right. A white and grey building with an expansive car park that was maybe half full, it was an inviting sight in the gloom of the night.

Rob parked up, recognising one of the force's pool cars already parked.

"I'll tell you what, I'm ready for this," Nick said, exiting the car before tipping the front seat forward, allowing Scarlett to clamber out.

"Very dignified," Nick quipped as she came to her full height. He smiled at her and winked.

"Piss off," she answered and stepped out of the way so he could close the door.

"Children," Rob said in a mock warning voice.

"Sorry, Dad," Nick replied.

Making their way inside, they soon found Ellen, Tucker and Guy sitting at a table waiting for them. Rob spotted Nailer at the bar buying some drinks and joined him.

"Hey, can I help you with those?"

"Aye, you can," he said. "How'd it go?"

"Alright. Not as successful as I'd have liked, but not as hopeless as I'd feared," Rob replied.

"So you learnt something?"

"Possibly. We'll have to look into it tomorrow. I'll tell you more once we're sat down."

"Fair enough," Nailer replied before he finished off his order and paid.

"What about you? How'd your meeting with Landon go?"

"Fine," Nailer answered as they started to pick up the drinks between them. Scarlett came over and helped. "She just wanted to know how the first day had gone."

"Fair enough," Rob replied as they ferried the drinks over to the table and handed them out.

Nailer took his seat. "Let's order, then we can talk."

Rob nodded and picked up the menu, finding a wide selection of options and some truly delicious-sounding meals. In the end, his empty stomach steered him towards a burger and chips, while the table agreed on a couple of plates of nachos with salsa, cheese and dips as a starter.

With their order placed, Nailer waited for the waitress to walk away before he leaned in. "Right then, let's see where we all are with this. Ellen, Tucker, why don't you start with your chat to Emmett?"

"Sure," Ellen said. "Emmett didn't deny that he had a brief confrontation with Nigel yesterday morning and was quite open about it. But he played it down. He didn't seem to think it was terribly important and reiterated his belief that he didn't think Nigel would kill anyone. Valerie, however, was less sure. According to her, they've had a long-running feud that dates back to their mining days, and Nigel just won't let it go. It's developed into violence once before, which I think we've got on record, so she's convinced that Nigel is to blame, that he killed the girl and is attempting to discredit Emmett."

"And what do you think?" Nailer asked.

"I think that's plausible," Ellen answered. "He's a councillor, and we all know how divisive politics can be, so I wouldn't put it past someone who disagrees with Emmett on these things to do that."

"I agree," Tucker said. "The Wilkinsons seem like an upstanding couple doing good work for the community, but people tend to have strong reactions to anyone in politics who doesn't agree with their view. That and they're also Christians, something which seems to be a dirty word, these days." Tucker didn't look happy about this.

"So perhaps politics is a motive," Nailer suggested.

"Or religion," Tucker added.

"I think that's a stretch," Nailer replied. "But, I'll bear it in mind." Nailer turned to Rob. "So that's the Wilkinsons' point of view. What about Nigel? How did he react to you questioning him?"

"He didn't deny it either," Rob replied. "Nigel took a similar view to Emmett, by the sounds of things. He dismissed it, saying it was an issue from their mining days. He did say he'd had a bad morning the day of the confrontation, although he didn't elaborate on what he meant by that, and when he saw Emmett, he just chose to take it out on him. A case of wrong place, wrong time, by the sounds of things."

"I see," Nailer replied. "But that also suggests something about Nigel's temperament, if waking up on the wrong side of the bed can lead to him assaulting someone in the street."

Rob shrugged. "Yeah. It's not a good look for him."

"No, it's not," Nailer agreed.

"There was something that one of Nigel's employees said, as well." He turned to Scarlett. "What was her name?"

"Caprice Randell," Scarlett answered, checking her notes.

"That's right, Caprice. She said that Nigel left them working at the bar without him between nine and ten PM. He disappeared until Caprice went looking for him."

"Does that fit with the possible time of death of the victim?" Nailer asked.

"It does," Rob confirmed. "Meaning Nigel doesn't have a foolproof alibi for that night unless he can find someone who can vouch for him."

"Or I find CCTV that incriminates him," Guy added.

"Indeed," Nailer replied, turning to DC Gibson. "Speaking of which, how about the Wilkinsons and their movements the night of the murder? Have you been able to work anything out?"

"I got their phones' GPS and cell tower data, and I also spoke to their friends who they say they met. Their friends confirmed they saw Emmett and Valerie that night. Emmett was with his friends for a few hours after work, then his phone moved around Clipstone, to various locations, including the Social Club and the allotments—which was an odd one—and then to the Chinese takeaway. He hangs out there for a while, probably eating his food in the car or something, until he comes here to the Dog and Duck at about nine-forty. He returns home at about ten-forty-five."

"So he was in the vicinity of the murder, or at least, his phone was, when the victim was murdered," Nailer summed up.

"He was, yes. Just up the road, in fact."

"And Valerie?"

"Her phone goes from work in Mansfield to her friends at a new estate in North Clipstone before returning home for eight-forty-five. So she was returning home around the time we think the girl was murdered, or maybe slightly before. She doesn't go out again after getting home."

"Good work," Nailer stated. "What else do you have for us?"

"I found the footage of the confrontation between Emmett and Nigel. It's from a distance, and the view is partly obscured by the trees, but it does show Nigel confronting Emmett and seems to follow the description we got from Father Aaron, Emmett and Nigel. I think there was at least one other person involved in ending the scuffle, but I'll need to examine the footage more to find out who that was."

"Excellent." Nailer turned to Nick. "Have you been speaking to people on the parade of shops?"

"We started that," Nick replied. "We got a little sidetracked when we found the body and we've been focusing our attention around there, but we will be going back to the shops as soon as we can."

"Good, okay, keep going, but try to get back to the shops as soon as you can."

"Will do," Nick said. "And a few more officers wouldn't go amiss."

"I'll see what I can do. But you know all about the staffing issues we have."

"Yeah, I know. We'll keep going. We've got a long way to go yet."

"Good, and what about your little escapade tonight. Rob said you found something out?"

Rob gestured to Scarlett. "I'll let Scarlett answer that."

Scarlett smiled. "We spoke to a few girls who we think were engaging in prostitution. Unfortunately, we were quickly interrupted by several men in two cars, claiming to be their friends, who got them out of there pretty sharpish. So, we didn't have much time with them. However, I did overhear one of the girls say that she wished she'd stayed at Phil's, and that there were no issues like this at the parlour."

"A parlour?" Nailer asked. "Like a massage parlour?"

"That would be my guess."

"Okay, then we need to look into that too, see if we can't find out more about this parlour and how it links in. Okay, I think that's about it, isn't it?"

"Well, there is the issue of the men who came and picked up the girls we were speaking to," Rob said. It was an issue that had been bothering him since the confrontation out on the street, as it added another dimension to this investigation and could muddy the waters. "The fact that these young and vulnerable women were being watched by these men who seemed about ready to tear me a new one until I showed them my ID, suggests there may be another layer to this."

"Gangs," Nailer replied, nodding sombrely. "I guessed that too. Prostitutes can be a good money maker for them, and it's not difficult to keep the girls in line when they're hooked on drugs. We need to keep an eye on that angle as it could be key to unlocking this case. We all know how violent they can be."

"Aye," several of them confirmed.

"Tomorrow then," Nailer continued, "we have the post-mortem of the victim, and hopefully we'll have a name for her too. Nick, Scarlett, I want you both at the post-mortem in the morning."

"Okay," she confirmed. "I'll be grateful for the company." Scarlett turned to Nick. "Not squeamish, are you?"

"I can't say they're the most enjoyable of things to watch," he replied. "You'll hold my hand, right?"

"Yes indeed, sweetie."

"Any other business," Nailer asked.

"Only that I've seen Vincent Kane sniffing around," Rob added. "He was at the murder site where we found the rest of the body."

"Kane?" Nailer asked. "Wonderful. Where's Pilgrim when we need him? Will he be any trouble?"

"Hopefully not," Rob replied.

"Keep an eye on him. I don't want him screwing this case up."

"Will do, guv," he answered as the waitress returned with the first of their food.

22

The following morning, Rob drove north out of Nottingham towards Mansfield. He'd managed to get out of town before the early morning rush hour, and the school traffic started to slow things down, leading to an uneventful drive through the countryside.

He was grateful for the lack of drama on his morning commute, as it gave him time to think, especially about something he felt a little guilty about after getting home late the night before.

On walking in through the front door of his apartment, Muffin was immediately on him, meowing around his legs as loudly as he could, making it quite clear Rob was late, and he was hungry.

After everything he'd been through, arranging for Erika to have a key and be able to feed Muffin for him, it made him feel bad. He knew he had to change how he did things. It was too long for the poor cat to wait for his food.

He was also craving some affection and companionship, something that Erika could give Muffin when Rob was away.

So he vowed to make sure he called on Erika more frequently to take over the care of Muffin on those evenings when he would be late home. It was the only fair thing to do.

Leaving home that morning, Rob had contemplated knocking on Erika's door to check everything was ok and that she was happy with the arrangement, but he'd decided against it. There was no need, really. They'd discussed it over the phone, and she'd been perfectly happy to help out when he'd spoken to her, so he felt sure nothing had changed over the following few hours. Besides, it was early, and she might have been sleeping or even had company.

He'd call her later and get her to pop in on Muffin at some point later today.

Rob reached the Clipstone Village Hall without a problem and made his way inside after parking up. He found Guy working on his laptop.

"Aaah, Rob, just the man I wanted to see."

"You're in early." Rob wandered over to where he was sitting.

Guy shrugged. "Had nothing else to do."

Rob nodded, feeling the same. "Fair enough. What have you got for me?" Guy's laptop screen was filled with a poor-quality still image of Clipstone's high street.

"This is the CCTV video of the confrontation between Nigel and Emmett. I've run it through a few filters and cropped into the area of interest, but it's tough to make out. Anyway, have a look and see what you think."

Guy hit play, and the video sprang into jerky life. It wasn't a smooth, high-quality piece of footage, and there seemed to be maybe one or two frames a second if that. But Rob could distinguish two figures facing off in the street that he recognised as Emmett and Nigel. They seemed to swap a few words before Nigel grabbed him by the collar. A moment later, Father Aaron and a woman appeared and pulled the pair apart. Emmett turned and went on his way, as did the woman, while Aaron had a brief chat with Nigel before they, too, walked away.

Throughout the whole sequence, the branches and leaves of a nearby tree were blowing, occasionally obscuring their view of what was going on and making it difficult to make out who the woman was throughout.

However, the video did seem to match the various accounts of the event they had been given so far.

"Okay, that seems to fit with what we've been told," Rob said. "I'd like to know who that woman was, though."

"Yeah, I'm not sure about that. I'll need to track back and see if I can figure it out." With a couple of clicks, Guy zoomed out so Rob could see the full width of the footage. Guy had been zoomed right into just a small part of the video.

"I guess there's no way to enhance it anymore?"

"No," Guy replied with a knowing smile. "Despite what the CSI shows would have you believe, there are limits to what is possible. If the pixels aren't there, that is, the image data isn't there, I can't just magically create it from nothing. Even the AI tools available now aren't useful on a forensic basis. They just magic stuff up out of nowhere, which just isn't useful."

"Okay, no worries."

"There is this, though." Guy riffled back through the footage to a few moments before the confrontation and hit play. He pointed to a pair of legs sticking out from where the tree covered the screen. "That's Nigel."

Guy's finger tracked Nigel's feet. They walked along the road, and after disappearing behind a branch, reappeared a moment later before they stopped. Guy hit pause.

"He stops here for a moment, and I think he's talking to whoever these people are." He pointed to what looked like maybe two more pairs of feet.

"Is that all we have, some feet?"

"That's it. He talks for a moment, then some wind blows, and we can't see him." Guy hit play. The leaves blew in the wind, hiding Nigel and whoever he was with. When Nigel appeared from behind the tree, it was moments before the confrontation, which Rob now watched play out in a small section of the frame.

He sighed, annoyed there wasn't better footage. "Well, whatever happens, we need to get the council to cut back that tree."

"Aye," Guy agreed. "Anyway, thought you should see what I've figured out so far. I'll keep going, see if I can't figure out who this woman is."

"Sounds good," Rob agreed. "While you're at it, have a hunt and see if you can't find a massage parlour or brothel that would fit with someone calling it Phil's."

"Sure, I'll have a look, see what I can find."

"Cheers," Rob thanked him and went to settle in for the morning.

23

"Thank you, dear," Bill's mother said as he placed the two bags of shopping on the countertop with a grunt of effort.

"That's okay, Mum," he said and started pulling the various groceries out of the bag and setting them on the side.

"Oh, you don't need to do that, dear."

"It's fine, Mum. I don't mind. Let me help you," Bill insisted.

She silently relented but started to busy herself by grabbing some of the items and moving them to the cupboard or fridge, as needed.

Bill let her do it, there was no need to argue with her, and if she wanted to help, that was fine. He didn't mind doing their shopping for them, although he kept meaning to do it online but forgetting. Besides, even if he did do that, he'd probably need to be there to help them pack it all away.

His parents needed help, and that was fine. It did occasionally get in the way of his work, which was annoying, but it could be worse.

He'd finish up here and then get himself over to the Lodge. He wanted an update from Vincent, but so far, the man was ignoring his texts. He'd taken a huge risk by bringing Kane in, and he wondered if he might have made a colossal mistake. Hopefully not.

"So, have you been out with any nice young ladies recently?" his mother probed.

Bill sighed. He didn't really want to talk about this, but his mum meant well and only wanted to see him happy. "Not really, Mum, no. I've been a little busy with work, so."

"Bill. You need to make sure you have a life outside of work. You need to take care of yourself more. I'm not getting any younger, and I'd love to see you settle down with someone."

"But, I'm happy, Mother. I'm quite settled."

"You know what I mean, William."

Bill sighed, annoyed at his mother's use of his full name. "Yes, I know. You want to see me married, right? With kids?"

His mum's eyes lit up as she smiled at him. "Oh Bill, that would be so lovely. I can just see you in a nice suit, getting married to a lovely woman. You'd make an old lady very happy."

"I know, Mum. I know." To a certain degree, she was right, and he wondered how much she could read between the lines with him. He did want those things. He'd like to find someone he could spend time with and maybe marry. He most certainly didn't want to end up like Rob Loxley, a life-long bachelor living alone in some flat somewhere. He'd just been preoccupied with his work and had neglected that side of his life. Maybe he needed to take some personal time and get back into the dating game...

His phone rang. Pulling it out, he saw Kane's name on the caller ID.

"I need to take this, Mum," he said.

"Oh, don't mind me, dear, you carry on." She continued putting the groceries away and paid him no attention.

Bill answered, "Kane. I was wondering when you'd call."

"I'm guessing you want an update, judging by all those texts this morning?"

"Yeah, I do." Bill walked out of the kitchen and into the empty front room.

"They found a body to go with the head that they discovered. Not much to say about that, really. It all looked pretty routine. Rob recognised me, though."

Bill grumbled. "Thought he might."

"Is that a problem?"

"I don't know, is it?" Bill threw the question back at him.

"Nah, I don't think so. Anyway, more interestingly, I followed Rob and his team last night. They went to talk to some of the local prossies up Mansfield Road. I've got some photos of him chatting up a couple of hookers. I thought they might make for a nice story, you know? Local detective seen with prostitute. Has a ring to it, don't you think?"

"No," Bill snapped, annoyed. "Absolutely not. I have no interest in a smear campaign based on lies. If you run that, we're done. That's not what I want at all. I want proof, actual proof that Loxley is crooked, okay? Got that?"

"Sure, I got it," Kane replied dejectedly. "You want to do things the boring way. Fine. But a headline like this will sell papers though, and might well get him suspended. That's what you want, isn't it?"

"It might also bring us some unwanted attention, which I do not want. So no. We do this right, or not at all."

"Okay, fine, if that's what you want. I can do that."

"Good. Keep me updated." Bill ended the call before Kane could answer. He sighed to himself, annoyed with himself. He was starting to regret bringing Kane in now. He was a liability.

"Nice to hear that you have some integrity."

Bill turned to see his father at the door, watching him. "Oh… Did you…"

"Yeah, I heard enough to read between the lines. Who's this Loxley bloke?"

Bill hesitated, but only for a moment. "A detective. He's… aaah. He's got some links to organised crime."

His father's eyebrows rose up his forehead. "That's a hell of an accusation."

"It's true. It's his family, who he claims he's estranged from."

"I take it he passed vetting if he's a serving officer."

"Yeah," Bill answered. "Look, don't worry about it, okay?"

"You're not being nosey, are you Graham?" his mother called out from the kitchen. Talking to his dad. "Leave the poor boy alone, will you? He's got enough to deal with."

She wasn't wrong.

24

"I'm scared," Izabela said as Caprice drove them across town. She'd got little in the way of sleep last night, but only because she'd spent much of the night in a cold sweat, worrying about what the next few days would bring, especially her meeting with Nigel this morning.

After waiting in Caprice's car for an hour last night, half expecting Nigel to appear, Caprice walked out alone and drove Izabela back to her flat.

She'd spent the night on Caprice's sofa, which was perfectly comfortable and far more inviting than the dirty mattress she'd been sleeping on at Abel's place. But despite the warmth and softness of the sleeping arrangements, her mind refused to still itself and continued to race the whole night through.

She kept thinking through what she would say to Nigel tomorrow, how she would explain herself and what he might say in return. And when she wasn't thinking about that, she was worrying about her previous pimp, Radek, the murder spree he was surely on, and how he was targeting Abel's girls. He must have been the one to kill Penny. It was the only explanation she could think of. But that meant he knew what had happened to her, he knew she'd joined Abel's group of girls, and he was taking revenge by killing them.

She'd hated abandoning them and leaving these girls to their fate, but what choice did she have? She couldn't stay because Radek would find her and kill her, too, eventually. But, if she left, maybe he'd stop attacking Abel's girls.

She hoped she'd done the right thing, but she couldn't be sure.

By the time morning rolled around, she'd barely managed two hours of fitful sleep and felt utterly shattered, stressed, and strung out.

Caprice had been the perfect host, though, and had continued to reassure her that Nigel wouldn't see her out on the street. He might not agree with what she'd done, but he still wanted the best for her.

Izabela was less sure. She'd run away, and in the time between then and now, on the few occasions when they'd crossed paths, she'd told him to get lost, including very recently. Of course, what Nigel didn't know, was that she'd done and said those things to protect him. She'd been aware of Penny and Abel watching and didn't want him incriminating himself after everything he'd done for her.

But he wasn't to know that. Instead, he just saw her being rude to him.

"You shouldn't be scared," Caprice reassured her as they approached the club. "You just need to talk to him. He'll listen to you, and I'm sure he'll help you again. He helped you before."

"But that was before I ran away."

"You just need to explain it. I'm sure he'll have you back. Look, you can stay at mine if he won't help you. It's okay."

"No. I can't do that to you. You don't have the space, and... I won't put you at risk."

"I'm at no more risk than Nigel is."

"Are you sure about that? Nigel knows people..."

Caprice shrugged. "Yeah, maybe..."

Caprice was being nice, offering to put her up, but there was no way she'd pull her into the world she'd just run away from. If Radek or Abel found out she was staying with Caprice, they wouldn't care about hurting Caprice to get to her. But Nigel was different. He knew people, had contacts, and knew how to hide her. He also had room for her to stay, which Caprice did not.

She refused to drag anyone else into her troubled life.

The final few moments of the drive to the club were done in silence until Caprice pulled into the rear staff car park and pulled to a stop.

"Ready?" Caprice asked.

"No."

"You'll be fine. Come on."

Izabela took a long, deep breath as she quickly steeled her nerves and got out of the car into the cool morning air. At least she felt safe out here. She wasn't worried about anyone appearing, bundling her into a car and taking her back to Abel or Radek.

"Come on." Caprice led the way over towards the back door. As they approached, it opened and two people stepped out.

"Thank you for coming over, Susan. It's always good to see you."

"Good to see you too," the woman said as Nigel stepped out ahead of her, holding the door open.

The woman smiled at them before she turned back to Nigel. "Bye. See you later."

"See ya," Nigel said, glancing at Susan before he focused his attention on Caprice and herself. Izabela forced herself to smile, but there wasn't much joy in it.

Nigel visibly sighed. "What's all this?"

"She stayed the night at mine," Caprice explained. "She needs to talk to you."

"Oh, really. What is it this time? Do you want to screw me over again?"

"No," Izabela muttered.

"Just listen to her," Caprice asked.

"Why? She's already told me to piss off. She doesn't want me around anymore."

"Nige, I really think you should listen."

"Give me one good reason."

"They killed my friend," Izabela snapped. There really wasn't a better answer than that.

Nigel clamped his mouth shut, pressing his lips into a thin line as he stared at her with searching eyes. The moment seemed to drag out forever as he assessed her and what she'd told him.

"I saw you just the other day," Nigel said eventually, but his tone was much calmer now. "You were pretty quick to blow me off then."

"That was before all this happened."

"All what?"

Izabela took a moment to herself before she launched into describing the predicament she found herself in. "Someone killed Penny, the girl you saw me with the other day. She didn't come back, and we think she was the one who was in the news yesterday."

Nigel stared at her with serious eyes. "Is that so?" He glanced at Caprice, and they shared a silent look before he turned back.

"It has to be Penny. I know it, and I think I know who killed her. If they find me, I think I'll be next... in fact, I know I'm next."

"You know?"

"I know."

"Okay, who killed her?"

"Radek."

"Really? The same man who trafficked you and set you to working the streets? Are you sure?"

"You don't know him. You don't know what he's capable of. He'd do this in a second. I know he would. He's found me. He knows I'm part of Abel's girls now, and he's taking revenge."

Nigel sighed and shared a long pregnant look with Caprice.

"You need to listen to her," Caprice urged.

Nigel closed his eyes and shook his head. He looked up at her. "You need to tell the police. If you think you know who did this, they need to know. It's as simple as that."

"No. I'm not going to the police. No way. I'm not meant to be in this country. If they find me, they'll send me back, and what good am I to my mother then? They'll tell her what happened to me and... No, just no. I can't put my mother through that. It would destroy her. This is my problem, not hers. I'll deal with it. But I'm not going to the police."

"Just give them something, an address, maybe? Anything. You can do it anonymously. They don't need to know where it came from."

"No, I'm not doing that. It's too risky. If I send them to Abel's, that puts the other girls at risk. But I can't anyway. I don't know where he lives. I was always driven everywhere."

Nigel looked tired as he thought through her predicament. It was as if he was doing everything in his power to avoid having to have her stay with him again, and it made her wonder if this was a good idea. If he didn't want her here, was this really the best place for her? Would she be safe here?

But she had to remember everything she'd put him through, from his initial aid, to her running away and then telling him to piss off in the months since, and now turning up on his doorstep again. It was no wonder that he had reservations about the whole thing.

"Okay," he said. "Then I think you should stay with my friend, Susan. The woman who just left. She can look after you better than I could. She has a few girls she helps with who are in a similar position to you. She'd be perfect and could really help you."

"No," she said quickly. "I don't know her…"

"You didn't know me when you first came here."

"But I know you now, and I know you won't turn me away. Please, I'm begging you, help me. I need your help."

He sighed, clearly unsure.

"I'm clean, by the way. I've managed to keep off the gear even while working for Abel. That's got to stand for something."

Nigel seemed to chew on this for a moment before he eventually sighed and seemed to deflate.

"Okay, fine. You can stay here, for now. I can't say I'm very happy about this, though. I need to think about this."

"I'm not going back to Abel, or Radek. No way."

"I hope not," Nigel replied. "I hope not."

25

Scarlett's drive across town ended up being quicker than she'd anticipated. She'd found her way to the mortuary's rear entrance easily and knew she'd be waiting at least ten minutes before Nick turned up. But, she didn't mind. This was only her second visit here. The first time she'd arrived, she entered via the hospital's main entrance and wandered the corridors for what felt like hours before finding where she needed to be. Home Office Pathologist May Shephard had then shown her where to go next time, and honestly, she was quietly pleased with herself for remembering the way.

She parked up her VW Polo up in one of the free spaces, making sure not to block anyone in or the access to the main rear entrance, where they brought the bodies in. The morning wasn't overly cold, so she got out and walked to the rear of her car, where she leaned against it and waited.

With any luck, they'd find out the identity of the murdered girl this morning, and they'd be able to open a new line of enquiry.

Knowing who the victim was could often be the key to finding out the motive, which would then allow them to narrow the field and work out who had committed the murder.

Right now, they didn't know, and it felt like they were chasing their tails somewhat. Scarlett pulled out her phone and started going through her notifications. Spotting one from Rob, she opened it. It seemed that Guy had discovered CCTV footage of the confrontation between Emmett and Nigel the morning before the murder, which lined up with what both Emmett and Nigel were saying.

Scarlett frowned. Was it odd that Emmett and Nigel, who according to everyone—including both men—were supposed enemies, both agreed on the events of that morning and downplayed their rivalry? Was there more to this than met the eye? Were they in this together somehow? Or was she starting to get paranoid and looking for complications and conspiracies that simply were not there?

Easily done when a simple explanation was yet to show itself.

She was probably chasing shadows and parked the idea for the time being as one of their pool cars turned into the delivery space she was waiting in.

Moments later, Nick Miller climbed out of the car looking fresh-faced and full of energy.

"Mornin'," he said, locking the car behind him. "Hope I didn't keep you waiting too long?"

"No, you're good. I was early, but you're more or less on time."

"You get any sleep?"

"Some," she admitted.

"I'm terrible on the first night after a major crime comes in," he replied. "I find my mind is just racing with all the details, and I struggle to get to sleep."

Scarlett nodded her understanding. "Yeah, I've had nights like that too, but I was just so tired last night, I was out like a log."

"Light."

"What?"

"Out like a light, but you slept like a log. You got your similes mixed up."

"Analogies, not similes." She smiled.

"Whatever," he waved off the correction, "Rob wants us to call him as soon as we know who the victim is. I think he's keen to try and get ahead of this."

"I don't blame him. It feels like we've been playing catch-up this whole time. We need to find out who she is and why she was killed."

"You've got no argument from me there," he agreed as they wandered over to the back door of the mortuary.

"What do you think of the team?"

Scarlett pursed her lips in thought. "They seem okay. Friendly, you know? I'm just grateful to be included. I kind of feel like the odd one out, really. You guys all know each other, but I'm the new girl from down south. The only link I have to any of you is my first case with Rob."

"I think you made something of an impression, though. Taking down a serving DCI is no mean feat."

She snorted. "I certainly didn't set out to take him down. We just followed the trail. It's not really our fault where it led, is it?"

"Absolutely not. I'm with you there," Nick agreed. "You did some good solid police work on that case, and it's obviously not gone unnoticed."

"Thanks." Unsure how to take the compliment, she flushed with embarrassment. "What do *you* think of Ellen, Tucker, and the rest?"

"They seem competent enough," Nick replied. "Rob knows some of them better than I do. I only know Ellen and Tucker through Rob, and I've never met Guy before, but Nailer clearly knows him."

"Well, you're all new to me, so…" She shrugged, and he smirked.

Reaching the rear door to the mortuary, Scarlett pressed the buzzer. Moments later, it crackled into life.

"Hello?"

"Hi. It's Detectives Miller and Stutely. We're here for the post-mortem?"

"Can you hold up your IDs to the camera, please?"

Scarlett did as the woman asked, and Nick followed suit. Moments later, the door buzzed, and she was able to push it open.

"I take it you've been here before," Scarlett asked.

"Too many times to count," Nick confirmed.

"Yeah, and too many lives cut short."

"You're not wrong."

They walked up the corridor and were soon shown through to one of the examination spaces where the Home Office Pathologist, May Shephard, was waiting for them.

"Good morning, detectives." Behind May, on the slab, was the decapitated body, her head placed just above the shoulders, where it would normally have been attached at the neck. It was odd to see the girl's head separated like that. It gave Scarlett's stomach a bit of a churn. "Thank you for coming." May fixed Scarlett with a look. "You found your way to the back door this time?"

"I did, thanks," she confirmed before glancing back at Nick, who raised an eyebrow at her. "I didn't know there was a back door the first time I came and went through the hospital."

"Aaah. Easily done."

"Mmm." She turned back to May. "Let's get started, shall we?"

"Well, first things first, we do actually have a name for you," May stated. "Her fingerprints returned with a match, and she's on the system. So she's obviously been through a custody suite at some point. I also have a good idea of her time of death, and while these things are never totally accurate, I think we can narrow it down."

"To what?" Scarlett asked, making notes.

"Well, between perhaps eight and eleven at night, and if you really pushed me, I'd guess it was between maybe nine-thirty and ten. There's a massive body of research on how bodies decompose and how quickly, so while it's not an exact science, I think we have a fairly good idea."

"Excellent. And what about her identity? Who is she?"

"She's Penny Lynn, age sixteen."

"Jesus," Scarlett hissed. "So young."

"They often are," May replied, with a hint of sadness in her voice.

"Do you want to call Rob and tell him while I get started on the exhibits?" Nick asked Scarlett.

"Sure, why not," she answered and pulled out her phone while the others started to go about their business around the body. She watched Nick move to the side room, where he would bag the exhibits that the mortuary staff would pass his way as they removed them from the body.

Rob answered after two rings.

"Scarlett. How's it going?"

"We have a name," she announced.

"Wonderful. Finally, some progress. Who is she?"

"Penny Lynn. A sixteen-year-old girl who is apparently on the system."

"Is she? Right, hold on." Sounds of movement could be heard on the line as Rob adjusted his hold on the phone. Moments later, she heard typing that ended with the slap of the return key. Seconds after that, Rob was muttering under his breath as he read from his screen. "Aaah, yeah, she is. She was picked up on a couple of minor offences, shoplifting and stuff. Then we have a Misper report issued months ago by the family for her, and this is then followed by being picked up for soliciting."

"Soliciting? Then we were right," Scarlett said. "She was a sex worker."

"Seems that way. And that's the last entry we have. Until this, of course."

"Okay."

"We have the family's details too. Her father is Richard, her mother's Hilary and she has a sister too, Dena. There's an address here. They're in Mansfield. Chatsworth Drive."

"I don't know it." She was only just starting to get the lay of the land in Nottingham.

"No, of course, you don't. It's a quiet, middle-class area. Nice houses and stuff on the south side of the town." He paused. "Right, now we know who she was, we need more information on what she was doing. We need to talk to other working girls who knew her, that kind of thing. We need to find out what kind of life she led. I'm guessing there's probably some gang ties in there somewhere, so was her death linked to those? Or was it a disgruntled punter who dumped her head in a bin, not realising that the owner was a local councillor?"

"Or, is there still more to this," Scarlett suggested, her voice full of unstated meaning. "You never know."

"No, I suppose not. Right then, Scarlett, I want you to send Nick back. He can come with me to meet the family. I need you to stay there, finish off the post-mortem, and report back."

"Will do, guv."

26

"Fuck," Abel yelled and kicked the cabinet door under the sink. The hinge finally gave up the ghost, and the door came loose at the top. It hung at an angle. "Fuckin' pigs, messin' with my biz."

"Babe, chill," Sal said, her voice calm and measured.

Abel planted his fists on his hips, took a moment to calm himself, and looked over at his girlfriend. She sat with her legs crossed, taking a drag from a spliff. "Easy for you to say."

She shrugged. "No one got nicked. You're golden."

"Yeah, but I've got to be fuckin' careful now, ain't I. They're sniffing about, causing me stress. As if I haven't got enough going on with Carter breathing down my neck, now I've got police hanging about and I'm losing girls every night..."

"More of them?" Sal sounded surprised. She didn't know.

"Izabela. She was banging a John when the police turned up, screwing up my plans to pick her up. She was long gone when we got there. It's a right fucking mess. First Penny, and now Izabela. Who's next?"

"She was nuthin' but trouble, that one," Sal said. "Don't know what Penny was thinking, bringing her in."

"She was good for business, not like some of these skanky hoes." Abel waved his hand at the house around him. He didn't care if some of the girls heard him.

"Aye," Jerome agreed. One of Abel's crew, Jerome was young, less jaded than some, and full of enthusiasm. He was standing in the nearby doorway, close to Baz, Abel's muscle. "She was hot. Not like some of these diseased bitches." He worked his hips as he crooned, pretending to thrust into an imaginary partner. "Aww yeah. She had one hell of an ass on her and a tight, juicy—"

Beside him, Baz lashed out and cuffed him across the top of his head. "Shut it, dick face."

"Oi, what was that for?" Jerome looked pissed off, but fell short of squaring up to Baz, who was over a head taller than him.

"For running your mouth. We don't wanna hear that shit."

"Chill, Baz," Abel said. "He's cool, and he's right. She was hot and brought in some good clients. It's a bloody shame."

"So, what happened to her?" Sal asked, having watched the interchange between them dispassionately. "Why'd she run?"

Abel screwed his mouth up as he remembered Izabela's words and her assertion that Radek was the one behind Penny's disappearance. He'd not given it much credence at the time, but now Izabela was gone too. Maybe she'd been on to something? Could it be that Radek and his Polish crew knew about Izabela and were taking their revenge on him?

He couldn't dismiss the idea quite as easily as before.

"I don't know for sure that she ran. What if she was taken?"

Sal stiffened and looked up. "What do you mean? Who took her?"

Abel shrugged. He wasn't sure how they'd react to what he was about to say. "Radek Lewandowski and his crew."

"Radek? The Polish crew?"

"That's where she came from. Izabela thought he was behind Penny going missing, too."

Sal pulled an unconvinced face. "Really? And you believe her?"

She had a way about her sometimes that made him feel two feet tall. Sal was one of the few people he allowed to speak to him like this. "I didn't... But now? I think she was onto something. I think he wants his girl back."

Sal took a long pull on her spliff, enjoying its effects. "You heard about the dead girl that showed up yesterday, right?"

He had, and he harboured his own suspicions on who that was. Suspicions that he guessed Sal shared, judging from her look. "Yeah, I heard, and I know what you're thinking."

"They killed Penny?" Jerome asked. "Fuck me. Those bastards."

"We don't know that," Sal barked, shutting Jerome up.

"I'll tell you what, if he did, I'm going to fuckin murder him," Abel vowed, feeling his fury rise, hot and impatient.

"I'll join yeh," Jerome added, almost bouncing on the spot in his excitement. "I'll fuck 'im up, good and proper. No one messes with us."

"Jerome," Sal snapped, turning to him, "go and bang one of the girls and let the grown ups talk, will you? Burn off some of that energy. You're doin' me head in."

"What?"

Baz chimed in. "What she means to say is, get lost. You're not helping."

"Oh, yeah, okay then." He looked a little un-manned and sheepish, but with false pride on his face, he nodded and walked out. Moments later, Abel heard him shouting at one of the girls. "Oi, you. Come here."

Abel's phone sounded in his pocket. He pulled it out and noted the caller ID.

"Carter," he announced. Sal nodded, and Baz shut the door, minimising Jerome's grunts in the background.

For a brief second, Abel wondered what his boss was calling him about. It was highly unlikely he knew about Izabela going missing, unless someone had grassed him up... He glanced up at the two people in the room but doubted that either of them would be stupid enough to turn on him. Christ, he was getting paranoid.

He answered the call. "Hey."

"Abel," Carter said in a bright and sunny voice. "Busy night?"

"Kinda," Abel replied. Did he know about the police and Izabela? Or, was he just being polite?

"Good to see you're up and about. I hope you've been working hard for me. Well, working those girls of yours hard for me."

"Always, boss. Always."

"Good. Pleased to hear it. I'm calling to let you know that I've just had word that the girl on the news yesterday, the one who was killed, was Penny. Your Penny. She was one of your whores."

"Fuck," Abel yelled. "You're sure?"

"Do you doubt me?"

"No, boss."

"Good. I'm doing you a favour by telling you, Abel. I don't know who did this, but..."

"I might know," Abel said, as his suspicions started to crystalise in his mind. He'd read the news stories of the murdered girl yesterday, about how the killer had chopped off her head and dumped it in a bin. This wasn't some random killing, it sounded more like a gangland hit. You don't chop someone's head off without good reason, it's too much work. No, whoever did this was either an unhinged psycho or a professional killer, and either way, there was meaning in the act.

They were sending a message, and it was one that Abel heard loud and clear. Radek was making it known that he knew about Izabela before he took her back.

Radek would have no issues with this kind of violence. He knew how brutal they could be. But regardless, he could not allow this to stand. No one dissed Abel, his crew or the people he worked for. No one.

These actions demanded a reaction. They demanded revenge.

"Good. I hope you do know. I like that. Is this going to be a problem going forward, or can I trust you to sort it?"

"You can leave it with me."

"I hope so," Carter replied and hung up.

His boss didn't tolerate failure for long. He needed to act fast.

27

"Guv, hold up."

Rob turned as he went to walk out the door. Guy was following him. "Walk with me," he said as he continued out the door. "What's up?"

Guy caught him up. "I think I figured out who the woman is that helped Father Aaron break up the fight between Emmett and Nigel. If I'm right, it's one of the hairdressers at the salon on the high street. In fact, it might be the owner."

"How'd you figure that out?"

"I followed her on the footage before and after the fight. She was hanging around the salon a lot, but I couldn't see her going in or out of the building when she helped with the fight. So I went to earlier in the day and spotted the same woman open up the salon that morning. The tree was a little more obliging, so I could see her unlock the door and walk in, letting the other hairdressers in."

"If she had the key, then you might be right. Good work. I've got to go and speak to the parents of the victim..."

"Penny. Yeah, I heard. Poor kid."

"I know. Have Ellen and Tucker chat with this woman, will you? Find out her name, too, while you're at it."

"I already know that." He sported a smug grin. "Her name's Colleen Shaw. I found her business on Companies House."

"Excellent," Rob replied as they walked around to the rear of the village hall, where Rob spotted Nick pulling into the car park. "Get Ellen and Tucker on it then."

"What about Nick?" Guy pointed at the car Nick was sitting in.

"He's with me, and Scarlett's at the post-mortem."

"Alright, will do, guv." Guy turned and jogged back into the hall, as Rob strode over to the waiting pool car. He'd have preferred to drive Belle there, but there was no need, and Nick was already waiting for him with the idling car.

Resigning himself to being the passenger, he climbed in. "Ready?"

"What's the postcode?" Nick asked, his hand hovering over the sat nav. Rob looked it up, and seconds later, it was programmed into the navigation system telling them to leave the car park behind. Nick set off, heading southwest, towards Mansfield.

"How was the autopsy?" Rob asked.

"I wasn't there long," Nick replied. "We only just got started when Scarlett called you."

"Fair enough. Hope she didn't mind being lumbered with that job?"

Nick shrugged. "If she did, she didn't say anything."

Rob nodded.

"What do you think of her?" Nick asked after a few moments of silence. "Scarlett, I mean."

Rob gave Nick side-eye, sensing that this wasn't a professional enquiry.

"Why?"

"I dunno. Just wondered, yeh know. You've been working with her, so..."

"Don't go there, buddy. She's engaged and seems quite happy. I don't think you should be sniffing around her, it'll just end in tears." Rob shook his head. "Christ, first Guy and then you. Leave the poor woman alone."

"Sorry. I was only asking."

"We've got enough on our plate without dealing with this crap too."

"We're not all perpetual bachelors, Rob. You need to find yourself a good woman."

Rob sighed, having heard the same line from Nick before. "Yeah, maybe. I don't know. I'm not that bothered. Besides, you're not in any place to lecture me about relationships, Mr Miller. You're single too."

"Yeah, but I'm younger than you."

"By three years!" Rob gave him an incredulous look.

"A lot can happen in three years," Nick protested. "I could be married by thirty-eight."

"Fat fuckin' chance of that, mate... No offence."

"None taken. But don't you worry, I'll have the ladies lined up before long."

"Keep dreaming, soldier boy."

"Soldier boy?" He smirked. "Yeah, those were the days. I went through a few girlfriends in the forces, but ever since joining the police? Nothing. Why is that?"

"There was Judy," Rob replied, wondering if he'd remembered her name right.

"Julie," Nick corrected him.

"Sorry, Julie. What happened to her?"

"I don't know. She just didn't want to see me again."

"Shame. She looked nice, going by the photo you showed me." Nick had shared a photo from her online dating profile with Rob just before their first date.

"Yeah. Aaah, well, listen to us, pining for lost loves. Whatever's become of us?"

"I've no idea. We're just sad old men at this point," Rob replied, as his mind returned to the task at hand. "I sent an FLO over as soon as I found out the victim's identity. She'll break the news and get the family back to the house for us. She should have been there for a while by now."

"Okay," Nick replied. "Sounds good."

Rob smiled, enjoying the back and forth between them. He'd worked with Nick for years before his previous boss had separated them, and Scarlett came along. This felt like old times, and he was pleased that Nick was with them. He was a good detective, and Rob felt better with him on the team.

"What do you think is going on here? We've got a murdered prostitute from a middle-class background whose head was dumped in the bin of a District Councillor, but so far, we've got no idea why this happened other than ever-deepening theories.

"I know, it feels like the more we look, the deeper the lies and animosity go. Is it a political disagreement that got out of hand? Maybe it's the rivalry between these two former coal miners? Or, could it be a disgruntled punter, or is she a casualty of some kind of gang warfare? Right now, I'm really not sure. We need to find out more about Penny. Who was she involved with? Who would want to kill her, and why?"

A short time later, they pulled into the long suburban Chatsworth Drive on the southern side of Mansfield. It was a middle-class haven of well-kept detached houses and bungalows, each one surrounded by emerald lawns and greenery.

"Nice place," Nick stated.

"Mmm," Rob agreed. "Too nice for a teenage prostitute to call home, but here we are."

"Money doesn't mean you've not got problems."

"It certainly doesn't," Rob agreed as they found the house they were looking for and pulled up outside. Another pool car was parked up a short distance ahead of them. It probably belonged to the FLO.

"Alright, let's see what we can find out."

"At least the Liaison Officer should have broken the news to them by now. I hate doing that."

"Yeah. I know what you mean," Rob agreed as he climbed out. Breaking the news of a death to the victim's relatives, especially to the parents, was always tough. It was one of the most heartbreaking things to do, and he'd done it several times over. It never got any easier, either.

Steeling himself for whatever this meeting was about to reveal, Rob walked up and rang the doorbell. Moments later, the door was answered by Detective Knight, the Family Liaison Officer who'd been assigned to Emmett and Valerie the previous day.

"Mornin'," she said in greeting.

"Hi. How's things?"

"They're ready for you. Upset, naturally, but they want to help. They're all in the front room."

"Good. Thank you."

"Drink?"

"Not for me," Rob replied.

"I'm good," Nick agreed as they walked into the house. Heather led them through the modest entrance hall, into the main front room on their right. Rob walked in after her, taking in the large room in a quick glance. It stretched from the front of the house to the back, with a grouping of soft sofas surrounding a coffee table and a dining table at the back, beside a pair of large glass patio doors that led out to a modest garden.

The three people in the room were all sitting on a single sofa, hugging each other, and talking quietly. They stood up as Rob entered, their eyes red, with expectant looks on their faces. They were looking to him and his team to help them, to bring them and Penny some justice, and he could feel the weight of that responsibility settle around his shoulders as he walked into the room.

"Hello," he started, going for a neutral greeting. He avoided phrases like, good morning, because there was certainly nothing good about the start of this day for these people. Greeting them with a bright and happy phrase felt wrong, so it was best to keep things as neutral as possible. "I'm Inspector Loxley, and this is Sergeant Miller."

"Hello," Nick said.

The family did their level best to offer them smiles, but they were brief and quickly dropped. "Hello detective," the father said. "I'm Richard. This is my wife Hilary, and our other daughter, Dena."

"Hi," Dena said.

"So, it seems our worst fears have been confirmed," Richard began.

"I'm afraid so," Rob replied. "Shall we sit?"

"Of course," Richard replied, and they all took their seats.

"We're sorry for your loss. I'm sure this is a very difficult time for you, but we need to find out as much about Penny as we can so that we can find out who did this and bring them to justice."

"How did this happen?" Hilary asked. "What was she doing in Clipstone?"

"Well, I can't go into too much detail. I can tell you some of it, but I warn you, this might be difficult to hear."

"Oh god," Hilary sobbed. "What was she doing? What was she involved with?"

"I want to know," Richard said. "I want to help."

"Well, why don't we start with what *you* know. When was the last time you saw her? We know you reported her missing a few months ago."

"That's right," Richard replied before taking a moment to himself ahead of delving in. It seemed like there was a lot of baggage surrounding this, and he was doing the distressing mental equivalent of digging it all up again. "Okay, so, for a long time, she struggled with friendships at school. There was always some kind of drama with her, you know? We thought it was the usual girl stuff, but as she got into her teens, she started to hang around with a crowd of kids who were skipping school and getting up to no good. We didn't know at first. She hid it from us quite successfully until Dena saw her do it and told us."

Dena nodded. "I saw her with these older boys and girls, walking away from school. She was smoking and drinking. I think she thought it was cool."

"She always struggled at school," Hilary added. "She developed early, and that led to some bullying."

"More bullying," Richard corrected her. "She'd been struggling with bullies for ages, but these new friends she was skiving with got her out of all that. I think she saw them as a way out. I don't know."

"I wish I'd spotted it sooner," Hilary cried. "If I'd just checked her phone and kept a closer eye on her, maybe I could have caught it?"

"You'd be surprised," Rob said. "With some of these social media platforms that delete messages after they've been seen, it can be tough to keep track."

"It certainly was with Penny," Richard agreed. "We just had no idea what she was doing. Then she started to hang around with one of these boys more than the others. I think they were dating."

"Jerome," Hilary said. "We saw his name come up on a message on her phone."

"Yeah, that's him," Richard replied. "She hid him from us, too."

"Jerome," Rob replied. "You're sure?"

"We're sure," Richard replied.

"Jerome, what? Do you have a surname?"

"No, sorry." Richard looked tired and at the end of his tether. "She changed in the last few months she lived here. She withdrew from us, becoming isolated and introverted. She wouldn't come home for days on end, and when she did, she'd have new clothes, shoes and all sorts. He was buying her stuff, and she seemed to think we hated her and wanted to ruin her life."

"Aaah, I see," Rob stated. "He was gaslighting her."

"Yes," Hilary confirmed, latching onto his comment. "That's exactly what he was doing. It must have been coming from him. From Jerome."

"Let me take a guess," Rob suggested. "One day, she just stopped coming home?"

"That's right," Hilary replied. "It felt like just another day when she didn't come home, like the countless times before, but that was the last time we saw her. Her phone hasn't been turned on since, and we had no idea where she was."

"I spent hours driving around, looking for her. I went all over Mansfield and Nottingham, but... I never found her."

"So it was around then that you reported her missing?"

"That's right," Richard replied. "Not that it helped."

"I understand," Rob replied, making a note of the name Jerome in his pad. He wished he had a surname, but a first was at start. He'd heard of similar things happening before, where individuals or gangs targeted someone they saw as vulnerable, and started to gaslight them. They typically targeted teenagers, who were often disillusioned with their family anyway, and then just stoked that fire. Making them believe that their parents hated them and it was best for them to distance themselves from those who loved them. But once they'd done that, then the gang pounced. They'd rip them away from their friends and family and use them for their own ends, be it drug running, prostitution or whatever else they needed them for. It sounded very much like Jerome was one of these people.

"So, what was she doing?" Hilary asked. "You said you knew."

"We think we do," Rob clarified. "And we think she was engaged in prostitution."

"What?"

"Oh my god!" Dena exclaimed.

"Oh, my poor baby." Hilary wept as Richard pulled her close.

Rob gave them a few moments to take that in before he continued, knowing there was more to come. "We think she was working the streets in the Clipstone area when she was murdered. Given your separation from her, I doubt you will know more than you've already told me, but were you aware of anyone who might want to do this to your daughter? Other than Jerome, I mean."

"No. No idea," Richard answered. Hilary and Dena agreed. "Did Jerome do this?"

"I can't say at this stage," Rob answered.

"How did she die?"

"Are you sure you want to know? You will find out soon enough anyway, but we don't have to discuss the finer details right now. We can wait a little bit."

"No, I want to know. I need to know if she suffered or not," Hilary said, her tone insistent.

"It would have been quick," Rob replied. "She suffered a severe hit to her head which would have incapacitated her. So, she probably didn't feel much after that. But, and I'll warn you again that this might be difficult to hear, but the killer decapitated her. They cut her head off."

"Oh god," Hilary gasped.

"I'm sorry you have to hear this. But as you now know, there is a detail that I would like to ask you about, because it seems that the killer left some of her remains in the bin of a local District Councillor. Now, we're not sure if this was just random chance or if there's a deeper meaning to this, but are you in any way linked to the local council? Are you aware of any government links between you or Penny and the council or government?"

"No, not at all," Richard answered. "Apart from voting, of course."

"Was she alive when they... you know..." Hilary pointed to her neck.

Rob sighed. He hated having to give them these details, but they would find out in due course anyway, and it was better they heard it from him than from a sensationalised newspaper story or news report. "We're not sure. We're doing the post-mortem right now, so we'll know more after that, and our liaison officer can pass along that information if need be. I really am so very sorry. I can't imagine the loss you must be feeling, but you need to prepare yourself because there will be news coverage about this, and some of it might be sensationalised to sell papers. That's just the reality of it. So I suppose it's better that it comes from us."

"Thank you, yes. We understand," Richard agreed.

Rob nodded as he thought through the information he had. "If what you said about her befriending this Jerome is accurate, along with her behaviour and the gifts, I think it's likely that Jerome was grooming her. He was turning her against you so it would be easier for him to get her away from you. It wouldn't surprise me if this Jerome is a gang member, and they planned to do this to her; to turn her into a prostitute and use her to make money."

"This is sick," Richard stated as his wife and daughter sobbed beside him.

"It is. It's unusual for them to target someone like Penny, but they must have sensed a weakness in her, something they could exploit, perhaps. You've helped us out immensely today. I'm just sorry that I couldn't bring you better news."

Richard sighed. "She was a troubled girl," he mused. "She struggled with friends and life in general. I'm sad she went through this, but at least she's at peace now."

"Absolutely," Rob agreed. Everyone processed these things differently but Richard's stoic nature and loving strength for his wife and remaining daughter were both respectable and devastating. Rob took another moment to consider the tragedy that murder caused innocent people and their forever-broken lives. Nodding at Nick, they brought the meeting to an end and left them in the care of their FLO.

"That was devastating," Nick said as they walked away from the house.

"It was. But we have a new lead, Jerome."

"You think her death is gang related?" Nick asked.

"I'd be surprised if it wasn't linked to a gang in some way," Rob mused as they returned to their car.

28

Ellen climbed out of their car after parking outside the parade of shops in Clipstone. The day seemed like any other, with people going about their business, shopping, eating and getting their hair cut.

They'd parked close to the hairdressers that Detective Gibson had sent them to, and she could see several women inside the shop, sitting in adjustable chairs with stylists going about their work behind them.

"Here we are," Ellen said, giving the shop an appraising look. "Let's see what Mrs Shaw has to say for herself."

"Aye," Tucker replied. "Lead the way."

Making sure she had her ID close at hand, she walked over the side road to the main entrance of the salon and stepped inside. A bell jingled as she opened the door, announcing her presence to the entire shop. People either turned to look or glanced at her in the mirrors on the walls. Nearby, the girl at the reception desk smiled.

"Hello. How can I help you?"

Ellen smiled brightly and approached. "I was wondering if Colleen Shaw was available for a quick chat?"

The girl glanced into the shop at one of the stylists, an older woman who was chatting to her customer while dying the lady's hair. If this was Colleen, she made no signs that she'd heard Ellen ask for her.

"I'm afraid she's with a client right now. You're welcome to wait, however?" The receptionist gestured behind Ellen to the collection of chairs beside the door, where another customer was waiting. "Also, we're fully booked today, so you might want to make an appointment for another day?"

Ellen always enjoyed this part and relished pulling out her warrant card and showing it to the receptionist. "I'm sorry, but I really must insist that we speak to Mrs Shaw right away."

The girl frowned, then looked down at the ID. She seemed a little confused for a moment, as if she wasn't sure what she was looking at before it suddenly seemed to click. "Oh. I see."

"Don't worry, she's not in trouble, and there's no need to make a scene. But we will need somewhere private to chat."

"Aaah, okay. Hold on one moment. I'll see what I can do."

The rush of excitement and power she felt whenever she got to pull out her ID and make people dance to her tune was intoxicating and never got old. She'd once been told not to let it go to her head, but she didn't think that would ever be an issue for her. While that rush was a wonderful feeling, she always harboured doubt that she wasn't worthy of the power the badge gave her.

Was it a distinctly English thing, this nagging lack of self-confidence that she felt? After all, we were usually always the first to put ourselves down in any given situation, she thought as she waited for the receptionist to sort things.

The receptionist walked over to the woman Ellen had assumed to be Colleen and had a quick and quiet whisper in her ear. As the girl spoke, Colleen looked over with a confused expression on her face.

Colleen informed her client that something urgent had come up and dashed about the salon, shuffling the stylists around to make sure someone could take over from what she'd been doing.

It took a few moments, and there were some unhappy looks from the affected customers before Colleen was finally free and waved Ellen forward.

She glanced back at Tucker, who'd been standing awkwardly in the doorway. She nodded, and he followed.

Ellen crossed the salon and followed Colleen to a door in the back, through a messy break room and out through another door into the back alley behind the shop.

"Will this do?" Colleen asked, waving at the area around them.

"This is fine, Mrs Shaw," Ellen said with a smile. She'd have preferred a more private room where they could close the door, but this would do for now. "I'm Detective Dale, and this is Detective Stafford. I'm right in thinking you're Colleen Shaw, right?"

"That's right. Sorry for the chaos in there. What can I do for you?"

"That's okay. Firstly, don't worry, you're not in any trouble. We just wanted to have a quick chat with you because we believe you were witness to something of interest to us."

"Oh? And what would that be?"

"Two days ago, on the morning of the fifteenth, we have reason to believe that you witnessed an altercation between Emmett Wilkinson and Nigel Wild, out here on the high street. Is that right?"

"Aaah, yes. I was. I helped break it up." She sighed. "It was Nigel. He's nothing but trouble."

"That's the owner of the Clip Club? Just up the street?"

"Yeah, that's him. It's not the first time he's caused trouble with Emmett, either."

"So this has happened before?"

"Several times."

"Would you mind running through the events of that morning for me?" Ellen got her notebook ready.

"Sure." Colleen pulled out a cigarette, lit it up and took a long pull while she frowned in thought. "It was a typical morning, I think. I opened the shop, let the staff in, and... No, wait. Oh yeah, that was it. Yeah. I'd just opened up, and I noticed a couple of hookers hanging around outside, over here." Colleen walked to Ellen's left.

Ellen had her back to the building and the high street beyond. She turned left to follow Colleen as she took a few steps to the edge of the building. There was a cut-through between the salon and the fish and chip shop next door that led back to the high street. It was wide enough for a car or van to get through, and it seemed that the shop owners used it to reach the rear of their properties.

Colleen pointed down that cut-through, towards the main road. "They were hanging out over there, beside the chip shop."

"Were they being a nuisance?"

"They're a pain in my arse," Colleen spat. "They're always hanging around, causing trouble, stealing things. Everyone knows what they are."

"They've caused trouble for you, specifically?"

"Oh yeah, because I refuse to cut their hair. Ever since they started hanging around and flaunting themselves, things have got worse. There's more crime, more trouble, and people getting hurt. It's the gangs. They're a nightmare. So, I refuse to cut their hair, and in return, they've broken my windows twice now."

"The prostitutes have?" Ellen asked.

"Yeah! Who else would do it? The first time it happened was the night after I threw them out of my shop. I told them to sling their hook, and the next day, I come in, and I've got a smashed window. They did it again later too. They smashed the same window after I fixed it, broke in, and nicked stuff. Fucking cockroaches, I hope they all die."

Ellen grimaced quietly at her words. They were unfortunate, given the circumstances, but she understood her frustration. Colleen was a salt of the earth kind of woman, and far more relatable than she'd expected. She kind of liked her no-nonsense approach.

Ellen summarised what Colleen had told her. "So, these girls, they've broken into your shop at least twice and caused criminal damage?"

"That's right. They've cost me a small fortune in repairs, and not only that, they hang around scaring off my customers, so I'm getting less business. They're scum, and I fucking hate them."

Ellen nodded in understanding, but wasn't sure she agreed with Colleen's point of view. Most of these girls and young women were victims either of circumstance or predators. They'd been dealt a shitty hand in life and were making money with the last thing of value that they had: their bodies. And yet, they were demonised for it, categorised as immoral, dirty and the lowest of the low. "And on the fifteenth, you saw these prostitutes outside your shop, along there." Ellen pointed up the cut-through.

"That's right. So, I went out and told them to piss off, then I hung around the front of my shop to make sure they didn't cause any more trouble or scare anyone away."

Tucker was making notes as Colleen spoke. Ellen could hear his pencil scribbling on the paper.

"I see," Ellen answered. "When did you see Emmett or Nigel?"

"I saw Nigel first. He was going to the news agent's or something, I don't know. But he walked over and started talking to the girls."

Ellen frowned, wondering if she'd understood what Colleen was telling her. "You mean the prostitutes? He was speaking to them?"

"Oh yeah. He's really friendly with them. He's always serving them at the club and talking to them. He's a bloody idiot 'cos he encourages them to keep coming back here. If he'd stop being such a letch, then maybe we could get rid of them."

"So, he's friendly with them?"

"Very. I dread to think how they're paying him for the drinks. Blow jobs under the bar, probably." She looked disgusted. "Why else would a man like him be friendly to a bunch of young women selling their bodies for money?"

Ellen dismissed that last comment, but her observation that Nigel was friendly with the working girls was an interesting one. "Okay, so what happened next?"

"I was watching him talk to them when these two guys come over, little and large, they were. They walked up to him and told Nigel to piss off and leave the girls alone. I bet they were their pimps. You know?"

"I know," Ellen assured her. "So, he left?"

"Yeah. They talked. I didn't hear all of it, but I think they threatened him. Nigel looked angry when he walked off."

"He walked away," Ellen asked.

"That's right. Then the two men walked the girls back to their car and drove off. I wasn't watching Nigel at that moment because I was more interested in the hookers leaving. Anyway, the next thing I know, I look up, and Nigel's about to thump someone. So, I ran over and pulled them apart just after the vicar jumped in."

"Do you know who he was attacking?"

"Of course. It was Emmett Wilkinson. He's a piece of shit, too. One of these wealthy, corrupt politicians."

"Corrupt?" Ellen asked, curious.

"Well, they all are, aren't they?" Colleen asked.

"I wouldn't like to say."

"I should have guessed it would be him, though. Those two have been at loggerheads for ages now. Nigel's always swearing at him, calling him a scab."

"So, you helped break up the fight?" Ellen pressed.

"Yeah. If I'd realised who it was, I would have let them fight it out, but I didn't recognise Emmett until I was pulling them apart. Anyway, we separated them and they went on their way. That was it."

"Nothing else?" Ellen asked.

"No, nothing. That was it. Then, of course, I heard about the girl yesterday. The one that died. She was a hooker, right? Well, serves her right, don't it? Hopefully, they'll all piss off now that one of them's been killed."

"I can't comment about the identity of the victim, but you think it was one of the prostitutes?"

"That's what I hear. Maybe someone's more fed up with them being around here than I am and has taken it in hand. I mean, Councillor Wilkinson has been doing fuck all about it, and neither have you, either, have you? People can only take so much. They can only deal with so much crap before they snap. I know I'm at the end of my tether with 'em. They can all piss off and die, as far as I'm concerned. Good riddance to 'em."

Ellen gritted her teeth at the words of the hairdresser. She was clearly frustrated and annoyed both by the presence of these sex workers, and by the inaction of the police and the council, and rightly so, given the effect on her business. Ellen didn't blame her for trying to protect her investment.

But it made her wonder if they'd been looking at this all wrong. A pissed-off shop owner, like Colleen, has ample motive to hate and potentially kill one of these prostitutes and then dump the head in the bin of the councillor who was doing nothing to help get rid of them. It made a scary amount of sense, but was it Colleen or someone else?

They'd need to do a lot more investigation to find out, including talking to Nigel again, as it seemed like he was friendly towards these girls.

Ellen proceeded to get a description of the girls and their pimps before finishing up and walking back to their car. They needed to report back.

29

Returning to the village hall, Rob stretched as he walked around to the front of the building, working out a few knots on his back, no doubt brought on by the stress of the day. Glancing across the road in front of the hall, he spotted a few reporters hanging around, including Vincent Kane, who watched Rob walk by with cold eyes.

Let him look, Rob thought, annoyed that this parasite of a man was staring at him as he did his job. Who did he think he was? He was the one who'd disrupted a previous investigation and torpedoed his own career for the last few years.

Was he planning another stunt like that soon? He hoped not.

"We need to run Jerome through the PNC, see if anything comes up," Nick suggested as they walked through the front door.

"Aye, we do. Hopefully, someone fits the bill."

He spotted a couple of people standing just inside the hall and recognised one as Janette, the woman he spoke to at the first crime scene. She turned, and her eyes flashed in recognition.

"Aaah, Detective," she said. "I'm Janette. We met on Edmonton Road."

Rob put on his best and most honest smile. "I remember." It wasn't what he'd call a pleasant memory, however.

"Good, this is my husband." She gestured to the man on her right.

He smiled at Rob through his salt-and-pepper beard. "Pleasure to meet you. David. David Radcliffe." He offered his hand, and Rob took it, giving it a solid shake.

Nick edged past them and nodded to Rob. "I'll check the PNC while you stay here and chat."

"Alright," Rob replied with a nod.

"I've heard a lot about you," David said.

Rob returned his attention back to David. "Oh, really?"

"I'm the Chair of the local Neighbourhood Watch Committee," he continued, ignoring Rob's question. "And I'd like to suggest that you liaise with us and that we have a town meeting. We have a lot to discuss, and I think it could be valuable to your investigation."

Rob felt his eyebrows climb up his forehead. "Oh, in what way?"

"We have problems in this town that need addressing. The recent influx of gangs and their harems of prostitutes are damaging the area. They're attracting the wrong kinds of visitors, they're scaring the good people of this town and hurting the local businesses. So far, the District Council is doing nothing to stop it, but it needs to be dealt with before this killing becomes the first of many."

"You think it's that bad?" Rob was curious.

"Worse, probably. I'm sure there's more going on than we know. But it needs to be stamped out quickly before it bubbles over. And mark my words, it *will* bubble over, one way or another."

A frown creased Rob's brow as he considered the man's words. "What do you mean?"

"Well, I'm no expert..." David began. Clearly, Rob thought, as David continued. "But I can see this descending into a gang war of some kind, or worse still, the local residents taking to the streets and taking the law into their own hands. I do not want to see that, but if something isn't done soon to turn things around, it wouldn't surprise me."

"That's a bleak picture you're painting." It sounded extreme, but perhaps some of these residents really were that upset. Maybe this was a real risk.

"But it doesn't have to be, Detective. The people of Clipstone are good people, and we love our small corner of England. We want to see it grow and thrive for everyone. But that can't happen with these violent gangs roaming the streets, making them unsafe for everyone else."

Rob had to admit he had a point, and it might be that there were local people with crucial information that could help them with the case. So, maybe a town meeting here at the hall wasn't a bad idea.

He'd need to run it by Nailer, but the idea of it was growing on him. "Alright, I can't promise anything," Rob admitted, "but I can speak to my superior and hopefully arrange some kind of meeting."

"That's all I ask," David replied, apparently pleased with the result.

"Thank you, Detective," Janette said, smiling smugly. "God bless."

Rob watched them go, finding the slightly superior attitude they had distasteful, but he couldn't deny that they seemed to love and care for this town, and he had no problem with people fighting for that.

Rob walked into the main room of the hall. One side had been partitioned off and served as an area for the wider team to work, while the other half had some chairs set out for larger meetings or for people to wait on. Rob made his way beyond the partitions and spotted Nailer walking out of the back room, which served as their main incident room.

Nailer spotted him and walked straight over.

"Rob. Good to see you. How's things?"

"Well, actually. We have a few new leads to follow up."

"Good. We're about to have a meeting to pool everything we know and decide on next steps. You and Nick are last to arrive. So, we should get started."

"Sounds good," Rob agreed and followed Nailer through to the back room. "I just had an interesting chat with a couple from the local Neighbourhood Watch association."

"Let's discuss it in the meeting, shall we?" Nailer suggested.

That sounded like the best plan, and would save him from repeating himself. "Sure," he answered and said no more as he walked into the back room.

He found Nick sitting at a laptop, accessing the PNC, while the rest of the team were either sitting around the table facing the evidence board, or clustered near the coffee machine. Alicia Aston, the CSM from the Scene of Crime team, was joining them too.

"Right then, everyone. Settle down. Let's see where we are," Nailer began, taking his seat and waiting for the others to join him before he continued, "Okay, Scarlett, let's start with you. How did the post-mortem go?"

"Riveting, you should have been there," she quipped, raising an eyebrow.

Nailer, who was about to start making notes on his pad, looked up and raised an eyebrow.

"Sorry, inappropriate," Scarlett said, sounding sheepish.

Nailer smiled. "That's okay, Constable. It's been a tough few days for all of us. I think we could all do with a laugh. However, let's save it for another time for now. Please, continue."

"Sure thing. The procedure was interesting, though. Obviously, we found out the victim's name, Penny Lynn, and I'm sure Rob will fill us in on how his meeting with her parents went and who Penny is, exactly?"

Rob nodded but said nothing as he sat ready with his notebook, listening and occasionally glancing at the evidential photos stuck to the board.

"Okay. We believe that Penny was struck on the head with something solid and metal, with a rounded end. She was hit hard enough that the blow cracked her skull, causing brain damage that could have been fatal in and of itself. It's likely, however, that although she would have been impaired by the attack, she was certainly alive when the killer took what we think was a knife to her neck and cut her head off. We don't know how much she understood about what was happening to her, but it's certainly possible that she did."

Rob swallowed at the thought of being in that situation and watching someone hack at his neck while incapacitated. The idea didn't bear thinking about, as it turned his stomach.

"In addition to this," Scarlett continued, "it seems that Penny had very recently had sex, just before her murder, and we found semen deposits inside her that have been collected. They're running DNA tests on them now to see if we can track him down."

"Do you think a punter did this? One of her clients?" Nailer asked.

"No idea. But if we can find him, we can see if it goes anywhere and potentially eliminate him."

"Alright, great work, Scarlett. Thank you." Nailer scanned the table briefly. "As we're on the subject of evidence, Alicia, what have you got for us?"

"Thank you, sir," Alicia said. "I can report that we've finished with both crime scenes for the most part, and we have a few things to report. We found some partial footprints, but nothing significant that narrows it down enough, as well as some hairs and fibres, so we'll see if they throw up any matches with anything. One other thing we did find was a fresh scrap of violet-coloured rubber that had been ripped from something." She pointed to a photo on the board. "It was covered in blood and caught in one of the bushes. We're doing some analysis to see what we can glean from it."

It seemed like a curious bit of information to Rob, and he wasn't sure how it linked in, but he noted it down anyway in case it was of use.

"Alright, Rob. What have you got for us? You and Nick went to see the victim's family, right?"

"That's right," Rob confirmed as he consulted his notes. "We saw both parents and Penny's sister. They're upset, obviously, and we have an FLO liaising with them to keep them updated. They were very helpful. They'd been having some trouble with Penny over the last few years. She fell in with the wrong crowd, and from what we were able to glean from them, I think one of these new friends of hers saw Penny as a target and started to gaslight her, turning her against her parents. It's certainly got all the classic signs: not coming home, resentment towards her family, presents and gifts, money, all the usual things, until she finally disappeared. They reported her missing, and she was later picked up for soliciting, confirming our prostitute theory, but it looks like she never reconnected with her parents."

Nick leaned in and spoke up. "The report from her processing when she was picked up has her telling the Desk Sergeant that she wasn't interested in seeing her parents, and she didn't call them while she was in custody, either. Looks like one of her friends came to pick her up."

"Was this not reported back to her parents?" Nailer asked.

"I don't think so," Nick replied. "There's no record of that, anyway. It could be an oversight, maybe?"

"A fuck up," Nailer grumbled. "That's what that is." He sighed. "Okay, fine. Continue."

"Well," Rob said, "the only other thing of note is that the Lynns gave us a name. They said the boy she was apparently dating at this time was called Jerome. They spotted the name on her phone, but that's all they know, just his first name."

"I've just been running a search," Nick said. "There are several Jeromes on the system local to here, but I think it's fairly clear which one it is. We have a Jerome Clifford on file who's been arrested several times but never sent down. We have a Clipstone address for him that seems to be his parents' address, but there's nothing on here saying if he's still living there or not. He's in the right age range, and it says here that he has ties to the local gang culture."

"That sounds like our man," Rob agreed.

"Great. I'll come back to that," Nailer said before he looked around the table again. "Okay, Ellen, Tucker? What have you got for us?"

"If Penny *was* a local prostitute, she and her mates have been pissing off the locals for months," Ellen said. "We spoke to Colleen Shaw, the owner of the hairdressing salon on the high street. She's had trouble with prostitutes smashing her windows and stealing stuff because she refuses to cut their hair and moves them on when they hang around. Not only that, according to Colleen, one of her neighbours on that parade, Nigel Wild, is quite friendly with these girls. He apparently serves them in his club, which pisses off the locals as it draws the girls back. Colleen also saw him talking to two prostitutes moments before he had his little confrontation with Emmett. We have descriptions of the girls and the two men who moved him on. Based on these descriptions, I think one of the girls might have been Penny, but I could be wrong. Also, the two men who moved Nigel on sound similar to the two men that approached Rob last night when they were out talking to the girls."

"Do we have names for them?" Rob asked.

"Not yet," Ellen answered.

"So, you're saying that Nigel Wild was friendly with Penny and her friends and spoke to Penny the morning before she was killed?"

"It seems that way," Ellen confirmed.

"Which means Nigel's been holding out on us," Rob mused, wondering why he'd lie about something like this.

Ellen had more to say. "One other thing that Colleen got me thinking about is that maybe we're looking in the wrong place. There's a whole bunch of pissed-off shop owners and residents out there, who hate what these gangs and girls are doing to the area, and they're equally frustrated with local government who seem to do nothing about it. So, could the killer be an angry business person, taking out his frustration on Penny and then dumping her head in the councillor's bin?"

"That's an interesting idea," Nailer admitted. "It certainly fits. I think that's worth pursuing."

Rob agreed, finding himself drawn to the theory. So far, few of their ideas seemed to cover all the bases of what had happened to a satisfactory degree, but this one did. But if that was so, who was it?

"What I can say," Ellen added, "is that Colleen was more than happy to express her anger at both the working girls and the local government's response to this."

"Do you think she did it?" Nailer asked.

"I don't have anything to prove that she did, but she certainly has a motive. She definitely didn't hold back any of her anger."

"Okay, something to keep in mind as we push forward," Nailer said. "You also said that Nigel is quite friendly with these girls?"

"He lets them into his club and serves them drinks. Colleen suggested that the girls were giving him sexual favours in return, but that's just speculation on her part."

"Probably, but I think this merits a return visit to Mr Wild to find out why he didn't volunteer this information." Nailer thought about this for a moment before he turned to Guy. "Okay. Anything new?"

"I'm still gathering footage from doorbell and security cameras while going through statements. But, I have found what I think might be the massage parlour after a long hunt online and chats with contacts. It's just a random house on a corner not too far from here, and it's known as Phil McCracken Massages."

"Fill-my-crack-in?" Scarlett scoffed, her eyes wide.

Guy laughed. "Close enough."

"Jesus," Scarlett exclaimed.

"Excellent work. We need to pay them a visit," Nailer replied. "Right then, we have some new leads and some promising suspects. This is good. I've got plenty to report back to Landon about, which is great news."

Rob coughed, getting Nailer's attention. "I just spoke to one of the local residents, who's also on the Clipstone Neighbourhood Watch team, and they're keen to help. I'm not sure what they can offer, but they might be worth talking to. He also suggested that we host a town meeting to keep the local community informed."

"Aaah, yes." Nailer nodded along with what Rob was saying. "A town meeting might be a good idea. We've been here for a few days now, so I think we owe it to the community to keep them up to date. We can speak to the Neighbourhood Watch members at the same time."

"Sir," Rob replied with a nod.

Nailer scanned down his pad at the notes he'd taken. "Right, this is how I want you to proceed. Rob, Scarlett, I need you to return to Nigel Wild's place and have a quick chat with him. He's been less than honest with us, and I want to know why."

"Guv," Rob answered.

"Guy, you've spent long enough in front of a screen, so I want you and Nick to check out Jerome's parents' address and see what they know. If you're lucky, you might catch Jerome there… But I doubt it."

"Thanks, guv," Guy replied.

"Will do, sir," Nick added. "I'll make sure Guy gets plenty of sun. Wouldn't want him getting vitamin D deficient."

"Indeed not," Nailer commented. "Which leaves Ellen and Tucker. You get the fun job of checking out this so-called massage parlour. Be gentle with this. We just want to find out what they know of the girls working the streets. Don't get all aggressive with them. Keep it friendly. You're not there to shut them down. That can be done later."

"Will do, sir," Ellen confirmed.

"Thank you. I'll report back to Landon, and I'll speak with the local councillors and Neighbourhood Watch to arrange this town meeting. I'll try to get it set up for tonight, and I'll need you all there for it, okay?"

"Of course, guv," Rob agreed. It looked like he needed to arrange for Erika to go and see his cat, then.

"Right," Nailer continued. "It sounds like we're getting somewhere. But now we know who the victim was, we need more information on her. We need to know who she was, who her friends were, and who was she hanging around with? It sounds like she got involved with some of the less savoury aspects of our society, so we need to find out who they were and pursue those leads. Also, as it looks like she was a sex worker, we need to find out who her clients were. In addition to all that, we need to keep going on that house-to-house, keep looking through the footage we're bringing in and wait for the DNA results. We have lots to be getting on with, so let's keep going while we still have this momentum and bring this home. Okay?"

"Yes, sir," they all chorused.

"Alright, you're dismissed." Nailer got up.

Rob did the same and leaned into Scarlett. "I've just got a quick phone call to make."

"Sure," she replied with a smile. "I'll be here."

Rob turned and left the room, plucking his phone from his pocket as he walked and made for the back door to the rear car park. He found Erika's number on his phone and called.

"Rob, hello," she answered. "Good timing. You caught me on my lunch break."

"Hi, Erika. I was wondering if you could check in on Muffin for me tonight? Just make sure his bowl's full and that he's okay. Is that alright?"

"Of course. Happy too," she replied, brightly. "Is it another late one?"

"I'm afraid so."

"Alright, no problem. I'll call if there's anything wrong."

"That's great, thank you."

They said their goodbyes, and Rob ended the call, feeling a little better about potentially staying at work a lot later than he'd planned. He had a feeling he'd be calling on Erika to do this again before too long.

30

Nick glanced out the window of the car at the tiny terrace house they were parked outside. It would have looked practically derelict if it wasn't for the lights that were on inside. The garden was overgrown, with discarded furniture and scattered, moss-covered children's toys that hadn't been played with in years. One of the windows was boarded up, and a couple more were cracked and barely hanging on inside their peeling wooden frames.

"Nice place," Nick commented in a dry tone.

"Well, someone's not house proud," Guy said as he turned the car off. "That's it, is it? Jerome Clifford's address? His parents' address, I mean."

"His mother's address," Nick clarified, checking his notes. "There doesn't seem to be a father on record for him from what I can see."

"Single mother? I thought we were told parents, as in plural?"

Nick shrugged. "Maybe it was, once upon a time."

"Whatever," Guy commented, chewing on his lip. "I think I'm getting an idea of the life Jerome was born into."

"Yeah, me too. He probably didn't have much hope of a normal life."

"Probably not," Guy answered. "So this is the guy who Penny's parents mentioned as possibly being her boyfriend? The one who showered her with gifts?"

"That's what they said," Nick confirmed and looked back at the house. "I'm guessing he didn't share his money with his mother."

"I think this'll be a dead end."

Nick shrugged. "Maybe. It's worth a chat, though. She might know something. Come on."

Nicked climbed out the passenger door and scanned up and down the street. He could hear children playing in the distance, but there wasn't much in the way of pedestrian or vehicle traffic, leaving the road quiet.

"What do you think?" Guy asked as he walked round to him.

"I don't know. It looks like a fairly deprived area. All fairly typical."

"Aye," Guy replied as he looked over the houses before him. He sighed and leaned against the side of the car. He didn't seem to be in a rush. "What about our team? What do you think of them? I know Nailer, but I'm not as familiar with the others."

"Oh. Yeah, they're a good bunch. I've worked with Rob for years, actually, and I know Nailer through him mainly. They're a good bunch." Nick gestured to the nearby front gate, which was hanging off the frame of the fence. "Shall we?"

"Yeah," Guy answered and followed before continuing the conversation. "They seem it. And the others?"

"Ellen and Tucker have been working with Nailer for a while…"

"I'm aware of them," Guy answered.

Nick nodded. "Scarlett seems nice enough, but I don't really know her. Pretty, though."

"Aye, she is that," Guy answered enthusiastically, keeping his voice low. "She's a bit of alright."

Nick paused on his walk up the garden path and raised an eyebrow at Guy's obvious interest in Scarlett. "You know that she's engaged, though, right?"

"I spotted the ring," Guy said. "That just means she's not married yet, you know? There's still time."

Feeling uncomfortable, Nick snorted at his gall. He seemed confident that he could woo Scarlett, but in Nick's opinion, Guy was doomed to failure. "I think you're barking up the wrong tree there, mate. She seems quite happy, and Rob thinks so too." He continued his slow amble up the path.

"You asked, did you?"

Realising he'd made similar comments, Nick sighed, hoping he'd been a little more tactful. "I made a passing comment, and Rob picked up on it. But seriously, I wouldn't bother. Both as your mate, and senior officer, don't go there."

Guy met his gaze, and Nick felt for a moment that the man was about to take issue with what he'd said, but a moment later, the edge to his demeanour dulled, and Guy shrugged. "Sure, whatever."

Nick eyed him for a moment, feeling sure that Guy wasn't about to be dissuaded by a few words. He mentally shrugged, feeling sure he was setting himself up for disappointment. But that was up to him. He'd done his part and warned Guy off. He promised himself to keep an eye on Guy's behaviour, though, just to be sure he didn't overstep the mark.

Setting that aside, for the time being, Nick stepped up to the front door and knocked. He noted how the carcass of the doorbell was still partially attached to the door frame, but the thing was clearly quite dead and unusable.

Two knocks later, the door was finally answered, revealing a shell of a woman just inside the doorway. She was drawn and thin with skin that sported open sores and flaking dry patches. Her bloodshot eyes looked up at him, and she seemed to have difficulty focusing. She squinted while pulling the strap of her old, stretched and dirty vest top back onto her shoulder.

"Yeah? What you want, ay?"

Nick held up his badge. "I'd like a quick word with you about Jerome, if that's okay?"

"What's the little shit been up to now?" she asked.

"Can we come in?" Nick pressed, preferring not to do this on the doorstep.

She seemed a little surprised that he wanted to enter her house but then shrugged. "If yeh like."

She turned and shuffled back through the corridor, kicking discarded junk out of the way as she went. The house was a mess, and that was being generous.

Nick followed her along the path she'd created, noting the worn-through carpet and the stained wallpaper that looked like something straight out of the 80s. The front room wasn't much better, and apart from the space on the sofa, which the woman took and lay down on, there really wasn't anywhere for them to sit.

Not that he wanted to sit anywhere in this mess. There was no telling what he'd be sitting on.

"Mrs Clifford, we need to discuss Jerome with you," Nick started while Guy scanned around the room, taking a look at some of the photos on the mantel.

"You said that," she muttered.

He ignored the jibe. "When did you last see him?"

"Dunno. Weeks ago, maybe? He don' come round 'ere much. He only shows up when he wants sumink, don' he? Scrounging little brat."

"So you've not seen him for a while?"

"You deaf or summat?"

"I'm just clarifying what you're telling me," Nick said, doing his best to try and keep calm.

"Well, you're gonna be 'ere a while then, ain't yeh."

Nick chewed his tongue in frustration. "Do you know where he might be?"

"Nope."

"Or what he's doing?"

"No idea. 'As he been a naughty boy again?"

"He's suspected to have been engaged in some criminal activity, Mrs Clifford, and we need to speak to him as soon as possible."

"I see. Well, I ain't got any idea where he is or what he's doin' like. I can tell yeh, though. He's always in trouble. Always. He's a little shit, he is. He's been a pain in my neck for ages. He's nicked things from me, and he's bloody hit me." She pointed enthusiastically to her lip, but Nick couldn't discern what was a bruise or cut, and what was a sore or skin condition.

"He's been violent towards you?" Nick asked.

"Oh yeah. Several times. Like I said, a little shit."

"Okay, well." Nick thought for a moment, wondering if there wasn't something they could ask that might help them. "Is there anything you know or have heard that might help us?

Have you overheard any names or anything? And phone conversations? Anything at all?"

"Err, no, not really... I mean, I think one of the guys he knows is called Abel, but that's all I know."

"Abel? He's one of Jerome's friends?"

"Aye. That's right."

"You're sure?"

"Sure, I'm sure. I heard him mention him one time. No idea who he is, though. Is that helpful?"

"It might be," Nick replied. "It might just be."

31

"Who were you on the phone to?" Scarlett casually asked as he drove them the handful of roads over to the Clip Club.

"Erika," Rob answered.

"Oh. Sorting out your cat sitter?"

"Yup. She said she'd pop over and make sure Muffin is okay. I felt really bad yesterday when I got home late. He was meowing like crazy and had an empty bowl."

"You bad dad," Scarlett remarked, her voice full of mirth.

"I know. He'll survive, but I did feel terrible, and I promised him I wouldn't do it again."

"You promised your cat?" She sounded incredulous and shook her head. "It's like I don't know you at all."

"Well, I promised myself more than the cat," Rob admitted before he changed the subject. "Sounds like the post-mortem went well."

She pulled a face. "Yeah, as well as those things ever go. I'm not sure I'll ever get used to them."

"I can send someone else if you'd prefer?"

"No, no. It's fine. I can cope. But yeah, they picked up on a few interesting points. No idea what that piece of rubber was, but if we can find out who her last client was, it might be that he saw something, maybe?"

"You never know your luck," Rob agreed. "He might even be our killer."

"Mmm."

"You don't sound convinced."

"That's because I'm not. I don't think this is some disgruntled or obsessed customer of Penny's taking out his rage on her. I think the method of killing and the place the head was discarded have meaning. I just don't know what that meaning is yet."

Rob nodded as she spoke. "I'm inclined to agree," he admitted as they closed in on their destination.

"Do you think Nigel has anything to do with it?"

"Maybe..." Rob muttered and shrugged. "Right now, I wouldn't assume anything. We've not narrowed it down enough. We need to dig deeper and find the thread that links all this together."

Rob pulled into a space close to the Clip Club and climbed out of his car. The pair of them walked over to the front door and stepped inside. Several customers were drinking in the front room, and Caprice was cleaning glasses behind the bar. Recognising them as she looked up, she placed the glass down and waited for them to approach.

Rob walked over with Scarlett close behind and smiled at her. "Afternoon. Is Nigel around?"

"Yeah, he's over there." She pointed. Rob turned to see him hidden around a corner, out of sight of much of the room. He was doing some paperwork on a nearby table.

"Thanks," Rob said and wandered over. "Nigel."

He looked up, briefly shocked, and then smiled. "Oh. I wondered when you'd be back."

"Have you got a moment?" Rob asked. "We have a few more questions."

"I'm sure you do. Apparently, you're not the only one, either."

Rob frowned at the comment. He nearly let it go, but he sensed a hidden meaning, and it felt like Nigel was offering it to him. "What do you mean?"

"I had a nosey reporter in here earlier from the Gazette. He was asking all sorts of questions, making a nuisance of himself. Told me I could sell my story and make a mint."

"Did he now?" Rob had a fairly good idea who this might be and silently cursed Vincent Kane.

"Don't worry," Nigel continued, "I know he's talking out of his arse. The Gazette relies on advertising to keep going, so they're unlikely to have any money to buy my story off me."

"Yeah, probably not. Besides, do you have much of a story to sell?"

"Well, exactly. So no, I'm not going to be talking to him, that's for sure."

"If you're referring to the man I think you're referring to, then you have good instincts. He's just looking for dirt, that's all. I'd recommend you stay well away."

"Noted," Nigel replied as he started to get up from his seat. "And in the interests of openness, I have something else I'd like to share with you if you don't mind."

Rob frowned, thinking of the busy evening they had before them. "Is it relevant to this case?"

"I would say so, yes." Nigel wore an inscrutable smile, as if he was relishing this moment.

"Then please, go ahead," Rob said, waving him out from the booth he'd been sitting in. "Lead the way."

"This way," Nigel replied and led them to a back room. Caprice watched them walk by suspiciously, frowning and looking a little confused. They followed Nigel through a staff-only door, along a corridor, and into what looked like a break room. Inside, a young woman who still looked like she was in her teens was sitting at the table. A plate of half-eaten food sat before her. She held her fork in her right hand and rested her head on her left, looking fed up as she pushed the remains of pasta bake around the plate with her utensil.

She looked up as Nigel walked in, and for a brief moment, a smile flickered on her face. Then she spotted Rob and Scarlett, and the smile fell away.

"Errr, who are you?" She had a slight eastern European accent, but her English was excellent. Behind them, Rob heard a door bang and the clatter of running footsteps. He turned to see Caprice running towards them, before stopping short.

"Nigel, what are you doing?" Caprice barked.

"This is Izabela," Nigel said in a factual tone, ignoring Caprice. "I think you might want to talk to her. She's a prostitute and a friend of Penny's. I'm helping her get off the streets."

"I thought I could trust you," Izabela raged. "What are you doing?"

Nigel turned to her. "This is the best thing for you. I said we should go to the police, and here they are.

"What?" Izabela snapped.

"We need their help, Izabela. *You* need their help. They're on *your* side."

Rob felt a little overwhelmed by the sudden revelations. "Wait a moment. You're a friend of Penny Lynn's?" he asked Izabela.

"You said I could trust you," Izabela spat, ignoring Rob.

"You can, and you need to trust me now," Nigel answered.

Rob grimaced.

"He's right," Scarlett said, taking a step towards her. "We want to help. We want to find out who killed Penny and bring them to justice. That's all."

"How can I trust you?" Izabela asked. "How do I know who you are?"

Scarlett pulled out her ID and showed it to her. "Look, see. We're not lying."

Rob held up his own ID as well. "Someone out there is brutally murdering young women like you. I don't want you to be next, or anyone else for that matter."

"Rob's right," Scarlett added. "You might be able to help us and stop anyone else from suffering the same fate as Penny. So, please, work with us."

Izabela seemed to deflate as she sighed in resignation. "Okay, fine. But I'm not happy about this." She looked over at Nigel. "You've betrayed my trust."

"I understand," Nigel answered.

"So, you're a friend of Penny's?" Rob asked, keen to get answers while he could.

"Kinda."

"What's your full name?"

"Izabela Nosek, and yeah, I knew Penny. She, err. She watched over me... a bit. She got me back into the game."

"Izabela first came to me a few months ago," Nigel cut in. "She'd been working as a prostitute for a Polish gang who'd trafficked her from Poland, but she escaped and came to me for help. I hid her here for several months, but she got talking to Penny when she'd visit here for a drink, and Penny got her back onto the street." He sighed. "I'm sorry, I should have been more honest when you first came to see me, but I was worried. Scared of what it might mean."

"I understand." Rob glanced back at Scarlett, who shrugged. They needed to talk to both Nigel and Izabela. "Right, I think we need to talk to both of you separately. Scarlett, can you take Izabela to another room and have a chat?"

"Of course," Scarlett answered and approached Izabela. "Can you follow me?" The fire seemed to have faded inside Izabela, and she did as she'd been asked. Scarlett turned to Caprice. "Can you show us somewhere we can talk in private?"

"Aaah, yeah, upstairs would probably be best," Caprice said with a glance at Nigel. He nodded.

"That works," Scarlett confirmed, and the three of them disappeared up the corridor, leaving Rob alone with Nigel.

"Sorry," Nigel muttered.

"That's okay," Rob replied before he closed the door and waved to the table and chairs. "Shall we?"

"Yeah, why not," Nigel answered and took the seat opposite. The chairs were the uncomfortable plastic kind and reminded Rob of a school canteen.

"You've been holding out on us, Nigel. That's not going to look good for you."

"I know," he admitted. "I just, I wasn't sure what you wanted to know or... Well, I was worried. I don't go shouting about this stuff from the rooftops. It's not a popular position; helping out the girls, I mean."

"The prostitutes," Rob clarified. "Let's call them what they are."

"Yeah, them." He sighed. "They're just people. I wish they weren't demonised as much as they are. These young women have been dealt a shitty hand in life, and they're either being exploited or making the best of what they have left. If I can help by giving them a place to drink and relax, well, why shouldn't I?"

"No, you're right," Rob admitted. "You're doing the right thing there. You're helping them in their hour of need. I congratulate you, honestly. It's good work you're doing. Where I have an issue is that you should have told us about it. You should have volunteered the information as soon as you knew it was relevant."

"I'm sharing it now," Nigel muttered.

"You are, which is good. But let's get down to brass tacks, shall we? You know why we're here, in Clipstone. One of these prostitutes, a girl named Penny Lynn, was killed. She had her head chopped off," Rob said, opting for shock tactics. "We need to find her killer."

"I had nothing to do with her murder," Nigel insisted. "I'd never kill anyone, let alone one of these young women."

"But you'd punch a man in the face?"

"Emmett's different. He's a scab, so he has it coming. But I still wouldn't kill him. I couldn't."

Rob sighed. "You see, I have difficulty with that. On the one hand, you say you wouldn't kill anyone, but then you go and make an exception for someone."

"I didn't say I'd kill him."

"No. You said you'd attack and hurt him." Rob fixed him with a knowing look.

"No, I get it," Nigel answered. "But I would not hurt or kill one of those girls."

Rob stared at him for a long moment, trying to read him, wondering if he was being truthful. It was tough to know for sure. He decided to try a different line of questions. "Tell me about Penny. How do you know her?"

"I only know her through Izabela, and I've seen her in the club, before. She started being friendly to Izabela during the last few weeks of Izabela's time here. I guess I wasn't being careful about who she hung around with. The next thing I know, Izabela has left and is getting back on the game, but this time with Penny. I tried to tell her not to do it, that it was dangerous, that she was throwing everything she'd gained away, but she wouldn't listen. You know what kids are like these days." Nigel sighed. "So yeah, that's it. One day she's here, she's clean, off the drugs, getting healthy, and thinking about her future... Or so I thought. And the next thing I know, she's back on the streets." He paused for a moment, but Rob let it hang. "I saw her a few times, you know. She'd hang around out here, around the shops, causing Colleen to have an aneurism." He chuckled. "I tried to speak to her, to convince her to come back, but Penny would always shut me down, and Izabela would join in. I saw her the day she died, you know."

"Really?" Rob asked, as he made notes. "When?"

"Just before I threatened Emmett. That's why I was pissed off. I'd just been blown off by them again, Penny and Izabela I mean. They told me to piss off."

"So you did?"

"No. I wasn't having any of it, but then their pimp showed up, him and his goon. They moved me along."

"Do you know who they are?"

"Penny's pimp? Yeah, sure. I've seen him in here before, drinking. He's called Abel. He's nothing but a thug."

32

"This'll be a first for me," Ellen said as they drove towards Forest Town. "I've never been to a massage parlour before." She had images of seedy little rooms with cheap beds and furnishings, populated by skinny, malnourished girls who looked like strung-out drug addicts.

"Fuck. You've never had a massage?" Tucker asked. He sounded surprised.

"Oh, yeah, I've had a massage. I've been to spas before. But this isn't really a massage parlour, is it? It's a brothel. People come here and pay for sex, not for a spa treatment."

"True," Tucker replied in clipped tones that drew her suspicions.

"What about you?" Ellen asked.

"Me?"

"Yeah," she pressed. "Have you ever been to... One of these places?"

"Errrm..." he answered, drawing out the sound as if he was racking his brains to try and remember, but Ellen wasn't buying it. It was a very guilty-sounding 'Erm' to her ears.

"You have, haven't you!"

"Well..."

"You dirty sod," she gasped. "So, was this while you were a priest or a police officer?" She hoped it was the former.

Tucker sighed. "Neither. In-between." He sounded sad and guilty as he admitted to it. "I was in a dark place. I'm not that man anymore."

Ellen gave him side-eye as she changed gear while turning a corner.

There it was again, a reference to that time between him stopping being a priest and joining the police. Clearly, there was a history there that Tucker wasn't keen on revealing. But then, everyone had little secrets they kept locked up in their closets. She wanted to press him and ask for more details. She would have loved to find out more about why he left the clergy, but she also had the feeling that this was an intensely personal issue for him. Something that went to the core of who he was, and it didn't feel right for her to try and pry it out of him.

And honestly, what did it matter if he'd used a brothel or two, especially if it was between these two careers of his? The answer to that was, it didn't matter, and it wasn't her place to keep asking questions, either.

"I understand. We've all had difficult times in our lives."

"Yeah... It's not something I really want to talk about. Not right now, anyway."

"That's fine. No pressure from me, and um, I'm sorry I asked."

"That's okay. No harm done." He checked the sat nav. "Nearly there."

He was right, they were. According to Guy, he'd had to trawl through some forums where clients of these places shared their experiences of the establishment and the women in them, giving recommendations and such. It sounded horrific and probably incredibly toxic. But he'd eventually tracked down the parlour's website and, from there, the address of the parlour itself.

As Ellen parked across a junction from the building, she gave it an appraising gaze. It was just a house on a corner. A fairly large one, but still just a house like any other. There was nothing exceptional about it at all and nothing outside to say what it was or what was going on there.

"Is that it? The house on the corner?"

Tucker was checking his notes. "That's the place," he confirmed. Tucker looked up and nodded. "Yeah, that's the one. Look, they've got blinds up during the day and lights on inside. I think that's the place, all right."

"Right, well, I'm eager to see inside. Let's go check it out, shall we?"

"Remember what Nailer said," Tucker cut in as she went to open her door. "We go easy on them. We don't want to spook them too much."

Ellen pulled an incredulous face. "Hey, it's me."

"Yes, yes it is," Tucker replied, deadpan.

Ellen climbed out of the car, and once Tucker had walked around to her, they crossed the street and made for the house. Drawing nearer, with a final road to cross, Ellen could see a front door straight ahead and what looked like a back way in, as well around the corner.

"Front door?"

"Certainly," Tucker said.

"Is it best if you..." Ellen asked.

"I don't think it matters. They'll smell a rat from the beginning. Come on."

Ellen walked with him across the road. "You know quite a lot about these places."

"Well enough to know that their police radar will be on point. Their business lives and dies based on their ability to spot suspicious customers early on. So yeah, they'll know. They've probably already seen us coming."

"Wonderful," Ellen said, glancing up at the windows, trying to see if anyone was up there, watching them approach, but she saw nothing.

They crossed the last few metres to the door, knocked, and waited. Ellen glanced left and right, wondering if they'd come to the right place or if this would turn out to be some random person's house.

Moments later, the lock on the door sounded before it opened just enough for a face to appear around it. The dark-haired woman wore a frown and looked the pair of them up and down suspiciously.

"Yeah?" Her tone wasn't at all friendly. "What do you want?"

"Hi," Ellen began, taking half a step towards the door. "We'd like to talk to the owner?"

"Oh, would you," the woman stated. It wasn't a question.

"Are they in?"

"What's this about?" she asked.

"We've just got a few questions, that's all. Nothing to worry about," Ellen said, trying her best to sound reassuring.

"What questions," the woman pressed.

Ellen bit her lip as she considered her answer. "We think they might know something about the situation in Clipstone that might help us find a killer."

"A killer of young women... Like yourself," Tucker added, his words laced with meaning.

The woman narrowed her eyes. "We don't know anything about that," she said and shut the door. Ellen heard it lock. She sighed.

"Damn," Ellen cursed, annoyed.

"What do you want to do?"

Ellen took a step back from the building and glanced at the various windows, spotting at least one twitching blind. "I'm not keen on giving up so easily." Filled with a sudden determination to get some answers, she stepped closer and knocked again. There was no answer. So, she knocked once more and then for the third time. The door unlocked before she finished knocking. A different woman stepped out, barely giving Ellen a chance to look past her, into the building. She closed the door behind her and planted herself on the doorstep with her arms crossed.

"Who are you?" she asked.

"We're with the police," Ellen said. "I'm Detective Dale, and this is Detective Stafford."

"What do you want?" She was older with a stern, gravelly voice and a solid physique.

"Are you the owner of this building?" Ellen began.

The woman met her gaze. "This is my home," the woman answered.

Ellen smiled at the dodge. She hadn't answered the question, not really, but she'd given them enough for them to assume she was in charge around here.

"Okay," Ellen replied. She glanced at the building behind the woman. She felt confident this was the massage parlour they suspected it to be. The woman would probably never admit to it, but that's what it was. She was sure of it. "We know what you do here, so don't try and deny it." The woman went to interrupt, but Ellen held up her hand. "We're not interested in that. That's not why we're here."

The woman closed her mouth and frowned. "Go on."

"You've heard of the girl that was found murdered? In Clipstone?" They were actually in Forest Town, the next area over, closer to Mansfield, but only just.

"I've heard," the woman answered.

"Well, it's come to our attention that you might know something about either the victim or the other working girls that she hung around with. She was a prostitute, and we believe there's a link between them and the... service, you provide here."

"You believe..."

"We do, and if you do know anything, anything at all that you think might be useful, we'd very much like you to share it with us, please."

"And, what do you believe we do here?"

"Massages... Maybe more?"

"More? I'm not sure what you mean by that. I provide spa treatments. And as for these prostitutes you're talking about, I'm afraid I know nothing."

"You're sure about that?"

"Quite sure," she answered without hesitation.

Ellen left a pregnant pause hanging between them for a moment and then shrugged. "Okay. If you say so."

"I most certainly do."

"Alright, thank you... um... Sorry, I didn't catch your name."

She seemed to consider the question for a moment before answering. "Susan."

"Susan what?"

"Just Susan," she answered. "Are we done here?"

"I suppose so," Ellen said before smiling.

Susan smiled back, but it didn't touch her eyes, and there was little joy in it. The conversation was over, but Susan didn't move. She just set her jaw and stared at them.

"Alright, let's go," Ellen said and started to walk away as Tucker slipped his notepad back into his pocket. A few metres away, Ellen glanced back and watched the woman open her front door and step back inside, giving them the evil eye the whole time.

"She seemed nice," Ellen commented sarcastically.

"Yeah," Tucker replied, matching her tone. "She was a fuckin' dream."

33

Caprice led the way from the break room where Rob was talking to Nigel, with Scarlett bringing up the rear and Izabela between them. Scarlett wanted to keep the young prostitute in sight in case she made a run for it, but to her credit, she never once looked like she was going to try.

They stepped into the upstairs apartment that she presumed Nigel called home and Caprice showed them into a dining room. Scarlett thanked her and left Caprice with no doubt that she wanted to be alone with Izabela.

"Thank you," Scarlett said, showing Caprice the door.

"Sure." She looked over at Izabela. "I'll be right outside, okay?"

"That's fine," Izabela answered.

Scarlett smiled one last time and then shut the door. She turned to the teenager and smiled. "Why don't you take a seat," she offered. Izabela accepted, and Scarlett joined her, readying her notepad as she settled. "Thank you for agreeing to talk to us."

The girl shifted in her seat and fiddled with the ties on her top. "No problem." She looked traumatised and scared, so going in hard wasn't going to work. She'd clam up, and then they'd get nothing. She needed to ease Izabela into the questions and let her tell the story in her own time. They'd get way more out of her that way.

"I'm Scarlett, by the way."

"I got that," she answered flatly.

"I know this is difficult, but it sounds like you're worried about some... people, maybe the same people we're trying to find. The people who killed Penny. So if you can help us find them, then you're going to be doing what Penny would want you to do, I'm sure."

"I know."

"How about you tell me a little about yourself? How did you end up here, in the UK?"

"Money," she answered. "I wanted money."

"And you thought coming here would get you that?"

"I did, once..."

"Why? What do you want to earn this money for?"

"To support my mother. She lives alone in Poland. She worked and always tried to provide for us when I lived with her, but it's hard. We never had enough. So, then I hear of someone who can get me a good job in England. So I can travel, I can see the world, and I can earn some money while I'm travelling. It sounded perfect. So I went to them, and they were interested. Before I knew it, I was on my way here, and then it went wrong. They take my passport, and they smuggle me into the country."

"Who's they?"

"Radek. He's the leader. He brings people over, girls, boys, men, women. I don't know what he does with them all, but they forced me to…" Her breath caught in her throat, and she took a moment to calm herself and get control of her emotions. Scarlett let Izabela take her time, never rushing her and waiting for her to tell the story. "I had to carry drugs… inside me, you know?" She pointed to herself.

"I understand."

"They wanted me to swallow the… things, but I couldn't do it. It was a nightmare. No one told me…" She sighed. "I was only here for a day before they forced me onto the street. They made me do it. They hooked me on drugs. They made me into this."

"I know. It's not the first time I've seen it."

"I didn't know what to do. I don't know this country. I didn't have my passport, my ID or anything. I didn't know where I was. But Radek didn't know that I could speak English. I kept that from him, and I listened."

"So, what happened?"

"I heard of the Clip Club. I heard Radek talk about how some of the girls from a rival gang used it because the owner was nice to them. So I waited, and as soon as I could, I ran, and I came here. I spoke to Nigel and Caprice, and they offered to help me. They helped me off the drugs. I don't know what I would have done if they hadn't offered to help. They saved me."

"But then you started working again, right? With Penny?"

"Yeah, I did. I was here for a few months, and I started to relax. I started to talk to some of the girls who came here, like Penny." She paused for a moment as she considered her words. "You have to understand, I was broke. I had no money, and I knew that Nigel was spending a lot to help me. I felt useless. I didn't want to rely on his help. It wasn't right, but I also needed to send money back to my mother in Poland. Penny assured me that I could do that, that her pimp would protect me and help me, and that I could earn money. It sounded good. I knew what I was getting into. I'd done it before. So, I convinced myself it would be alright."

"And it wasn't."

"No. It wasn't any different. They took most of my money, they hurt me, they forced me to do things I didn't want to do."

"So, Penny tricked you?"

"Yes. She did it because... She wanted to..."

"To curry favour with her pimp? She got stuff in return for bringing you into the group."

"Yeah," Izabela confirmed. "She lied to me, but... I know why. I don't blame her, she was only playing the game. She was doing what she needed to do to survive. I understand that. I would do the same."

"You're very forgiving," Scarlett commented, surprised that Izabela would be so kind to the person who'd pulled her back into this horrible life.

"She wasn't in a good place either," Izabela continued. "She had it tough, like me. We all did what we needed to survive."

"So, who was this pimp? What was his name?"

"Abel. He's a gang leader, I think. He deals drugs and stuff, too."

"Alright," Scarlett said, noting down his name. "Does he have a surname?"

"I don't know."

"That's okay. How about where he lives? Do you know where we might find him?"

"I'm so sorry," she answered. "I don't know where he lives. We were always driven from the house to where we worked. I'd recognise it if I saw it, but I don't know where it is."

"You're sure about that? You didn't see any road signs?"

"I… I can't remember. They blacked out the back windows, and it was dark…"

"There were others there with you? Other girls?"

"Just Penny," Izabela said, but it didn't ring true.

"Just you and Penny? That's it?"

"Yeah…"

"Izabela. I think you're lying to me. I think there were others there, but because of some misguided loyalty, you're protecting them, right?"

Izabela shook her head. "I'm not, no. It was just us two."

Scarlett narrowed her eyes. She was lying about this, but there was little she could do about it. She probably thought she was protecting the other girls, keeping them safe, when in reality, she was doing the exact opposite.

"Look," Izabela said. "This wasn't Abel; he didn't kill Penny. It was Radek. I know it. He found out about me and wants revenge."

"Revenge?"

"For me escaping. He probably found out I was working with Abel and wanted to punish him, so he killed Penny. He'll be looking for me now, so I had to get out of there. I had to escape."

"And how did you manage that?"

"I was out working, and a punter drove me to the allotments. Abel usually waits for me and picks me up, but he wasn't there."

"And this was last night?"

"Yep. I'm not sure why, but he wasn't there. So I ran."

Scarlett bit her lip as she considered what had happened the night before and then came to a realisation. Had they accidentally facilitated Izabela's escape by talking to the prostitutes and drawing Abel's attention.

She smirked.

"What?" Izabela asked.

"Nothing. Don't worry about it."

"Look, all I want is for you to capture Radek. He's out there, looking for me. I know it."

Izabela might well be convinced of this idea, but Scarlett felt like she had a way to go with it. While it was certainly possible that this Radek character was after Izabela and was embarking on some kind of gang war, she wasn't sure that this was the cause of Penny's death. Something didn't add up about it.

"Okay," Scarlett said. "And I'm guessing you don't know where we can find this Radek, either, right?"

Izabela's face looked apologetic. "Sorry, no. They keep that hidden, even from me. They always drove me in a blacked-out car, and sometimes they blindfolded me or put me in the back of a van. I never knew where I was. It's not far, though. It didn't take us long to get anywhere."

Sensing this was something of a dead end, she decided to focus on something else. "Tell me about the night Penny went missing. What happened?"

"She got a punter. It was the usual, you know? He just drove up, they negotiated, and then she went off with him." She sighed. "She didn't come back."

"Okay. What about this punter? Did you see him? Do you remember what he looked like or what car he was driving? Did you catch his number plate?"

"No, I... I don't know. He was in a car, I think. A dark one. I didn't get a good look at him, but he wasn't unusual or anything. Just a guy."

Scarlett frowned. "But, you were with Penny when she picked up this punter? So, he saw you too?"

"Aaah, yeah. I think so."

"Okay, so if he saw you and didn't pick you up, that means it's unlikely that this punter was working for Radek because I would assume that Radek would show his men a photo of you, at least. He'd want them to be able to find you."

"I guess. I didn't suggest that the John was the killer, though."

"No, you didn't. But it helps with the timeline. If we can eliminate this John from the investigation, then we know that whatever happened to Penny happened after she left her final client."

"I suppose," Izabela answered, sounding unsure. She sighed and glanced around the room while Scarlett made a couple of notes on her pad. "He doesn't like her, you know."

"Hmm? Who?"

"Nigel. He doesn't like Penny. Ever since I left him and went off with her, he's hated her. I know he has." Her tone was casual as she vocalised her thoughts.

"Then, is it possible that Nigel killed her? Was this revenge for what Penny did to you?" Scarlett frowned as she continued the thought, thinking it also made sense that he dumped the head in Emmett's bin, given he hated Emmett so much. Maybe he was trying to pin it on Emmett. That made a scary amount of sense.

"No," Izabela cut into her thoughts. "He couldn't kill someone."

"Are you sure?"

"Positive. Nigel wouldn't do that. I know he wouldn't. He's a good man."

"But you just said he hated Penny, the girl who tricked you into getting back into being a prostitute. That sounds like a very good reason for wanting to hurt someone."

"I don't care what you think," Izabela scoffed. "It isn't Nigel. It can't be Nigel."

"I admire your optimism," Scarlett replied sceptically, keeping her cool.

"No, don't say that. He didn't do this. He wouldn't. He's a good man. He saved me once before, and he'll do it again."

"I really hope that's true."

"It is."

"You know, I can arrange some accommodation for you if you like. I can find somewhere for you to stay where I know you'll be safe."

"I'm safe here," Izabela spat, apparently annoyed at this line of questioning.

"What about you?" Scarlett asked, changing her line of questioning. "Did you like Penny?"

"She was... err... She was okay, I suppose. We became friends, I think."

"But you're not sure?"

"I don't know..."

It wasn't a great answer, but there probably wasn't one that Izabela could give her.

With her questions answered, Scarlett suggested that they make their way back downstairs to find the others. As they got up, Caprice stepped inside. She'd apparently heard the interview end.

"Are you okay?" Caprice asked.

"I'm fine," Izabela confirmed as Caprice walked up and took her by the arm, leading her out of the room. Scarlett caught a judging glance from Caprice, but she didn't mind or care. It was her job to ask these questions and to find out the truth about what had happened. She wasn't here to try and make friends.

Scarlett followed Caprice and Izabela back downstairs to the break room. One of the other bar staff appeared out of the door at the back of the bar as they walked along the corridor.

"Caprice. We could really do with a hand back here."

"Okay," Caprice said before turning to Izabela. "Will you be alright?"

The girl nodded. "I'll be fine."

"Alright, but you come and find me if you need me, okay? You don't have to answer their questions."

Izabela nodded again before Caprice dashed up the hall to the bar while Scarlett led Izabela back into the break room.

"Successful interview?" Rob asked as they stepped back into the room.

"Informative," Scarlett answered before she turned and gave Nigel a look. It seemed like a good enough time to ask her questions. "I do have a question for you though."

"Go ahead," Nigel answered.

"What did you think of Penny?"

Nigel seemed a little surprised by the question and took a moment to consider his response before answering. "Um, she was okay, I suppose."

"You suppose?"

"Well, she wasn't terribly nice to Izabela, so..."

"No, she was not. Are you in the habit of liking people who do terrible things to your friends?"

"Well, no..."

"So, would I be right in saying you didn't like Penny?"

"I guess."

"You guess?" Scarlett asked.

"Alright, no. I didn't like her. Is that what you wanted to hear? I did not like Penny."

"Thank you for being a little more honest with us," Scarlett said. "But would it not be more accurate to say that you hated Penny? She tricked Izabela into joining Abel's crew, turned her back into a prostitute, undid all your hard work, and caused her a lot of pain and suffering."

Nigel gave her a glum pout and sank back into his chair. "I don't know about that. I don't think I hated her. Not really. Not enough to kill her, I can promise you that. I couldn't kill anyone."

"And yet, you had the motive and the opportunity, and the dislike of Emmett, too." She gave Nigel a knowing look. "It's almost as if someone was trying to pin this on Emmett, isn't it?" Scarlett noticed Rob nod out of the corner of her eye. He seemed to agree with this assessment.

"I can't deny that I dislike Emmett. I've been upfront about that, and I'm not the biggest fan of Penny, either. But I promise you that I didn't kill her. Besides, Izabela had larger issues with

Penny. She was the one who'd been tricked and forced to work as a prostitute."

"That doesn't exactly exonerate you," Rob suggested. "She still did this to someone you took in and helped. She undid all your amazing work. Penny ruined it all, destroyed it. I know I'd be upset if I were you."

"If you think I did it, then arrest me."

Rob met his gaze for a long moment before answering with a wry smile.

34

Erika walked to her apartment door and gripped the handle, ready to open it and step outside, but hesitated. Clutching the key to his apartment in her other hand, she took a deep breath to steady her nerves.

She could hardly believe she was about to do this, but from the looks of things, she'd need to get used to it because she doubted this would be the last time.

Opening her door, she stepped through and closed it behind her before turning to glare across the hallway. Rob's front door seemed to loom large in the hallway, tempting and calling to her. Once she stepped through it, there was no going back.

She'd be crossing a line...

But hadn't she already crossed several lines by agreeing to help Rob in the first place? Maybe she shouldn't have said she'd do this? Maybe this was all a big mistake?

It was too late now, though. She was committed, and there was no going back.

Sucking in another lungful of air, she strode across the landing, inserted the key, and opened the door. There was no room for half-measures. This had to be done. Otherwise, he'd start to ask questions, and she couldn't have that. She had to keep things as normal as possible and ensure he didn't suspect anything.

The door opened smoothly, revealing the open-plan living space beyond. A loud meow emanated from within, followed by the soft patter of feline footsteps.

Spotting the approaching cat, she moved inside and closed the door. The sound of the door shutting and its latch clicking into place echoed through her mind like a sonic boom. It felt like the gates of hell slamming shut behind her.

Back when she'd formulated her initial plan, she'd never thought this would happen. She'd believed this would be a long, drawn-out process taking months, if not years, and that was assuming that certain things fell into place. But she'd veered way off script and moved her schedule forward by… who knows how much? Her plan had been thrown out the window, and she was feeling her way in the dark without a light, groping blindly, hoping she didn't stumble. There was no telling where this new path would lead her.

Muffin meowed again, snapping her out of her daydream and the job she'd been asked to do. It only took a moment to find what she needed, and within seconds she'd filled the food bowl and topped up the water. Muffin was instantly munching merrily on his biscuits, perfectly happy and contented.

With the job done, Erika turned on the spot and swept her eyes over the surrounding apartment. It was fairly simple, with somewhat minimal furnishings. There was a comfortable-looking sofa with a huge TV opposite, a small dining table and sideboards. She spotted some photos and wandered over, almost sneaking through the apartment, trying not to make any noise.

On the wall behind the photos, she saw his framed police qualification, and below that, several photos on the side, showing Rob with what she guessed were work friends. She didn't recognise most of them, but she spotted John Nailer among them.

It seemed that Rob was rightly proud of the work he did. She appreciated that.

Feeling emboldened after walking this deep into his apartment, she crossed the rest of the way to the far windows that looked out over the River Trent. The view wasn't much different to hers, although her flat had a better view of the Trent Bridge. Directly opposite on the other side of the river was The City Ground, the home of Nottingham Forest Football Club, somewhere she'd never been and had no plans to. Then to her left was the tied arch, Lady Bay bridge, with its aqua blue arches, bright against the greens and greys beyond.

It wasn't a bad view at all.

She wondered how long Rob spent looking out of these windows, admiring the view after a long day's work hunting down criminals.

Behind her, Muffin meowed again and jumped onto one of the chairs. She wandered over and petted the black cat, scratching behind his ears and stroking him. He relished it, arching his back and meowing for more. After another minute with the cat, she felt she was starting to outstay her welcome and wondered if Rob might have any internal security camera's watching her.

He was a detective, after all. She glanced around but couldn't see any. It didn't mean there weren't any, though.

It was time to go.

Giving Muffin a final stroke, she walked to the door and glanced back, feeling pleased with herself. So far, so good. Her mother's fears about what this could mean or of her getting too close seemed unfounded for the time being.

For now, though, she needed to get on with her day. She'd have time to think through what this all meant later.

35

"How'd it go?" Nailer asked as they walked into the back room of the village hall.

"Good," Rob replied as he followed Scarlett inside. "Nigel surprised us, actually."

"Oh?" Nailer asked.

"Yeah. Turns out he's helping a prostitute called Izabela, who's been trafficked over here from Poland by a local gang. She escaped that gang and stayed with Nigel for a few months before she was lured back into the game to work for a rival gang. She's also run away from that one and returned to Nigel, who introduced us to her. Turns out, she's a friend of Penny's, so I interviewed Nigel, and Scarlett spoke with Izabela."

"And you've left her there?" Nailer asked incredulously.

"She refused to leave," Scarlett said. "She's not under arrest, and I wasn't about to force her to come with us."

Nailer shrugged. "Okay, so what did you find out?"

"Nigel admitted to serving some of the working girls at his place," Rob said. "He knows the other shop owners hate him for it, but he doesn't seem to care. He said he just wants to help these girls out and give them a safe place to visit."

"Admirable," Nailer remarked.

Rob continued, "We also have a couple of names we need to run through the system."

"On it," Scarlett said as she sat at the table and opened one of the laptops.

"What names?" Nailer asked.

"Abel and Radek," Rob replied. "They're both pimps and gang leaders based here in Mansfield, and they're very much rivals. From speaking to Izabela, she believes that Penny's killer is Radek. She thinks he killed Penny because he found out that Abel had recruited Izabela and wanted revenge. Izabela ran away because she thought she was next."

"I also think she's trying to protect the other girls working for Abel," Scarlett spoke up as she tapped away on the laptop.

"Makes sense," Nailer agreed.

"Okay, Radek is on here," Scarlett announced. "Full name: Radek Lewandowski. From reading this, he's a Polish national who's been here for years and is a wanted man. He's known for his trafficking and drug dealing, as well as his extreme violence. Mmm, not a nice man. I can see why Izabela is scared of him."

"I think I've heard of these guys," Nailer said. "I've not had direct contact with them, but I'm aware of their record, and from what I can remember, they're a really nasty bunch of people. Not the kind you want to cross. Good work. What about Abel?"

"He's on here too," she answered after another flurry of keystrokes. "Abel Underwood. Another violent pimp with his fingers in the drug trade. He's been linked to various gangsters, but he's mainly known for the prostitution ring he runs on this side of town."

"Underwood? Aaah, yes. I know him too," Nailer said, reminding Rob that Nailer had specialised in organised crime for a long time, hunting down some of the most violent gangs across the county. It was Nailer's specialisation in this field that had led him to find Rob back when he was a teenager. Had Nailer not stepped in and saved him, giving him an alternative, his life would, he was sure, be very different now. It was hard to overstate how grateful Rob felt towards Nailer, who went out of his way to help and support Rob in those early years and guide him towards a better life. It was unlikely he'd ever be able to pay him back, and his expertise with these gangs would be invaluable in their work for the EMSOU.

"Abel is another man you do not want to get on the wrong side of," Nailer continued.

"We have some photos of Abel, actually," Scarlett said and brought them up on her screen. Rob leaned in to get a better look and immediately recognised him.

"Shit," Rob cursed. "It's the same guy we saw last night, the one who picked up the girls we were questioning."

"Are you sure?" Scarlett asked. "I didn't get as good a look at him as you did."

"It's him," Rob insisted. "One hundred percent."

"So we know who they are," Nailer said. "What about addresses?"

"No listed address for Radek," Scarlett reported. "Looks like he moves around a lot from the reports we have on him. As for Abel… Oh, we have a bunch of addresses for him, including a very recent one."

"Excellent," Nailer complimented them. "So this is the man who'd been Pimping Penny, this Izabela you met, and it's the same man you met last night."

"That's him," Rob confirmed.

"Jerome's mum named him too," Nick said, walking over. "She said that Jerome mentioned him."

"So the boy who gaslighted Penny also knows Abel," Rob mused. "I'm willing to bet this Jerome was part of Abel's gang, probably still is."

"Of course he is," Scarlett added. "It all links together, and it looks like Abel is at the core of this, somewhere."

"He seems like a key part of it," Rob agreed. "But is he the killer? That's the more important thing."

"Not according to Izabela," Scarlett answered.

"But is she right?" Rob asked.

Scarlett shrugged. "If I knew that, I'd be a DCI by now."

"A DCI with a crystal ball," Rob said.

"Right then, looks like we have a couple more leads," Nailer said. "However, it's late, and we're having this town meeting soon. So, Ellen, Tucker, I want you two to check out Abel's most recent address. We need to find this guy as he could have some valuable info. Meanwhile, the rest of you will help prepare for this meeting. People will be arriving soon, and they'll have questions. My intention is to be as open and friendly as possible without compromising this investigation. We need the village on our side if we're going to see this through. It's no good fighting on two or more fronts."

"Yes, sir," Rob replied and looked over at Ellen and Tucker. "Good luck. You'd better get going."

36

In the heart of Forest Town on the northern side of Mansfield, Ellen paused at the start of the alleyway. She glanced each way along the main street they'd parked on. The road was lined on both sides with cars, leaving little room for passing vehicles. It was an odd road, Ellen decided. The main street was thin enough as it was, but with the parked vehicles, there was barely enough room for a single passing car, let alone two. God forbid you met someone driving the other way.

Branching off from the main road were thin alleyways every twenty metres or so. Between these were rows of terrace houses extending away from the main road, their front and back gardens facing the alleyways. From where Ellen was standing, she just saw the sides of the end terraces facing the road she was standing on. It was an odd set-up, but one designed to cram in cheap housing in the smallest space possible without resorting to flats or high rises. She wasn't sure she liked the look of it.

Peering down the alleyway closest, she saw a pathway hemmed in by fencing and walls surrounding each garden. Garden was perhaps a generous word for these postage-stamp-sized outdoor havens with barely enough room for a few chairs and maybe a small table. These yards or patios varied from well-maintained and neat to derelict and in desperate need of a makeover.

Partway along, two men were smoking, shooting suspicious looks their way.

Any woman who walked up here alone, day or night, probably wouldn't feel very safe. Tucker spotted the men as he reached the end of the alleyway and probably noticed Ellen's brief hesitation because he quickly took the lead.

"Come on," he muttered.

Ellen smiled. "Look at you, my knight in shining armour."

Tucker grunted and smiled, before waving to the houses. "Which one was it?"

"Number twenty-two," she answered, craning her neck to peer over the fencing. Their quarry was several houses in on the left and looked pretty much as she suspected it would. She could have picked it out with a casual glance had she thought about it. As they sauntered along the alleyway, the two men crushed their half-smoked cigarettes out under their boots and melted away into a house on the right.

Were they up to no good? Part of her wanted to follow them and take a look, as she often did when someone seemed in a hurry to get out of sight, but she resisted. That's not why she was here.

"Another shining example of home improvement from the community of druggies in Mansfield," Tucker commented while opening the garden gate, which threatened to fall off in his hand.

Ellen followed him along the short garden path, the long grass on either side brushing against her legs. She wondered what she might find in the undergrowth but knew better than to go looking without protective gear.

Tucker reached the front door and knocked as he touched it the whole door wobbled and swung open a few inches.

"Yo," someone inside called out. "Bruv, is that you?"

"Hey. I need to ask you something," Tucker called out, pushing the door wide.

"Come in, man, come in." Ellen followed Tucker into the front room of the house, to find what was probably meant to be a lounge in a sorry state. Graffiti had been daubed onto the walls, and there was crap everywhere. Everywhere she looked, there were food cartons and boxes, disposable fast-food drinks cups, rotting pizza and Chinese, but the drug paraphernalia dominated everything else. Burnt foil, spoons, crack and meth pipes, and needles as well as powders and residues.

Ellen stuffed her hands in her pockets and made a silent promise to herself not to touch anything.

"Who are you?" a guy slumped on the sofa asked.

He seemed a little confused. She spotted someone else collapsed on the floor, breathing but incapacitated.

"I'm Tucker. We're just passing through and wondered if you might know someone we're looking for.

"Oh yeah?"

"Yeah, if you don't mind answering some questions."

To their left, a figure stumbled into the doorway from another room and slumped against the frame. She surveyed the scene with half-asleep eyes before she said anything. "You the filth?"

"We're with the police," Ellen admitted. "We just have a few questions."

"Like what?"

"Do you know Abel Underwood?"

"Who?"

"I'll take that as a no, then, shall I?"

"Take it however you like. I don't give a shit," the woman answered before stumbling into the room and dropping into another seat.

"What about you?" Tucker asked the young man who'd invited them in. "Do you know Abel Underwood? We have this address listed as his."

"And?" the guy replied. "You can have it listed as my address too if you like. But no, I don't know him."

"You're sure?"

"Piss off, mate. He ain't here, is he?"

"Would you mind if we had a look around?" Tucker asked, changing his line of questioning. She'd have done the same given the state of these two. They were either high, drunk, or just generally messed up, making any statement they gave suspect at best, and useless at worst.

"Be my guest." The man waved at the house around him, urging them to go and leave him alone.

Tucker looked back at Ellen.

"You go. I'll stay here. PNC anyone you find, okay?"

"Noted," Tucker answered.

She turned back to the pair of crackheads as Tucker walked deeper into the house. "What are your names?"

What's that got to do with you?" the woman replied, cutting off whatever answer the guy was about to give.

"We're conducting a murder investigation, and unless you want to be a suspect, I can use your names to help eliminate you from our enquiries." She was being a little liberal with the truth, but she didn't care. She wanted their names.

"Alright, fine," the guy said. "My names Tyson Ellis."

"Thank you." Ellen turned to the woman. "And you?"

The woman gave her a long hard look as if weighing her up, wondering if she was telling the truth. "Angelina Good," she answered eventually.

As they talked, the unconscious guy woke up enough for her to get a name off him too.

Ellen noted their names, thanked them, and moved to the front door. Taking a step outside, she pulled out her phone and called into control. She asked them to run the names through the Police National Computer, and they came back with a laundry list of petty crimes between them, mainly drug possession and similar. These were just junkies, nothing more. Interestingly, they could all be linked to Abel through at least one associate, but these were not key members of Abel's crew and probably knew nothing of use.

Their links to Abel were hardly damning evidence, given they were drug users and Abel was a supplier. This was looking more like a dead end every moment.

Frustrated, Ellen hung up and turned back to the room as Tucker returned.

"Anything?" Ellen asked.

"No, fuck all," Tucker replied. "Just a couple more twats like these three, PNC was a dead end on them."

"These three, too," she replied, their voices low. "We're not getting anywhere here."

"Agreed," Tucker replied. "Come on, let's get the fuck out of here."

37

Standing at the back of the room with his arms crossed, Rob watched the steady influx of people into the village hall. They were being checked and their names taken as they entered, so they knew who was in attendance. Some of the earliest attendees to arrive were the press, and Rob was quick to spot Vincent Kane in there, prowling around the room like a shark, looking for his latest victim. Rob scowled at him, not bothering to hide his disgust.

Kane seemed to ignore him, though, and went about his business.

That was something, at least. Rob had expected the bottom feeder to approach him and try to get an interview or soundbite, so it was a pleasant surprise that he seemed to be giving Rob a wide berth.

Maybe he'd learnt his lesson? Or was that too much to hope for?

As more local residents and interested parties arrived, he spotted Father Aaron walking in and starting to make his rounds, talking to some of the press who approached him. He'd be one of the people up on the stage with DCI Nailer, leading the meeting later. Rob wondered how that would go down.

It wasn't long before Rob spotted another attendee due to be on that stage had entered the building.

Rob walked over, threading his way through the crowd to approach Emmett and Valerie Wilkinson. Valerie saw him approach and alerted Emmett, who turned and greeted him warmly.

"Detective Loxley, it's a pleasure to see you again."

"And you," Rob replied. "You seem well?"

He shrugged. "As well as can be expected, given the circumstances."

"That's good. I just wanted to check up on you and make sure you're both okay and coping with all this?"

"Coping, yes, I suppose," Emmett answered. "I can't say I'm very impressed with being moved into a hotel room," he shot his wife an inscrutable look, "but I'm sure we'll survive."

"It's not forever, darling," Valerie said, with a superior smile. "The police have a job to do."

"Obviously." Emmett sighed.

"Well, I think it's a disgrace." It was Janette Radcliff, who had appeared beside Emmett and Valerie with her husband, David. "It's sick that someone such as yourself, a District Councillor, a pillar of the local community, has been forced to live in a hotel room while your house is ransacked."

"We're just following procedure," Rob explained but didn't think for a moment that anything he said would assuage Janette's misgivings.

"Well, it shouldn't have happened in the first place, should it. It's just a mark of how far this town has fallen that people like Emmett and Valerie, people who really care about this community, are thrown to the dogs like this. Had this happened a few years ago, Reverend Mercer would have opened his doors to you because he was a true man of the cloth, not like that filthy imposter." She shot Father Aaron a look that Rob didn't care for.

"Now, now," David said to his wife. "We don't know the details of what Father Aaron can and cannot do."

"Well, you wouldn't want to go and live with someone like him, anyway, would you, Val?"

Valerie shrugged, glancing around at the others in the small group.

"Of course you wouldn't. It's not good to be seen with... them."

Feelings of utter disgust coursed through Rob's veins as he listened to the woman's bile-filled racist rant. But he wasn't here to cause trouble, and as long as she didn't kick off, she had as much right to be here as everyone else. Besides, her husband, David, was on the Neighbourhood Watch

Committee, and they might need their support. No need to go upsetting people who could prove useful.

"I mean, look, he's talking to that hairdresser, Colleen. Have you seen her salon?"

"I have," Valerie muttered. "That's not the kind of place I'd visit, admittedly."

"I know what you mean. I wouldn't trust someone like *her* with my hair." Janette turned to Rob. "Would you?"

Surprised by her question, Rob did a double take, his gaze tik-tocking between Janette and Colleen. "I'm not sure I'm in a position to comment."

"No, no, that's fine, silly me," Janette said. She leaned in then, coming closer to him. "How's the case going? Do you have a suspect yet?" Her eyes narrowed. "Are they here, in this room?" She glanced around suspiciously.

On more familiar ground, Rob found his reply came much easier. "I'm afraid I can't comment on the ongoing case."

"It was one of those filthy hookers, though, wasn't it? The victim, I mean. We've all heard about it by now." She pulled back a little, addressing the group. "I knew it would be. I said as much that first day, didn't I?" She sneered. "They deserve it if you ask me."

"Now, now, dear," David said to his wife, clearly aware of how offensive she was being.

Rob chose not to dignify her words with an answer.

Emmett stepped closer to Rob and turned him away from the conversation the two women were engaging in. "Sorry for their gossiping. I'm sure you don't want to listen to that."

"I wouldn't say that," Rob answered, thinking it was an interesting insight into their point of view on the town and its residents.

"Well, I know I wouldn't," Emmett replied and waved David to come closer. "You know David's on the Neighbourhood watch, right?"

"Yes, we've met," Rob replied, smiling at David. "Are you both okay with being on stage?"

"Fine, yes," Emmett replied. "We're fine."

"Looking forward to it," David added. "Will you be joining us up there?"

"No," Rob replied. "My boss, DCI Nailer will be leading the meeting today. He'll be up there, along with Father Aaron and Penny's father, Richard."

"Penny? As in the girl who was killed?"

"That's right," Rob replied. "He'll be here any moment. He confirmed last minute that they wanted to be here and to speak."

"I see," Emmett said and shifted his weight uncomfortably. He didn't seem pleased by the revelation, but there was little he could say without seeming insensitive. Besides, Rob could understand his discomfort, given he found their daughter's head in his bin. What on earth could he say to the girl's father? Emmett continued, "Are you sure that's a good idea? They've just lost their daughter."

"And they want to use this platform to appeal for witnesses to come forward. Richard's appeal could be a valuable tool and might help to persuade someone to give up their friend. I'm not about to deny them this."

"I see. I understand."

Did he? He didn't seem comfortable with the idea, but there could be a thousand reasons for that.

"Hey, look who's here," David said and pointed.

Rob followed his gesture and spotted Nigel Wild walking into the building with Caprice. He heard Emmett grumble beside him as Nigel scanned the room, his eyes coming briefly to rest on Emmett and himself. He made no sign that he'd recognised them, and looked away, going about his business.

"He's another one that should be arrested," David suggested. "Have you heard about him attacking Emmett?"

"I understand that there's an old rivalry," Rob answered, doing his best to remain neutral.

"I suppose that's one word for it," David said. "The man is a hooker-loving menace, and I wouldn't be seen dead in his bar."

Rob glanced at Emmett, who was keeping quiet. He still looked uncomfortable.

David spotted the look and glanced between them. "Emmett is just being coy because you're a police officer," he explained. "But expressing an opinion isn't a crime, Emmett. You didn't do anything. You didn't kill that girl. Nigel, however, well, we all know he's been seen with these girls before, don't we." Innuendo positively dripped from his words.

"We've had our differences, but the Detective is aware of this," Emmett explained.

"Then you have nothing to fear by talking about it," David replied. "You've told me how unsafe Nigel has made you feel on occasion and how you try to avoid the Clipstone shops in case you run into him." David turned to Rob. "Like I said, he's a menace."

As David spoke, Rob spotted Penny's parents, Richard and Hilary Lynn, walk into the hall. He needed to greet them and make sure they were okay. "As I said, I'm aware of the history between the two of them, Mr Radcliff. Thank you for elaborating on it."

"Of course, my pleasure," David replied.

"Now, if you'll excuse me, I need to make the rounds." Rob smiled, and with a quick nod of goodbye, he crossed the room, making a bee-line for the couple. They were standing just inside the entrance and seemed a little isolated amidst the sea of people, which wasn't a surprise given they weren't from the village. They might not know anyone here.

"Richard, Hilary, thank you for coming. We really appreciate it."

"That's okay," Richard answered, forcing a smile. It didn't last. "We needed to do this. We need to be here, for Penny's sake."

"We did," Hilary agreed.

"Well, it's very brave of you. You didn't have to come, but I'm very supportive of your desire to help. Please, come round here. We'll keep you out of the reach of the press as I'm sure you don't want to be answering their questions just yet."

"Thank you," they both said and followed Rob as he led them around and behind the dividers that separated the 'office' section from the 'meeting' section of the hall where the gathering was happening. As they stepped out of the scrum of bodies, Rob spotted Father Aaron talking with Nailer. They were close to where the stage had been set up.

Well, 'stage' was perhaps a generous word for what was a platform made from sturdy wooden boxes with a table and chairs on top.

"Sir," Rob said as they approached the DCI. "This is Richard and Hilary Lynn, the parents of Penny, the victim."

"Aaah," Nailer replied and offered his hand. "Thank you so much for offering to come tonight. We really appreciate it. This can't have been an easy choice for you."

"No, it wasn't," Richard answered. "But, we felt it was necessary."

Father Aaron offered his hand and introduced himself. "Thank you for coming. If there's anything I can do for you, you only need ask. Clipstone is a small but tight and caring community, and you have our deepest condolences."

"Thank you, Father," Hilary answered.

"Yes, thank you," Richard added. "That means a lot."

"How have you been holding up?" Rob asked.

"It's... a nightmare," Richard answered. Rob could feel the sadness pouring out of him and wished he could just snap his fingers and make it all okay again. No one should have to lose a child, no matter how estranged from them they were. "We just need to get through tonight and hope that our words here jog someone's memory or persuade someone to come forward."

"That's all any of us can hope for," Rob agreed, as he sensed a presence behind him. Hearing footsteps and hushed voices, Rob turned to see as Guy walked up with Emmett and David following. Rob watched as introductions were made, following which Emmett and David offered their condolences to Richard and Hilary. Emmett looked particularly uncomfortable, but he got through it just fine before Nailer started to talk them through the order for the evening, and how he wanted things to go.

"Sir?" Someone touched Rob's shoulder. He turned to see Ellen.

"Yes?"

"Have you got a moment?"

She wanted to talk out of earshot of the civilians, so Rob excused himself and walked a few metres away with the DC, to a gap in the dividers. "Sorry to interrupt, sir, but I thought you'd be interested in this."

"That's okay. What have you got for me?"

"If you look over there, straight ahead. Can you see the woman in the red jacket? She's not really talking to anyone. Do you see her? She's just taken a seat."

"I see her," Rob confirmed. The woman was well dressed and looked to be in her late thirties or early forties maybe. She was alone, but it didn't seem to bother her. She didn't look nervous or ill at ease and had walked with confidence through the room before sitting in a more or less empty row. "Who is she?"

"That is Susan. We believe she runs the Phil McCracken Massage Parlour. Tucker and I met her earlier when we visited the address that Guy discovered.

"Is that right?" Rob said. "So, what's she doing here?"

"She's a local, so it might be that she's just being a good resident and taking an interest," Ellen suggested.

"Or," Rob took over, "Penny was someone she knew or was aware of, and the details of this case are of interest to her."

Ellen shrugged. "Yeah, sure. That works too."

"Hmm, I might just go and introduce myself."

"Go for it," Ellen urged him. "A word of warning, though. She's a tough cookie."

"Noted." Rob stepped out from behind the barrier and started to make his way towards Susan when another woman, a short, slim woman with auburn hair, stepped into his path.

"Thank you for holding this meeting, Detective," she said with an easy smile. "I was just wondering what the order of play was?"

"Well," Rob said, glancing past her at Susan before looking back at the attractive woman before him. "We'll say a few words, then the vicar will speak briefly, followed by the victim's father and the District Councillor."

"He was the one who found the remains, wasn't he?"

"He was," Rob admitted but refused to say more, wondering who the lady was. She seemed well informed. "May I ask your name? You seem to know who I am."

"I've done my research, Detective Loxley," she replied with a stunning smile before offering her hand. "I'm Mary Day, from the Nottingham Echo."

Rob found himself unexpectedly distracted by her. He smiled and, for a moment, forgot that she'd offered him her hand. There was a brief awkward silence before he noticed her hand and shook it. "Oh, so you're a reporter?" Rob felt his hackles rise as his dislike for certain aspects of the press conflicted with his initial reaction to her.

He shook it off and forced himself to focus on the job at hand. He couldn't afford to get distracted by a pretty lady while in the midst of a case.

"I am. And yes, I'm aware that my profession might sour your opinion of me, or do you not subscribe to that stereotype?" She regarded him with narrowed eyes.

He grinned and then snorted. "Aaah, well, you've got me there. Although, honestly, my dislike is more towards certain individuals within the press rather than the profession as a whole."

She offered him an understanding smile. "Then, hopefully, I can show you that we're not all vicious hacks who'll do anything for a story. Some of us actually take our job and our reputation seriously."

"I look forward to being impressed." He wasn't about to hold his breath, however. He'd been disappointed by reporters before.

"Maybe we could talk over a drink, sometime?" she asked. "I'm always looking for friendly officers."

"Sources, you mean?"

She held both hands up in surrender. "That is one word for such friends."

Rob chewed on the idea for a moment. "Let me think about it. I have my own reputation to think of as well, you know."

"Of course you do. No one wants to be known as a grass."

"Way to sell it to me!"

She smirked and then shrugged. "I have a way with words."

"Indeed," Rob agreed with an amused smile. "Now, if you'll excuse me, I have people I need to speak to."

"Of course, Detective Inspector," she answered and stepped away with a smile.

Rob watched her go, finding himself drawn to her despite himself and his better judgement. Tearing his eyes away, Rob crossed the rest of the way to the suspected brothel owner and walked along the row of seats. The woman looked up as he approached.

"Is this seat taken?"

"Will it make a difference if I say it is?" She looked away as she answered him, apparently disinterested.

"Not really," he answered, apparently to himself. "Susan, isn't it?"

She turned back to him, frowning and held his gaze for a long moment before glancing away and then back. "Detective?"

"Surname?" Rob stood his ground. He wanted to know who he was dealing with.

She twisted her lips, screwing up her features as she considered his request. "Rennoll," she said eventually, sitting back.

"Yes, I'm Detective Loxley," Rob answered her earlier question. "And thank you."

She sighed, seemingly resigning herself to the conversation, or maybe steeling herself for the question she voiced next as she fixed him with an intense look. "I saw a couple of your team earlier. They seemed to think I was in the prostitution game."

"I take it you're saying you're not, right?"

"Of course not. I'm a massage therapist. I offer spa treatments, that's all. And I don't appreciate you dragging my name through the mud."

"So you don't run the Phil McCracken Massage Parlour, then?"

"The what?" She sounded convincingly incredulous. "No, I do not. And I don't know anything about what's going on, either. And before you move on to the next obvious question, let me answer it for you and save you the hassle. I'm a local resident, and I'm concerned about this turn of events, so that's why I'm here. Okay?"

"I understand," Rob replied. "You know nothing, got it."

She nodded in agreement, but Rob caught a note of suspicion in her eyes as their gazes briefly met. "I'm glad we're in agreement. Now, if you and your team would just leave me alone, I'd be eternally grateful."

Recognising the hint, Rob got to his feet. "My apologies. Have a good meeting." With that, he walked away, leaving Susan where she was sitting.

"Anything?" Ellen asked as he returned to where she was standing at the dividers.

He shook his head. "No, nothing. She stonewalled me."

"Yeah, she's pretty good at that. We can run her through the PNC, though."

"We're going to need proof if we want to get anything out of her."

"Do you think she might know something useful?" Ellen asked.

"I've got no idea. Probably not, but right now, I'll take anything that moves this case forward."

"Yeah, I know what you mean."

"If everybody could just take their seats, please?"

Rob turned to see DCI Nailer on the stand, calling the room to order. His deep voice filled the room and got everyone's attention, so it wasn't long before they'd settled into their places, cameras were recording, and reporters stood ready.

Rob scanned the room, picking out the faces he recognised while they listened to the proceedings.

On the stage, Father Aaron led Richard out and guided him to a chair. The pair sat to one side of Nailer, while Emmett and David took their seats on the other, their footsteps and chair scuffs loud in the now silent hall.

"Thank you all for coming today. We really appreciate it," Nailer began. "We understand this has been a very difficult time for all of you in Clipstone, and we wanted to have this meeting to keep you updated and aware of the investigation and its progress."

Already, hands had been raised by people keen to ask questions, and they didn't go unnoticed by the DCI.

"Please, there will be time for questions at the end, but for now, we all have a few things to say. So let's bring you all up to speed. Firstly, I have been joined by Father Kenyon Aaron of the local Parish Church, District Councillor Emmett Wilkinson, and Chair of the local Neighbourhood Watch organisation, David Radcliff. We're also humbled to welcome Richard Lynn, the father of the murdered Penny Lynn, who wishes to say a few words. But, before all that, it falls to me to update you on the investigation and the situation as it stands. As many of you already know, on the morning of the fifteenth, partial remains of Penny Lynn, age sixteen, were discovered in a wheelie bin on Edmonton

Road. Later that same day, the rest of the victim's remains were discovered on the side road that leads into the Clipstone Colliery. We have since identified these remains as those of Penny Lynn. We believe she was killed between eight and ten PM close to the Headstocks, and then part of her was transported to Edmonton Road before being deposited in the bin. We're obviously looking for anyone who might have seen something that night, that's the evening of the fifteenth, no matter how small or insignificant you think it might be. Someone must have seen something. Penny, we believe, had been groomed by a criminal gang, lured away from her family and those who loved her, before being forced out onto the streets to work as a prostitute."

Rob watched the stunned faces of the people in the room as they listened to the gruesome details of the case and took a long hard look at the TV displaying Penny's face to the side of the stage. She smiled out from the screen, the photo having been taken in happier times. Her gentle smile and youth stood in sharp contrast to the horrors described by DCI Nailer.

"It's possible there are people in here or watching on the news who might have associated with Penny either as a friend or through her time on the streets. If you are one of these people, we urge you to please come forward and talk to us so that we might eliminate you from the investigation. You might know vital clues or information that could help us find this vicious killer of an innocent young woman, and you might just be saving others from a similar fate."

"She wasn't innocent," someone called out.

Rob grimaced at the insensitive words, his eyes flicking to Richard Lynn to catch his reaction. Richard closed his eyes and hung his head but otherwise said nothing.

"Please, that's enough," DCI Nailer called out. "We won't stand for any more comments of that ilk. Penny was a victim of a coordinated criminal effort to recruit young girls against their better judgement in order for these gangs to force them into a kind of modern slavery they make money from. I don't believe for a moment that Penny wanted to be a sex worker. This wasn't a choice for her. The methods these gangs use are barbaric, and I can only imagine what she must have gone through and how scared she must have been before her brutal murder."

As Rob watched, a couple of officers moved around the room, found the heckler—who Rob didn't recognise—and escorted them out.

"As I was saying," DCI Nailer continued, "if you know anything, anything at all, we want to speak with you, no matter how irrelevant you think it might be. Okay, Now I'll hand over to Father Aaron, who wants to say a few words."

"Thank you, Chief Inspector," Aaron said, getting to his feet and smoothing down his jacket. "One bad-taste comment aside, I think I know this community well enough by now. I know I've not been here long, and I know some consider me an outsider, and that's fair enough. However, I'm not one to bear a grudge, and I hope that, in time, I can show you who I am and what I hope to offer this magnificent village. But right now, we have a family grieving over the loss of their daughter. She was taken from them in the most violent and horrific way. This is a loss that many of us find unimaginable, but I'm asking for you to take a moment and consider how the parents and sister of Penny are feeling today. Many of you have children of your own, so I'm going to ask you to try and put yourselves in their place and imagine losing one of your own, and then think about what you would do to find justice for them. This family needs your help. They need support, they need love, and they need justice. I know this village and this community is filled with good, loving, caring people, and I know that during this time of crisis, when one of our own is suffering so much, I know you will all come together, put your differences aside, and do what you can for them. Thank you."

Father Aaron sat back down, leaving the room stunned into silence. Rob spotted more than one person wiping away tears following his speech while DCI Nailer got to his feet briefly once more.

"Thank you, Father Aaron. I'm sure everyone here shares your opinion. I know I certainly do. Okay, I will now hand you over to Penny's father, Richard Lynn, to say a few words."

Nailer retook his seat and waited while Richard, sitting between him and Father Aaron, cleared his throat while holding a sheet of paper with trembling hands.

"Thank you, Detective," he began. "Penny was our beautiful daughter. She was kind, funny, intelligent, with an infectious laugh that I can still hear in my head today. She perhaps wasn't perfect, but who amongst us is? Like many teenagers, she had her struggles, like the stresses of life and friendships, but whatever issues she had, she didn't deserve this. We loved her with all our hearts, and she's left a gaping void that will never be filled." He sniffed and fought back tears. "Penny was a bright, clever, bubbly young woman with her whole life ahead of her, and I have little doubt that she would have gone far in life. She loved netball, romantic comedies, and crafting handmade jewellery that she'd give to her friends. She had so much to offer this world, and the world is poorer for her loss. So I beg you, if you know anything, if you saw her, if you knew who she was, or you were a friend of hers, please, come forward, contact the Nottinghamshire Police, in confidence if you need to, and help us find her killer. Thank you."

He placed the paper on the table before him, closed his eyes, and let tears fall down his cheeks. Father Aaron and DCI Nailer offered him some hushed words of comfort. The silence in the room was palpable. Apart from the occasional sniff or rustle of tissues, you could hear a pin drop.

Moments later, Nailer introduced Councillor Emmett Wilkinson.

"Thank you, Chief Inspector," Emmett started. "My deepest condolences to you and your family, Mr Lynn. I can only imagine what you must be going through." He paused for a moment before continuing. "I don't have much to add to what's already been said other than to ask this wonderful community that I care so deeply for, to come together—"

"You don't care about this community!"

Rob turned to see Nigel Wild, standing beside a seated and flustered-looking Caprice, shouting at Emmett.

"You've never cared for this community," Nigel yelled. "All you care about is lining your pockets. That's all you've ever cared about."

"Mr Wild..." Emmett called out, trying to interrupt.

"No, you listen to me," he continued shouting Emmett down as Rob started to cross the room, trying to get to him. "You pander to big business, selling your soul and this town to the highest bidder, turning Clipstone into a soulless husk of what it once was."

"Mr Wild, That's an unfair characterisation—"

Janette jumped to her feet. "Shut up, Nigel," she yelled in defence of Emmett.

"I will not be silenced," Nigel shouted. "You, and your harpy wife, you've destroyed this town, gutted it, and now you say you love it? That's horse shit!"

Other officers were approaching Nigel, trying to get to him. But he was in the middle of a row, and people were in the way.

"And now, you're trying to blame all this on me," Nigel continued. "You're trying to frame me as the killer when I'm the only one in this bloody room that actually cares about these poor girls. The rest of you would throw them to the dogs, especially you, Janette."

Taking the last few steps past the final person in his way, Rob stepped in front of Nigel, just as Scarlett got there with a couple of uniformed officers in tow.

"That's enough," Rob snapped, getting in his face. "You're done."

"I've not even started," he growled, lost in his anger and fury.

"You either turn around and walk out with me right now, or I drag you out. Your choice."

"I ain't movin'."

"So be it." Grabbing his arm and twisting it, Rob turned Nigel around and manhandled him out of the hall with the help of the other officers. Rob passed Janette and Valerie as they guided Nigel out of the building. Janette's face was filled with rage, and for a moment, she looked like she was about to spit on him. Beside her, Valerie buried her head in her hand, shaking it from side to side in disgust.

Bundling him out through the door, into the courtyard out front, Rob turned him left, away from the people standing out there, over to one side, where he finally let Nigel go.

Nigel straightened to his full height, flustered and shaking his arm where Rob had twisted it. "Jesus, that hurt."

"That's the point," Rob said. "This was not the place to kick off, Nigel. What the hell were you thinking?"

"He's a corrupt piece of shit. That's what I was thinking," Nigel answered. "He goes on and on about caring for this community, but he doesn't care about it at all. Not the in the way he makes out. The only way he cares about Clipstone is when he can get it to line his pockets. That's all he and that bitch of a wife of his care for. Money. Nothing else. You know she works for the Coal Board, right? She was one of the people involved in helping to sell the Headstocks, and now they're going to be turned into a bloody leisure facility. It's sacrilege. That's our history, that is, and they want to turn it into some kind of cheap attraction? It's sick."

If he ever needed a reminder that Nigel was a former miner and that his issues with Emmett went right back to the miner's strikes in the eighties, this was about as big a reminder as he'd ever get.

Rob sighed. "Well, you can't go back in there, so I recommend that you head back to your club and get a drink."

In the silence that followed, Rob heard the sudden distant rapid-fire snaps of gunfire echo over the village.

He frowned and turned to Scarlett. She'd heard it too and looked up at him with wide eyes.

"Is that..." she asked.

"Gunshots," Rob confirmed as his stomach fell through the floor.

Scarlett gulped. "Shit."

38

"Christ, I thought we'd never get out of there," Nick exclaimed as they drove away from the village hall, making for this new crime scene. All around them, the local residents were walking back home, leaving the village hall behind. Some seemed scared or panicked and were half-jogging along the pavement. The announcement that the meeting was over and they needed to head home was sudden, and although Rob and the others tried to keep the news of the gunshots within the ranks of the police, it soon spread. Within moments Rob could hear people talking about it, embellished to the point of ridiculousness. But it did seem to get the attendees to leave the hall that bit quicker and head home.

It still took what felt like ages, though, before Rob, Scarlett, and Nick were in their car and driving towards this new crime scene. Police and emergency services were already on the scene, according to the chatter on the police bands.

"Do you think it'll do any good, that meeting?" Scarlett asked.

"It'll be all over the evening news, especially with these gunshots going off," Rob replied.

"Yeah, 'Breaking news, gunshots interrupt meeting at a Mansfield Village Hall'. It'll get eyes on this, that's for sure," Nick said.

"Attention is good," Rob replied. "We need witnesses, and we need them soon. However, it'll also mean more press, which is less good." His mind drifted back to his brief chat with the reporter Mary Day in the village hall. Was his general attitude towards the press becoming more nuanced? Mary seemed nice, so maybe they weren't all bad... Maybe.

"You love them, really," Scarlett teased.

"If you say so."

"Well, here's hoping something good comes from it. You never know," she added. "Are you okay, Rob?"

"Yeah, I'm fine. I'm just wondering what we're going to find and who the hell's shooting guns around here because that was not a farmer's shotgun."

"You recognised the sound?" Scarlett asked.

"I've had some experience of firearms... once upon a time," he answered, thinking back to his childhood, before he'd left his family for good. Guns had been around during those years, and he'd even shot a few of them, recreationally. If he had to guess, the shots he'd heard in Clipstone were from a handgun. He also had a sinking feeling he knew who was behind this, or at least which group or faction was behind it, anyway. He just hoped he was wrong.

They found the cordoned-off area on the main Mansfield Road, meaning this was the second diversion in as many days that had been put into place on this street, disrupting traffic ever further. He could imagine the local residents were cursing them, wondering what they were doing to help protect the locals from whatever was going on.

They were soon parked and could see the small crowd of people standing around outside the outer cordon, watching proceedings from a respectful distance.

As they approached, Rob spotted Vincent Kane and rolled his eyes. How do they move from place to place so quick, he wondered. Rob gave him a wide berth but couldn't resist a couple of sideways glances.

On his second sneaky look, he saw Mary Day over there too, and she'd seen him approaching the cordon. She smiled and winked.

He looked away. He needed to concentrate. After signing in, Rob was soon greeted by Sergeant Jolly, who'd spotted them coming.

"We've got three dead," she said, wasting no time on greetings. They'd been working together for several days by now, after all. "Two female and one male. They look like more prostitutes and a punter who got caught in the crossfire."

"Witnesses?" Rob asked.

"Several," Megan answered as they approached the pair of tents that had been erected. Walking up, he stopped where he could see into both as the forensics people worked.

The first tent was beside a car, and on the ground inside were the man and one of the women, motionless and covered with blood. Inside the other tent was the second prostitute, splayed out in an ungainly manner with blood pooling around her.

"Shit," Rob whispered, feeling sure he knew where this was going.

"The general consensus by the witnesses is that these girls were working the street, here, with one of them talking to this guy," Megan pointed to the dead man, "when a car pulled up, and a hooded man rushed out with a gun. He shot them, firing indiscriminately, before getting back into his car and driving off."

"This isn't the same killer, is it?" Scarlett asked.

"I'd be shocked if this guy killed Penny," Rob replied. "No, this is different, completely different. This stinks of a gangland hit." Rob turned back to Megan. "Has anyone offered any additional details on the girls?"

"Like what?"

"Did they know who they were? Have they spoken to them before? Are they British or do they speak with an accent? Did they see their pimp?"

"Aaah, I see where you're going with this. They weren't being complimentary, but someone did refer to the women as 'them Polish hookers'."

"It's what I thought. This is Gangland, and I'm betting it was one of Abel's crew, or Abel himself, that did this."

"Oh," Scarlett exclaimed. "Yeah. Izabela. She's run off, so maybe he thinks the Polish gang kidnapped her or killed her as retribution."

"And this was Abel's way of paying them back," Nick added.

"Has to be," Rob agreed. "This is escalating."

"Radek and his crew won't take this lightly, either," Nick ventured. "They'll want revenge."

"They will." Rob agreed. "This will get worse before it gets better."

39

Following Valerie into the hotel room, Emmett slammed the door shut in a fit of rage. It caused an almighty bang, making Valerie jump.

"Gosh," she squeaked.

"Bastard!" Emmett barked, his mind fixed on Nigel and their exchange at the village hall. "That bloody bastard. Why does he have to turn up and ruin everything?"

Valerie shrugged. "He was entitled to be there."

"So, the fuck what!"

"Don't swear, Emmett."

"Oh, shut up. Don't tell me what to do," he grumbled, lost in his emotions as he thought back. He dreaded to think how it would look on the news and what the knock-on effect would be. He knew the other council members would want to have their say on things, and it might be that the Executive Mayor would take issue with him still being a sitting councillor. He hoped that wouldn't be the case, but he couldn't be sure. It wasn't as if this was an isolated event, after all. Was he becoming a liability?

Angry thoughts ran through his head as his hyperactive mind jumped from one idea to another. He'd been dealing with his idiot for years, insulting him in the street, causing a scene, and occasionally getting physical, but none of those things had been as high profile as this. There had never been news cameras filming or photographing them before. Nigel's little rant would be all over the morning news with pundits talking about it and his career, and there was no way that publicity like that would go unnoticed by the District Council.

Emmett paced up and down the room with his fists clenched, working it through in his head, trying to make sense of it and how he would deal with it, but it felt like a lost cause. What the fallout from this would be, was anyone's guess.

And how dare Nigel accuse him of not caring for this community! He wasn't the one being friendly to whores, after all. He was the one working for the council, trying to make things better for the local residents. He was the one securing investment into infrastructure and redevelopment. He had dedicated his life to serving the community and wasn't hiding in a pub making out he was some kind of hero for those without a voice.

No, if anyone was doing more for this community, it was him, not Nigel-fucking-Wild.

"I thought you handled it well," Valerie said in a vain effort to calm him. "You'll be fine, you'll see."

She reached out for him, but he pulled away. He didn't want her near him, and the idea of her touching him actually filled him with disgust. She didn't do anything for him anymore and hadn't for a while now.

Staying with her in this room these past few days had been torture. He couldn't get away from her. There was no space.

"Emmett, don't be like that."

"Like what? I'm pissed off. Leave me alone."

"We need to talk about this. We can't leave it," Valerie replied. "He can't be allowed to get away with this. Can't you do anything?"

"Do anything?" he asked, incredulously. "Like what? What are you suggesting?"

"Can you revoke his licence, so he can't sell alcohol anymore?"

Emmett gave Valerie a disdainful look as if she was a particularly dense child. "What the hell are you talking about. No, I can't do that. There are processes in place for these things. Don't be an idiot."

"I'm not an idiot," she snapped.

"Could have fooled me."

"You don't mean that. You're stressed and need to calm down. You'll see this in a new light in the morning. I know you will. We can spin this easily enough and make sure everyone's on your side. I can make a few phone calls and call in a few favours. You'll breeze through this. You know I'm right."

"Stop trying to control me," Emmett yelled, frustrated by her apparent need to manipulate him all the time. She was always trying to mould and shape his life into something she could approve of. It was maddening.

"I'm not controlling you. I'm helping you. That's what partners do for each other. We help."

"Well, you're not helping," he snapped, angry.

"And you're not seeing straight." She stood up and walked closer. "You're acting like a child, Emmett. You're an adult with responsibilities now."

"Stop patronising me," he demanded, letting his pent-up anger and frustration get the better of him. He rounded on her and, for a brief moment, wanted to grab Valerie by the neck and throttle her. Anything to get her to shut up or shake some sense into her. He took an angry step towards her and was about to raise his hands when he caught himself. A flash of fear in her eyes brought him to a screeching halt.

He stared at her for a long moment, shaking with fury, before turning on his heel and striding to the door. "I'm going out," he hissed through gritted teeth and stormed out of the room.

40

"Looks like we're not getting home anytime soon," Scarlett said as they walked back into the village hall and made their way towards the back room.

"Not with this latest killing," Rob agreed, thinking about all the paperwork and coordination that went along with this new crime scene, as well as continuing to guide the current investigation into Penny Lynn's death. "That's okay," he added. "Sleep's overrated, anyway."

"Yeah, who needs it," Scarlett replied.

"Well, I'd love some if you're offering," Nick added.

Rob laughed. "Yeah, fat chance."

"Looks like it's time for a coffee," Scarlett suggested.

"Damn right, that sounds good," Nick replied, full of enthusiasm. "The stronger, the better."

"Rob? You want one?"

Rob spotted Nailer nearby and knew he'd want an update. "Later," he replied to Scarlett. "I'm gonna update Nailer on what we found. I'll join you in a bit. I'll get my own drink. Don't worry about me."

"I won't," Scarlett replied with a sweet smile before she smirked and walked off with Nick. Rob approached Nailer, who broke off from his conversation with another officer and greeted Rob.

"You're back," Nailer remarked. "How'd it go?"

"Fine. The situation's under control, but things are getting worse. We've got two more dead prostitutes and a man who we think was talking to them. They were shot by a lone gunman, just mowen down in the middle of the street."

"This is nothing like the first murder, then," Nailer said. "Sounds like a gang hit."

"That was my conclusion too, guv. If I had to guess, based on what some eyewitnesses said, I think this is either Abel or his crew taking revenge on Radek and his gang. Abel probably thinks that Radek kidnapped or killed Izabela and took his revenge, when in reality, she ran away."

"Radek takes two of his girls, Penny and Izabela, so he takes two of Radek's girls."

"Something like that."

"Do you think Penny's murder was a gang thing, too?" Nailer enquired.

"Right now, no. I can't see it. Penny's death was different. It feels more like a crime of passion, not a dispassionate gang hit." Rob knew he could be wrong, of course, but his gut was telling him he wasn't. It just didn't feel like that. "No, I think Abel's got the wrong end of the stick, and rather than wait to find out the truth, he's taken action so as not to look weak."

"Hmm. Makes sense. But let's not discount the idea that Penny's killer is in one of these gangs. We need to take a holistic approach to this and see where the clues lead us."

"I agree. I have my opinions, of course, but I'll investigate every angle."

Nailer nodded. "I know you will. How you holding up, by the way?"

"Yeah, I'm fine," Rob replied with a smile. "Tired, but that's nothing unusual."

"Don't I know it," Nailer agreed.

"I might have five minutes alone outside in a moment to get my head in order."

"Alright, do what you can tonight, but try to get some kip later, okay? Even if it's on a chair or the floor."

"Will do, guv."

"Alright, on you go, then."

With a smile and a nod, Nailer turned and walked away, leaving Rob with his thoughts. With everything that had been going on, he felt a little overwhelmed and needed a moment to himself before he carried on.

Making his way outside into the cool night air, Rob pulled his coat tighter around his neck and walked around the building into the side passage between the front and rear car parks, where he leaned against the wall and looked up.

Shadowy clouds scudded across the heavens, and behind them, the velvet black night sky twinkled with a smattering of stars blinking in the darkness. For a moment, he wondered what might be out there in the depths of deep space. Were there other life forms on distant planets, and were they looking back at him, right at this moment, contemplating similar big thoughts.

Did his job really matter in the grand scheme of things? Was what he did worthwhile? Probably not on the cosmic scale, of course. The sun didn't care who lived and died and who did what. It just burnt merrily away, waiting for the day when it would expand and consume the earth and everything on it.

But what he did wasn't for the moon or the stars, he worked for the people he lived with, the good citizens of Nottingham and beyond, and they needed him to do his job because what he did mattered to them. He could bring comfort and justice to those who needed it.

Rob sighed and turned away from the stars, and fixed his gaze on the worn concrete he was standing on, bringing his mind crashing back down to the cold reality of earth and what he needed to do. These families were counting on him and his team to find the killer responsible for these horrific crimes, and he had no desire to let them down at all. He felt the weight of these responsibilities more or less most of the time, especially when he stopped to think about the damage this killer had done to Penny's poor family. She might have run away from her parents, but they still loved her, no matter what, and now their precious daughter was gone forever. Having never had children, he couldn't say for sure that he knew how they felt, but he'd lost friends over the years, and then there was the disappearance of his mother when he was seventeen.

She might very well still be alive out there, somewhere, but it did often feel like a death, given the utter lack of contact since. He'd mourned her in a manner of speaking, and he often drew on that sadness to put himself in the position of these families who had lost so much to these brutal criminals.

Closing his eyes, Rob pushed those deep thoughts away and tried to clear his head. It might be late, and he was certainly tired, but he needed to focus and consider the information he had. Was there a clue in there that would lead him to the killer, and end all this?

"Penny for your thoughts?" someone asked.

Rob looked up to see the reporter, Mary Day, stepping around the corner with a curious look on her face. She smiled as they locked eyes.

"Oh, hi," Rob said.

"Getting some fresh air?"

"Yeah, something like that. It can get a little much, sometimes. I just needed five minutes."

"Understandable, given what you have to deal with every day."

"You must see some crap, too," he suggested.

She smirked as she walked closer before putting her back to the wall, mirroring his pose. "Yeah. Sure I do. We deal with the same people, we just have different roles and come at things with a different agenda."

"I guess so." He sighed.

"I was a nosey kid when I was younger," she said. "Always wanted to know what was going on, who was doing what, you know. I suppose I should have guessed I'd end up as a reporter. It makes sense, really, when you think about it." She smiled to herself. "I started early, writing articles for the school bulletin and magazine, interviewing students and teachers. I loved it, and as soon as I knew what a reporter was, I knew that was what I wanted to do. I just knew it. From that point on, I knew where my life would take me."

"So this is a passion then, a calling?" Rob suggested.

"I suppose so. I love it, too." She sighed contentedly. "What about you?"

"Me?"

"Yeah, you. Did you always want to be a detective?"

Ron smirked, amused that she hadn't heard any rumours about him. "No, actually. I didn't. It happened later in life. I was on a very different path before my boss, John Nailer, found me and helped me. I suppose I saw another side to the police, and he encouraged me to join up."

"Aaah, okay. And do you like it?"

"I love it, yeah. It's a very... satisfying job. I get to help people and bring closure to their problems. It's good."

"That's good, then. If you enjoy what you're doing, then you're on the right path. Life's too short to do anything else."

"Absolutely," Rob agreed, as all the lives he'd seen taken from people over the course of his life and career flashed before him. Life was way too short for regrets. He looked at her and smiled. He liked her point of view. "Sorry if I was a little rude when you first spoke to me. I've had some issues with... certain reporters in my time."

"Any in particular?"

"Yeah, but I'll keep that to myself if you don't mind."

"Of course not, although my professional curiosity is certainly piqued." She grinned, a cheeky twinkle in her eye.

"Feel free to do your research. It's not as if I can stop you, after all."

"I might just do that," she answered. "But, this is my job. I have to ask questions, sometimes tough questions, questions you might not like. That's just who I am and what I do."

"I know that, and I'm all for freedom of the press and free speech, just to be clear. I'm not looking to censor you or any reporter."

"Glad to hear it," she replied approvingly. "We're here to speak truth to power and tell the world what's going on, that's all. And in regard to that being my job... It looks like this latest incident, these three killings, they look very different from Penny's murder."

Rob grinned. "You noticed?"

"I take my job seriously, Mr Loxley," she stated, her tone firm. "It looks more like a gang killing than a crime of passion."

Rob nodded, feeling the shutters come down and his defences go up. He couldn't talk too openly, no matter how friendly or attractive the reporter might be.

She sighed. "Look, I'm not trying to be a problem. I'm just asking questions."

"I know," he confirmed. "But, there's a limit to what I can say. Even if I did totally trust you, I could not reveal the full details of this investigation. You know that."

She went to answer him, but he got in first.

"I know there are exceptions to that rule. I know your lot offer bribes and get more information than you should strictly have, but I won't be doing that."

"So, you're a boy scout," she suggested.

Rob shrugged. "My first responsibility is to the case and the families of the victim, always, not the press."

"I understand, but to be clear, I only want to help. I want to report the truth, not the sensationalist crap that some put out. The truth is often shocking enough, anyway."

"You're not wrong."

"So, what are you happy to tell me?"

"Right now? I don't know. I'll have a think." He pushed himself off the wall. "Sorry."

"That's okay," she replied with a conciliatory smile. "Just remember me when you're ready to talk to the world, okay?"

"I will. Thanks for the chat, but I've got a mountain of paperwork that won't do itself, so..."

"Of course, have a good night."

"I'll try," Rob replied with a final smile.

41

Jerome pulled on the joint, sucking in a long deep breath, taking the smoke down into his lungs to get the full hit from the ganja in the roll-up. The smoke coiled inside his lungs, infusing his bloodstream with the drug and sending his mind to a far more relaxed and pleasant place as his consciousness soared into the stratosphere.

He relaxed into the seat and closed his eyes, enjoying the moment.

When he opened them again, he had no idea how long had passed, but the girl sitting on the arm of his comfy chair had taken his joint and was enjoying a long pull on it herself, savouring the effect. He ran his hand up her bare thigh, enjoying the feel of her soft skin.

Around him, his mates were partaking in similar delights. Several were smoking joints, filling the room with the familiar smell of burning marijuana resin that was a dead giveaway to anyone who knew the smell of it. A couple of the guys had taken some hits of cocaine, too, the remnants of the lines of white powder still visible on the coffee table before them. It was a mix of young men, some of them teenagers, and similar-aged girls. Most of the young women came from Abel's stable of hookers and were here to entertain them in what was a celebration. A couple of the guys were indulging in this more deeply than others, with one having a full-on blow job and another with his hand up the girl's skirt and hers down his sweats. No one cared. Jerome would be sure to bang the girl sitting beside him, smoking his joint, soon enough, but for now, most of them were listening to Abel as he bragged about the night's events and the revenge he'd taken.

"You should have seen it, man," Abel remarked. "It was easy. I just rolled on over to Radek's girls, got out, and 'pap, pap, pap', blew them bitches away. It was easy, dog. Easy."

"Yeah, man," one of the others added, his tone full of enthusiasm. "Fuck the Poles."

"Damn right, bruv. Fuck 'em. They kill my girls and kidnap my whores? I will not take that lying down. This shit demands revenge." He was still holding the gun in his hand and waved it about carelessly as he spoke, making Jerome feel a little nervous. "No one fucks with Abel and gets away with it."

"Hell no, dog," another added.

Abel jumped up, pointed his gun at the window directly behind Jerome, and pretended to shoot through it into the street beyond.

"Pap, pap, mother fuckers! Yeah, fuck you, bitches." Abel held the gun sideways and looked damn fucking cool to Jerome's eyes. He had no idea where Abel got the gun, but he hoped to shoot one himself someday. He knew it was a way to earn respect and move up on the street. One day. One day he'd have his own piece and make these idiots dance to his tune.

Abel laughed and dropped back down into his seat. "It's so fuckin' easy, man. So easy. And I'll tell you what, if that fucker tries anything ever again, I'm gonna put one right between his eyes. He won't know what hit him."

A cascade of rapid-fire bangs sounded in the street outside. The window behind Jerome exploded into the room in a shower of twinkling, razor-sharp glass. People shouted and screamed. The girl beside him jerked as blood exploded from her shoulder and then her face as two bullets ripped through her.

Jerome watched in horror as the far walls were peppered with bullet holes, sending paster into the air. Soft thuds sounded behind him as the bullets hit the chair he was sitting in.

And then came the pain.

Sudden, mind-numbing, terrible pain exploded through his back as the gunfire continued.

Bang, bang, bang!

On and on it went as deep dark wetness spread over Jerome's chest. Everyone was on the floor, shouting and screaming. Abel fired back wildly without really aiming. Bullets were zipping over Jerome's head in the chaos until a final wet, cracking thud exploded through his head.

42

Scarlett looked down at Rob, where he lay on a mixture of blankets and coats that served as a makeshift bed. He snored loudly and shifted in his sleep.

It would be a shame to wake him. He'd been working so hard on the case. She felt that he needed to get some sleep. She'd given up before him in the early hours of last night and managed to get a little shut-eye sitting on a chair with her head resting on her arms on the table.

It wasn't a great night's rest. She'd woken up with a cricked neck and an aching body after what must have been just a few hours of restless, broken sleep to find it wasn't even five AM. But there was no way she was getting any more sleep here. There just wasn't anywhere even remotely comfortable to lay her head down. Besides, there was work that needed doing.

The phone call had come in barely fifteen minutes later.

"Morning," someone whispered behind her as she contemplated waking Rob.

Scarlett turned to see Ellen getting to her feet and stretching. "Christ, I feel like shit."

"You're up."

"Well, there was no way I was getting any more rest down there." She pointed to the corner of the room where she'd sat on a folded-up blanket and rested her head on a rolled-up coat. "I'd better be able to sleep at home tonight."

"I know the feeling," Scarlett sympathised, attempting to turn her head again and grimacing with pain as she did so. It would likely take a few days to get rid of that.

"Well, he seems well out of it," Ellen commented as she walked over and looked down at Rob. "How does he sleep there?"

"No idea," Scarlett answered before looking up at Ellen. "Well, seeing as you're up, you might as well make yourself useful."

"Aye, what's up?"

"We've got a call out. Seems we have another crime scene to visit. Come on, I'll give you the details in the car."

"You're not waking Rob?" Ellen enquired.

"No. Let him rest. We need at least one member of the team compos mentis."

Ellen shrugged as they walked to the back door and made their way into the car park. Scarlett led Ellen to her purple VW Polo, and within moments, they were driving away from the village hall through quiet streets.

"So what's this all about?" Ellen asked.

"Seems like we've had another shooting. A drive-by this time. A house got shot up in Forest Town."

"Casualties?"

"Two fatalities from what I was told," Scarlett answered, remembering the details dispatch had relayed to her.

"Wonderful," Ellen replied drily. "What a perfect way to start a new day. How come this got referred over to us?"

"PNC linked at least one of the casualties to the same gang we've been dealing with."

"The Poles or…"

"Nope, Abel and his crew," Scarlett corrected her.

"Okay, cool."

At this time in the morning, the drive didn't take long through the quiet suburban streets, and they soon turned onto a road filled with people and emergency vehicles, their blue flashing lights strobing crazily off the windows of the houses and cars.

Parking up, they got out and walked into the cordoned-off area, where several of the attending officers pointed the way until a uniformed Sergeant Scarlett didn't recognise approached.

"Evening, ladies," the man said, sounding a little too patronising for her liking. "I'm Sergeant Anderson. I take it you're CID?"

"Something like that," she replied airily and showed him her ID. Ellen did the same.

He nodded that he'd seen them. "Cheers. Right then, do you want to have a look inside?"

"Sure," Scarlett agreed, and he directed them to a nearby van where they could don their forensic suits to match the gaggle of Scene of Crime officers going about their business. "What do you know so far?"

"It was a drive-by," he said, waiting and watching as they pulled on the over suits. "Witnesses say they saw a dark car drive away at speed. It had people in the front and back, but they couldn't see who was inside. They shot the house from the car windows, aiming for that main front window there." He pointed. "They've made a right mess of the place. Anyway, we found what we think is the car they used, dumped and burnt out down a nearby country lane."

"Okay. And what about the house and victims?" Scarlett asked, having now pulled on the main over-suit.

"We have the owner over here." The sergeant pointed, and continued in a sarcastic tone of voice, "A lovely and highly cooperative individual called Baz Winfield, who swears blind the only people inside the house were him and a few mates playing FIFA on the PlayStation. Says he's got no idea who did it or why. But he doesn't seem terribly upset that two of his friends are currently dead on the floor of his front room."

Scarlett looked over to see a young man in his twenties arguing with another uniformed officer who was making notes in his pocketbook. She watched for a few seconds as the man ranted and raved, spittle flying everywhere as he yelled, and decided to let others conduct that initial interview.

"Seems like a stand-up citizen," Scarlett said dryly.

"Oh aye," the sergeant grumbled. "He's only been out of prison a few months and swears up and down that he's done nothing wrong. Says he's turned a corner in his life," the sergeant waved to the house, "despite evidence to the contrary."

Scarlett grunted.

The sergeant continued, "Is this to do with what's going on over in Clipstone with you lot, then?"

"Possibly," she confirmed. "Time will tell, I guess."

"Alright," the sergeant replied. "Well, I'll let you ladies head inside and get an eyeful. It's not a pretty sight. The CSM is in there somewhere. Have fun."

"Will do," Scarlett said and led the way up to the front door of the house. She spied people in white in the garden, combing through the bushes and grass, looking for evidence. It was meticulous work.

Stepping onto the footplates to keep their feet off the carpeted floor and any evidence it might hold, they made their way inside and walked through to the front room on their right.

It felt like she'd stepped into a warzone.

The wall to her left was peppered with scattered bullet holes. A fine dust of plaster covered everything, illuminated by the work lights that had been set up in here.

Several comfortable seats and sofas were arranged around the room, all of them sporting rips where bullets had slammed into them, sending their stuffing flying. But the focus of the work was around the two bodies. One of them, a young man, was slumped in a chair with his back to the front window. Scarlett's eyes were automatically drawn to the large, ragged hole where his left eye and cheek had once been. It was now a ruddy mess of flesh and bone, with his one remaining good eye staring out at them, lifeless and vacant.

His clothes were covered in dried blood, and he sported a couple more wounds on his chest. Despite his ruined face, Scarlett felt sure she recognised him.

"I know him," she said. "I've seen him before. I think that's Jerome. I recognise him from his mug shot."

Ellen peered at him, pulling a face as she looked at the horror before her. "Yeah, I think you might be right."

"I don't recognise her, though." Scarlett pointed to the young woman sprawled on the floor in front of the chair Jerome was sitting in. She lay on her front with her head turned sideways, a look of terror on her marred face. She too, had taken a bullet to the head and several more to her back, shoulder and neck. The carpet beneath her was a deep crimson.

It was a bloodbath.

"Morning, detectives," one of the white-suited people said, approaching. "Ava Saunders, I'm the Crime Scene Manager."

"Scarlett and Ellen," Scarlett introduced them. "This was a massacre."

"Indeed it was. We don't see much of this kind of thing, so it's always shocking when we do."

"Two fatalities, then, right?"

"That's right," Ava replied. "But I think I can say with a high degree of certainty that several more were injured."

"How so?" Ellen asked.

"From these." Ava pointed to splatters on the walls. "It's certainly possible that some of these came from our two fatalities over here, but the splatter pattern is all wrong for most of them. So, I'd say with a fair degree of certainty, pending further investigation, that several more people were hit with bullets, but walked out of here. This theory is further backed up by the trail of blood leading out the front and back doors. We're taking samples and we'll run DNA tests on them to see if we get any matches and let you know."

"Thank you," Ellen said, and turned to Scarlett. "What do you think?"

"Rob said it would escalate," Scarlett remarked. "Looks like he was right."

43

Rob jerked awake, the hazy memory of a dream fading into the mists of forgetfulness as he sat up, feeling stiff and not entirely rested. As he rose, his back cried out with a shooting pain, making him hiss and hold his back.

"Aww, jeez. I'm not getting any younger," he muttered before wiping the crusty nuggets of sleep from his eyes.

Around him, the back room of the village hall, their temporary incident room, was already in full swing for the morning, with most of his teammates hunched over their laptops, inputting data while slurping on morning coffees, running searches or scouring through footage. He could see Tucker, Nick and Guy all sitting around the main table, joined by several uniformed and civilian officers doing similar jobs. The operation was in full swing, and they were making what he hoped was good progress.

He couldn't make out Scarlett or Ellen, though, but his attention was drawn to Nailer as he approached carrying a steaming mug. "Morning, sleepy head."

Rob took the coffee and savoured the rich smell and the heat on his hands. "Thanks."

"Pleasure. How'd you sleep?"

"Not well. I honestly have no idea how I slept on that. Everything aches, but clearly, I was tired enough to doze through you guys getting up. You should have woken me."

"We thought you needed your sleep, so we left you. But you're with us now, so welcome back to the chaos. It's still early."

"What's been going on?"

"We've had another shooting," Nailer announced, a serious look on his face.

"Aww, shit. What's happened this time?"

"Drive-by on a house. We've got two fatalities and possibly more injured. Scarlett and Ellen are attending. I doubt they'll be much longer."

"We'll talk to them when they're back then," Rob said, taking a sip of his coffee and nearly burning his mouth.

"Aye," Nailer confirmed, then waved towards the team at their laptops. "We've been inputting data, reading statements and reviewing security footage from these latest incidents and Penny's murder too. We have weeks worth of footage to get through."

"Okay. I'll freshen up and then join them."

"Good man," Nailer replied, and with an approving nod, left him to his drink. Rob pulled out his phone and checked his notifications, finding the usual endless junk emails and updates. Placing his mug down, he fired off a quick text to

Erika, letting her know he'd not been home, wouldn't be home until tonight and asking if Muffin was okay when she fed him.

That done, he finished his drink, savouring the five minutes he had to wake up before he jumped into the day's work. After a quick trip to the bathroom to freshen up, he walked back into the incident room at the same time as a uniformed officer. He spotted Rob and walked over.

"Sir, someone's come in asking to speak to a detective. Says he saw Penny the night of her murder and that he was one of her clients."

"Oh, really? Where is he?"

"Out in the main hall."

"Alright," Rob looked around the room, and then turned back to the officer. "I'll come and speak to him."

"Of course, sir." Leading him back into the main hall, the officer directed Rob to a nearby table where a man was sitting. He was perched on the edge of his seat, his right leg bouncing nervously while he chewed on his nails. He seemed young, with fair skin, a shock of messy hair and casual clothes.

Rob wandered over. "Morning. I'm Detective Inspector Loxley. My colleague tells me, you think you saw Penny the night of her murder?"

"That's right, yeah. I did. I err, I wanted to come forward because... Well, I guess, you'd find me anyway."

"Oh?"

"Yeah…"

Sensing a story, Rob grabbed his pocketbook and decided to restart the conversation. "Right, before we go any further. Let's get some basics, what's your name?"

"Dillon. Dillon Bradshaw."

Rob proceeded to get the rest of the man's address and phone number, which Rob briefly tested with a quick call and passed the details to another officer to check while he continued the interview.

"You're local, I see. You live here in Clipstone."

"Yeah. I've been here for a few years now."

"Okay. So you've been aware of the investigation so far?"

"I have, yeah. I saw it on the news, but I didn't realise the murdered girl was… was the one I spent time with until the meeting last night when I saw her photo."

"I see. And how did you know Penny?"

"She was a prostitute, and I've um… paid for… you know."

"You're one of their clients," Rob clarified.

"That's it, yeah. I've been with a few of 'em."

"You're a regular user, then?" Rob asked, noting how nervous the guy seemed to be about talking about this. Rob wasn't judging him at all, but Dillon did seem kind of embarrassed about it.

"I've used them a handful of times, I guess. Penny once, though, the other day."

"The fifteenth?"

"That's right."

"The day she was murdered? That's when you paid her for sex?" He needed Dillon to be honest, open, and speak plainly.

"I did, yes." He seemed sheepish.

"Can you run me through what happened?"

"I just needed a release, you know? I'd been paid, and I just really needed to, you know, have sex."

"Okay."

"So yeah, I drove up Mansfield Road, where they've been hanging out, and saw Penny. I didn't know her name. She used a different one. But I liked the look of her, so I picked her up."

Rob made notes as the man talked. "And where did you take her?"

"To that little side road by the old coal mine. We did it in the back seat. It didn't go on for very long, but, yeah, that's what we did."

"Did you use a condom?"

"That's part of why I wanted to talk to you. I did wear one, but it split. She wasn't very happy about that and started shouting at me. So I got her out of the car and drove off. I paid her, but not the full amount."

Rob gave him a look, but Dillon was staring at the floor. He seemed ashamed of his actions.

"So you left her on the side road, is that right?"

"That's right."

"What time was this? Can you remember?"

"I think we got to the road about half past nine, and I left about nine forty-five."

"Alright, so you drove to the side road around nine-thirty, had sex, and then left her there alive and well at quarter to ten. Is that about right?" This seemed to fit with the timeline of events that they'd worked out so far, including Emmett's stop at the parade of shops to eat Chinese, just a short walk up from the road where Dillon had left her, and it fit with Nigel's break from work when no one knew where he was.

It also aligned with what the pathologist said about the approximate time of death as they worked it out.

"And you're sure she was okay at the end of your time with her?"

"Absolutely. I wouldn't hurt her. I wouldn't hurt anyone. I was annoyed with her shouting at me, but I just got out of there."

"Did you see anyone else on or close to that side road? Was anyone watching you?" Rob asked.

"No, nothing. But it was dark by then, and I wasn't really looking outside."

I bet you weren't, he thought. "Alright. Well, thank you for coming forward and talking to us. I'm going to get someone to sit with you and take your statement, and if you wouldn't mind hanging around, we'd like to make a few checks. We'll take a DNA sample, too."

"Yeah, sure. Anything. I was at the meeting last night, so I heard what happened to her. I can't quite believe this, but I think I might have been the last person to see her alive. Apart from the killer."

"That's certainly a possibility," Rob confirmed.

"I just…" He sighed and started welling up, his eyes glistening in the morning light. "I wish I'd been a little more vigilant, or taken her back to her patch, maybe? I shouldn't have just left her there."

He seemed genuinely upset, and as incriminating as his position was, Rob had a feeling that he was telling the truth. After years of talking to criminals and innocent people, he'd started to get an idea of when someone was being truthful, honest and open, and when someone was hiding something. It wasn't always accurate, and it didn't mean they were guilty of the crime he was investigating, but it was usually a good barometer of where the truth might lie.

With Dillon, that was the feeling he was getting. He seemed embarrassed that he'd paid for sex, but apart from that, he seemed genuinely concerned about Penny, and he appeared to want to do the right thing.

Rob's gut told him to believe the man. He didn't get a bad feeling about him, and he didn't seem to be holding anything back. Still, he'd been wrong before, so he couldn't be one hundred percent certain.

"You've done the right thing by coming here and telling us what happened, and if you're being honest with us, you have nothing to worry about."

"Sure. Okay, thanks."

"Stay here," Rob said and got up from the table. It was a matter of a few moments to arrange for one of the other officers to take Dillon's statement and DNA, and with that done, he wandered back through to the incident room. He walked in to find Scarlett and Ellen talking to Nailer.

"Sleeping beauty's arrived," Scarlett announced with a smile. "How are you? Sleep okay?"

"Well," Rob answered, "I slept, but I wouldn't call it a very restful night."

"No?"

"No! That floor's not comfortable," he exclaimed. "I'm looking forward to being back in my bed tonight, hopefully."

"Me too." Scarlett then muttered, "Chris will start to wonder if I have too many nights away."

"So, the guv was saying you've been to another crime scene?" Rob asked.

"Indeed," Scarlett confirmed. "A house was shot up in Forest Town. It was a drive-by from a passing car that we've found burnt out a few miles away. There were two confirmed casualties on the premises, with possibly more injured still at large. One of the victims was Jerome Clifford."

"Jerome?" Rob asked. "The guy that Penny's parents said groomed her?"

"That's him," Scarlett confirmed. "He'd been shot through the head from behind. We found him still sitting in his chair, his back to the shattered window."

"This was retaliation," Nailer said. "I'd bet good money this was Radek and his gang hitting back at Abel after he killed two of his girls. These aren't random killings, this is gang warfare."

"That was our assessment, too," Scarlett agreed.

"I agree," Rob said. "Damn it, I knew this would get worse. We can't have these thugs driving around shooting at houses. More innocents are going to get killed, and this is going to get totally out of control."

"Then we need to end this quickly," Nailer replied. "We need to find Penny's killer and these gang members, and arrest them."

"Were there any useful witnesses?" Rob asked.

"We have several people who saw the car but not who was in it," Ellen said. "And we have the house owner, who swears it was just him and a few mates playing PlayStation. According to him, he got no idea who did this or why."

"Naturally, we don't believe a word of that," Scarlett added. "But the blood trails leading out of the house suggest there were others and that some of them were injured from the attack. Witnesses back that up, too, saying they saw people leaving the house after the shooting."

"Okay, we need to keep the pressure on the house owner and keep hunting for Abel and his gang," Nailer suggested. "And what about Penny's murder? Any more progress there?"

"Nothing much yet, guv," Rob replied. "Her death looks like it sparked all this trouble, but I'm convinced it was someone else who killed her for reasons we're still not clear on. I have just spoken to a man who came forward, saying he saw Penny on the night of her murder. He was one of her clients, and going by the timings he's given us and the location where they engaged in intercourse, it all fits. They were in the sideroad where her body was found, and when they'd finished, he kicked her out the car and left her there alive and well."

"He kicked her out and abandoned her?" Ellen asked. "Charming."

"He claims the condom split, and she was upset with him over it."

"That fits," Scarlett said. "The pathologist said she found traces of semen inside her. If his DNA matches…"

"Then that all but confirms his story," Nailer finished. "Get that DNA test expedited, will you?"

"Can do, sir," Rob replied. "We've got his address too. We should probably search his house."

"Agreed," Nailer confirmed. "Hold him here for the time being until we know more. For all we know, he's the killer, and he's just trying to throw us off the scent."

"Already on it," Rob said with a smile.

"Do you think he's the killer?" Ellen asked.

"Honestly, no," Rob replied. "He doesn't strike me as a murderer, and my gut says he's being honest. Plus, if he was, why would he come forward?" Rob gestured to Nailer. "Unless this is a somewhat elaborate and risky plan to throw us off the scent. But I doubt it."

"You never know," Scarlett suggested.

Rob grunted. "Alright, well, maybe. But I don't think he's the killer."

"Alright," Nailer cut in, stalling any further conversation. "Enough speculating. We've all got work to do. Let's get on it and have a good day."

44

One of the great things about owning the club was the friendships he'd accrued over the years in all strata of society. He knew people in all kinds of roles and liked to think he was one of the most well-informed people in the village, although he had no way to verify that.

But this also came with several downsides. Namely, the less savoury people he'd come to meet and know.

Nigel sat at his own bar in the empty club. It was early, and they wouldn't open for several hours, and he should really be in bed, catching up on his sleep. Running a bar was hard work and led to countless late nights. But last night, after the shooting of the two girls up the street, he'd struggled to find any peace. His mind had been racing the whole night through until a text appeared from a friend telling him there'd been a second shooting in nearby Forest Town.

He didn't know the details or if anyone had been killed, but it seemed fairly obvious to him that the two shootings would likely be related. Penny's death and Izabela's disappearance had sparked the simmering tinderbox of rival gangs, and now it had finally exploded.

After the news of the second shooting, he'd finally given up. There was no way he was going to get any sleep. So he'd stumbled downstairs and done the only thing he could think of that might silence the voices in his head.

Gripping the tumbler with his fingers, he tilted the glass, causing the smoky amber beverage inside to slosh around. The medicine he'd prescribed himself didn't appeal, and he'd only had a couple of drinks, so his solution hadn't really worked.

He still couldn't get these intrusive thoughts out of his head and remained frustratingly sober.

He kept thinking about Izabela, how she'd caused this, and how she was probably in some very real danger. Her disappearance had resulted in two shootings so far, and from what he'd heard, at least two deaths, probably more.

Did they want to kill Izabela too?

The thought gave him chills as he took another sip of his drink. It wasn't as if he was neutral in all this, after all. He'd been friendly with the working girls for months, giving them free drinks and space. Even Abel, who was only an occasional visitor, knew about his sympathy for the prostitutes.

How long would it be before he put two and two together and paid him a visit? He'd been careful while Izabela had been here the first time, keeping her away from him, but that would probably not be enough to keep Abel off his doorstep. It would only be a matter of time before he showed up to have a friendly chat.

But if that was the case, then Izabela couldn't stay here. She had to move on and go somewhere safe whether she liked it or not.

The club's rear door sounded, and he heard footsteps approaching through the back of the building. Nigel took a final swig of his drink and tensed.

Caprice appeared through a side door. "Hey." She seemed perky and rested.

"Hi," he said but looked back down at his glass.

"Is everything okay?"

When he looked back up, she wore a frown on her face, her eyes tick-tocking back and forth between him and the glass he'd been nursing.

Nigel sighed. "Not really."

"You're worried about the shooting last night, right?"

"Shootings," he corrected her, putting the emphasis on the plural 'S' at the end. "There was another one. This one *against* Abel."

Her expression dropped. "Shit. So Radek hit back?"

"Looks like it," Nigel confirmed. "It's getting out of control, and all because of her." He pointed to the ceiling, meaning Izabela, upstairs.

"I know. But as long as she stays out of sight..."

"How long can I do that, Caprice? I know Abel, remember. He comes in here sometimes. He knows I serve his girls, he knows I know them. Hell, Penny probably told him that she met Izabela here. Does he know that Izabela lived here with me? Does he know that? Because if he does, how long will it be until he pays me a visit?"

"Aaah, yeah, I see. That's a problem."

"No shit, Sherlock." He didn't mean to snap at her, but he'd said it before he knew what he was saying. He bit his lip in embarrassment.

Caprice grimaced and then nodded. "Okay, so we need a plan. We need to get her out of here. She can come to mine."

"No. No way. Your flat would be the first place they'd look. I'm not doing that. Besides, you don't want these guys knocking at your door."

"Alright, then where?"

"I don't know... I mean, I have ideas, but some of them are a bit tricky, and she might not want to go."

"Like what? Tell me."

"Well, I had one idea, and I know she'd take her, but it's not really ideal."

"Where?" Caprice's tone was insistent and demanding. She needed to know.

Nigel went to answer. A loud bang echoed from behind him. He turned in surprise to see the front door had been kicked open. A large man, nearly as wide as he was tall and made of thick, bulging muscle, walked in, barely fitting through the door.

"Aaah, we're not open yet," Caprice called out. But Nigel had seen the man behind the brute and stopped himself from joining her protests.

"Caprice, don't."

"What?"

Three men walked in, while a fourth—another huge thug—stood outside, his back to the door. Following the first bald man-mountain were two others that Nigel knew all too well. He'd been fearing the arrival of one of them all night, but this was much worse.

For a brief, utterly crazy moment, he considered making a break for it, and running, but he quickly dismissed the idea. There was no way he could abandon his friends. Izabela wouldn't want to leave, and he didn't want to disappear and let Caprice or any other staff deal with these guys. This was on him. This was his responsibility, and he needed to fix it.

The thug who kicked the door open stopped just inside it, allowing Abel Underwood and his boss, Carter Bird, to approach.

Wearing an immaculately tailored suit, Carter was the epitome of the gentleman criminal. He dressed sharply and kept himself well groomed, but his appearance masked a dangerous, violent man who many in the underworld rightly feared.

He'd heard the rumours about him many times, about the people he supposedly tortured and killed, although none had ever been found or linked back to him. He'd even appeared in this very club once or twice, but that was a rarity.

Carter led Abel through the bar like he owned the place, full of confidence and without fear. Nigel, however, felt his breath catch in his throat at the sight of them. He'd known it would only be a matter of time before Abel appeared, but this was quicker and much worse than he'd anticipated. Abel was a dumb thug, but Carter was no idiot.

He stopped a short distance from Nigel, adjusted his cuffs, and then placed his hands in his pockets as he looked between him and Caprice.

Nigel looked over and saw concern and worry in Caprice's eyes, but he knew what Carter wanted. He smiled at his employee, trying to be reassuring. "If you wouldn't mind, I'd like to talk to Mr Bird in private and without *any* interruptions." With his gaze locked onto hers, Nigel flicked his eyes to the ceiling and back, hoping she understood his meaning. "Thank you."

A flash of understanding passed over her features. "Oh, yeah, sure. Will do." She picked up her bag and hustled out of the room with a couple of backwards glances. Moments later, she disappeared through a door, and they were alone.

Nigel turned back to Carter, and despite his gut-wrenching fear, he smiled. "We're alone."

Carter inclined his head. "Much obliged," he said and regarded him for a moment more. He took a breath and started to slowly pace back and forth as he spoke. "I take it you heard what happened last night?"

"I'm aware," Nigel replied. "I hope no one was badly hurt."

"Mmm," Carter muttered. "Abel tells me two of his friends were lost in this latest act of aggression. There were some minor injuries too. But we've dealt with them."

"I'm sorry to hear that." Narrowing his eyes, Nigel felt the hint of a frown crease his forehead as he wondered why Carter was telling him this. He knew Carter mainly by reputation. He had served him drinks before and swapped pleasantries, but they were by no means close. But here he was, almost admitting he was involved in the criminality the rumours accused him of. What the hell was he doing?

Carter smiled. "I'm sure you're wondering why I'm telling you this. But here's the thing, you see. Unlike some, I know you're not an idiot, and neither am I. I know all about the rumours surrounding me, as I'm sure you do. So, I'm treating you with respect, and in return, I ask that you do the same. Do you see how this works?"

"I do," Nigel replied cautiously. He noticed Abel looking around the room and wondered what Caprice was doing upstairs with Izabela.

"Good. That's good. Let me reassure you that we will be taking care of things. But all this seems to have started because of one girl's murder and another's disappearance. Do you know what I'm talking about?"

"I heard about the girl who was killed but not about any disappearances." He did his best to keep his tone neutral as he tried not to give away that he knew Izabela or that she was upstairs right now. "I'm aware of the killings last night, too."

Carter's eyes narrowed. "I see. And you know of nothing else?"

Feigning ignorance, Nigel shrugged. "Sorry, no. What happened?"

Carter regarded him for a long moment as if trying to read his expression. Behind him, Abel stared at him with rage-filled eyes. Did he know? Did he suspect?

Carter shrugged. "Well, we've had a disappearance, a girl who was a visitor here, a customer of yours, called Izabela Nosek. A Polish girl. Do you know of her?"

Lying through his teeth, he drew on the truth of running this club whenever anyone said he should know everyone who came through his doors. He smiled in incredulity. "Look, I'm sorry, but hundreds, maybe thousands of people walk through these doors each week." 'Thousands' was perhaps a little exaggeration, but only a small one. "There's no way I could ever know everyone who comes here, even if they're returning visitors who show up each week. So, unless you've got more for me to go on, then I'm sorry, but no, I don't know who this girl is."

Carter turned to Abel and pointed at his hand. Abel held up his phone. There was a photo of Izabela on it. It didn't escape Nigel's notice that the photo had been taken in here, in the club, and he recognised the outfit that Izabela was wearing too.

With his heart thundering and adrenaline surging, screaming at him to run, he gazed sceptically at the screen.

His and Izabela's lives depended on him selling this fiction, and as he stared at her smiling face, he felt like a bug beneath the magnifying glass of a particularly cruel child.

"You're sure," Carter asked, his eyes fixed on him.

With a mouth like the Sahara, Nigel nodded. "Yeah, I'm sure," he croaked. "I don't know her. I see girls like that in here every night."

Carter took a slow step forward, coming closer, his eyes locked onto Nigel's. "I hope you're not lying to me, Mr Wild. I don't like people who lie to me."

"Absolutely not." He needed a drink. "I'd never lie to you."

Carter didn't rush into his reply. "Well, if you do see her, I'd ask that you do me the courtesy of giving me a call. Can you do that for me?"

"Of course. Absolutely. Happy too. What number should I call?"

Carter reached into his jacket's inside pocket and pulled out a simple white card that had only his name and a phone number on it. He offered it to Nigel.

He went to take it, only for Carter to jerk it back. "You call right away, the moment you see her. You understand?"

"I understand," he replied before Carter allowed him to finally take the business card.

"Then we have an understanding, Mr Wild." He smiled suddenly, and the mood in the room lifted. "Well then, I can't hang around here all day. Good day to you."

Nigel watched as Carter turned and walked out without a backwards glance, unlike the thug and Abel, who both fired looks back at him. Abel's glare was by far the most accusing and seemed to have only intensified over the course of this meeting as if he knew Nigel was lying. The thug was the last to leave and pulled the door shut behind him, even though his kick had splintered the lock, damaging it.

Nigel sighed and returned to his stool, taking a much-needed breather. He'd feared they would demand a look around, and they would have had to somehow hide Izabela, but he'd dodged that particular bullet for now.

He'd bought himself time, but that was all. He needed to get Izabela out as quickly as possible before the worst happened.

***

Fuming with pent-up rage, Abel walked away from the club, following Carter back to where they'd both parked and met up before entering the club.

Nigel was lying, he was sure of it, but he knew better than to question his boss's methods or to voice his objections too much. Carter only stood for a certain amount of insurrection before he took action.

At the car, one of Carter's enforcers opened the door for him. His boss stopped and turned. "Stay here, and watch the club. Report anything suspicious. Got it?"

Abel wanted to do more than just watch. He wanted to storm in there and turn the place upside down, but that could be disastrous for him. "Okay," he hissed through a grimace.

"Good." Carter got in the car, his thug closing the door behind him and giving Abel a disgusted look. Moments later, the car pulled away, leaving Abel by the side of the road.

He'd do as Carter asked, for now. For now…

45

The previous night's events led to the day being spent dealing with paperwork and managing the main thrust of the investigation. Rob reviewed reports and statements while overseeing the ongoing house-to-house investigations and interviews all through the day. Security footage from cameras close to all three incidents was still coming in and being reviewed by the team. Most of it was useless or of limited help, and as the day wound on, it started to feel like they hadn't made much progress on the overall investigation at all.

No new leads had come in, and there was little progress towards finding out who had killed Penny and why.

They'd been looking in detail at Abel's life and criminal record, and mapping out who was in his gang and how they were connected to the broader criminal fraternity. Who were their allies and enemies, that kind of thing. But it was a dark and murky world, and when they started looking at those above Abel in the pecking order, things became less certain. They had to rely on rumour and hearsay and less on hard evidence. They didn't have a single name to go on or look into. They had several possibilities and no solid chain of evidence.

Rob wondered if there might be links to his own estranged family in there somewhere, further up the chain, but so far, nothing had come up.

The rivalries were easier, and they had a good starting point with the Polish gang Abel's crew were already clashing with.

Rob stared at the big board they'd set up in the corner of the room, complete with photos of the victims and likely suspects. To one side, they'd also mapped out some of Abel's gang, as well as Radek's crew. Interlacing his fingers behind his head and stretching out, he grimaced to himself.

Did all this really bring them any closer to finding out who Penny's murderer was or why they did it? He had a horrible feeling it didn't. As he tensed and worked out a couple of the knots in his back, a full-bodied yawn stretched his mouth wide, making his cheeks tingle with the power of it.

God, he hoped he was in his own bed tonight. He didn't fancy another night on the floor or worse on those bloody chairs. His back would never forgive him if he subjected it to more of that.

Maybe he needed to invest in a camper bed and keep it in his car, just for these occasions? It would make sense, both on a health front and on a work front. Their job demanded that they be at their best at all times. Lives depended on them, and he didn't want to miss a valuable clue just because he'd had a bad night.

He made a mental note to look into that as soon as he found a moment. They should probably invest in them as a team.

While his mind wandered through the possibilities of how best to get that done, he heard his phone buzz on the desk and picked it up.

It was a text from Erika. Accessing his phone, he opened the message and was greeted with a selfie of Erika grinning at the camera while holding Muffin in his apartment. The caption read: 'Thought you'd like to know, Muffin's been a good boy today.'

Rob smiled, pleased that his arrangement with Erika was working out, and after a moment's consideration, he decided to check in with her properly and got up from his desk.

"You all right?" Scarlett asked from where she was sitting, around the side of the table.

"Yeah. I'm gonna get some fresh air and make a phone call." He jabbed his thumb at the back door.

"What time is it?" she asked.

Rob checked his watch. "Five-twenty."

"Christ, where's the day gone?"

"I know," Rob sympathised, equally shocked that hours seemed to have passed without them really noticing. "I won't be long."

"No worries," she replied and returned to her work.

Slipping out through the back door, he stepped into the back of the rear car park and glanced around to make sure he was alone before tapping the screen of his device to call Erika.

She answered a couple of rings later.

"Hiya," she greeted him. "Checking up on me?"

"Something like that," Rob answered. "How's he been?"

"He's fine. I fed him this morning, and I'm at yours now, giving him some fuss. He's not destroyed anything yet, but I think he's missing his dad."

"Well, I don't know if I'll be back tonight either. If I am, it'll be a late one. I'll let you know either way via a text. Hope that's okay?"

"It's fine. It's not a problem. I'm happy to help out."

As she spoke, movement ahead of him caught his eye, and he looked up.

A man stepped out of a gleaming black BMW, his eyes fixed on Rob, and closed the door behind him. Rob stared at the man for a moment, realising that he recognised him and not quite believing what he was seeing.

As the man started to approach, Rob's stomach dropped.

It was Owen, his brother. The youngest of his three older brothers.

He'd not seen him in years, but Owen was just as he remembered him. The largest of his three siblings, he clearly worked out. He'd shaved his head and seemed to have cultivated a clean but brutal look that left you in little doubt as to who you were dealing with.

The voice on the end of the phone snapped him out of the brief trance he'd dropped into. "Rob?"

"Sorry, Erika, I'm here. Something's just come up, and I've got to go. Thanks again. I'll text later."

"Oh, okay, sure. See ya. Don't work too hard…" But Rob had already pulled the phone away from his ear and ended the call.

Owen smiled. "Robert," he said, his voice deep and gravelly. "How are you, you little twerp?"

Rob grimaced as nervous energy coursed through his blood. He was well aware of the reputation that Owen had and didn't fancy provoking him. Rob kept his eyes locked onto his brother, hunting for signs of threat. "I don't want to talk to you."

"Fuck you," Owen spat. "You think I want to spend my time talking to a traitor like you? Fuck that."

"Then why are you here?" Did he really want to know?

Owen stopped a couple of metres away and fixed him with a steely glare. "Shut it," he snapped. "I've come here for one reason, and one reason only, to tell you to keep your fucking nose out of things that aren't your concern."

"Things? What things?"

"We're watching you. Remember that, *Inspector*." That last word was filled with contempt and hate as Owen straightened up and stuffed his hands in his pockets, before turning away. Rob watched the man go with a racing heart, wondering if he'd somehow just dodged a bullet.

What did Owen mean by his warning to keep his nose out? Was Owen connected to all of this somehow? Did his family have a hand in Penny's murder, or was Owen referring to the gang war angle? He knew which was most likely.

As Owen started his car and drove out of the car park in a cloud of dust, Rob sensed another presence and turned to see Vincent Kane nearby, watching the car pull out of the gravel car park and leave.

"Who was that?" Vincent called out. "A friend of yours?"

"Get lost, Kane," Rob replied with a sigh, and turned back to the rear door into the village hall.

"He didn't look like police? Maybe I should look into whoever it was?"

"Do what you want," Rob replied, annoyed, and stormed back in through the rear door, slamming it shut behind him.

Nailer was in the corridor, just stepping out of the rear room, and looked up at the noise. "You all right, Rob?"

Rob pulled a face, annoyed and frustrated by the interactions he'd just been through and what they might mean for the investigation. He peered at Nailer and briefly weighed up whether he should talk to his boss about this or keep it to himself. Would it paint him in a bad light or jeopardise the investigation. It had a possibility of doing that if it got out, but the chance of that would be higher if he kept this to himself.

"Not really," Rob answered, exasperated. "My bother just appeared in the car park, and told me not to look into stuff that doesn't concern me."

"Really? Which brother?"

"Owen. I've not seen him in years, and he just appears and says that? Makes me wonder..."

Nailer frowned as he considered Rob's words. "I would doubt they're involved in Penny's murder. I've been following gangs like theirs for years, and it's not really their style unless someone's gone rogue."

"No, I agree. If I had to guess, I'd say he was referring to the gang war angle, but there's no way to be sure." Rob leaned against the wall and shook his head. "What the hell have we stumbled on here?"

"I don't know, but your brother's not going to scare me off. I can tell you that. But how do you feel? He's your brother, after all."

Rob looked back at Nailer. "I'm fine, and I'm not going anywhere. If you're still happy to keep me on the case, then I'll stay. I know this could constitute a conflict of interest, but you know my feelings about my family."

"Yeah, I know. They're not really your family anymore, right?"

"Right. I left them behind twenty years ago, and I am not going back, just like my mother did."

Nailer nodded, his expression tense. "I understand. Shall we get back to it?"

"Yeah, I'm done talking about my brother." The less time and brain power he gave to them, the better as far as he was concerned.

"Good. Come through. I was just looking for you anyway. We've had some info come through from Forensics that might be of use."

"Oh?" Rob followed Nailer through into the back room and over to DS Nick Miller's desk.

"Nick, show him what just came in," Nailer asked.

"Yeah, no worries," he replied while switching to another window on his laptop and adjusting the screen so Rob could see it clearer.

It took him a moment to read it through, and according to the report, the scrap of purple rubber that was found snagged on the bushes beside Penny's body was PVC, and the closest match was to a rubber found in washing-up gloves.

"Wait," Rob said, standing up straight. "So, you're telling me the killer wore a pair of Marigolds when they killed Penny?"

"Maybe," Nailer replied. "This doesn't mean the killer wore them, though. It just means this scrap of rubber was there, covered in Penny's blood, and looked fresh."

Shouting echoed from the main hall.

Rob glanced at Nailer, and then bolted from the room, running through to the main hall as quick as he could. He found Janette Radcliff being manhandled away from Dillon Bradshaw, the man who'd admitted he was one of Penny's clients.

"You're sick," she yelled. "You're disgusting. People like you shouldn't be allowed to live around here."

Sergeant Megan Jolly turned and walked over on seeing Rob run in, followed by Nick, Nailer and Scarlett.

"What's going on?" Rob asked, seeing that the officers in the room had the situation under control.

"She either guessed or overheard that Dillion had been using the prostitutes and kicked off."

"Shit," Rob hissed under his breath.

"Inspector Loxley, you should lock him up. We can't have people like him here, in Clipstone. He's probably the killer! Arrest him!"

"We'll deal with her, sir," Megan reassured him and followed the officers as they escorted Janette out of the hall.

Tensions were high, it seemed. They needed a breakthrough and fast.

46

With his camera hooked up to his laptop, Vincent sat in the driver's seat of his car, reviewing the photos he'd snapped of DI Rob Loxley talking to an unknown man behind the village hall.

The man hadn't looked like a police officer, although he had been wearing a suit. He sported a shaved head, a goatee and was a big man. Not someone he'd want to piss off. But the real question was, who was he and what was he speaking to Loxley about?

He'd been following Loxley and the case for the past few days, and this was the first thing he'd seen that even came close to being worthy of reporting to Bill Rainault. He had no idea if it was anything dodgy, but if it was, Bill would probably figure it out.

As the images continued to download, Vincent grabbed his phone and called Bill. He answered moments later.

"Good evening, Kane."

"Bill," Vincent replied. "I might have something for you."

"Oh? Anything good?"

"I don't know. I saw Loxley speaking to some guy behind the village hall. I've got no idea who he was or what they were talking about, but thought you should know so you can look into it."

"Did you get any photos?"

"I did, actually. I'm downloading them to my PC now, I'll fire them over as soon as I can. Any idea who it could be?"

"What did he look like?"

"Big, bald, with a goatee. He was wearing a suit."

"And you've never seen him before?"

"Nope."

"Okay, good work, fire them over." He hung up.

Vincent gave his phone a quick glance over at the sudden end to the call when the driver's door was suddenly yanked open.

Huge hands, like slabs of meat, reached in and grabbed him by the front of his clothes and hauled him out of the car. There was no fighting it. The huge arms were like pneumatic power arms, an unstoppable force that just ripped him from the car.

"What the hell."

A massive, giant of a man lifted him and then slammed Vincent against the side of the car. The man's ugly, brutish face was just inches from Vincent's own.

"Ooof. Um, ouch." Fear flooded his system with adrenaline, but there was no fighting this beast, and he knew it. Better to do what they wanted and survive to tell the tale. "Hey, chill, man. You can have whatever you want."

The man grunted but said nothing. Movement beyond his attacker caught Vincent's attention. It was the man he'd seen speaking to Loxley. He was watching dispassionately, a short distance behind the monster that was holding him.

"Oh…"

"I don't appreciate having my photo taken without my permission," the man said as he walked over. He reached inside Vincent's car and grabbed his camera and laptop. "So, I'll be taking these."

Vincent glanced at the beast and then at the mysterious man. "Fuck you."

The beast shook him with a grunt.

The man held up his hand. "Phone."

"Aww, come on. I've got my whole life on that thing."

"And if you want to continue living that life, I suggest you do as I ask," the man said, while the beast tightened his grip, and growled.

"Shit," he hissed, and handed it over.

The man glanced at it, then held it up. "Unlock it."

"God damn it." But he did as the man asked as the beast continued to hold him aloft and pressed against his car. It cut into his back in an excruciating way. The man tapped the screen a few times before he held it up for Vincent to confirm his security code again and remove the security features from the device.

"Thank you. You see? Easy, wasn't it. And now I don't need to ask my friend here to do something you wouldn't enjoy."

The beast lowered him to the floor.

"Arr, yeah, thanks." There was a sudden flash of movement, and the beast's fist appeared out of nowhere, moving quicker than he'd have thought possible. The punch slammed into the side of his face and sent him sprawling into the car with a thud.

"Still, wouldn't want to deprive him of some fun, would I. Good day to you, Mr Kane, and stay out of my business."

Dripping blood from his mouth, Kane looked up from the concrete and watched the pair of men get into the same car he'd seen at the village hall but noticed the number plate was different. He guessed these would be false plates, too, as he rolled onto his back while the engine of the car roared into the distance.

There was no denying it now. He'd stumbled onto something juicy.

47

Slumped in his car, Abel slurped on the dregs from the bottom of a can of Coke. Finishing the drink, he crushed the can and threw it into the passenger footwell, where it joined the others.

"Fuck!" He'd been here for hours, bloody hours, and nothing had happened. No one had walked in or out of the shitty little club the whole time he'd been here, making this a monumental waste of time. He could have been out there, hunting down those bastard Poles and exacting his revenge. But, oh no. He wasn't allowed to do that because Carter-fucking-Bird had ordered him to stay here and waste a god damned day watching this shitty place and the creepy fucker inside it.

What the ever-lovin'-fuck was he doing with his life?

He sometimes wondered. He'd nearly left several times to go and do something more worthwhile but had so far settled on ordering his crew to go hunting for Radek and his guys over the phone, on strict instructions to call him if they found any.

He'd need a good reason to leave, otherwise, Carter would...

Carter would what? Kill him?

Well, fuck Carter. He'd spent far too long running around being scared of that bastard when it should be people like him and his crew running things.

He needed to find Radek and take his revenge. That's what he needed. He needed to teach that shit-stabbing cock-gobbler a lesson once and for all. Only one crew could put their girls on the streets around here, and that was his. No one else.

There was a reckoning coming for Radek that would flatten the twat once and for all and leave the streets open for him to use as he saw fit, and it couldn't come too soon.

He'd had enough of being ordered around by the likes of Carter and these so-called bosses. It was time the real power on the streets took control and showed these old shits how it was really done.

His phone buzzed, the screen displaying the name "Sal".

Abel answered, "Go."

"You'll never believe who I've found wandering around Forest Town, bold as brass like she owns the fucking joint?"

"Who?" Abel asked, in no mood for mind games.

"Only fucking Apolonia. Radek's right-hand girl. Baz and I have her behind the Chinese joint, just up from the school on Clipstone Road."

"About fucking time," Abel hissed with enthusiasm down the line. "You keep her there."

"She ain't going nowhere."

"I'll be there soon." Abel ended the call, turned his phone off, and threw it into the passenger seat. Glancing up at the club, he pulled a face, knowing he was about to disobey a direct order from Carter. He focused his anger towards Nigel who was hopefully somewhere inside. "You stay fuckin' there."

With a turn of the key, the car fired up, and within moments he was out onto the road and driving South West, shouting and swearing at slow drivers.

He had a simple plan in mind. Get to Forest Town, deal with Apolonia, and get back. He should be gone for minutes at most. There's no need for Carter to even know about this, and there was no way he was letting Sal or Baz deal with it without him.

These bastards had ruined his fuckin' life, and he wanted revenge.

It seemed to take forever to drive the short distance to the outskirts of Mansfield when in reality, it was only a few minutes. But as he finally reached his destination, he saw the overgrown, weed-covered driveway down the side of the takeaway but opted to park at the pub next door.

Pulling in, he whipped the car into a space and jumped out, his hot, angry energy filling him up and urging him to do what needed to be done.

Striding out to the road, he made his way round to the driveaway and turned into it, keeping his ever-vigilant eyes on the streets, looking for anything suspicious.

The back of the takeaway was little more than an overgrown wasteland of a garden, with only the part closest to the building in any kind of regular use, and that was only for bags of rubbish.

He spotted Sal tucked in close behind a shed that had seen better days. She waved him over. As Abel rounded the corner, he saw Baz holding a gun against a kneeling woman's head. Apolonia was dark-haired with ruddy skin and a face like thunder, but she couldn't speak due to a gag stuffed in her mouth.

"We found her out on the street, just walking along the road, bold as you like," Baz said.

"What you gonna do to her?" Sal asked.

The sight of one of Radek's close allies kneeling before him, vulnerable and defenceless, was intensely satisfying, but there was only one way to deal with this, send the right message to Radek, and get back to the club and his watch in as short a time as possible.

"Send a message," Abel muttered and reached into his jacket.

"What kind of message?" Baz asked, but before he could finish, Abel pulled a knife, stepped in, and thrust the blade into Apolonia's chest.

"That's for Penny," he muttered as his whole body shook with the emotion and anger that was flooding his system.

Apolonia gasped, her eyes wide with shock as he withdrew the blade and slammed it home again. "That's for Izabela, and these are for Jerome and the others." He stabbed her twice more in the chest, making his fist wet with blood.

Withdrawing the blade one last time, he stepped back as she dropped to the overgrown grass and writhed in agony, leaking blood all over this patch of garden.

Abel watched dispassionately. His only thought was that she deserved it. She'd sided with the wrong crew and had paid the price, and so would Radek. She was an important member of his gang, from what Abel understood. A former prostitute turned pimp, she'd recruited most of the girls she currently used, and managed them for Radek, keeping them in line and dishing out punishments when needed.

Her death should hit Radek hard. He'd be pissed and would make mistakes, which was exactly what Abel wanted.

As Apolonia's face grew vacant and she stopped moving, Abel wiped the blade of the knife against his black tracksuit bottoms and put it away.

"Good work, but get away from here and keep looking," Abel said as they walked around the main road. "I need to bounce. I've got somewhere to be."

Within moments, Abel was back in his car and using one of the napkins he'd picked up from the chippy to clean his bloody hand before he drove back into Clipstone. It felt like he'd been away for ages. He needed to get back before anything happened to put him up shit creek for good.

Arriving in Clipstone, he pulled into the sideroad that ran parallel to the main road in front of the parade of shops, only to find himself caught behind a couple of cars that were waiting for a third car. Abel briefly considered backing out, but a car pulled in behind and blocked him in.

"Shit." Abel craned his head. A little further up, separate from this tiny traffic jam, he saw Nigel standing at the side of the road, waving to a car that turned into traffic and drove away.

"What the fuck," he cursed, jiggling about in his seat, trying to get a better view as Nigel put his head down and strode back into his club.

Turning back to the road, the car Nigel had waved off was gone, having disappeared into traffic. Who the hell was in that car? What had he missed? Carter would want to know!

Furious, Abel screamed. He wanted to sound his horn, but that would attract too much attention. He slammed his steering while with his fists and shouted at the drivers ahead of him, until moments later, the jam cleared, and he could move. He pulled into the first space he saw, jumped out and stormed over to the club. Fury raged and roiled around inside him as his mind raced with thoughts and possibilities, but whichever way he looked at it, none of them worked out well for him when Carter found out.

Reaching the entrance of the closed club. Abel slammed the door open and stormed inside. Nigel was a short distance inside the main bar, and turned in shock as Abel appeared.

"Hey, whoa, hold on for a minute. Just wait…"

Abel launched himself at Nigel and slammed his fist into the older man's face. He dropped like a sack of potatoes.

"What the fuck was that?" Abel raged.

"What?" Nigel asked. "What are you talking about?"

"The car, who was in the car? What were you doing?"

"I don't—"

"Don't fuck with me. Tell me what the hell is going on," Abel raged. "Because if you don't, I will make what's left of your miserable life a living hell!"

"Okay, I get it."

"Who was in that car, and where the hell are they going?"

48

Parking on the residential street in Forest Town with his heart pounding, Emmett pulled on the hand break and killed the engine, all without looking up. It wasn't until the car had fallen silent that he glanced across the street to the house on the corner.

He'd resisted his desire to do this for so long, but spending several days in close proximity to Valerie in that tiny hotel room had finally broken his spirit. He'd hoped to resist and get through this without succumbing to these base desires. He should be able to do this easily, especially given how this could look to certain authorities, but in the end, there was no stopping it.

He couldn't hold this off any longer. The need for him to be here was too strong.

He chuckled to himself. At least he wasn't resorting to picking them up off the street again. At least he had that going for him. After all, he had to remember how this would look to people if they found out about it.

It sometimes amazed him that he'd been getting away with this for so long, and that Valerie hadn't picked up on it. But then, she wasn't the sharpest knife in the drawer and was a little too self-obsessed to look too closely at what he was doing, unless it was to nag him and try to control his life.

But despite his confidence, he still harboured doubts about what he was doing. Was this a terrible idea that he needed to rethink? Was it too soon?

Could he really not resist the pull to be over there for a few more days?

Shaking his head, he wondered if he wasn't the pathetic one. He should really be able to go a few days without treating himself like this, and yet, these indulgences had become more frequent of late, as he found he couldn't go a few days without doing something to scratch that itch.

Looking at the building again, his mind wandered as he imagined the fun he'd have over there, fun that Valerie had leached from their marriage years ago.

Because, ultimately, that was why he was doing this. It was her fault, really, not his. She was the one to blame. If she hadn't changed and turned into the vile controlling bitch that she'd become, he wouldn't be here now. He'd be with her, having fun in their hotel room at the Nottinghamshire Police's pleasure. But she wasn't into all that.

Was it so wrong that sometimes, he just wanted his dick sucked?

She didn't understand and possibly never would, at least not anymore. Thinking back to those early days in their relationship and the fun and games they got up to, he lamented losing that spark.

And yet, he wondered if he wasn't just looking at things through rose-tinted glasses. Had things really been that good?

He wondered if there might perhaps be a deeper reason behind Valerie's change in personality? Was there something wrong or rotten at the core of their relationship?

Neither of them had wanted children, so they'd not gone down that path, preferring to live for themselves rather than have their comfortable life ruined by a psychotic tiny person or two.

But, was he so sure that she agreed with him when he said he didn't want kids? Was she agreeing just to please him, or did she honestly not want children?

Well, it was getting a little late for that now, anyway. Neither of them was getting any younger, and it wasn't as if he wanted to get that close to her anyway. Her touch made his skin crawl. She disgusted him. He doubted he'd be able to perform for her, even if she did get down on her knees and do the business.

Emmett sighed and shook his head, clearing his mind of these troubling thoughts. He needed to get over there and just satiate these desires, get them out of his system before they drove him to distraction.

Who knew what he'd end up doing to Valerie if he was forced to stay with her for much longer without doing what he needed to do.

Emmett climbed out of the car and made his way across to the house. He'd been here a few times and knew it well enough, although there was always a new girl or two for him to choose from whenever he visited. None of them stuck it for very long.

He didn't blame them, not really. For many of them, he was old enough to be their dad, if not their grandad. It couldn't be much fun for them, even if he did tip them well for their work. He appreciated their attention.

Emmett crossed the road without issue and without being recognised, which was always his biggest fear, and rang the doorbell. Within moments, a young woman appeared and opened the door, keeping it on the chain. She gave him a quick look and recognised him.

"Oh, hello again." She closed the door, removed the chain, and opened it again. "Come in."

"Sorry for showing up unannounced. I don't know if you have space or…"

"We do. Come in. We have a few new girls since your last visit." She led him through to a well-heated room where several young women, some of them looking like they were still teenagers, were sitting and talking between themselves. Most of them wore some kind of lingerie, silk robe, or nothing at all, chatting and sipping on drinks. An older woman sat close by, watching. Emmett recognised her as the owner. He'd spotted her at the recent town meeting, which was possibly where the desire to return here had come from.

The owner, Susan, gave him a quick smile and a nod. She'd probably already spoken to the police, and it seemed as though she'd not revealed that he was a regular of hers.

That alone would be incriminating enough because, if he was a regular at her brothel, the police could rightly assume he picked up the occasional prostitute as well. It would be a swift fall from grace from that point on.

His dalliances with street walkers might well be a guess on her part, but it wouldn't be wrong.

"So," the girl who let him in said, waving her hand to present the girls to him. "Who would you like to choose today?"

"Girls," Susan barked from her seat at the table, her voice strong and commanding. "We have a guest."

Instantly the demeanour and posture of the women in the room changed, from relaxed and slouching, to poised and alluring as they sat up, stopped talking, and smiled at him.

Emmett scanned the room, feeling like he was at an all-you-can-eat buffet serving his favourite food. As his eyes skipped from beaming face to sexy smoulder, he spotted a girl further in who seemed a little less comfortable, but there was something about her nervousness and vulnerability that piqued his interest. He found her coy glances endlessly seductive and instantly, desperately wanted to see more of her. He wanted those dusky eyes fixed on him while she did unspeakable things to him.

But there was something else about her too, something that just danced at the edges of his conscious thoughts. He strove to reach it and figure out what it was, and then suddenly, it came to him.

He recognised her.

"The dark-haired girl in the white lingerie," he enquired, "what's her name?"

49

Sitting at his desk, Rob found it difficult to settle and focus on his work after the brief encounter he'd been through with his estranged brother in the car park outside. He'd not seen Owen in years, although they had crossed paths once or twice between his departure from the family twenty years ago and today. But those chance meetings had only been in passing, and the words exchanged had been few.

But this was something different. This was no chance meeting. No, Owen had sought him out and waited for him. He wanted to see him and to have his say, which meant something had changed. Something was different, and the only thing he could think of was to do with their current case. He'd not gone looking for gang ties, but that's just how it had developed, and here they were, on the cusp of a brutal gang war that looked like it was about to blow up.

The situation was on a knife edge after the drive-by. Radek's crew had killed one of Abel's gang, and now everything depended on how Abel reacted to this. If he lashed out and killed one of Radek's crew, then all bets were off, and they would be plunged into a brutal gang war that would be waged in the streets of Clipstone and

Mansfield, and there would be inevitable casualties, both innocent and not.

Was that perhaps what Owen was warning him about. Was he saying to stop and keep out before things turned to shit? Was this something that his brother would be dealing with and stopping on his own, and would the interference of the police make things worse rather than better?

Or maybe it was the other way around, and Owen wanted the gang war but to keep the police out of it. Was Owen being protective of him? But the instant he thought it, he knew that to be wrong.

There was no way on earth that his brother would care enough about him to stop him from getting hurt. No, the only thing he cared about would be the family business and nothing else. But if that was true, then maybe the real reason for Owen showing up was that his team were getting a little too close to things.

Had they actually worried Owen's firm?

He supposed it was possible...

While Rob languished deep in thought, his focus on the angles and possibilities of the case, he noted absentmindedly the squawk of the radio in the background and the rise in voices surrounding him. He didn't take much notice until Scarlett grabbed him by the shoulder.

"Rob, are you with us?"

"Wha?" It felt like he was rising from a dream. As if he'd been napping in the day and been shaken awake. "What's going on?"

"Didn't you hear the radio?"

"No," he admitted, feeling a little embarrassed.

"Another body's been found at the Clip Club."

It took a moment for the full implications of that sentence to fall into place as his mind raced to catch up. The Clip Club could mean Nigel, Caprice, or even Izabela. "Who is it?"

"We don't know yet."

Rob jumped to his feet, noticing for the first time that many of the eyes in the room were on him. He was the most senior detective in the room, after all, so they were waiting for their orders. But for whatever reason, at that moment, he'd forgotten this tiny detail.

As his mind fell back into more familiar territory, putting aside thoughts and worries about his family, he ordered the room to organise a response while directing a couple of uniforms to join Scarlett and himself as they attended the scene.

Within minutes, they were out of the building and driving across the village. They might only be a few streets away, but driving was still quicker, and they could use their cars to block the road and restrict access.

"Who called it in?" Rob asked as he drove, the tiredness he'd been feeling falling away from the corners of his mind.

"I don't know. We just got word from dispatch that a body had been found. That's it. I guess we'll find out when we get there."

"Shit."

"It'll be Izabela," Scarlett speculated. "Another young woman with her whole life ahead of her, cut short by a monster."

"We don't know that yet," Rob replied. "Not that anyone else is a better option, but..."

"I know."

Rob raced around to the side road that ran along in front of the shops and found no other emergency vehicles. They were the first on the scene, which wasn't surprising given their proximity to the club, but he'd hoped to find at least an ambulance here.

No such luck.

"Let's go," Rob ordered and jumped out. They raced to the front door and barged into a silent bar. Just a handful of lights were on, and straight ahead, a single chair had been placed centrally, away from any tables, with a figure slumped into it.

Even with his badly beaten head bowed, Rob recognised Nigel.

Movement to his right drew his attention. The reporter Mary Day stood up. All the colour had drained from her face, and she held a phone to her ear.

"Okay, they're here now," she said into the device. "Thank you."

"Mary?" Rob said, frowning. "What..."

"I came here for an interview. I wanted to speak to him, but I found him like this. She waved her hand towards him and noted some blood on it. She shuddered and wiped it away.

"You called it in?"

"Yeah. I called 999, that was them." She indicated her phone.

Rob nodded, making a mental note to check the recording of the call later. "Do you know what happened?" Around him, Scarlett and the officers who had accompanied them started to move through the room, taking a closer look at the body.

"No, I... I don't know. I just found him like this." She seemed shaken by her experience. "Who would do this?"

Rob grimaced as he looked back towards the body. "I don't know," he muttered. He wasn't lying. He didn't know, but he could probably guess.

"He's been beaten up," Scarlett said. "He's covered in bruises and cuts. Judging from the amount of blood, I think he's been stabbed."

Rob could see it too. The dark carmine liquid had stained the carpet around the base of the chair and soaked through his shirt. "He's been tortured."

"That would be my guess, too," Scarlett agreed.

"Jesus," Mary gasped. "What is this?"

Rob glanced over at her, knowing the answer. It was the gangs. Had they found out Izabela was staying here? Had they tortured him to find out the truth and then taken her. They needed to check the rest of the building.

"Sir!"

Rob looked up to see one of the uniformed officers standing at the end of the bar. He was looking behind it and waving him over.

"What?"

"This one's still alive."

"Shit. Stay here," he said to Mary before rushing over with Scarlett. Behind the bar, Rob saw another bloodied body. It was Caprice, sitting up against the back wall, clutching her bloodied flank. With half-closed eyes, she was breathing fast, hyperventilating.

Rob rushed down to her while waving to the uniform. "Ambulance, now. Caprice?" He lifted her sagging head. "Caprice, stay with me. Can you hear me? Caprice?"

"I... can hear you..." she croaked, her voice small and weak.

"Hang on, we've got an ambulance on the way. What happened?" Beside him, Scarlett peeled Caprice's hand away from her side to reveal a puncture wound that was bleeding badly. Scarlett then pointed up. He followed her finger and spotted a bullet hole in the wall. "You were shot?"

Caprice nodded.

"Who did this? Who shot you? Who was here?"

"It was... Abel..."

"Abel? Abel Underwood?" What was he doing here? Did he know about Izabela?"

Caprice nodded.

"Shit." He turned to Scarlett. "Get upstairs and find Izabela."

"On it." She nodded and stood up.

"No," Caprice hissed. "Not here."

"What?"

"Izabela. She's..." Caprice coughed and brought up blood that splattered down her front. "She's not here. She's... Gone."

"Gone? Gone where? Where is she?"

"Brothel. Susan." Tears streamed down her face. "He told Abel…" Another cough. "Oh, god, it hurts."

"Bollocks," Rob muttered and then looked up at Scarlett. "Izabela must be at Susan's brothel, and Abel's going after her."

"We need to stop him," Scarlett said.

"Damn bloody right," Rob agreed before he turned back to Caprice. "I'm going to leave you with my colleagues, okay? They'll look after you."

Caprice nodded and winced with pain. "Go. Stop him."

"We're going," Rob reassured her and got to his feet. He glanced at Scarlett. "Let's go."

50

Emmett gazed down, his eyes locked on hers as he savoured this incredible feeling. Her young lips were wrapped around him, her head pumping smoothly back and forth, sucking hungrily on him while she stared into his eyes.

Seeing her young face pleasuring him was incredibly intoxicating and wildly satisfying.

"My god, you're beautiful, Izabela." He'd first seen her that night. She'd been standing with Penny when he'd picked her up, and he remembered being attracted to her even then. He'd hoped to return to her one day and have his time with her, and then this whole thing happened and ruined everything.

His mind briefly flashed back to the moment he opened the bin that fateful morning and saw Penny's vacant, lifeless face staring back at him from inside that black plastic bag.

He looked away from Izabela and shook his head, closing his eyes as he tried to banish the memory from his thoughts. It put him off his rhythm, and sent his train of thought down a track he didn't care for.

Squeezing his eyes shut tight, he cleared his head and focused on the wonderful warm feeling of Izabela's mouth and the wonders she worked with her tongue.

The sensations were enough to distract him and send the memories of the head, memories that had plagued his nightmares in recent nights, spinning off into the darker recesses of his mind.

He'd barely slept since that morning. Every night he'd woken up in a cold sweat with images of Penny's head in his bin. Sometimes the head moved in those nightmares. It looked at him with those dead eyes and taunted him. She mocked him and called him a pervert, an adulterous philandering freak who got his rocks off by fucking teenagers. Sometimes she called him a paedophile, too.

Was he one?

He didn't see himself as one of those disgusting sub-humans, but... Penny had barely been at the age of consent. He hadn't known that at the time. How was he supposed to know? They all made themselves look older. He wasn't attracted to kids, but would that matter to the police?

As his mind continued to spiral off into darker waters, he remembered sitting at that table beside Penny's father, listening to his moving tribute and asking for help in finding Penny's killer. Emmett had listened, knowing that just a few days before, she'd been in his car, fucking him and doing everything he'd asked of her in return for money.

He'd felt small and embarrassed, and part of him had wanted to confess to him or the police about what he'd done.

"Mind elsewhere?" Izabela asked.

His eyes snapped open. He looked down, and she smiled back while holding him in her hand, working to arouse him once more.

"Sorry. My head was elsewhere."

"That's okay," she said seductively and went back to work.

Emmet relaxed as he felt himself stiffen once more.

A loud explosive bang echoed through the house. Emmett's attention snapped to the door. He held his breath. Izabela froze in place as she watched the door and whimpered.

"What was that?"

"I…"

Several more ear-splitting bangs followed, now mixed with shouts and screams.

"Oh god," he gasped. "No, no, no…"

"What… What's going on?" Izabela said as she backed away from the entrance to the room.

Part of him wanted to run. He stared at the door, wondering if he could get out of the building. Was there a back door? Could he escape? He was butt naked, though, and his clothes were scattered all over the room where Izabela had thrown them.

She crouched beside the bed, as nude as he was apart from a pair of heels, her eyes wide with terror as she stared at the door.

Emmett rushed to grab his boxers and trousers when the door was smashed open with another bang.

A man Emmett had never seen before walked in. He was tall, fit, well-muscled, and was dressed in black. A coating of stubble wrapped around his jaw while dark hair in close curls hugged his head. The man's dark eyes spotted them both and flicked back and forth between them.

Emmett stared at him, and it was only after a few moments that he noticed the large handgun in the man's hand. He shrank back, his breathing quickened as his heart thundered.

Emmett raised his hands in surrender.

The man spoke, but apart from one word that sounded like Izabela, he couldn't understand anything he said. He sounded eastern European or Russian, maybe? He was talking to the girl, though, not him. She replied in the same language, getting to her feet and holding her hands up in a calming gesture. She looked terrified but seemed to be trying to calm him down. If she used the man's name, Emmett didn't recognise it.

The man replied, angry, barking at her in short sharp words that seemed to almost slap Izabela around the face. She approached him, still trying to calm him while tears streamed down her face.

With the man's attention firmly on her, Emmett picked up his trousers and shirt, got to his feet, and started to slowly walk towards the door. Two steps in, the man's head turned.

"No," the man snapped and pointed his gun at him. "You stay here."

"Radek, no. Not him," Izabela said, switching to English. "This has nothing to do with him. Let him go."

Radek shook his head. "You are clever girl," the man answered in heavily accented English. "You know English, and you no tell me. You are clever, yes? No! You think you are clever, but no. You are silly bitch whore who does not know what I will do. No one make me look like idiot. Not on. You understand?"

"I do," Izabela replied. "I'm sorry. I'll come back. I'll be yours again. I don't care, but please, no more deaths. No more killing. Please."

As naked as the day she was born, Izabela knelt at the man's feet, prostrating herself before him as she begged for their lives.

"Why should I take you back?" the man asked. "You just run away again. You make trouble for me again. That's all you do. You are just trouble." He waved the gun around. "I can end trouble today." He pointed the weapon at Izabela.

She whimpered and fought back more tears. "Don't do this, please, I'm begging you. I'll come with you now. I'll do anything you want. Anything. I don't care. Just please, put the gun away."

As they went back and forth with Izabela trying to justify her life and why he should let her live, Emmett watched, paralysed with fear as he waited for the judgement on their lives.

Then Valerie walked into the room.

Emmett did a double take as his wife silently walked in behind Radek, who didn't seem to realise she was there. With a face filled with incomprehensible rage, she locked eyes with Emmett and then looked over at Radek's back. She frowned, looking confused as she looked between Emmet and then Radek again.

Emmett tried to form words, but nothing came out. What the hell was going on? Why was she here? How did she find him? Was she insane? He'd kill her too!

Valerie spotted Izabela, and her lips twisted in disgust. Turning, she spotted a metal ornament, grabbed it and swung it at Radek's head without a moment's hesitation. She put her whole body into the swing and slammed the statuette's base into the man's head right above his ear.

He dropped to the floor instantly, all strength disappearing from his legs as he collapsed.

Emmett stared, utterly agog, at the scene before him, his mouth open in shock.

"What the hell?" Izabela gasped, looking between Radek and Valerie. "Who are you?"

"Valerie?" Emmett squeaked. "I… What the… How…"

His wife threw the metal statue to the floor and pointed to him. "Shut your face."

"Aaah…"

She stared at him for a second more before she reached behind, into her waistband, and pulled out a knife. Emmett watched as she took a single step and plunged the blade into Izabela's bare chest.

Emmett's jaw dropped as blood oozed from Izabela's chest. Above the bloody knife, Valerie glared at him, her eyes wild. "You've made me do it again!"

Emmett's stomach dropped as he suddenly put two and two together. In his mind's eye, he saw Penny's head in his wheelie bin, staring at him, decapitated and lifeless.

"It was you."

"You pathetic excuse for a man," she hissed.

"Valerie, no. Please, stop." He glanced at Izabela, who was staring over at him, her eyes wide with fear as she held out her hand, pleading to him.

"Help…" she gasped. "Please."

"Don't do this," he begged. "She might live. We can save her."

"And why on earth would I want to save her, Emmett? Why would I want her to live after what you've done with her?"

Emmett got to his feet, his own nakedness forgotten and held his hands up towards her. "Please, Val. Don't…"

"Get back," she snapped. Ripping the blade from Izabela's chest, she crouched and grabbed something from the floor. Izabela fell back against the bed, clutching her chest as blood, deep and crimson, fell over her hand and breast. It glistened in the soft light of the room as it poured over her.

Valerie held Radek's gun in her hand and pointed it at him. "You stay there. I'm not done."

"No, Val. Please don't…"

Holding the knife with the blade down, she stabbed Izabela again and again, grunting with the effort as the young girl wailed and whimpered, before falling silent. She slumped to the floor, lifeless.

Emmett stared at Izabela in utter shock before his gaze tracked back up to Valerie. Standing over her prey, breathing hard, Emmett saw her in a new and terrifying light. Not only had his attraction to her ended years ago, but now, he didn't recognise this woman. Who was this crazed harpy standing before him? Because it certainly wasn't his wife.

Somewhere in the distance, at the edge of his hearing, sirens wailed.

Valerie heard it too. With the focus of a big-game predator, she turned her head to listen, then trapped him with her gaze. "We're leaving."

51

"We need assistance as soon as possible," Scarlett said over her phone, having called in to report events at the club, and let dispatch know where they were driving to and what they could encounter there.

Rob was under no illusion about it either. Abel was, by all accounts, a violent and dangerous criminal, and he was clearly on the warpath both against the Polish gang, led by the mysterious Radek and now Izabela. Her antics had caused much of the troubles Abel and his crew had faced, leading to the death of at least three of his prostitutes and one of his gang members.

There was no telling what kind of mental state he would be in, but Rob guessed that it wouldn't be a rational one.

He'd insisted on them both donning their flack vests before they set off for Forest Town, and into the unknown.

"What?" Scarlett said, still on the phone beside him. "And that was when? Okay, thanks." She ended the call.

"What was that about?" Rob asked, sensing she'd heard something new.

"A body was discovered in Forest Town. A woman that's been identified as Apolonia Bartosz. She's a known associate of Radek's, part of his crew. Years ago she was picked up on prostitution offences, but it looks like she graduated to full gang member status some years back."

"Damn. Who says there's no room for advancement in the criminal underworld? Huh?"

"I know, right? Just look at this girl, working her way up from hooker to right-hand woman of a local crime lord!"

"The girl done good," Rob added in a fake American accent with a shake of his disbelieving head. "Jesus. So, she was found dead?"

"Stabbed to death," Scarlett confirmed.

"Executed," Rob added. Another gang hit, he resolved. Things were spiralling out of control quicker than he'd anticipated. These guys were actively going after people on the sidelines now, like Nigel and Izabela, and catching innocents like Caprice in the crossfire.

They needed to get on top of this and fast.

With the siren of the unmarked pool car blaring, they bullied their way through another junction, hoping they might arrive before things descended into more of a blood bath than they already were.

Rob had his doubts they'd make it in time, though. They seemed to be playing catch-up the whole time, following the trail of bodies as they were left behind by these morally corrupt individuals.

"I bet you're glad you chose a pool car and not Bella for this run?"

Rob smiled. "We had to get there as quick as we could. It was the right choice to make." But, he took her meaning. He always preferred to drive his pride and joy, but there were times when it just wasn't the right choice.

"How very pragmatic. You should get a siren fitted to Bella and one of those magnetic lights you whip out and slap on the roof."

"You mean, I need to go 'full sweeny'?"

"Sweeny? What's that?"

"Oh, sweet Mary and Joseph and his wee donkey. You young uns!"

"What? Is that a TV series I don't know?"

"Only one of the best TV series!"

"Is it on iPlayer?"

"Christ knows." Rob shook his head and concentrated on the road, throwing the car round a final corner and skidding to a stop outside the suspected massage parlour and brothel.

Judging from the people standing outside their houses and cautiously approaching the building, they were in the right place. Rob jumped out as the front door of the house opened, and a young woman in skimpy clothing stumbled out. Covered in blood, she crumpled to the floor. Gasps and at least one scream sounded from the onlookers.

Scarlett was already on her phone, demanding that emergency services get here on the double as Rob rushed over to the girl.

"Hey, are you okay? Are you hurt? We're with the police."

"I think I'm okay, nothing too bad," she answered. "You need to get in there. You need to help the others."

A nearby civilian woman joined them.

"You're police?"

"Yeah," Rob answered, focusing on the girl.

"You go, I've got her," the woman said, crouching beside the girl, and waving for others to help.

Seeing other locals rush to help, Rob nodded and got up as Scarlett ended her call.

"An ambulance is on its way," she informed him. "No idea how long it'll be, though."

He thought he could already hear sirens in the distance, but they could be related to the scene at the Clip Club they'd just left. Hopefully, some of them would divert here. But there was no time to waste.

"Come on," he said and carefully eased past the front door, through a small hallway into a larger room. Rob spotted several bullet holes in the walls and a number of bloodied, lifeless bodies on the floor, most of them young, possibly teenage girls wearing next to nothing. The house was silent, the eerie silence associated with the dead, the only noise coming from outside as people gathered.

It was like a scene from a horror film.

"Shit," Scarlett hissed. "Look."

Moving to Scarlett's side, he followed her gaze. At her feet, was a body he recognised, who looked out of place in this room. It was Abel, the gang leader who'd just killed Nigel and injured Caprice. He sported a single gunshot wound to the head, mimicking the report of the body that had just been found not too far from here.

As Rob looked up at Scarlett, he heard movement echo from deeper in the house. A door slammed, and a girl screamed.

Pulling their batons out, they moved to the next room and over to another open door leading to a corridor beyond. Rob peered along the shadowy hallway, noting the doorways on either side. There was a dog leg bend part way up, concealing the end of the hall.

They heard more movement and a yelp, followed by a shout of pain.

Rob jogged down the hall, holding his baton ready. At the left and right switchback, he slipped around the corners until he could see the final stretch of the corridor. He spied a couple more doors to either side and a final fire door standing ajar at the end, but no people. The first door they came to on the right was open. Rob edged around it until it revealed the carnage inside. Two more bodies lay motionless on the bedroom floor.

A man he didn't recognise, dressed in black with dark hair, lay crumpled on his front, a pool of blood next to his head and no obvious signs of life. Beside him, on her back up against the bed, the naked body of Izabela lay covered in blood from the multiple stab wounds that had been inflicted to her chest.

It was a sorry and gory sight. Feeling deflated, Rob sighed as he took a step into the room.

They were too late.

"Bollocks."

"Oh no? Damn it," Scarlett exclaimed as she approached Izabela, crouched, and placed her fingers on the girls wrist, looking for a pulse. "What the hell was she doing here?"

"Christ knows." Rob grimaced in anguish over failing to protect Izabela. She'd not deserved to die like this, at such an early age.

With a sigh, Scarlett dropped Izabela's wrist. "She's dead." She pointed at the other body. "Who's that?"

"No clue," Rob answered dejectedly, sighing at the scene before him. He wasn't too interested in the guy at this point. He was probably a gang member, here for revenge. Radek maybe, the Polish guy? Who knows. Instead, his focus was on Izabela and his own failure to keep her safe. He should have insisted that she leave Nigel and come with them back when they first met her.

"I'll check him," Scarlett said and made to walk over to him.

A girl screamed.

Suddenly alert, Rob turned and darted back out into the corridor with Scarlett right behind him. A young woman stumbled in through the open fire door. She held her blood-splattered thigh in both hands and collapsed against the wall, hissing in pain.

"What happened?" Rob demanded.

Scarlett crouched beside her, reaching to assess her wounds. "Are you okay?"

"Don't worry about me." The girl grunted in pain and nodded to the fire door. "They're outside. She stabbed me, and she's got a gun."

"She?" Rob asked, curious.

"But, you're hurt," Scarlett countered as Rob got to his feet and looked at the door, gripping his baton.

"Forget about me. Get them. Go on, go!"

The sirens were close. They'd be here any moment. Rob knew they needed to end this, and after seeing Izabela, he was not about to let the killer slip through his fingers. "Come on, help is nearly here. We need to end this."

"Okay, okay," Scarlett said, clearly torn about what she should do as the injured girl continued to shout at them, telling them to get outside.

Throwing caution to the wind Rob rushed out, leading the way. At this point facing an assailant and ending this murder spree was more important than his safety.

He exited through the fire door into a small off-road parking bay. As he stepped outside, a car wheel spun backwards out of one of the spaces into the road. Rob spotted Emmett in the passenger side window, his terrified face staring out at them. They locked eyes for a moment, and Emmett mouthed the word 'help' at him as the shadowy driver put the car into gear and accelerated away at speed, heading towards Clipstone.

"That's Valerie's car," Scarlett remarked.

"Shit." Rob turned, spotted their own car just metres away, and instantly made up his mind. "Come on."

He sprinted for the car, pulling the key and jumping in. Scarlett followed and landed in her seat just as he fired up the engine. Putting it into gear, he dumped the clutch and squealed through a doughnut to face the right way. The car's spinning tyres kicked up a wall of smoke before they caught, and G-Forces slammed Scarlett's door shut. Rob floored the accelerator and tore off up the road.

He hit the switch for the siren and settled in for the drive. They were just seconds behind the car carrying Emmett, and with the siren clearing the way, he soon had the fleeing car in sight.

"There she is," Scarlett called out.

"Do you think it's Valerie?"

"Who else would it be?"

Rob considered the possibility and shrugged. "Fair point."

Scarlett got on the radio to control and started to call out a running commentary as they gave chase, reporting their speed and every road they took.

It was clear to Rob they were heading back into Clipstone, but as to where she was going, he had no idea. Valerie had clearly noticed they were giving chase and was pushing as hard as she could to try and get away. Flouting every rule of the road, she endangered drivers and pedestrians but luckily didn't seem to hurt anyone as she sped along Mansfield Road and past the parade of shops in Clipstone.

Ahead, the Headstocks of the former Colliery jutted high above the surrounding homes.

To his surprise, as they made for the edge of the village, passing the fenced-off wasteland where the Headstocks rose up, Valerie suddenly turned hard right. She bombed down the side road where Penny's body was found and accelerated towards the gates that led into the Colliery.

"What the hell is she doing?" Scarlett hissed.

"She knows she can't get away," he replied. It was a guess, but it made sense.

"Fuck," Scarlett grunted.

"Language, Timothy."

"Piss off..." she snapped before adding, "Sir."

Rob smiled and tore through the gate after Valerie's car. They bounced over the uneven ground until Valerie's car skidded to a halt in the shadow of the Headstocks. Rob hit the brakes and opened his door, jumping out. He could see some commotion on the far side of their car. The driver was pulling Emmett across the driver's seat and out her side, and as they both stood up, he saw Valerie's face for the first time in this chase. With her jaw set and her eyes wide, she looked like a wild animal, ready to lash out. She held Emmett by the back of his collar with a gun pointed at his head.

"Christ," Scarlett gasped. "Where the hell did she get that?"

"No idea," Rob said, staying behind his car door. It wouldn't stop a bullet if she fired at him, only the engine block could do that, but it was better than nothing. He yelled over to Valerie. "It's over!"

"It's not over. Nothing's ever over."

"Don't be naive, Valerie. You're not getting out of here, and you know it. It's done."

"She killed Penny," Emmett shouted, confirming Rob's guess. "And Izabela."

Valerie pistol-whipped him, slamming the butt of the gun's handle into Emmett's head. He yelped and dropped to his knees.

"Emmett, be quiet," Rob shouted. They were maybe ten metres apart and nowhere near close enough to stop Valerie if she decided to use the weapon.

"Do we approach?" Scarlett asked in low tones out the side of her mouth.

Rob nodded. "Slowly, keep your distance from me." He stepped out from behind his car door and took a cautious step towards her, keeping his hands in view. "Valerie. Please, put the gun down. There's no need for more death."

"They deserved it," she snapped. "Those whores. I hate them."

He needed to keep her talking. "*Why* did they deserve it?"

"Because of him." She was behind Emmett, where he knelt in the grass.

As Rob took another step closer, Valerie raised the gun. "Don't come any closer. I'm warning you."

Rob froze and held up his hands. "Wouldn't dream of it."

Valerie pointed the gun at Scarlett, then back to Rob. "You wouldn't understand."

"Try us. We can talk this through."

"You're just trying to delay things, waiting for your friends to get here." They could hear more sirens, not too far away.

"No," he lied. He was trying to delay her, but it wasn't the only reason he wanted to get her talking. "I'm trying to understand why you did this, and for that, you need to talk to us. Please. Why did you kill Penny?"

He could see the storm of emotion cross her face as she thought things through before answering. "He should have just done as I asked. I was trying to help him."

"By killing these girls?" Rob asked, taking another slow step closer.

"They don't deserve to live. They're scum. They tempt and seduce and ruin the community."

"And you believe that you were the one to judge them?"

"If not me, then who? We don't need their kind in this village, corrupting our men. Corrupting him." She jabbed her gun into the back of Emmett's head. "Someone needed to stand up to them. I needed to show this idiot the consequences of his actions. If he had just listened to me and done as I asked, we wouldn't be in this mess. It's his fault. He drove me to it. He made me kill them. I didn't have a choice. If more people in Clipstone followed my example, the village wouldn't be in this state. We need more people like me."

"Are you insane?" Emmett shouted, turning to her and starting to stand. "We need more murdering psychos?"

"Shut up," Valerie raged.

"No, I won't shut up. I've put up with your controlling shit for too long. You don't own me. You don't run my life. I'll do what I damn well want, and you can't stop me."

The gun barked. Emmett staggered, then fell.

"No," Rob yelled.

"Oh god," Valerie gasped as she stared down at Emmett writhing on the ground. "No. No. This can't be... I didn't mean...." She looked up and met Rob's shocked gaze. All he saw in her eyes was madness, the fragments of a shattered psyche falling into the yawning void of her mind. As he watched, she raised the gun and put it to her temple.

"No, Valerie. Don't."

She fired.

52

With his hands stuffed deep into his pockets and his collar pulled up around his neck in a vain attempt to keep the cold out, Rob watched the paramedics do their job. Naturally, they trampled over the scene, focusing on saving Emmett's life above everything else.

Rob has no issue with this because, of course, it was the right thing to do, and Emmett was in desperate need of medical help. But a part of him still cringed as he watched the paramedics trample over the scene.

As the ambulance crew worked, getting Emmett onto a stretcher ready to carry him to the waiting ambulance, Rob's eyes wandered over to the covered body of Valerie.

It was her all along.

She'd watched her husband discover the head in their bin, where she'd dumped it, and then watched as he and Scarlett had turned up to assess the scene.

She'd killed Penny here and then both Radek and Izabela at the brothel, all because Emmett was playing away. The true reason why she'd cut Penny's head off and placed it in their bin might never be fully known, but he could take a guess.

It was probably a warning aimed squarely at her husband. They'd need to check with Emmett once he was able to talk, but Rob guessed Emmett had paid Penny for sex, and somehow Valerie had found out, which led to Penny's murder. But not satisfied with just killing the girl, she then needed to send a warning to her husband.

Rob could only guess how it must have felt to open the bin and see a face he recognised staring back at him. It would probably haunt Emmett's dreams for the rest of his life.

"Do you think that'll be the end of the fighting?" Scarlett asked.

"Between the gangs?" Rob clarified.

"Yep."

He shrugged, unsure. "I hope so. Both Abel and Radek are dead now, so..."

Scarlett nodded as the paramedics and a couple of helpful police officers carried Emmett past on a bright orange stretcher. Emmett offered them a brief smile and a grimace as he went.

He looked a little ashamed of his actions, and he wasn't yet aware of the full extent of these consequences. All these lives ruined or lost could be traced back to Emmett's inability to keep it in his pants.

It was sad, really.

The paramedics bundled Emmett into the back of the ambulance, and as the vehicle pulled away, Rob saw a car pull up, and Nailer climb out. He spotted Rob and made his way over.

"The gaffer's here," he remarked to Scarlett, alerting her to his arrival before turning to greet his superior. "Guv."

"Well done, you two. That's a good job done, from what I hear."

Rob grunted. "Well, she killed herself, so it could have gone better. I would have preferred to take her in alive."

"As would we all, but things are what they are, and ultimately this means we have our woman, and maybe, just maybe, things can settle down again."

"Here's hoping," Scarlet agreed. "With Abel and Radek out of the picture, the gangs might actually call it a day."

"Radek?"

"He was the body dressed in black at the brothel," Rob explained. "We saw him in the same room as Izabela. Emmett confirmed it was him before the paramedics got here when we were helping staunch the bleeding."

"I've just come from the massage parlour," Nailer replied. "There was no other body in Izabela's room."

Rob frowned. "You're sure?"

"Positive. And I was one of the first on the scene. No one had been in there before us."

A feeling of dread spread through Rob's body as he considered the options, but there was only really one that seemed to fit. "Damn. He was alive, and playing dead."

"He ran away?" Scarlett added. "Damn it. So that means, between us leaving and the authorities arriving, he legged it."

"Bollocks," Rob cursed. "I knew it was too good to be true. Crap."

"Yeah, he was gone," Nailer confirmed, screwing his face up in frustration. "Well, I have faith in my team. We'll find him. So, Emmett's on his way to the hospital, I take it?"

"Yeah, that was him leaving as you pulled up," Rob confirmed. "Valerie shot him in the back, but didn't kill him outright. With any luck, he'll pull through."

"Valerie wasn't as lucky," Scarlett added. "Her headshot killed her instantly."

"That depends on your definition of luck." Rob shook his head, removing the image of Valerie's last action.

"So, she was the one who killed Penny?" Nailer asked.

"She admitted as much, and Emmett seemed certain of it. We're hoping to get the full story from him when he's in a more stable condition, plus, we know what we're looking for now. There'll be proof, I'm sure of it."

"I hope so," Nailer said.

"What about Caprice and Nigel?" Scarlett asked. "Any news on them? We left them with a couple of officers."

"Yeah. Unfortunately, Nigel's dead," Nailer answered. "But Caprice should be at the hospital too by now. As far as I know, they're hopeful she'll pull through. So, here's hoping."

"That's great news," Rob said, relieved that it wasn't a total loss.

"That's good," Scarlett agreed. "I was a little worried about her."

"Me too," Rob agreed then turned to address Nailer. "We'll need to talk to her as well, and anyone who survived the massacre at the massage parlour. Our work is far from done."

"Indeed it's not. No rest for the wicked," Nailer quipped.

"Or those who chase them," Scarlett added.

53

"You look like shit," Bill said as Vincent Kane walked into the back street greasy spoon in the heart of Nottingham and sat opposite him with a scowl on his face.

"So would you, if you'd been punched in the eye by a seven-foot tall ogre," Kane grumbled while gingerly taking his seat. "Would you like to know how it feels? I can oblige."

Bill half closed the laptop he'd been working on and pushed it to one side. Kane was pissed and was taking it out on him. He couldn't let that go. "Try it. See how assaulting an officer of the law goes down with the police and your employer."

Kane smirked, sending a shiver of doubt up Bill's spine. "I am tempted just to see how your employer reacts to the recording I have of you asking me to stalk Inspector Loxley."

Every muscle in Bill's body tensed at the revelation. Balling his fists and gritting his teeth, he stared at Kane's smug face. It took a great deal of effort to regulate his breathing and not punch the gobshite, giving him another black eye to match the first. But that would only land him in deeper water when Kane released the file, effectively ruining his life. Closing his eyes for a moment, Bill sucked in a long, cleansing breath and pushed his emotions back and away. He needed to be calm and focused to deal with this bottom feeder.

Eventually, Bill felt settled enough to continue. "So, what happened? Where are my photos?"

Kane sighed. "I don't have them."

Bill frowned. "What?"

"Just as I got off the phone with you yesterday, I was attacked. They did this to me," he pointed to his eye, "and stole my laptop, phone and camera. I don't have anything anymore. They even got into my online storage and raided that."

"Who? Who did this?"

"The guy I saw Rob meeting with. Him and his thug."

"Okay." A thought occurred to him, so he opened his laptop and navigated to a folder he accessed regularly. He had an idea who it might be, but he needed to be sure. And do you remember what this man looked like?"

"Of course." Kane shrugged, uninterested. "But I need new gear, Bill. You wanted me on this job, so you need to replace the gear I've lost."

Bill glanced up and gave Kane an incredulous look. The man seemed pissed, but there was no way he was shelling out for a new laptop and camera. "Aren't you insured?"

"That's not the point."

"I think it very much is the point. You didn't need to take this job. You could have told me to shove it."

"Wish I had now," Kane grumbled.

Finally getting into the file, Bill scanned through the folders. After a moment or two's hunting, he finally found what he was looking for. This was a long shot, and he could be way off about this, but he had to know. He had to find out if Rob had met with... with them...

Taking a deep breath, Bill fixed Kane with a stare. "I want you to take a look at these photos and let me know if you recognise anyone in them, okay?"

Kane's lip curled up in disgust before he shrugged. "Yeah, sure. Whatever. What's this about?"

"We'll see..." Bill spun the laptop and started scrolling through the various photos in the folder, watching Kane carefully for a sign that he recognised anyone in the images.

It didn't take long.

"Wait. Him." Kane pointed. "That's him. That's the man that Rob met and then attacked me with his goon."

Bill looked at the screen and then back to Kane, his heart fluttering with excitement. "You're sure? Him? This man?" Bill pointed to the face on the screen.

"One hundred percent. I wouldn't forget that face. Why? Do you know him? What's his name?"

"His name is Owen," Bill replied as he turned the screen back towards himself and looked upon a face he knew all too well. "He's Rob's brother."

54

"Morning, everyone," Rob said, perched on the edge of the desk with the big whiteboard close behind. He then nodded to Nailer as he approached. "Morning, guv."

Nailer took a seat with the others. "Morning. I'm looking forward to hearing where we are with things since we wound everything up in Clipstone. I know you've been busy these last couple of days."

"We have," Rob confirmed, thinking back over the whirlwind of interviews and information gathering they'd been neck deep in once they knew the truth. It was much easier once they knew what they were looking for and where to focus their efforts and resources. "And we believe we have an excellent idea of everything that happened and also why it happened too. It's been a lot of work, but we got there."

"Okay, what have you discovered? Don't leave me swinging in the wind, will you?"

"Certainly not, sir. Wouldn't dream of it. As you know, we've been conducting a lot of new interviews surrounding Valerie and what happened, speaking to Emmett, Janette and David, as well as Valerie's parents, but also Caprice and others. We've also been going through Valerie's phone and such too, and we've found some useful information. For a start, it turns out Valerie's father was a very domineering man who openly used call girls and escorts, with the full knowledge of his wife, Valerie's mother. He controlled the household, provided for them financially, and saw it as his right to have a little fun in return for providing for the family. Valerie saw this, of course, and hated both her father for what he was doing and her mother for her weakness, for letting her father get away with it."

"This goes some way to explaining Valerie's state of mind," Nailer remarked.

"Absolutely," Rob agreed. "So when Valerie's marriage became strained, and Emmett started pulling away, she tried—out of fear—to control him and his life more and more. This, in turn, led to him seeking companionship elsewhere, and he started to use prostitutes.

"Naturally, she eventually found out about it and ended up tracking his phone and following him, which was how she found out what he was up to. She was able to drive out, find him, and see what he was doing."

"Okay, so what happened the night of Penny's murder?" Nailer asked.

"Well, from tracking the movements of their phones and talking to all those involved or connected to them, we know that Valerie went to her friends but was tracking Emmett, who she knew was out and about. Emmett picked up Penny and took her to the Clipstone allotments, where, according to Emmett, they indulged in oral sex before parting ways. Based on her tracking data, Valerie was just up the road at the time and probably watched at least part of it. We think Valerie saw who the prostitute was when she left Emmett's car and started to walk back to her patch. From there, Emmett went about his night out with his friends elsewhere in Clipstone. Meanwhile, Valerie went home and gathered a few things but left her phone at home."

"She was of sound mind, then, if she knew to leave her phone at home while committing a murder."

"Indeed," Rob agreed, having come to the same conclusion. This was premeditated. "She then went to find Penny and saw her picking up another client, Dillon Bradshaw, who we've spoken to. She waited until they'd finished, probably watching from her car. When Dillon threw her out of his car, she approached through the undergrowth and took her by surprise, hitting her on the head with a lug wrench from her car which we've recovered. Valerie then dragged her into the bushes and cut her head off. She then took Penny's head back to their house. She placed it in their wheelie bin on her way back inside, where she hid the tools she used, washed her clothes and took a shower shortly before Emmett returned home.

"We matched the scrap of rubber we found at the scene to a pair of ripped rubber gloves we found hidden in the loft of Valerie's house, along with the lug wrench and knife. These items had not been thoroughly cleaned and still had Penny's blood on them. The DNA was a direct match to Penny."

"So there's no doubt?" Nailer asked.

"Not as far as I'm concerned," Rob replied. "Valerie is our killer."

"And she killed Izabela, too, then?"

"She did," Rob confirmed. "From talking to all those who survived that night at the brothel, it seems that Emmett arrived, picked out Izabela, and then went to a room. Abel was next to arrive after killing Nigel and injuring Caprice. But before he could get to Izabela, Radek burst in, shot Abel and several of the women in the first room, and then went hunting for Izabela. Valerie was the last to arrive. She walked through the carnage and into the room behind Radek, where she knocked him out with a metal ornament before stabbing Izabela and fleeing with Emmett, who she held at gunpoint. You know the rest."

"So, Radek is still at large, then?" Nailer asked.

"He is. We're no closer to finding him." Rob sighed, annoyed with himself. "We should have checked him when we entered the room where we found Izabela. If we'd realised that he was alive..."

"We didn't have time, and there were no signs of life and a pool of blood," Scarlett said. "There's no point wondering 'what if', Rob."

"I know," he replied, still frustrated.

"No one holds that against you," Nailer added. "You had an active situation with Valerie and Emmet with a life in danger, you did the right thing. Now, tell me about our wounded witnesses. How are they doing?"

Rob knew his colleagues were right, but he couldn't help but feel annoyed that Radek, a known violent criminal, was still out there somewhere. For the time being, however, Rob banished those thoughts and answered Nailer's question. "Emmett and Caprice should both make full recoveries," Rob replied. "They've been very helpful. Emmett remembers that he noticed the rubber gloves his wife always uses were missing from the sink the morning he found the head, but he didn't read anything into it at the time. He wishes he'd taken more notice and has expressed great remorse over the death and destruction his actions have caused." Rob remembered seeing the realisation on Emmett's face when he finally grasped the full extent of the consequences of his actions. He was understandably devastated.

"And the gangs?"

"Everything seems to have calmed down. We're no closer to finding Radek, but the conflict between the gangs seems to have cooled, from what we can tell and find out."

"Good to know," Nailer said, standing to address the team as a whole. "I have to say, I am really pleased with these results and how effectively you all worked together on this. You've brought this case home, and while I understand and sympathise with your frustration that Valerie will not see her day in court, we did bring this to a satisfying conclusion, and that is what counts. Good job."

"Thank you, sir," Rob replied, followed by a chorus of similar responses from Scarlett, Nick, Guy, Ellen and Tucker.

"Job's not over yet, though," Nailer added. "I know how much paperwork you have to deal with. Have a great day." With that, Nailer turned and made his way back to his office.

"Great talk," Scarlett said as she approached, followed by Nick.

"Good job, guv," Nick added.

"Thanks. Everyone played their part and pulled their weight. That's all I can ask. I have to say, though, I'm glad to be sleeping at home again after two nights away. That village hall was a nightmare."

"A very uncomfortable one," Nick agreed.

"I bet Muffin was pleased to see you, too," Scarlett said.

"He was," Rob confirmed. "He hadn't wrecked the place, either."

"Oh, good kitty," Nick said.

"You've met Rob's cat, then?" Scarlett asked Nick.

"Oh yeah. He's a cute one."

"He is," Scarlett added with a cheeky smile. "But I never thought Mr Grumpy here would have such a soft spot for his cat. It's cute."

"Does your fiancé know you speak about Rob like that?" Nick asked.

Scarlett scoffed. "What? I think it's cute."

"I bet you do."

Scarlett shook her head, dismissing the playful accusation. "Hey. But I'm not the one looking after his cat when he's away. That's Rob's pretty neighbour." She turned to Rob. "What's her name?"

"Erika," Rob confirmed, rolling his eyes. "And before you start, I have no interest in Erika. Not in that way. She's young enough to be my daughter."

"She's not that young. She's in her early twenties, maybe?"

"Is she now," Nick replied in a suggestive tone, smiling the whole time. "You might have to introduce me."

Scarlett snorted. "Down, boy."

"Don't you start, Soldier Boy. We've got work to do."

"Moi?" Nick said flamboyantly.

"Soldier Boy?" Scarlett asked. "You were in the army?"

"Yeah," Nick confirmed. "That's a few years ago now, though. Ancient history." Rob sensed Nick's walls suddenly go up when Scarlett enquired and wondered if she felt it too.

"Okay," she replied but pried no deeper. "Well, let's get to work, shall we? I want to be at home on time tonight. Otherwise, Chris will start asking questions."

"Aye," Rob agreed. "Muffin too. He needs to know I'm still his owner."

"You don't own Muffin," Scarlett commented. "He owns you."

"Don't I know it," Rob agreed. "Now, back to work."

55

Owen pulled to the side of the road at the edge of Kings Park in Retford and scanned the street before he got out, making sure there was no one around who might cause trouble. He walked with purpose across the street, rounded the corner from Chancery Lane onto Exchange Street, and walked up to the entrance of The Old Police Station.

It was an odd feeling walking in here. The building had once been the town's police station until cuts and such had forced the police to close it and move their operations elsewhere.

Now, it was an upmarket pub and hotel, but kept much of the old aesthetic of the original building. Stepping inside, he knew exactly where his father would be, where he always was, and made his way round behind the bar into a back corridor. A couple of heavy doors lined this passage to the function room, and in the shadows of the corridor, he could make out lights inside the rooms.

These were the former cells of the police station, but these days, they were used as private dining areas for those who wanted to enjoy the ambience of a police cell while sampling the establishment's excellent food.

Owen's father had a particular fondness for these rooms, having spent a couple of nights in them as a younger man, and found the idea of coming here to eat and take meetings deliciously ironic.

Owen approached the usual door and stepped inside to see his father sitting opposite a man Owen recognised. He was a local District Councillor, and he looked up in surprise when Owen appeared.

"That's just my son," his father said, reassuring the man.

"Oh, okay. Well, thanks, Isaac. I appreciate the help."

"My pleasure. I'm always happy to support my local councillors in their work for the community. You know that. Come back any time, and my people will be in touch."

"Of course, thank you," the councillor said and shook Isaac's hand as he rose from his seat.

"Good day," the man said to Owen as he passed and disappeared up the hall.

Owen watched him go before he closed the door.

"I wasn't expecting to see you today, son," his father said, standing up to hug Owen. Owen accepted the gesture of affection before he joined his father at the table. "Can I get you a drink?"

"No, I'm good," Owen replied. "Thanks."

"As you wish. What can I do for you today? Or is this just a social visit?"

"Actually, no, I have some interesting news that I thought you should know about."

"Oh, really?" His father relaxed back into his seat. "Well then, go ahead. Regale me with this information."

"It's about Rob."

His father frowned and sat forward, suddenly attentive. "Go on."

"I met with him a few days ago in Mansfield. He was part of a unit investigating the death of the prostitute there."

"Was he? And you're only just telling me about this now? I thought you'd dealt with that little turf war you were having with the Polish traffickers."

"We have, but I'll get to that."

His father frowned again before his expression turned inquisitive. "So Rob's part of the Nottinghamshire EMSOU now?"

"And he's an Inspector."

His father seemed surprised. "Going up in the world. Interesting.

"I thought so," Owen agreed. "He might be of use to us..."

His father grunted and didn't sound quite as convinced. "Someone of that rank is useful, no doubt, but Robert is a true believer, or was at least. This will require more investigation and a great deal of care, Owen. I do not want you charging in there like a bull in a China shop."

Owen nodded, knowing not to cross his father. "Of course, sir."

"But as you say, this is interesting. Thank you. Is there anything else?"

"Yes. As you know, Carter and his man, Abel, had been fighting with Radek and his gang over turf and their girls. We know that Radek killed Abel at the brothel outside of Mansfield before he escaped the police by apparently playing dead." Isaac smirked at this, but Owen continued, "Radek's been quiet for a few days since then. We've been looking for him, but he's been laying low until now. We found him today."

"What's happened?"

"Radek and his crew were found dead. Every single one of them had been professionally executed. The scene was clean of any clues, apart from this." Owen pulled out a simple white business card and placed it on the table between him and his father. The only marking on the whole card was the image of an ornate red hourglass printed on one side.

It was a calling card left behind by whoever had killed Radek.

His father regarded the card before he picked it up and turned it over in his hand. "And there was nothing else?"

"No. The place was completely clean. No fingerprints anywhere and no other clues. They'd even turned off the local CCTV. This was a professional job."

His father took another look at the card, turned it over in his hand, and then crushed it in his fist. "Then we have a new player on the scene."

56

Pulling into the parking space outside his building, Rob turned the engine off and took a moment to himself. It was the first time he'd been back in days, and frankly, seeing the familiar building he called home was a welcome sight. This first case with the EMSOU had been one of the most full-on and draining cases he'd ever worked on. The loss of life and misery on display was mind-numbing in its viciousness, and yet, it had served to bring the team together as nothing else could, and working with the newly formed unit had been incredibly rewarding.

He had high hopes for it and was already looking forward to returning to work tomorrow as they moved towards bringing the case to a close.

Scarlett had been his steadfast partner once again, showing integrity and resolve that few others could match, and it was great to work with his long-time friend Nick again after they had been separated by his previous DCI.

He had nothing but good things to say about the rest of the team, too, with Ellen, Tucker and Guy all working well together and putting in whatever time was needed to close the case.

Unlike Peter Orleton, his previous DCI, John Nailer, had been a revelation to work under. They'd been friends for a long time, of course, with Nailer mentoring him since before he'd even joined the police, but this was the first time he'd actually worked in a unit run by his friend.

It reminded him a little of those early days after leaving his family under the guidance of Nailer and setting up in Nottingham, which led to a feeling of nostalgia about the unit which he hadn't expected.

As for the case, well, it hadn't gone exactly to plan with Valerie committing suicide, but at least it was fairly cut and dried as to who the killer was, and there was no need to prepare the case for court in the usual way.

Silver linings and all that.

He did, however, feel terrible for Penny's family, Emmett, and Caprice, all of whom had their lives destroyed over the last few days. He wasn't sure what any of them would do now. Would they choose to stay in the area or move out? If they did stay, he'd seen many genuine acts of kindness on behalf of Clipstone's residents that warmed his heart. The vicar, in particular, had offered so much to them, visiting them in the hospital and arranging all kinds of help to see them through these difficult days.

This was a side of Clipstone that he'd not seen much of during the last week, a side that had clearly been there but had been hidden by the vile acts committed in the village.

Ultimately, the vast majority of people were just good, hard-working folks who wanted to live their lives, do their jobs, raise their families, and live in kind, caring communities. It was always the obnoxious few that ruined it for the majority.

But then, that was his job, was it not? To protect the majority of law-abiding citizens from the minority of criminals and reprobates.

But as much as he loved and believed in his job, he also loved getting home, sinking into his sofa, and spending time with his cat.

Climbing out of his car, Rob set off for the main entrance when someone called out his name.

"Rob?"

"Hmm?" He turned to see Journalist Mary Day climbing out of her car. "Oh, hi."

"I was hoping to catch you," she said as she approached. "I thought you'd like to know that my report, the one you helped on, is being published tomorrow."

"Oh. That's come around quickly," he replied, feeling his insides tense.

She smiled. "Hey, don't worry, it's not as bad as you think. You're not mentioned in it, I don't even say I used a source, so you're good. Here, this is a copy of it for you." She handed him a card folder with some sheets of paper inside. "If you have a genuine objection, I won't run it. But I need to know in the next hour or two."

"Fair enough. Were my clarifications and insight useful?" Rob asked, taking the folder she offered. Mary had approached him right after Valerie ended her life in Clipstone, asking for his help crafting her report. It was something that Rob had ultimately agreed to, on the proviso that it was just in an advisory capacity and that he not be named in the report. Mary had agreed, and Rob had chosen to trust her. It felt like a huge leap for Rob to trust this reporter in such a sensitive matter, but Mary had been nothing but professional and responsible throughout.

"You were very useful, yes. I hope we can do this again sometime."

"I'll let you know after tomorrow."

She smiled. "Fair enough. I can't ask for more than that. See, we're not all bad."

"Perhaps not." He offered his hand. Mary glanced at it and pulled a face. She seemed disappointed. "A handshake? Alright, I'll take it." She shook his hand before winking and saying her farewells. "See you around, Loxley."

Holding onto the folder she'd given him, he watched her return to her car and drive off before entering his building and climbing the stairs to the first floor. He came to the top, facing Erika's door, and briefly considered knocking on it to thank her face-to-face but then decided against it. She probably wouldn't appreciate having her evening interrupted, and he could thank her over text.

Then her door opened, and Erika's face appeared in the gap.

"Hey. You're back."

"I am. I was going to knock to say thank you, but I didn't want to disturb your evening," he explained.

"Oh, no, disturb away, any time. It's fine."

"Okay." Rob smiled. "How was he?"

"Muffin's fine," she replied easily. "I think he's missing you, but he's good otherwise."

"Okay, great. Thank you for doing this. You're a lifesaver, really."

"That's okay. I've enjoyed looking after him. I'm happy to do it any time. Just let me know. You have my number now."

"I do, thanks." Rob grinned and remembered Nick asking that he introduce him to Erika. For a moment, he briefly considered mentioning his colleague but then decided against it. If Nick wanted to introduce himself to Erika, he could damn well come here and do it himself. Why should he make an ass out of himself when Nick could do it just as easily.

She seemed to notice that he was about to say something and then changed his mind, causing a flicker of a frown to appear on her forehead. "Everything okay?"

"Yeah, I'm good, thanks. I'll let you know the next time I need some help."

"Of course," she replied before they said goodnight to each other, and Rob turned to his apartment.

The moment he entered, Muffin ran over and started to headbutt his shins, meowing loudly. Rob crouched and gave him a good scratch around the neck before picking Muffin up and walking over to the far window that looked out over the River Trent, the stadium, and the city beyond.

It was good to be home, he thought, feeling the most relaxed he'd felt in about a week.

Glancing at Mary's report in his hand, he walked over to the sofa. "Right then, let's see if she can write, shall we?"

"Meow!"

THE END

Join me in book 3
For An Eye

A L FRAINE

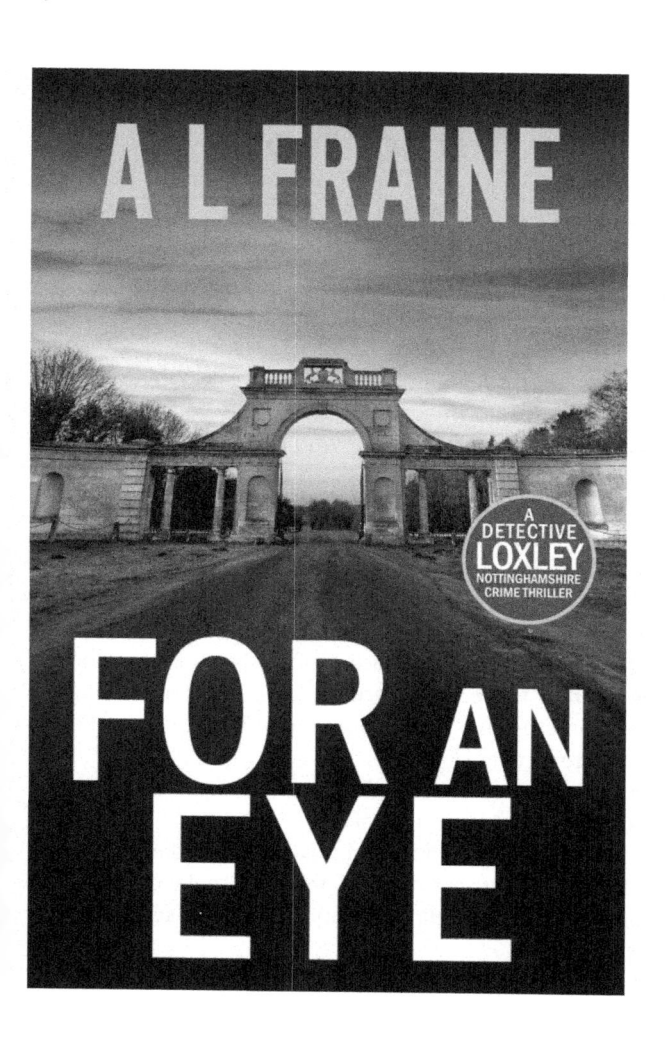

FOR AN EYE

A DETECTIVE LOXLEY NOTTINGHAMSHIRE CRIME THRILLER

Author Note

Thank you for reading book 2 in this series. I hope you enjoyed the story. I've loved writing these books, and setting them in my home county has been great fun as I revisit places both from my childhood and places I've been to more recently.

I've driven through Clipstone many times over the years, and its iconic Headstocks are a very recognisable landmark, and I'm sure anyone who's been through the village will remember them.

All the landmarks or road names are either real places or inspired by real places or landmarks, with small changes to make them my own. For instance, there is a bar on the main street, although it's called The Top Club, not The Clip Club. Also, The Old Police Station is a real place in Retford, and I recently had the pleasure of looking around it and having a drink there. It's a great place, and I'm looking forward to returning there soon for another drink and maybe a bite to eat.

You should check it out. I'm sure there are no crime bosses hanging out there in real life.

But then, the world in these books is a little darker and more dangerous in some respects than our real world.

Thanks again for reading this book. I hope to see you in book 3 soon.

Kindest Regards

Andrew

Come and join in the discussion about my books in my Facebook Group:

www.facebook.com/groups/alfraine.readers

Book List

www.alfraineauthor.co.uk/books

Printed in Great Britain
by Amazon